Plea
on t'

To rei
or con

Your b

4 4 0082518 7

ALL THAT
IS BURIED

By Robert Scragg

What Falls Between the Cracks
Nothing Else Remains
All That is Buried

ALL THAT
IS BURIED

ROBERT SCRAGG

Allison & Busby Limited
11 Wardour Mews
London W1F 8AN
allisonandbusby.com

First published in Great Britain by Allison & Busby in 2020.

Copyright © 2020 by ROBERT SCRAGG

A CIP catalogue record for this book is available from
the British Library.

First Edition

ISBN 978-0-7490-2464-2

Typeset in 12/17 pt Adobe Garamond Pro by
Allison & Busby Ltd

The paper used for this Allison & Busby publication
has been produced from trees that have been legally sourced
from well-managed and credibly certified forests.

Printed and bound by
CPI Group (UK) Ltd, Croydon, CR0 4YY

For my wife, Nic,
the best partner-in-crime a writer could wish for

CHAPTER ONE

He can't remember exactly when he lost his children, only that he has. Lost? No, she took them. Cut them from his life, and he from theirs. How long has it been? Even now, the memories are hazy, painful to touch, a wound that won't ever scab over.

Around him, the ebb and flow of people is a chaotic palette of colour. Sounds swirl, overlap, conversations impossible to separate from the cloud of white noise as he picks his way between rides. Oversized teacups spin in lazy circles. Squeak of socks on rubber as children launch themselves skywards on a bouncy castle. Seems like the entire village has been lured out by the promise of fun in the sun.

How long since he's seen them? Too long. Months? Longer? Today will be the day though. Today he gets to take them home. He looks around, smiling at the wide-eyed wonder of the children that pass, nibbling at clouds of flamingo-pink candyfloss larger than their own heads. Rows of stalls plug the gaps between rides. Hook-a-duck, Tin-Can Alley, and a dozen more like them, all promising prizes for those willing to part with pocket money. Behind these, the woods, pressed up against the back of the stalls and tents, stretching back half a mile, maybe more.

Up ahead, he sees her. Breath catches in his throat. Could that be . . . ? Is it . . . ? The blonde ponytail is a carbon copy of the one in his memories. She's peering over a counter, watching tiny plastic horses race towards a finish line, calling for number four to hurry up. No sign of her brother or their mum. What to do? Wait and greet them together? He's more nervous than he thought he'd be. Stands for a full minute, frozen by indecision as the next race runs. This time, she doesn't hand over any more money. Instead she spins away, looking left and right. Maybe she has lost them?

There's a bounce to her step that seems to keep time with his heart. He'll follow her to them. They'll turn and see him. Smile at him. Both kids will run towards him, clamping to him like barnacles to a rock. She'll see how much they love him. Might still have feelings for him herself. Maybe enough to paper over the cracks. He can't even remember what they argued about, only that it was his fault. His mistakes to make right.

Her head is down now, bowed over a phone as she walks. He doesn't remember her owning one. Since when has she been allowed that? He'll speak to her mother about it when the time is right. Not today though. No disagreements today. He frowns as she pauses to take a picture, a selfie judging by the way she's angling it, half a smile visible as she turns her head. She repeats this twice more, in front of another stall, and one of those image-warping fairground mirrors. After that, some furious tapping on her screen. Sending a picture to a friend, maybe. She angles left, around a corner and out of view, behind the tent flaps of a sweet stall. He picks up his pace so as not to lose her.

He hustles around the corner, but she's nowhere to be seen. Maybe she's gone behind, and he turns left again, almost bumping into her where she stands, phone held at arm's length, like she's about to take another selfie, but there's some sort of game on-screen now. It's as if she's using the camera, but with strange creatures superimposed in shot. A grunt of surprise pops out of his mouth and she turns to look at him, the spell of the screen broken.

Eyes blue as sapphires stare up at him, and a lump forms in his throat, corners of his eyes prickling. His baby girl. His little princess. He goes to speak, lips parting, but it's as if he's slipped into neutral and nothing comes out. Struck dumb by happiness. It's her who breaks the spell.

'Are you OK?' she asks.

Her voice is like a splash of cold water, snapping him out of his trance.

'I am now.' He nods.

'Are you lost?'

He shakes his head, feeling the beginnings of a smile tug at his mouth. 'No, no. I was just looking for you and your brother.'

'Why?' she asks, a concertina of tiny creases on her forehead.

'What do you mean why?' he says. 'I've come to take you home.'

'I can't go home with you. Mum always says I shouldn't talk to strangers.'

'I'm not a stranger, though, Marie, am I? I'm your dad.'

'My name's not Marie, and you're not my dad.'

CHAPTER TWO

Jake Porter traced a lazy swirl across the back of Evie Simmons's hand with his index finger. Three months in, and he still felt whispers of guilt in moments like this. Stupid, pointless even. Almost three years since he lost Holly. She of all people would have wanted him to be happy, to find someone else. Might be different if they'd drifted apart, broken up after a fiery run of arguments. Anything that might have given him a better sense of closure. As it was, whoever had been driving the car that mowed her down was still out there. Breathing, laughing, living.

'Penny for them,' Evie said, cocking her head to one side.

He blinked his way back into the room, forcing a smile. 'Not even worth that,' he said. 'Sorry, just a bit tired.'

He felt about as convincing as a kid standing next to a smashed lamp pleading ignorance, but she mirrored his smile, covering his hand with hers and squeezed. Their waiter appeared at his shoulder like a genie, popped the cork from a bottle of red and poured half an inch into Porter's glass.

'I'm sure it'll be fine,' he said, looking up, seeing disapproval in the waiter's face. He'd never been one to do a swirl and sniff. To him it was red wine, nothing more. No base notes of blackberry, no hints of plum. Wine came in three types: red, white and rosé.

Across from him, Evie's eyes twinkled as the disgruntled waiter poured, sensing Porter's discomfort. He looked around the restaurant as her glass was filled, a lazy sweep of the room. No familiar faces, but then again why would there be? They were nowhere near the station, closer to her place than his. What would it matter even if there were?

It wasn't as if they worked together. She was part of the drugs squad, while he was on Homicide and Serious Crime Command. No rules broken. More of a force of habit. Only a handful of people knew they were an item yet. Of those, only one was on the force: Porter's partner, Detective Sergeant Nick Styles.

Evie raised her glass, holding it out towards him. 'To a quiet weekend,' she toasted.

'I'll drink to that,' he said, his glass singing a clear note as it clinked against hers.

A waitress ghosted past them, plates stacked high, defying gravity as they balanced along a slender arm. Porter caught a glimpse of a juicy-looking steak and a mini haystack of skinny fries that only served to remind him of how little he'd eaten today. A plate like that would do him just fine.

Two large mouthfuls saw off half of his wine, and he'd barely had time for his glass to hit the table when he felt a vibration from his pocket. Whether Evie heard it or noticed him stiffen, he saw a tiny crease between her eyebrows. Disappointment, maybe, but she knew he had to take it.

'DI Porter,' he said, looking longingly at his glass, wondering if he'd get the chance to finish it.

'Sorry to disturb you, sir,' said the voice on the other end of the line.

'It's DC Benayoun. I tried to get DS Styles first, but he wasn't answering.'

'It's OK,' Porter said, wondering what his partner was up to, wishing he'd taken a leaf out of his book and not answered. 'Everything alright?'

'Not really, sir,' she said. 'Missing child, seven years old.'

CHAPTER THREE

Voicemail. Again. Where the bloody hell was Styles?

'Call me when you get this.'

Short, brusque, to the point. Porter clicked to end the call, and got out of his car. The block of flats loomed high above him, each floor a slice of pale green and dirty cream, layers on a cake. Named after a former councillor, John Walsh Tower and its neighbour, Fred Wigg Tower, dominated the skyline. Both looked in sore need of TLC. Porter had even heard talk of demolition and rebuilding. Two patrol cars bookended the path leading up to a set of steps. Seventeen storeys, and they just had to live at the top. Porter's silent prayer to the lift gods was answered, and he waited patiently as the gears groaned their way upwards.

He worked his way along the corridor, knocked on the door and was greeted by a young female officer he recognised from a previous case. PC Dee Williams nodded and stepped aside to let him in. First thing that hit him was stale cigarettes, the kind of ingrained odour that takes years of dedication to seep in. A sweeter base note too, though, suggesting it wasn't just tobacco that had been smoked.

This was a part of the job that never got easier. Different from the death knock, delivering the news that a loved one was never coming home. Missing persons meant hope. A chance, no matter how slim. When it was a kid, that hope was all that kept some parents from sliding over the edge.

A young woman sat hunched forwards on the sofa, elbows on knees, paper hankie scrunched like a loosely packed snowball in one hand. Mid-thirties he guessed, no make-up, hair in a tight ponytail, and a pink tinge around nose and eyes. No mistaking her for anyone else but the child's mum, Ally Hallforth. A second officer perched next to her – family liaison officer, most likely.

By the window, a man paced back and forth, stopping when he realised somebody had joined them in the room. Presumably Simon Hallforth. He had a lived-in face, deep lines scored across his forehead. Fingers twitching by his sides as if playing a keyboard. Eyes that wouldn't look out of place on a rat: small, close-set, dark.

'Mr and Mrs Hallforth,' Porter said, making no attempt to sit. 'My name is Detective Inspector Jake Porter—'

'Have you found her then?' Simon Hallforth cut in before Porter could say anything else.

'Not yet, sir, but it'd really help if we can have a chat, help us get to know a bit about Libby, any friends she might have wandered off with. The majority of these situations end up being along those lines, but it goes without saying we'll pull out all the stops to find her and bring her home safe.'

'Yeah, that'd be just like her,' Simon sneered. 'Wandering off without a care in the world. She's done it before a few times at the supermarket. She knows it winds me up. Probably done it for a laugh this time. I tell you, if she's done this on purpose . . .'

He stopped short of finishing the sentence, and Ally's head snapped up, glaring at him.

'You'll what, Simon?' She stared him out until he dropped his eyes and turned back to look out of the window. 'She's a good kid, Detective,' she said, dabbing at her nose with the hankie. 'Ignore him. He'd already got out of bed on the wrong side before any of this.'

Porter looked over at Simon Hallforth. Watched him clench and unclench his fists. Anger wasn't the norm in these circumstances. Fear, yes. The anger usually came after any search failed to find the missing person. He used the lull now to introduce himself to the FLO, DC Moira Kelly, then took a seat in the chair opposite Ally Hallforth.

'I know you've already been through this with one of my colleagues, Mrs Hallforth, but if you could walk me through Libby's day, when you last saw her, what she was wearing, whether you saw anybody acting suspicious.'

She nodded, took a deep breath and puffed it out loudly, steeling herself to go over it again.

'There's a fair at Epping Forest, near the visitor's centre. Libby's been harping on about it all week.'

'You can barely call that thing a fair,' Simon cut in. 'I said we shouldn't have gone. I told you.'

'Enough, Simon,' Ally snapped. Porter looked at her, then back to her husband. Something in both faces, a subtext they weren't sharing with him. Her anger gave way quickly to uncertainty, like a line had been crossed. His expression was more one of surprise, possibly not used to his wife snapping at him. Either way, Porter doubted they'd played happy families even before today.

'She's a good girl, Detective. She doesn't wander off. Does as she's told.'

'When it suits her,' Simon muttered, but this one went unchecked.

'And what do you remember leading up to Libby disappearing?' Porter asked. 'Take your time.'

Ally Hallforth had a thousand-yard stare now, unfocused, playing back loops in her head.

'She hadn't even been on many of the rides,' she said in a faraway tone. 'Just stuffed her face with candyfloss and watched other kids, mainly. Said she wanted to watch all the rides before she made her mind up. I only took my eye off her for a second. Just wanted to grab a coffee, told her I'd only be a minute, and then . . .'

The rest of the sentence disappeared behind a veil of sniffles. This would be the perfect time for Simon Hallforth to swoop in, curl an arm around her, tell her their baby girl was safe, that she'd be home soon. Instead, he huffed out a loud breath, pulled an e-cigarette from his pocket and started puffing away. Clouds of fruity-scented vapour shrouded his face. Porter couldn't stand those things, and kept his focus on Ally.

'She was watching that horse race one, you know where you back a colour and the little metal horses race along a track. You win a prize if yours finishes first. One minute she was there next to me, then she was just gone. Do you think someone took her?'

She came back alive for that last sentence, eyes snapping into focus, voice trembling at the very real possibility.

'We can't rule anything out, Mrs Hallforth,' Porter said with a shrug. 'Statistically most missing children have just wandered off. Either that or run away. Can you think of any reason why she'd want to run away?'

'And what the bloody hell do you mean by that?' Simon barked between angry puffs. 'You're saying we had something to do with this?'

'I'm not saying that at all, sir,' Porter said, keeping his tone level. In reality, though, he couldn't rule that out at this stage. Tia Sharp, a high-profile case back in 2012, had proved that families are capable of doing awful things, even to ones they're supposed to protect. Something about the dynamic between Simon and Ally was off. Not necessarily enough to have caused Libby to go missing, but definitely something Porter would have to follow up on.

16

'What about friends?' he asked. 'Were there any other kids she knew at the fair? Friends, or friends' parents? Anyone she might feel comfortable wandering off with.'

'She doesn't have many. Just a couple of other girls from school really, but I don't think any of them were there today,' said Ally.

'It'd be helpful if we can get their names to follow up just in case,' he said, and waited as she scribbled on a Post-it note, idly looking around the room. A picture behind the sofa caught his eye.

'Libby's brother and sister?' he asked, gesturing towards it.

Ally nodded. 'I was only nineteen when I had Marcus, same age as he is now. Chloe turned four last month.'

'Are they here?' Porter asked.

She shook her head. 'Marcus moved out last year. Got a flat in the block next door. My mum came around and took Chloe for a walk. Didn't want her seeing me upset.'

Porter's phone purred in his pocket before he could ask anything else about the other children.

'Excuse me just one second,' he said, sliding it out and seeing Styles's name blinking at him. Nick would have to wait. Disrupting the flow of a sensitive debrief like this could mean facts were missed, misremembered, even embellished. He rejected the call and fixed his attention on Ally again.

'And what did you do when you realised you couldn't see her any more?'

His phone buzzed again: same caller. Porter felt his hackles rising. Styles should know if he didn't take the call there would be a damn good reason. Seemed lately that his partner's judgement was just a fraction off on the little things. Understandable to a degree, baby on the way and all, but little mistakes could easily add up, make life difficult, cases harder to solve.

'I really am sorry about this. Let me get rid of the call,' he said, pressing to answer.

'DS Styles, I really can't talk right now. I'm interviewing the parents.'
Formal title in place of a Christian name intended to send a message.

'I know, boss, and I'm sorry to be a pain, but it's about the girl. We've found something.'

CHAPTER FOUR

Anger leached from Porter, heat draining from his cheeks. He tried to keep his tone neutral, not wanting to give anything away to Libby's parents.

'Go on,' he said, offering a silent prayer that his partner had misspoken, that it was a someone, not a something.

'It's her mobile phone, boss. Smashed up pretty bad as well.'

'Where?' he asked, instantly regretting his choice of word, seeing Ally Hallforth's eyes widen. He mouthed the words *Not Libby*, saw a fresh wave of disappointment crash over her.

'Hundred yards or so from the edge of the fairground. Screen's all cracked, but it still powers up so we should be able to check through it fairly quickly.'

'OK, good. You out there now, or did someone reach you at home?'

'On my way to the scene now,' Styles said, puzzled tone to his voice. 'I was at the midwife's appointment with Emma. Remember, I told you about it last week.'

Porter had a flashback to a conversation over a coffee. He had mentioned it alright; Porter had just forgotten, preoccupied with a hundred other thoughts.

'Yeah, of course I do. I'll see you back at the station when I finish speaking with the parents.'

He ended the call, feeling bad for doubting Styles, but didn't have time to dwell as both parents peppered him with questions, volume rising to be heard above each other. He held up both hands.

'That was a detective sergeant on my team. We've not found Libby yet, but we have found her phone.'

'Her phone?' Ally said. 'Where?'

'Not far from the fairground.'

'So, she did wander off then,' Simon said. 'Wandered off and lost her bloody prized possession that cost me a fortune. That's what all this is about. She's either still out there in the bloody long grass looking for it, or hiding cos she knows she'll get a bollocking for losing it.'

'What if someone took her?' Ally sniffed. 'Took her and got rid of it so the police can't use it to find them?'

'I know you've got questions,' he said, addressing both of them, 'and I want to get you answers, believe me I do. But trust me when I say that second-guessing things like this isn't going to help.'

'And neither is sitting here chatting like we've got all the time in the world,' snapped Simon, grabbing a photo frame from a shelf. 'You know what she looks like, you know where she was. Us telling you what a great kid she is won't help you find her any quicker.'

Porter felt his hackles rising. He'd dealt with his fair share of anger being thrown his way. Criminals, relatives, witnesses; he crossed paths with people at their worst or most vulnerable, liable to lash out at the nearest target. There was something about Simon Hallforth, however, that suggested that Porter could walk in here any day of the week and get the same reception. Quick to anger, to lash out. What kind of husband and father was he behind closed doors?

Porter decided to change tack. He didn't have time for this angry little man routine. Not with a seven-year-old girl missing.

'You know what, you're right, but first, may I?' he said, gesturing to the picture with his phone.

Simon took a second to realise what he intended to do, but handed it over, and Porter took a picture. All three wore beaming smiles, sitting on a beach somewhere. Had to be fairly recent from the ages Ally had given. Happier times.

'Thank you,' he said, handing it back, watching as Simon practically thumped it onto the shelf. 'Now if you'll excuse me, I'm going to head out there now and help look for her.'

He stood, walked over to where Simon Hallforth leant against the wall and held out a hand. Simon left him hanging for a second longer than necessary, and when he did grip Porter's hand, he went for the testosterone option. Porter squeezed back just as hard, then added a few extra ounces of pressure for good measure. Still on the right side of the professional line, just. Hallforth was first to release, scowling as he turned away, sucking in another lungful of whatever rubbish was in his e-cigarette.

'I'll leave you with DC Kelly. She'll be able to arrange a time for you to finish giving your statement down at the station.'

Ally Hallforth nodded and smiled, rising to see Porter out, but Porter was more interested by her husband's reaction. The mention of a station visit creased his forehead. Not something he was keen to do, presumably. Had he been inside one before, for the wrong reasons, maybe? Easy enough to find out. He'd already shown he had a temper. Maybe he had form for losing it as well. Five minutes in an interview room would be enough to see for himself. Definitely hiding something, that one.

CHAPTER FIVE

Styles was leaning against his car when Porter pulled up. He peeled himself away, straightening up as Porter approached, like a Transformer unfolding, to reach his full height. At six-four, Styles had a clear five inches on him but often seemed to slouch to minimise it, as if he was self-conscious.

'Sorry about before,' Porter said as they shook hands. 'Just wound up a bit too tight, what with it being a young 'un.'

'Honestly, it's fine, guv, I should have reminded you yesterday,' said Styles, waving away the apology. They'd worked together for around four years now, and he'd always had Porter's back. There had been one misunderstanding a few months back, when Porter had thought Styles was feeding information back to Superintendent Roger Milburn, Porter's boss, undermining him. There had been tension there, sure, but he'd been wrong, and had admitted as much to Styles. Water under the bridge.

'What do we know, then?' Porter asked, scanning the car park and surrounding area, taking in the unmanned stalls and silent rides. A group of people, a couple of dozen maybe, milled around just beyond the line of police tape. 'And who are the spectators?'

'They're the people who own this lot,' Styles said. 'All ecstatic at losing the afternoon's takings, as you can see. I've tried pointing out there's more serious things going on than whether some bloke from Chigwell can buy two and a half minutes of peace for a fiver so his kids can spin round in a giant teacup, but I must be losing my touch.'

Porter looked at the crowd again. A small sea of scowling faces, pacing, muttering, racing their way through a day's worth of cigarettes.

'Tough. They can get back over here when we're finished.'

When that might be was unclear. With so many vehicles, stalls, no CCTV and no clear picture of exactly how Libby Hallforth had disappeared, the scene would take a fair chunk of time to process. Two roads penned in the long green triangle of grass where the fair had set up shop. Behind him, a few hundred metres of open ground. Over the far side of the fair, the Kings Oak Hotel. All in all, a tiny patch carved out of over three hundred square kilometres of woodland.

'What have we got in motion so far?'

Styles rattled through what he knew. Crime scene manager logging everyone in and out. Names of staff and customers, over a hundred combined already. Number plates from the car park. Twenty officers making a start on searching nearby woodland. The only CCTV was at the hotel. No one there had seen her, but they'd asked for copies all the same.

'Does anyone remember seeing her? Her mum mentioned she was keen on some horse racing game at one of the stalls.'

Styles nodded. 'Spoke to that guy myself. He remembers a girl who matched her description. Said she stuck in his mind cos she reminded him of his granddaughter. Didn't see anyone with her, though, or anyone that looked out of place hanging round. He also remembered her because she was on her own the whole time she was at his stall.'

That sparked something at the back of Porter's brain. 'Ally Hallforth told me she'd been with her there, and then walked off to get a coffee.'

Styles shrugged. 'The guy must see hundreds of people a day. If she wasn't playing, he probably wouldn't pay as much attention.'

'No, it's not just that,' Porter said, shaking his head. 'She said she'd been standing next to her, told her she was going for a drink, then left. He would have seen them talking.'

Ally Hallforth had lied to him. Her little girl missing, and she'd lied within five minutes of him walking through her door. What could be more important than telling the truth with so much at stake? The same thought he'd had in the Hallforths' living room swam to the surface. Even families are capable of doing awful things to those they love.

CHAPTER SIX

Porter sent a pair of constables over to the hotel to speak to staff and guests. They'd already searched the place before Porter arrived in case she'd wandered over and decided to explore any of the rooms. Apart from her phone, though, there was no sign she'd even been at the fair. What he'd give for this to have happened in a street full of CCTV, or for her to have kept hold of the phone so they could put a trace on it and go straight to her. He and Styles took the opportunity to speak with a few more of the fairground staff, but with the exception of the man Styles had already interviewed, none of them remembered seeing anyone matching her description, although Porter worried that some of the answers were a little too quick for his liking. Too keen to move them along to the next person. He could have sworn there were a couple of dozen people here before, maybe a few more, but now he counted only nineteen. No matter; they'd have names from the list taken earlier.

Follow-up conversations with the Hallforths needed to happen, and fast. Libby had last been seen by the stall owner a little after one this afternoon. Ally had called up to report her missing around two hours later. Porter checked his watch. Almost 8 p.m., and the sun had long since sunk behind the treetops; the sky behind them was a dark, inky black. Seven hours missing, give or take, already. If Libby was out there, lost in the woods, she'd be scared witless by now.

Please let it be something stupid. An argument with her mum or dad, and she's hiding somewhere to teach them a lesson.

'Are you OK to stay here and coordinate the search?' Porter asked Styles. 'I need to go and speak to the parents again, clear up the part of the mum's story at the stall.'

'Yeah, I'm good to stick around,' Styles replied.

'There was something off with the dad as well. Really weird vibe going on between him and his wife. He was an angry, mouthy one. Seemed more pissed off that Libby was causing hassle than actually worried about her. The glances they were giving each other, though, it's like they were trying to tell each other things they didn't want to say out loud with me in the room.'

'Could be a run-of-the-mill domestic, guv?' Styles asked. 'Her giving him evils for saying the wrong things, and that pisses him off cos she's making him look bad to us, so he gets angrier.'

'Yeah, maybe, maybe not. There's a brother as well,' said Porter, snapping his fingers. 'Moved out and lives on his own, but they didn't say if he'd been out with them today. Can you pick that up first thing tomorrow? Track him down and have a chat?'

'Yep, no worries,' Style replied. 'Oh, before I forget, Emma asked me to invite you and Evie around for dinner this weekend if you've got no plans.'

It seemed surreal to be discussing something as casual as dinner plans in the middle of working a potentially delicate case like this, but Porter was used to Styles having no filters most of the time. It didn't mean he was any less concerned about Libby Hallforth. He just had a habit of spitting out thoughts as they popped into his mind.

'Don't think we're doing anything. I'll check with Evie and let you know tomorrow if that's OK?'

Saying her name triggered his own memory. Shit, he'd said he would call and let her know if it was worth her staying over at his tonight, or whether he'd not be back till late. He was still feeling his way around the idea of being in a relationship again, and with a job like this, there were always plenty of distractions to push all thoughts of home life from your mind.

Styles's phone buzzed. 'Lorna, that's a new record. I'm guessing I owe you a week's worth of coffees for this one?'

Lorna Shields worked in the lab that processed most of the evidence gathered on their cases. The rule of thumb was the faster the evidence came back, the more it cost you. Porter was sure she had a soft spot for his DS. He seemed to be able to get her to overlook that at times, to undercharge and overdeliver. She was in her early sixties, and he was happily married, so not that kind of soft spot. She had told him that he looked like Denzel Washington, if Denzel had been stretched on a rack for a week, and that he was lucky she wasn't thirty years younger.

Porter watched Styles's face as he listened. Saw his expression darken, fresh furrows appearing across his forehead. He waited until Styles ended the call.

'What's up?'

'She's been taking a look at Libby's phone.'

'And?'

'And there's more than just cracks on her screen. Says there's some photos on there we need to see.'

CHAPTER SEVEN

Porter called DC Moira Kelly on the drive back to the station, and she promised to bring the Hallforths along to the station to take their full formal statements. He smiled at the thought of Simon Hallforth walking into a small boxy interview room. If the look on his face earlier was anything to go by, it'd be like sticking a claustrophobe in a suitcase.

The rest of his drive was more sombre, though. Lorna hadn't elaborated on what the pictures showed, apart from to say they'd been taken in the half hour leading up to Libby's disappearance. Could be the best insight they'd get into where she'd been, what she'd seen. *How did the phone get cracked in the first place?* he wondered. Maybe wherever she was, she had a story ready about some bigger kids stealing it. Maybe it had been forcibly taken away from her.

He shook the thought away. This was the kind of hopeful tangent Ally Hallforth would explore. He needed to stick to the facts, and the simple truth was they were already well past the golden hour: that crucial sixty-minute window that starts when an offence is committed, before evidence gets trampled, witnesses wander off or a suspect vanishes. The longer that clock ticks, the harder a case will be to solve. Not that he would admit as much to the Hallforths, but once it went past twenty-four hours with children, especially as young as Libby, forty-eight tops, the chances of a happy ending dropped like a stone.

He did a double take as he walked into the office. Simmons sat there at his desk, sipping from a cardboard cup, holding a matching one out to him as he approached. Her dark brown hair was pulled back into the customary tight ponytail. His sister, Kat, had said on more than one occasion that she had something of a young Audrey Hepburn about her.

'Figured you could use a coffee before you speak to the parents,' she said.

'How did you . . .'

'Know you were on your way in?' she finished his sentence for him. 'I'm a detective, sir. It's what we do,' she finished with a wink. 'Guessed you'd be on a late one, so thought I might as well catch up on some admin myself. That, and Styles texted me about dinner at theirs, and mentioned you were heading back in. Must have figured you'd forget.'

There weren't many others in at this time of day, but Porter did a quick check of those closest, looking for a reaction, anything to show they might have heard about the dinner plans.

'Don't worry,' she said, leaning forwards, talking in a stage whisper. 'We're not office gossip just yet.'

'Hmm? No, no, it's not that I . . . well, you know what it's like. It's just easier if we keep this to ourselves for now.'

She leant back, held her palms up, smiling. 'It's all good. I get it, and that's fine with me.' The cheeky glint came back in her eyes as she leant in again. 'It's actually more fun that way. You know, illicit.'

29

He felt his cheeks burn, hating that he was so easily embarrassed, but didn't try and hide his own grin. 'I might be a while in there,' he said, gesturing towards the interview room.

'That's fine.' She shrugged. 'Not like I have anywhere better to be.'

He toasted her with the coffee cup. 'Better get started then. Thanks for the cuppa.'

Wandering over to the door to interview room five, he felt a lightness to his step that hadn't been there when he'd trudged up the steps at the entrance. He liked that about her. The effect she could have, even just in small doses. He'd had that with Holly. Hadn't thought he'd find it again. He still wasn't sure what they had, or where it might go, but for now at least it felt right.

Ally Hallforth visibly jumped as he opened the door and strode in. Just her and DC Kelly. Simon Hallforth was in another room down the hall, as per Porter's instructions. Better to hear both sides without the background static of a domestic. That, and both of them had set him on edge a little. Different reasons for each, but he'd learnt to trust his gut. Still needed to tread carefully, though. Even if they were coming across as obstructive or evasive, it wouldn't do to have a complaint land on Superintendent Roger Milburn's desk. He'd become Porter's boss after a case that exposed corruption in the team, and had taken some convincing that Porter's methods were the right side of the line. They seemed to have reached an unsteady truce, for now at least.

Ally had changed since he'd seen her at her flat, now wearing jeans and a baggy plum-coloured jumper. Same eyes, though, heavy with worry, like clouds ready to burst.

'Here's the info you asked for, boss,' said DC Kelly, handing a folder to Porter. He flicked through it quickly as he took a seat. The contents of Libby Hallforth's phone: call log, texts, photos, browser history. A couple of items caught his eye, and he filed it as something to ask about, along with the other questions he'd composed in his mind on the drive over.

'Mrs Hallforth, sorry you had to wait. Can I get you another drink?' he said, gesturing at the almost empty water beside her.

'No, I'm alright, thanks. I'd just like to get this done, so I can go and pick Chloe up from my mum's.'

'Of course,' Porter said with a reassuring smile. 'Won't keep you any longer than we need to. We just need to finish walking through what you remember, then I've got a few extra questions. After that you'll be free to go. How does that sound?'

She nodded, looking down at her hands clasped in her lap. 'That's fine.'

'Good, OK, we'll make a start then,' he said, starting the recording, calling out the date and time, then identifying the people in the room.

'So, Mrs Hallforth, you said earlier that you saw her next to the stall that ran horse races. She was there when you went to get a coffee, and when you came back, she was gone.'

She nodded, but said nothing.

'How long would you say you were gone for?'

She frowned. 'Only a couple of minutes. Two or three, maybe.'

'But before that you were standing at the stall with her?'

'Yes, that's right.'

'How long would you say you were with her for at that stall?'

She looked puzzled. 'Why is that important?'

'I just want to build up a picture of the events leading up to her disappearing.'

'I don't know, maybe another couple of minutes. I can't remember exactly.'

'Where was your husband when you and Libby were at that stall? Did he have Chloe on one of the other rides?'

'No, she was with me. He kept wandering off then coming back,' she said. 'He kept moaning that Libby was wasting her time, that she should try some rides.'

31

'But he wasn't with you all of the time?'

'Why do you keep asking about us?' she said, a hint of anger creeping around the edges. 'Aren't you meant to be working out where she went?'

Porter gave a patient smile, the kind that said he'd done this a hundred times before, that he knew what he was doing.

'Like I said, Mrs Hallforth, the more we know the better. We weren't there, you were.' He left it there for a few seconds, giving her time to wind back in. 'How far away was the place you got your coffee? I'm just wondering how big a window she had to wander off in.'

'Over towards the cars,' she said. 'Can't remember the name, but it wasn't that far. Fifty metres away, maybe.'

The fair had been sandwiched between two roads, a hundred metres or so apart at their widest. Stalls and rides were arranged in four rows at that end, narrowing to just two near the point of the grassy triangle. He had made a beeline for the horse race stall earlier. Made a point of mapping out what was around it, the line of sight to and from other parts of the fair.

'Really?' he asked, sounding surprised. 'You went all that way for a cuppa? Why not just get one from the place next to the stall where Libby was?'

'What do you mean?' she asked, looking wary, unsure of herself.

'I mean there was a place right next door. You even had to walk past it to get to the one you went to. Why go that far away when you could have stayed a few feet away?'

Her mouth opened, closed, and she started to blink her confusion like Morse code. 'I, ah, I don't remember . . . I didn't see that other one. The place you said.' A tremor in her voice, barely audible, but there nonetheless. 'I must have just been looking the other way.'

Her shoulders, tense and squared, eased a touch, happy that she'd batted back his question.

Porter nodded and leant back in his chair. 'OK, yeah, that makes sense.' He looked over at DC Kelly for the first time since he'd started with his questions. Saw it in her face that she wasn't sure he was fishing in the right direction, but she knew better than to interrupt.

'I went out there to look around. Bumped into one of my colleagues, who spoke to the owner of that stall. He remembers seeing Libby. Funny thing is, he doesn't remember anyone being with her.'

'Well, he's wrong then, isn't he?' she said, and Porter fancied he saw a flash of fear in her eyes, glinting like gold in a pan.

'Mmm, could be,' Porter said, rubbing a hand over the first prickles of stubble. 'Here's the thing, though – I don't think he is, and I'll tell you why. I asked him about her, and he could describe her to a T. What she wore, the bobble in her hair, the lot. Wish all my witnesses were that good. But what he remembers thinking in particular is that no one was with her. She only paid for one race that he remembers. On her own the whole time though. Stood out because of it. Not many kids that age get left on their own.'

She was shaking her head now, creased ridge between eyebrows. Small movements, like watching the world's smallest game of tennis.

'She was there, at that stall. I definitely saw her there,' she mumbled.

'Saw her but weren't right next to her?' he asked. 'Possibly standing off to one side?'

'I might not have stood next to her at the stall,' she admitted in a quiet voice. 'We were walking past, and she ran over to it. I remember Simon saying something about it being a mug's game. How the man could fix the winner depending on how the punters bet.'

'So, Simon was with you at that point?'

'At *that* point, yeah.'

Something about the way she said it, all the emphasis on the second word, make Porter pause a beat.

'But not all afternoon?'

She looked down at her hands again. Started worrying away at the edges of a nail. What was she not telling him?

'What about after you left her at the stall?' he asked. 'Did Simon go with you for the coffee?'

'No, he can't stand the stuff. He went off to get a beer, I think.'

Porter felt heat in his cheeks. He wouldn't wish their situation on his worst enemy, but the pair of them had left a seven-year-old girl to her own devices, with no regard for who might be lurking around.

'And remind me, Mrs Hallforth, this happened just after one this afternoon?'

She nodded, but said nothing.

'Can I ask you why you waited as long as you did to report her missing?' he asked, a little more steel in his voice.

'Pardon me?' she said, looking startled by the question.

'The stall owner saw her around one this afternoon, but you didn't report her missing until just after three.'

'We, um, I just thought she was messing around. She couldn't have gone far. You just never think . . . I wanted to call it in sooner, but . . .'

She stopped mid-sentence, and Porter saw something flash across her face; a split second, then it was gone. Not the same fear he saw there when she talked about Libby being missing, but not far off.

'But what?' he prompted.

'I tried, but . . . I just . . .'

Porter glanced down at the printouts DC Kelly had prepared for him, spun one around and slid it towards her.

'What's that?' she asked.

'That is a call log from 999 earlier today. This' – he tapped – 'is the call we took from you a little after three, and this'– he slid his finger down to the next line – 'is a 999 call made from your mobile at quarter past one, not long after you last saw her.'

He saw colour seep from her cheeks, lips drawn in a tight line, eyes flitting across the page.

'Now what I'm hoping you can help me understand, Mrs Hallforth, is if you were worried enough to call us at one-fifteen, why you hung up and waited another two hours to actually tell us your daughter was missing?'

CHAPTER EIGHT

Ally Hallforth looked from Porter to DC Kelly, then down to the sheet of paper. When she picked it up, he could see a tremor around the edges. She chewed nervously on her bottom lip, staring with such intensity at the page, as if doing it could make it read differently.

'Mrs Hallforth?' Porter prompted. 'Anything you can share could make a difference in finding out where Libby is. Why did you end that first call?'

She swallowed hard, coming to a decision. 'I didn't.'

Porter shook his head. 'Why you did, only you can say, but this' – he reached over and tapped the top of the page – 'proves that you did.'

She shook her head. 'That's not what I mean, Detective. The call was ended, but not by me.'

'Your husband?'

She nodded. 'He said she was just messing around, overexcited. She'd probably turn up any minute, and he didn't want us looking stupid by panicking and calling the police over something as silly as that.'

The instant dislike Porter had taken to Simon Hallforth grew, morphing into outright anger. His own stubbornness might well have put his daughter in danger, but hey, as long as it didn't make him look stupid.

'You were obviously worried enough to have tried that first call. Why didn't you call back?'

'He took it.'

'Your phone?' Porter asked, incredulous.

'Mm-hm. I called you as soon as he gave it back.'

'He kept your phone for two hours?' said Porter, careful not to let any anger at her husband seep through into this conversation. 'Seems an extreme thing to do. The controlling type, is he?'

'I know what you must think,' she said, 'but he does what he thinks is best.'

'And what about you, Mrs Hallforth? Do you think it was a better idea for us to start searching when she went missing, or wait a few hours?'

He knew he was close to crossing the line now, that he should rein it back in. He could practically see the complaint on Milburn's desk already. That last question hit home, and he watched as her eyes filled, tears streaking their way down her face. DC Kelly reached over, put an arm around Ally Hallforth's shoulder and looked over at Porter.

'Maybe a good time for a break, boss?'

Porter nodded. Good time to switch rooms and speak to her husband.

'We'll do everything we can,' he assured her, 'but I need you both to be honest with me. Libby needs you to be honest with me.'

He left her dabbing at her tears with an already grubby hankie, and headed along the corridor to where Simon Hallforth waited. He wasn't quite the cornered rat that Porter had expected, having checked for prior arrests and seen form for minor offences. Nothing huge in the grand scheme of things: arrested fifteen years ago for possession of

37

cannabis, picked up a few times drunken and disorderly, and one arrest for assault, but charges were dropped.

Hallforth was early forties, but it was unlikely that anyone would peg him for that. Scores of frown lines criss-crossed his forehead. Dark hair and darker eyes. Definite contender for little man syndrome.

'Why are we in separate rooms?' he asked as Porter sat down.

'Helps with the statements,' he said. 'Avoids one person filling in the other's blanks with things they might remember differently.'

'I dunno what more you think we can tell you,' said Hallforth. 'Like I said before, you'd be better out there looking for my daughter.'

'And the more we know, the better we can direct the search. Now why don't we start with why you stopped your wife calling us two hours earlier?'

Straight in, no messing around, Porter slipped it in under his defences like a punch to the liver.

'You what? What the bloody hell are you trying to say?' Hallforth stammered, volume rising, folding his arms like a shield across his chest.

'I'm not *trying* to say anything,' Porter said, keeping his tone level. 'I know for a fact there was a call from your wife's phone to 999 around quarter past one. It was terminated pretty much as soon as it was answered, and nobody picked up when they called back. Why would you not want us looking for her sooner?'

'Cos she's a bloody liability that one,' he said, angry at being put on the spot. 'Working herself, hiding around the house, hiding my packet of fags. That's just what she does.'

'Seems your wife thought differently. She wanted to call us. Why did you stop her?'

'Didn't want to get in trouble for wasting police time,' he said, with a smug smile like he'd just won a battle of wits.

'It's Libby's time you're wasting, Mr Hallforth,' Porter said. 'Every minute she's out there, we're a tiny bit further away from finding her. Who else knew you were at the fairground?'

'What? You think someone was stalking her?'

'Please, sir, if you can just answer the question.'

'I dunno, it's not like I took out an ad in the paper,' he said, with a forced grin again, like the whole thing was one big joke.

Porter had already strayed far from his usual approach with parents of a missing child, but between the two of them they seemed to be holding back for whatever reason, answering his questions with ones of their own.

'How about friends, family, neighbours? Anyone who might have taken a particular interest in Libby?'

'Nope,' he said; short, to the point, as if Porter was an inconvenience.

'And how are things at home?'

That got a rise from him, more than Porter expected. 'No, no, no. You don't try and turn this round on me.' Simon Hallforth wagged a finger at him, like telling off a naughty schoolboy, eyes wide with indignation.

'If she has run away, these things tend to be linked to home or school. That's not to say you or your wife have done anything wrong, but right now, I need to rule things in or out as quickly as possible. So, I'll ask again, how are things at home? Could she have seen anything that would upset her enough to run away?'

Hallforth huffed out a loud breath. 'Gets upset at anything, just like her mother. Pair of 'em can barely watch a Disney film without tearing up.'

'What about her older brother, does she see much of him?'

'Hmph, comes round when it suits him.'

'Quite young to move out. Nineteen, isn't he?'

'That's right yeah.'

'Is he at college, university?'

'Got himself an internship at some software company. Always been too clever for his own good.'

'Have you got his contact details? I'd like to speak to him too.'

Hallforth copied out a number from his own phone, and scribbled an address beside it. 'Waste of time speaking to him anyway,' he said. 'He wasn't even there. Libby had texted him yesterday, but he said he had to work.'

'Still,' said Porter, 'I always try and speak to everyone in the family. Have you let him know what's happening?'

'Yeah,' said Hallforth, almost begrudgingly, 'his mum called him on the way here.'

Porter made a mental note to forward the details to Styles for him to follow up tomorrow, and moved on to the matter of Libby's phone, watching Hallforth's reaction closely as he did.

'We're still examining it, but there's a few things we need to talk about,' he said, taking the heat from his tone. As much as he'd taken a dislike to Simon Hallforth, the man's daughter was missing, even if Hallforth himself had a funny way of coping with it. That, and he had to be careful he didn't come across as too confrontational for the sake of the recording.

'I need to let you know that we found some photographs on there that I'd like you to take a look at.'

Hallforth's cocky I-don't-give-a-toss mask dropped away, eyes slowly closing as he leant forward, resting elbows on the table.

'What kind of photos? Of her, d'you mean? Have you found her?' he asked quietly. 'Is she . . .' He couldn't bring himself to finish the sentence.

No disagreement there. Porter went to reply, but guilt hit him like a slap in the face. He'd been preoccupied with Ally Hallforth, so fixated on the notion of her husband controlling the situation, and why he might do that. So much so that he'd switched rooms to get his answers without mentioning the photos. He'd have to go back in and get her to look at them too. Couldn't leave it to Simon to tell her about them; he looked like he had the tact and compassion of a spoilt child. Porter tuned back in at the tail end of a rant from Simon.

'. . . those bloody fairground lot. I bet you any money one of them has got form.'

'We're speaking to everyone that was there, Mr Hallforth, I promise you that. Now, we're nearly done for this evening. DC Kelly will arrange for someone to take you home. Before we finish, though, I need you to take a look at these pictures we found on her phone.'

Hallforth's forehead crinkled as he watched Porter delve into the folder he'd brought with him, unsure what to expect. The photograph Porter pushed across the table made Hallforth suck in a deep breath, hold it for a three count. Libby's expression in the picture reminded Porter of his nephews, twin boys, forever being told by his mum that their faces would stay that way if the wind changed. Tongue out, eyes crossed. An arm's length selfie, a slight tilt to the camera.

For a second, seeing him stare at the picture of his daughter, it was as if Simon Hallforth had forgotten she was missing, where he was, why he was here. The corners of his mouth tugged up, hinting at a smile.

'She must have bloody hundreds like that on there,' Hallforth said, picking it up, nodding.

'She took this at two minutes past one,' Porter said. 'This one less than sixty seconds later.' He slid a second across beside it. More of the same, except this time Libby looked like she was blowing a kiss to the camera. 'And this one a few minutes later,' he added as a third was laid down beside its companions.

'OK, how does that help us find her, though?' he said, looking between the three pictures, unsure what Porter was getting at.

Porter tapped an index finger in the corner of the first picture, and again on the second picture, to the right of Libby's face. Finally, on the third. He watched Simon's eyes widen as he took it in, looking where Porter had indicated. Seeing the man in the background. The same one each time, judging from the clothes. Blurry, not quite in focus. Watching. Waiting.

CHAPTER NINE

Pins and needles fizz in his ankles and feet, but he stays kneeling. Hasn't moved for twenty minutes, maybe more. Today was meant to be a new beginning. The first step to getting his old life back. Instead it's left him uncertain, confused. Everything is muddied, swirling like pond water after feet dredge up the bottom.

Why had she not recognised him? He closes his eyes, picturing again the confusion on her face. The way her eyebrows pinched in the middle as she looked at him. The way her eyes widened in fear as he'd reached for her.

Light is fading fast, replaced with dusk, settling like a cloak on the city, but here in this oasis of calm, all he can see are green canopies and gnarled trunks. A little over a hundred metres away, green gives way to grey, grass to concrete. The sounds of the city are little more than a backing track here. This place brings him peace, soothes the rapids that sometimes churn in his head. Not today, though. Today, his thoughts are a black whirlpool, drawing in everything around him, dragging them down, and him with it.

He squeezes his eyes shut tighter still, desperately trying to picture her face. It's fading again already, an overexposed strip of film. Same for his son. Even his wife feels like a figment of his imagination on days like this. A construct, with a connection to a past he can't dredge up. It's like he's walking down a hallway lined with doors, memories trapped behind them, voices whispering to him, just on the wrong side of audible.

When he opens his eyes, pinpricks star the edges of his vision and he blinks them away. Another half hour and it'll be dark. He rises to his feet, screws up his face as he stamps the feeling back into his legs. Time to leave, for now anyway. He'll visit again soon, though. He's a creature of habit, a man of routine. One last thing to do before he leaves. He squats down, pats the dry patch of earth by his feet.

'Goodnight, sweetheart. Sleep tight.'

CHAPTER TEN

Styles decided to give it one more go. Third time lucky, he hoped, as he rapped on the door again. Marcus Hallforth lived in a fourth-floor flat, less than a hundred metres away from his parents, in the neighbouring tower block. What had made him move out at such a young age? Lots of teenagers clashed with their parents; that was par for the course. Didn't have to have been blazing rows. Maybe he just wanted his own space, to strike out on his own. Surprising then that he stayed so close.

A lift pinged at the far end of the corridor. A tiny sparrow of a woman came out, dragging a dark green tartan shopping trolley behind her, so full it might even weigh more than she did. She did a double take when she saw Styles, giving him a look that he'd seen more often than he cared to remember. The kind that says, *If you're wearing a suit, and not white, then you must be the defendant.* He flashed her his best *I'm not a drug dealer* smile, but that only seemed to unnerve her even more, and she disappeared inside her flat, heaving the trolley in after her.

He turned his attention back to the door in front of him. Heard the soft rattle of a chain, and the faintest of shadows flickering across the peephole. Definitely home then, just deciding whether Styles was worth answering the door to. A few seconds passed, and just as Styles raised his hand to knock again, the door opened a few inches. Marcus Hallforth peered out through the crack, giving Styles a quick once up and down.

'Marcus Hallforth?'

'Yeah.'

'My name's Detective Sergeant Nick Styles, Met Police. I'm here to have a chat about your sister.'

No need for long explanations. Ally Hallforth had already confirmed she'd told Marcus what had happened yesterday.

'Oh, erm, OK, just give me one minute.'

The face vanished, and the door closed. Five seconds passed. Ten. Styles leant forwards, pressing his ear to the door as faint noises drifted through from inside. Hard to make out: footsteps, an occasional thud. He'd only just pulled his head back from the door when it opened again.

'Sorry, just tidying a few bits away. Place is a state,' Marcus said, standing to one side, gesturing Styles in. They went down a short hallway and into a living room that looked more like a teenager's bedroom. Pizza box on the coffee table, next to three empty Coke cans. A large flat-screen on the wall was paused with some sort of gun poking out from the bottom of the screen. First person shooter game.

'*Call of Duty*?' Styles asked.

'You play?' said Marcus, smiling.

'Me? No, but my wife's nephew is never off the thing. You a fan, I take it?'

'Homework.'

Styles looked at him, not sure he'd heard right. 'Homework?'

'Yeah, I've got an internship with Lycasoft. I want to design games, not just play them. Please, have a seat.'

He might live like a messy teenager, but Styles got the sense that there was a fair bit going on upstairs. You didn't get taken on by software companies unless you had potential. He looked like a younger version of his dad, but without the hard edges. Geek-chic in his skinny jeans, *Rick and Morty* sweatshirt and messed-up mop of dark brown hair.

Styles shuffled a PlayStation controller out of the way and perched on the edge of a couch that looked older than him. 'So, first things first. We haven't found your sister yet,' he said, 'but we've got dozens of officers and volunteers searching the area around Epping Forest.'

Marcus sat shaking his head. 'Just all a bit surreal, you know? You hear about these things on the news, but you never think it'll happen to you. Mum said you'd found her phone. Have you got any idea what might have happened?'

'Not yet,' said Styles. 'We're keeping an open mind, but it's really important that we learn as much as we can about Libby. Sorry to have to ask this, but would you mind telling me where you were between noon and two yesterday afternoon? Just gives us a chance to rule you out of the inquiry right at the start.'

'Here. I was gaming online most of the day.'

'Anyone who can verify that?'

'Yeah, my girlfriend, Susie. Susie Lim.'

Styles got her number and address from him to follow up later.

'Is there any reason you can think of why Libby might run away? Where might she go if she did? That type of thing.'

'She's a bright kid. I keep telling her she's smarter than I was at her age,' he said, a soft smile creeping in around the edges. 'She's not far off beating me on some of these.' Marcus nodded at the TV. 'Not *Call of Duty*,' he corrected quickly. 'She's got her own games.'

'So, no reason you can think of that she'd disappear herself?'

'There are a few kids in her class, mainly girls. They've been picking on her. Squirting water on her schoolbooks, making other kids ignore her, that kind of thing. I don't think she'd just up and leave because of that, though.'

'Do your parents know?'

Marcus gave a low laugh, no humour in it. 'Dad said she needed to toughen up, fight her own battles.'

'Is she close to your mum and dad?' he asked, but that sounded clunky in his head, so he rephrased it. 'I mean, is she a daddy's girl, or closer to your mum, that type of thing?'

'Mum dotes on her. Barely lets her out of her sight.'

Except at fairgrounds, thought Styles, but kept that little barb to himself. Maybe it was just the thought of impending fatherhood, Emma being due in a few weeks, but he couldn't imagine leaving their child for any reason at that age, let alone to grab a bloody coffee.

'It's not that Dad doesn't care,' Marcus continued. 'He just does a good job of making you feel that way.'

'You and he not get on, then?' asked Styles.

'Hmmph, that's one way of putting it,' said Marcus, his tone leaving no room to misinterpret.

'Is that why you live here, not over there?' Styles asked, tilting his head towards the neighbouring tower. 'Don't think I got my own place till I was twenty-five.'

'Let's just say one of us believes that knocking your kids around is a part of being a parent, and the other one disagrees.'

'Your dad hit you?'

'Look, man, it's alright. I tried telling people at the time, and nobody listened, so I left as soon as I could. Doesn't happen to me any more.'

The unspoken inference was there. Doesn't happen to Marcus, but that didn't mean it wasn't happening to anyone else. It had been reason enough for Marcus to up sticks and leave. What would the same treatment do to a seven-year-old girl?

CHAPTER ELEVEN

Last night's follow-up interviews with Libby's parents had given Porter a lot to mull over. Simon Hallforth, for all his attitude, had looked genuinely worried at the prospect of someone having followed them. The shady figure from Libby's photos had stunned him into silence for a good thirty seconds. The quality was poor; Libby's arm must have been at full extension and not steady when she snapped them.

Lorna Shields had a guy on her team who could work wonders with image enhancement, but Porter wasn't pinning much hope on it with these particular pictures. Styles had called in on his way back from visiting Marcus Hallforth. It didn't come as any real surprise to Porter that Simon was the kind of man to raise his hands to his kids. There was every chance Ally might have had the same experience. Could still be living with that now. The fact he'd taken her phone, kept it from her, stopped her from reporting their daughter missing, spoke volumes as to the kind of man he was. Coercive, controlling.

Porter made a few calls off the back of Styles's update. Turned out social services had a file on Simon Hallforth. There had been anonymous reports, three of them, from nosy neighbours maybe, going back ten years. Allegations of violence towards his wife and son. Nothing proven. No action taken.

A team of officers had already carried out a thorough search of the flat and surrounding area. Granted, it was almost eight miles from where she'd been seen last, but his mind flicked again to the Tia Sharp case. He owed it to Libby to make no assumptions, take nothing and nobody at face value.

Simon Hallforth had definitely bumped up a few notches on his list of suspects. Location was a huge problem, though. Most of the roads leading to the visitor's centre were single carriageway, some even single lane. No CCTV, no ANPR – automatic number-plate recognition. Cast the net wider to get back into a coverage area and the number of cars exploded into the thousands, with no way of knowing which had visited the fair and which were just passing through. Libby could have been in any number of those cars, willingly or otherwise. Proper needle-in-a-haystack territory. He'd make sure it was done, but it'd be a juggling act, sacrificing manpower from a physical search.

A dozen other thoughts bounced around his head like bluebottles against a window. Someone would need to look at her school, the kids picking on her, whether that had been enough to send her running. With missing persons, especially where kids were concerned, it always felt like you were up against an egg timer. Get past a certain point, the sand runs out and chances of a happy outcome drop fast, and hard.

Libby's brother would need to come in and give a formal statement as well. They'd even need to speak to her younger sister, Chloe. Speaking to a four-year-old, even in the room they had specially kitted out to look less intimidating, was tricky at the best of times, let alone when you're asking her about her big sister.

The late stint last night hadn't done him any favours. For all things seemed to be going well with Evie, he couldn't remember the last time he'd managed more than four hours' decent sleep, five tops. Hadn't since Holly died. It had started off as not wanting to sleep, preferring not to see her wandering around his dreams like nothing had happened. It was just par for the course now. He was pretty sure Evie hadn't noticed yet. He hadn't thought through what to say if she did, and asked why.

He grabbed a pen and started making a list of everything that had to be done today. Slotting things into a sense of order helped declutter his head. He'd just hit double figures on his list of actions when the phone on his desk rang.

'Porter.'

'DI Porter, it's Lorna Shields.'

'Oh, hi, Lorna. Wasn't expecting to hear back from you so soon. Has your guy worked his magic on those pictures already?'

'The pictures?' She sounded confused for a second, as if she'd forgotten about them. 'Oh, no, that'll take a little longer. There was something else we found, though.'

Something about her tone – grave, serious – reminded him of his own when he was about to deliver bad news.

'What is it?' he asked.

'Blood,' she said. 'We found traces of blood on the screen.'

CHAPTER TWELVE

Five months later

Porter held up a hand to Evie, indicating two minutes. She gave him a thumbs up and disappeared into her dad's house.

'Sorry, mate, you were saying?'

'Yeah, so Milburn is doing the press conference at three this afternoon. He wasn't happy when I reminded him you had the day off, but you know what he's like. He wouldn't have let you get a word in anyway.'

Porter grunted a half-laugh. 'Yeah, he's a proper shrinking violet when it comes to the press.'

Roger Milburn was a mix of many things – part policeman, part politician, part preacher, taking every chance he got to spew out a good sound bite or two. Today's fifteen minutes of fame was to launch a new community policing charter. Styles was bang on that Milburn would hog the limelight. Porter would have been window dressing.

There'd been an incident a year or so back with a suspect who'd been part of the gang that hospitalised Evie. He'd found the right words to push Porter's buttons, making a joke of her injuries. Stoked his anger to the point where he snapped back like an overstretched elastic band. Porter hadn't hit him. He'd only grabbed him, but it had been enough. Passers-by had whipped out phones, and it had been trending on Twitter before you could say 'police brutality'. Ever since then, Milburn had been even more vocal, if that was possible, about everyone doing their part to boost the image of the force.

'He's asked me to take your place, so I reckon that makes it your round next time we're out.'

'If you're that cheap to bribe, I'll get you to stand in every time from now,' Porter shot back.

'This is just a special introductory offer.'

'What about the hotline? Any calls?'

Five months of chasing shadows, no closer to finding Libby Hallforth, had felt like trying to run a marathon blindfolded. Apart from her damaged phone, there had been nothing, no other trace evidence. It was like a magic trick gone wrong. There one minute, gone the next. At Porter's insistence, and despite Milburn's mutterings about budget and manpower better used elsewhere, they had put together a reconstruction of Libby's last known movements that had been broadcast a week ago.

The results had been disappointing to say the least. Because she'd disappeared in an out-of-the-way location, that cut down on passers-by that could reasonably be expected to have seen anything. Some claimed to have seen her, but were easily ruled out because they were regular callers, previously claiming knowledge of anything from the Hatton Garden diamond heist to Madeleine McCann. Nothing that sounded even vaguely genuine.

'Checked in with the team this morning, but no calls for the last few days.'

Porter closed his eyes, pinching the bridge of his nose between finger and thumb. As much as he told himself he had done everything he could, still was, it didn't make him feel like any less of a failure when it came to Libby.

'Alright, cheers, Nick. Anyway, listen, I've got to go, but I'll call you later to hear how your moment in the spotlight with Milburn went.'

Porter ended the call, but rather than head straight inside, he sat for a minute, staring at nothing in particular. Much as he hated to admit it, maybe this was the last dead end. One he'd just have to let go. The reconstruction had been a long shot, hoping someone, somewhere, would have something jogged loose. Maybe someone from out of the area who'd been there for the fair, and left soon after she went missing. Milburn had already warned that if nothing came of it, it would drop down a notch on his list of priorities. That right there was the reason Porter couldn't do his super's job. Wouldn't want to. Making decisions that badged a missing girl as less important than anything else would stick in his throat like a bone. Even the thought of someone else making it pissed him off. Evie's head popped around a curtain, peeping out like a nosy neighbour. Porter made a show of putting his phone away as if he'd just finished the call, and headed inside. She'd left the door open for him, and he followed the sound of voices into the living room.

Evie had slouched back into the big leather armchair by the window, and her dad, Alan, sat on the sofa. He sprang up as Porter walked in.

'Jake, nice to see you again,' he said, reaching out with an overly enthusiastic handshake, then gesturing towards the chair opposite Evie's.

'We were taking bets on whether you were getting called back into work,' Evie said, only half-joking, knowing in their line of work it was always a very real possibility.

'I've got time for a cuppa first,' he said, seeing something between alarm and confusion on Alan Simmons's face. He arched an eyebrow. 'Joking, Alan.'

Alan Simmons broke into a smile, trying his best to make out he'd seen through it. 'Well, I know Julie's cooking has its off days, but people generally don't run away until at least after the starter.'

Smiles all round. Porter had taken an instant liking to Alan when they first met. Granted, not the circumstances you'd want to meet your girlfriend's dad, standing outside a room in A&E, Evie inside with more wires running around her bed than a badly wired house. She'd come a long way since then. They all had. There was something there bubbling beneath the surface, though; whenever work came up in conversation, Alan Simmons seemed to tense up, any smile becoming just that little bit forced. He'd almost lost his only child, so Porter couldn't blame him for worrying about her decision to come back.

It was hard for anyone not on the job to understand the obligation that came with it. It wasn't just a job, not if you did it properly. The types of people they chased after didn't keep office hours, so neither could they. They also weren't exactly the Marquis of Queensberry types when it came to getting physical either. For as long as she was on the job, there would always be an element of risk.

You didn't have to be a detective to pick up on where Alan's thoughts were headed. Both he and Julie had dropped a mention of other careers Evie had nearly followed. How at one point she'd wanted to be anything from a teacher to a social worker. Not that they weren't proud of her, more that her injuries had brought reality crashing in. There'd been a handful of blink-and-you'll-miss-it comments about grandchildren as well. Presumably, that's where Porter came in: their route to grandkids, Evie's to a life away from the force.

His thoughts skipped ahead like a stone across a pond, only letting himself be dragged back into the room when Julie Simmons popped her head around the door.

'Perfect timing, Jake. Lunch is ready.'

They trooped through into the dining room, where everything couldn't have been more perfectly positioned if Julie had used a set square. Slabs of roast beef lay steaming on a platter in the centre, making Jake's mouth water before he'd even sat down. *This is nice*, he thought to himself, pulling his chair out, its legs dragging through thick piled carpet. The notion of being part of a couple, adding their family and friends to your extended circle, had felt an alien concept at first, something to rail against. It had been like sliding into a hot bath, giving it time to work into his muscles, relax him, open him up to the possibilities.

'This smells amazing, Julie,' he said, stabbing his fork into a thick slice of beef, drowning it in gravy almost thick enough to plaster a wall with. Just how it should be.

'Must make a nice change both being off on the same day, eh?' said Alan.

Any other time, Jake would take it as nothing more than small talk, but with where his mind had been minutes ago, it felt more like a side swipe at the job, the hours, the commitment. It wasn't a coincidence that the police force had one of the highest divorce rates by profession, but that was a million miles away from where Porter's head was at, even now they'd been together a while. That was one of the things that made it work for him. Evie seemed happy to live more in the moment than years down the line. That had definitely helped him transition from being just a widower into someone open to possibilities.

'We saw *Crimewatch* last week,' said Julie. 'Still no sign of that poor girl, I take it?'

'Uhn-uh,' said Porter, caught with a mouthful of beef and roast potato. She waited politely for him to finish, hoping for elaboration. 'Nothing new, really. We haven't had the response we hoped for.'

'Hate to say it,' said Alan, 'but I'd bet my house on her not being found alive at this stage. It's been what, four months?'

56

'Five,' said Porter. 'We're not giving up hope just yet, though.'

'I don't know how you do it, you two,' Julie said with a smile.

'Neither do we half the time, Mum,' Evie cut in. 'Can you pass the carrots, please?'

'So, this community policing thing Evie mentioned,' Alan chipped in. 'Will that mean you're not working cases like this one any more?'

'Not if I have anything to say about it,' Porter said. 'Don't get me wrong, it's a good thing, building relationships with the communities and all that, but I couldn't do that full-time. I'd miss the rest of it too much.'

'Why don't you throw your hat in the ring for that, Evie?' Alan said. 'Get to spend more time with Jake?'

She looked down her nose at him, a stern look flipping the parent and child roles around.

'Cos of course that's your endgame there, Dad, isn't it? More quality time for us. Nothing to do with wrapping me in cotton wool?'

'Evie,' he said, with a hurt expression, trying to bat away her insinuation, failing miserably.

'Just let them enjoy their lunch, Alan,' Julie scolded.

For the next few seconds, cutlery clattered against plates as the conversation reset. Porter's mind scrambled for a safe topic to switch to. Evie had mentioned a holiday her parents had booked, but just as he opened his mouth to ask about it, he felt the insistent buzz of his phone under the table. It could wait. He'd not had a day off in the last ten. It soon stopped, but started back up almost immediately. By the third time he noticed the others looking at him.

'It's OK if you need to get that, Jake,' said Julie, but Alan's face told him that he didn't share his wife's view.

'Sorry,' he said, rummaging in his pocket as he stood. 'I'll just be a minute.'

He walked back through to the front room, expecting to see Styles as the culprit, but saw that all the missed calls were from Dee Williams.

'This better be important, Dee,' he said as the call connected. 'I was right in the middle of getting my back waxed.'

Whatever she was going to say turned into a series of confused stutters.

'Joking, Dee,' he said. 'What's up?'

'It's, um, sorry, it's the helpline for Libby Hallforth. We've got something.'

CHAPTER THIRTEEN

'Tell me again,' Porter said. 'From the beginning.'

'I took Milo here out for a walk,' said Madeline Archer, nodding down at the tan dog by her feet. Milo was all ears and tail, staring up at him with a *you're going to feed me, right?* expression. She started explaining how he was a Pomeranian crossed with Shih Tzu crossed with God knows what else, until Porter cut her off.

'He's usually so good, as soon as I shout he's back like a shot, except this time the little so-and-so ignored me, didn't you?'

She bent down, fussing over him and ruffling his ears. Could she last two minutes without petting the damn dog? He kept his best friendly smile fixed front and centre.

'That's when I saw her,' she went on. 'Looked just like the girl from that *Crimewatch* reconstruction last week. Even down to the clothes, that bright red jacket she was wearing.'

'And you saw her face?' he asked. 'You're sure this was the girl?'

He held out a copy of one of the pictures the Hallforths had given them when Libby first went missing.

'Mm-hmm. She was as close as that tree over there, the one with the split branch.' She pointed at a large yew tree, fifty yards away, a gnarled knot of roots fused together, one of its branches splintered, angling downwards like a broken arm. 'She was right there. I called out her name, and she ran off.'

Porter scanned the treeline over her shoulder as he listened. Grove Road cut north to south, through Victoria Park. The park was shaped like a giant boot, and Grove Road cut through north to south just above the foot. The treeline was twenty metres wide, give or take. Deep enough to lose sight of someone, but nothing on the scale of Epping Forest. Victoria Park Pond lay on the other side, paths and trails criss-crossing the area. Seemed improbable that a seven-year-old could vanish in such a public place, again.

Porter had an officer covering each of the nineteen entrances to the park, another dozen picking their way through various clumps of trees. If she was here, they'd find her. How she'd got here was another question entirely. Victoria Park was over ten miles from where Libby had last been seen in Epping Forest, from where she'd vanished like smoke on the breeze.

Truth be told, Porter hadn't expected much from the re-enactment that had been screened the week before. Once the blood in the cracks on the phone screen was matched to Libby, the weeks that followed had passed in a blur, a frenzy of activity, one disappointment after another. Simon Hallforth had been the nearest they'd come to a suspect, what with his temper, previous investigations by social services and his behaviour on the day: not wanting to call the police. All circumstantial, though. Barring Libby's phone, they had nothing. No physical evidence. No sightings, no sign of where she'd gone, or whether she'd gone there alone.

It had been around the one-week mark when the sense of inevitability had started to set in. If she'd run away, that was too long for a seven-year-old to fend for themselves. If she had been taken, then . . . well, that didn't bear thinking about. If this really had been her today, though, maybe she'd escaped from whoever had her. Maybe she was trying to find her way home.

'You said you followed her through the trees?'

'Mm-hmm, but when I came out the other side there was no sign of her. I even had a wander around the lake,' she said, as if she'd turned over every stone in the place.

Nick Styles appeared from the direction they'd been staring in.

'Anything?' Porter called out.

Styles shook his head. 'Nothing yet, boss.'

Porter saw Madeline Archer clock the DS, scrape back stray hairs from her face and run her tongue over her lips. He smiled despite the seriousness of the day, watching Ms Archer give Styles a quick once up and down. If the roles were reversed, Styles would be the first to poke fun at Porter, so he resolved to do exactly that as soon as it was just the two of them.

'Are you his partner?' she asked, holding out her hand. 'You could always take my statement if your boss is too busy.'

Styles wasn't often lost for words, but she managed to silence him for a few seconds while he tried to compose himself.

'There's no rush, we'll finish up the search first and you can always come in and give a formal statement later today or tomorrow,' he said, gently withdrawing from a prolonged handshake.

Porter couldn't resist. 'No, no, Miss Archer. I can spare DS Styles to buy you a coffee and take it here. I think there's a cafe by the lake.'

Porter saw Styles's expression, pleading at first, but it soon changed, looking past him, deep frown lines scored across his head. He turned to see what Styles was staring at. A van had parked up by the side of Grove Road; a man and a woman piled out and trotted over towards them. Porter could make out the logo on the vehicle from here.

'Who the bloody hell called Sky News?' he muttered.

Beside him, he saw Madeline Archer shrug. 'Oh, that was me actually,' she said, all casual, like she'd accidentally spilt a drink.

'You called them before you rang us?' he said, his accusing tone leaving no doubt as to what he thought of that.

'No, no. I called you guys first, but a friend of mine got paid once for calling them about this guy she dated, who had—'

'Miss Archer . . .' Porter started, but then the reporter and her cameraman were beside them.

'Amy Fitzwilliam, Sky News. Is it true that Libby Hallforth has been spotted in Victoria Park?'

Even as she spoke, her cameraman was rolling, lens pointed at Porter. He sighed, shook his head. 'There's nothing I can comment on at this stage. We're just here following up on a lead for a case.'

'But is it the Hallforth case?'

Porter gave a tired smile. 'Amy, was it? I'm DI Porter. Look, Amy, we've not met before, but you must know that all I can give you is a "no comment" at the moment. You take that any way you like.' He turned to Styles. 'Take Miss Archer to the cafe and get her statement. I'll handle this.'

Styles nodded and put a hand on Madeline Archer's shoulder, guiding her away.

'What do you say to accusations that not enough efforts were made to find her first time around, Detective? And what about the rumours that her dad is still a suspect?'

Porter heard the protests of Madeline Archer over his shoulder, bleating on about how they'd better not leave without speaking to her about her tip-off.

'I say you should know that you're not going to get an off-the-cuff comment from me about an ongoing investigation.'

She stared him out for a few seconds, frustration giving way to a wry smile, as she shouted at the retreating figures behind him.

'We'll be here when you're done, Miss Archer.' She turned her attention back to Porter, and shrugged. 'Worth a shot. We'll still get a sixty-second slot even just with the sighting.'

'Alleged sighting,' Porter corrected, seeing the cunning in her eyes a fraction too late.

'Oh, so it is Libby Hallforth then,' she said. 'Thanks for confirming. I'll leave you to it then.'

Porter hated being outwitted, played that easy. Before he could offer any kind of retort, she'd turned her back on him, gesturing for her cameraman to start recording. Porter sidestepped out of shot. Bad enough she'd be cobbling together some bullshit about *sources within the police confirm*. If Superintendent Milburn saw him in shot as she said it, he'd get a bollocking. Probably heading for one anyway. He began wandering towards the lake.

He'd worked a dozen cases since Libby vanished, but she'd never been far from his mind. That she could disappear, with not even a ripple on the surface, while others were forced to carry on, regardless of the hole her disappearance left in their lives. Last time he'd tried to update her parents, only Ally was home. Simon had left, she said. Left, or kicked out, Porter wasn't sure. Couldn't help but feel it was best for all concerned, but Jesus, how much more upheaval could the poor woman have lumped on her? Marcus had moved away too, putting extra miles between himself and what happened. Porter understood that more than most. The allure of running away, pretending the bad shit hadn't happened. Ignore it long enough and it'll go away.

Except it hadn't, not for him. That's what made this thing with Simmons surreal. He liked her. Really liked her. But he still loved Holly. Didn't know if he could ever reconcile the two.

He shook himself out of his mental slump, pulled out his phone and scrolled to find Ally Hallforth's number. They'd mobilised as soon as the call had come in. Hadn't even notified Libby's parents yet. No point getting hopes up unless there was some substance to it. He'd have to make the call now, though. No way could they be allowed to see this without some kind of warning. Parents first; Milburn could wait. He'd barely had time to raise the phone to his ear when he saw a figure trotting through the trees towards him. Not Styles returning. As they stepped out from the treeline, he recognised PC Dee Williams. Her trouser legs were dark, damp-looking from the longer grass, fringe matted to forehead, cheeks flushed.

'Boss, we found something,' she said, breathy from the jog.

'What is it?'

'One of the islands in the lake,' she puffed, drawing level with him now. 'One of the lads says there's something you need to see.'

CHAPTER FOURTEEN

Porter burst through the treeline and skidded to a halt by the side of the lake. Over to the left, a small wooden hut served as a hub for boat hire. Two officers paced along the side, calling out to the handful of rowing boats and pedalos still out on the water, telling them to return to the shaky-looking T-shaped jetty. Williams had lagged behind, but caught him up now, still breathing hard.

'Over there,' she puffed, pointing at the nearest of three small islands in the lake.

The guy in charge of boat hire had clearly resigned himself to a lost afternoon's takings, and pointed out one of the rowing boats, muttering under his breath that business had been slow enough without shit like this. Porter beckoned for Williams to join him and, after a brief pause, she stepped down into the boat, looking about as keen as if he'd asked her to wade across. Not a fan of boats or water, he guessed.

He grabbed an oar, shoving off against the side, and saw Amy Fitzwilliam walking across the grass, the cameraman with his back to the lake, filming on the move. Too far away to hear what she was saying, but suddenly the camera swung around, pointing straight at him. Nothing could be done about that now. A glance over his shoulder, and he caught a flash of movement from behind the trees.

'Couple of our team, boss,' said Williams. 'Tessier and Holloway. Tessier thought he spotted something out there. Flash of colour behind the branches, so they borrowed one of the boats to check it out.'

It only took a minute or so to row over. Not far at all, but Porter still felt the first tickle of sweat running down his back by the time he pulled up alongside the island. There was no obvious landing point so he made do with bumping up alongside the boat Tessier and Holloway had taken over, and lashing the guide rope around a rail, tying the two together.

'You can stay here if you want,' he said. Couldn't help but smile when he saw the look of horror on Williams's face at the prospect of staying on water any longer than absolutely necessary. She followed him, stepping across the two boats in long exaggerated steps, unsteady like a drunk as they bobbed up and down.

The first thing that Porter noticed was the worn trail between the trees. Where he'd first thought there was no natural entry point through the treeline, up close, the vegetation on the bank was trampled down, and not just from a few pairs of feet today. More like a faded hiking trail that nature is constantly trying to erase between footfalls.

'Where you at, fellas?' Porter called into the treeline.

'Bang in the middle, boss,' Tessier's low rumble came back, sounding fairly close.

Porter found them in a matter of seconds. The island couldn't be more than twenty metres by forty, give or take, but with a dense cluster of trees and bushes. Porter was surprised to walk out into a clearing of sorts. Couldn't have measured more than five metres square, but when he looked back, already the shoreline was practically hidden from view.

Gus Tessier stood in the middle, a giant of a man. Styles's height but twice the width. Half-French, half-Ghanaian, the kind of guy you'd want to have your back if things got physical. Porter clocked the look on his face. Solemn, serious; the usual perma-grin he wore was nowhere in sight.

'What is it, Gus? What have you found?'

'A body, boss. We found a body.'

CHAPTER FIFTEEN

Tessier nodded to where Holloway knelt off to one side, and for the first time Porter noticed the flowers. Roses, lots of them. A cluster of rose bushes, blazing colour. Must have been what Tessier had glimpsed. A mixture of blood reds, soft whites, pale peaches and buttery yellows.

DC Zach Holloway knelt by the base of the right-most plant. He stood up, sidestepping out of the way as Porter approached. Holloway held up his makeshift spade: the lower half of an empty Coke bottle.

'Don't worry, boss, I haven't touched it. The soil by this one looked fresher dug than the others. Just looked weird, you know. I mean, what the hell's going on here? It's like a private garden. So I thought I'd take a look, and I found this.'

Porter took another few steps forward, keeping as much distance as he could while still getting close enough. Holloway had scooped out a hole the size of a football. Jutting out by the base, Porter saw the skull, partially exposed. Dry brown earth packed into eye sockets, dark and solid like glass lenses. Bone stained grey-brown from the dirt packed around it. It was small. Not an adult. Could it be Libby? If it was, then the sighting today had been false. This had been buried a while. If not her, then who the hell was it, and if the remains had been there for a while, why had the soil looked recently turned?

With this discovery, the case had sprouted heads like a Hydra. Too many for Porter to wrap his own head around in the moment.

'Don't touch anything else,' he said to the two officers. 'Williams, get back in the boat. We need to get this place locked down. Find out who's in charge of the park – a manager, groundskeeper, anyone like that.'

He took in the rest of the clearing, noticing for the first time how carefully shaped it looked. Surrounding trees had been pruned back, branches cut on angles to let sunlight get to the roses. Not pared back completely, though, as if whoever had done this wanted it screened from nosy eyes. This clearing, garden, whatever it was, looked man-made for sure.

'Let's make sure every boat is off the water. I want CSIs across here within the hour. Doesn't change the fact that our witness claims to have seen Libby. We treat this as a new case until we have a reason to link them. Whoever that is, it's not the kid that Madeline Archer saw.'

A sharp crack, somewhere in the trees beyond Holloway. All three heads snapped towards it. Porter tensed, took a few steps forward, holding out a hand to signal the others to stand their ground. A chorus of crunches, cracks and rustling followed, voices muttering, getting closer. There, in the trees, pale between the branches. A face.

Porter cursed under his breath as Amy Fitzwilliam pushed past the last few branches, joining them in the clearing. 'Fuck's sake. You need to leave. Now.'

Without being asked, Gus Tessier stepped around the rose bushes, blocking any view of the hole. The nameless cameraman already had his lens pointed at them, scowled at Tessier and tried to sidestep him. Tessier held both arms out to the sides, a one-man crowd control.

'You heard DI Porter. I'm gonna need you to head back to your boat.'

'What's all . . .' Fitzwilliam's voice drifted, taking in the clearing, forgetting about her own camera for a second, then snapped back into focus like she'd been rebooted. 'Detective Porter, what have you found over here? Anything yet to confirm the sighting of Libby?'

She peered past Tessier, through the gap under his arms to be precise. Stick him in a white shirt and black overcoat, he could double as a doorman. Barrel-chested, biceps straining against his jacket.

'Pan around, Jamie, get a shot of all this,' she said, eyes roving upwards, turning a slow circle, before looking back down at the flowers. 'Whatever this is.'

Jamie the cameraman followed suit, panning around in a lazy arc. Tessier stepped forward, his hand the size of a hardback blocking the cameras view. Amy Fitzwilliam moved quickly, taking advantage of the big man's attention being on the camera, ducking under an outstretched arm and past the flowers, stopping only feet away from Porter.

He instinctively glanced down, and wished he hadn't. Her gaze followed his, dropping to the mini excavation by Holloway. He knew straight away that she'd clocked it, seen exactly what was in there. Eyes and mouth widening in tandem. Looking like she wanted to speak, but the words had gotten snagged on the way out. They stood, as if someone had pressed pause, and stayed like that for the full five seconds it took her to find her voice again.

'Is that her? Is that Libby?'

Shit. No putting this cat back in any kind of bag.

CHAPTER SIXTEEN

Styles stood alone on the side of the lake as Porter rowed back across. Off to the left, Amy Fitzwilliam and her cameraman were taking baby steps along the shifting jetty, deep in conversation. The damage was well and truly done. Porter knew she'd already broadcast one live segment earlier, confirming their tip-off about Libby. He was pretty sure Tessier's bulk had blocked the remains on the island from being captured on camera, but the young female reporter wasn't going to unsee that any time soon.

An ache spread down his neck, radiating out across his shoulders, moving upwards, a dull drumbeat of a headache. *Shit*, he thought. In the rush to get across to the island, he'd forgotten to call Ally Hallforth. *Please God, don't let her have been watching the news in the last half hour.* He dipped the oars, using them to brake, and bumped the boat against the side. Styles reached down, pinning it to the shore as he stepped out.

'That looked interesting,' he said, nodding over to the Sky News team. 'What have they found, anyway?'

Porter told him about the clearing, the roses, what was buried beneath one of the bushes. Styles looked back over to the reporter. 'How much of it did she get?'

'Just a general shot, not the skull, at least I don't think so. Bad enough that they've gone public with the Libby angle, though.'

'Like you said, though, that can't be her, not if what Madeline Archer says is on the money.'

'And?' Porter asked. 'Is it?'

Styles shrugged. 'She believes what she's saying. Described Libby quite well, but then again, her picture was all over the papers at the time, and the same piccies were on *Crimewatch* last week. Could be that she's just projecting.'

'Any luck with the rest of the search yet?' Porter asked.

'Nothing yet,' said Styles. Porter noticed his DS peering a little more closely at him. 'You OK, boss?'

'Course I am. Why?'

'Just look a little tired, that's all,' said Styles.

'I'm fine,' Porter said, a little too brusquely. 'Just fools like those two winding me up.'

Back towards Grove Road, the retreating figures of Fitzwilliam and her cameraman merged with a copse of trees as they disappeared through them.

'Listen, Nick, I need to go and see Ally Hallforth. Can you stick around here, coordinate the rest of the search? Think it's mostly the north-east part left. I've left Tessier and Holloway across there to guard the scene until the CSIs get here.'

'Course, boss. Get yourself away,' said Styles, clapping a hand on Porter's shoulder.

Porter thanked him and turned to leave. He pulled out his phone as he walked. Face-to-face was always best, but it was worth checking Ally Hallforth was in before he made the journey. Before he could call her, he spotted a missed call from Superintendent Milburn. Rarely good, but it could wait.

Ally's number went to voicemail. Sod it, he'd go there anyway. He owed her that much. He quick timed it back to where he'd left his car on Old Ford Road. A scrap of paper fluttered under his wipers. An unsigned note from one of the lovely residents calling him ignorant for parking on the residents-only side of the street, threatening to call the police if he did it again.

Yeah, good luck with that, he thought, scrunching it up and tossing it in the back seat. A text chirped as he slid his phone into the cup holder. Evie, wondering if he wanted to meet for a coffee. He fired off a quick reply saying he was tied up, and connected to Bluetooth to call Milburn along the way.

Sack off your girlfriend, and snap at your DS. Now you get to head round to drag a poor woman back into the same dark place you left her months ago.

Fair to say he'd had better days. Unlike Ally Hallforth, Milburn picked up after one ring. Must have been sitting with his hand practically hovering over it.

'Ah, DI Porter. So glad you found time to check your phone.'

Roger Milburn took passive aggressiveness to an Olympic level. Porter couldn't quite get a read on him. Milburn was straight down the middle, called a spade a spade, qualities that Porter believed they shared. At times, though, it was as if he chipped away for no reason, trying to get a reaction, to prove that everyone had shortcomings.

'Sorry, sir, I was dealing with a situation.'

'So that's what you're calling it.'

Porter knew then that Milburn had either seen or been told about the run-in with Sky News, and subsequent broadcast.

'Sir, if I can explain. The—'

'The only explanation you need to give right now is to that girl's

73

parents,' he snapped. 'I've had the father on the phone, reading the riot act, threatening to go to the papers about how you practically accused him of kidnapping his own daughter back then, and that we didn't even have the decency to tell him she'd been spotted.'

'Sir, we couldn't confirm the sighting. Our witness is sketchy at best.'

'Don't get me wrong,' Milburn continued as if Porter hadn't even spoken. 'He's an odious little man, but he shouts loud enough and this will make us look insensitive and incompetent. I only hope for your sake that he doesn't follow through and sell his story.'

Porter had never ruled Simon Hallforth out in his mind, but fought back the urge to lay into the man now. He'd heard that tone from Milburn too many times. More politician than policeman, all about the image. His and the Met, probably in that order. Porter had gotten on the wrong side of him last year, after a colleague turned out to be on the take from one of the biggest organised crime bosses in London, and Milburn had viewed everyone with suspicion. Guilty until proven innocent.

'Top priority is for you to speak to the parents. They should hear these things from us, not a bloody reporter.'

'On my way to see the mother now,' said Porter.

'Good. Right, I'm at a charity do with the assistant chief constable in an hour, so I'll leave you to it. Let's have an update first thing tomorrow morning.'

Porter swore as he ended the call. His boss had the knack of making him feel like a chastised child at times. Rattling off lists of tasks, as if Porter didn't have the experience or the brainpower to work his own cases. What was already a shitty day took a turn for the worse when he hit traffic. A handful of motorcycles and Deliveroo riders whistled past him while he inched forwards, tortoise to their hare.

Maybe just as well he didn't see Evie tonight. The day's events hadn't exactly left him in a sparkling mood, and it wouldn't be fair to take it out on her. What could take fifteen minutes on a good day became a forty-minute snail's pace of a drive along Eastway, past signs for Queen Elizabeth Olympic Park, bumper to bumper, cars shuffling along like a production line.

He pulled up outside John Walsh Tower, under the watchful eye of a trio of kids on bikes. The eldest couldn't have been more then twelve, the others a few years younger. The smallest of the three pedalled towards him, weaving around a blanket of glass fragments glistening in the disappearing sun like a layer of frost.

'Look after your car for a fiver, mister,' he piped up, glancing back at his mates, as if to say, *See, told you I'd do it.*

'You give police discount?' Porter asked, pulling out his warrant card.

The boy stared for a second, eyes widening in surprise, before whipping his front wheel around and heading back to join his mates. The other two watched him as he walked off, and he wondered if his car would get any special treatment. Banana up the exhaust, snapped aerial, dog shit placed carefully under his wheels.

No officer answering the door this time. Just Ally Hallforth. She looked smaller than he remembered. A sad smile when she saw who was at her door. The kind that said she'd accepted her new reality. The one where her eldest daughter had no place, where she had no resolution.

'Mrs Hallforth, I don't know if you remember me, I'm—'

'Detective Porter,' she said. 'Yes, I remember you.' The briefest of smiles, then the realisation that a policeman was at her door again. 'Would you like to come in?'

'Yes, please,' he said, following her inside.

As he walked into the living room, it was the absences he noticed. No overpowering nasal bashing from a liberal dousing of stale cigarette smoke. No undertone of weed. No obnoxious husband. Had Simon stormed out in a fit of the temper Porter had seen flashes of himself? A tinny melody made him whip his head around. Chloe Hallforth sat cross-legged, oblivious to his presence, holding a moulded plastic book, new nursery rhymes starting with each turn of a page. Ally looked tired, as if just dragging herself through the day was an effort. She tried a tired smile when she offered him a cup of tea, but it didn't reach her eyes.

He waited while she pulled clinking mugs out of the cupboard, squeezed teabags against the edges and carried their cuppas through to the living room. He realised then that she hadn't actually asked him why he was here today. That could only mean one thing.

'Simon called me,' she said, perching on the edge of the sofa. 'I've asked him not to ring. I'd usually ignore his calls, but he withheld his number. Anyway, he told me what he'd seen on the news, that a lady had seen our Libby. Is it true?'

This last bit came out as a loud whisper, rough around the edges.

'It's true we got a response from last week's re-enactment,' he began, not wanting to give her too much hope without cause. 'A lady claiming she'd seen Libby, red coat and all, walking in the woods at Victoria Park.'

'He told me I needed to switch the telly on. Watch it for myself. I tried, I wanted to, but I just couldn't do it, you know?' Her words were heavy with emotion, brittle, bordering on breakable. 'It's taken me this long to even start to get my head around the fact I might not see her again,' she continued. 'I say "get my head round", more like admit to myself that it's possible.'

'We've not given up on her yet, Mrs Hallforth,' he said, sitting down next to her. 'I haven't given up on her. You shouldn't either.'

'He tried calling back again, about ten minutes before you turned up. At least I assume it was him. Didn't answer that one, though. What exactly did this woman see, then?' she asked.

Her words came out shaky, tentative, not wanting to put it out there that she believed there could be any truth to this.

'Honestly, not much more than you already know,' he said. 'The

76

lady was out walking her dog. Says she saw a young girl, and that it reminded her of the reconstruction. Similar age, similar hair colour, similar coat. She called out her name, but the girl disappeared behind some trees, and she didn't see her again.'

'Could it have been her, do you think?' she asked.

Talk about rock and hard place. Do anything except sit on the fence, and he'd raise her spirits or undermine her hope. If he didn't commit, she stayed in limbo. He went with door number three, the lesser of three evils.

'It really is impossible to say just now, Mrs Hallforth. I've got two dozen men searching the park, and we're pulling CCTV from the streets around it.'

She leant forwards slowly, elbows on knees, palms flat together prayer style, eyes squeezed tight shut. So much to dredge up again. He tried to put himself in her shoes, imagining the choice she must face every day. Living in a constant state of hope, feeling hollowed out every day that passed with no news, or accepting your child wasn't coming home, hating yourself for giving up on them.

Chimes echoed down the hall, followed in quick succession by hammering on the door. Ally Hallforth jumped like she'd been plugged into the mains as the muffled voice shouted from outside the flat.

'Ally, it's me. Simon. We need to talk. You have to let me in. Please.'

That last word almost sounded sincere. Not one Porter would have used to describe the Simon Hallforth he remembered.

Ally stayed sitting, all the while looking ready to bolt, like a cornered animal. Porter wondered again what their marriage had been like when it was just the two of them around, no witnesses. There was no mistaking the nervousness. It came off her in waves. Eyes darting towards the door then back again, fingers on one hand rubbing at the knuckles of the other.

'Why don't I get the door?' said Porter.

'Just leave him be,' she said, almost a whisper, shaking her head. 'He'll just go away if we leave him.'

'You're sure? I can ask him to leave if he's bothering you.'

'It's alright,' she said, with a sad smile that spoke of countless times like this in the past.

'Ally!'

Louder this time, not just a knock, more like a fist bashing against the door.

'Open the bloody door.'

Any hint of sincerity was gone. Now he just sounded annoyed, entitled to enter. Porter went to stand, but Ally waved him down again, finger to her lips. He sank back down, respecting her wishes for now, but started a silent ten count. Any more than that and he'd do what needed to be done.

'If you won't listen to me, then turn on your bloody telly,' he shouted in between bursts of banging. 'There's a body. They're saying it's her.'

Porter had heard enough, and pushed up from the couch. He opened the door so quickly that Simon Hallforth, who had been just about to knock, swung his fist through the space where the door had been.

'Mr Hallforth, I'm going to need to you take a step back, a deep breath, and calm down. Whatever they're saying on the news hasn't come from us. It's speculation.'

Simon recovered from the surprise of a face other than his wife's in a heartbeat.

'Ally!' he shouted past Porter, then went to step around him to get inside.

Porter leant across, blocking the doorway, putting a hand out to stop him.

'Like I said, sir, I need—'

'Yeah, yeah, and I need to get inside my flat,' Simon said, trying his luck on the other side.

'From what I hear, it's not your flat any more,' Porter said, blunt and to the point.

Simon stepped back, giving Porter a confused once up and down. 'If it's a load of rubbish, then what the hell are you doing here?' he said.

'It's true we had a call saying someone had seen Libby, but we haven't been able to confirm anything much more than that right now.'

'Yeah?' he said, and Porter saw a malicious glint in his eyes. 'You might not have, but someone sure as hell has.'

Porter was about to politely, professionally, give him the party line again, when he heard a choking sob from inside the flat. He pointed a finger at Simon.

'Stay here, please.'

He edged back inside, turning to keep one eye on the doorway, glancing back into the living room. Ally Hallforth swayed ever so gently, like a tree in a soft breeze. Both hands cupped over her mouth. Porter followed her gaze. Saw the tickertape scrolling along the bottom of the television screen.

Police find human remains in search for Libby Hallforth. Sources confirm it's the body of a young girl.

CHAPTER SEVENTEEN

Nick Styles squirmed as stray beads of sweat worked their way down his back. Crime scene suits were paper-thin, but wearing one over a suit, coupling the extra insulation together with being on his feet for the last few hours helping scour the grounds of Victoria Park, wasn't exactly his idea of a perfect day.

Emma had called four times at last count. Could he pick up some eggs on the way home? Had Porter said whether he and Simmons could make it for dinner? Would he have time to build the cot-bed this weekend? All innocent enough, but he knew her well enough to pick up on the little comments here and there. She'd had a nervousness about her for a while now, ever since Styles had been injured last year by a member of an organised crime gang he and Porter had taken down. Those feelings had multiplied like bacteria in a petri dish when she'd become pregnant. She'd even tried to convince him to move jobs. Not leave the force, just a sideways step into a less risky role. They'd talked it through, but agreed eventually that he should stay put. Now, he was pretty sure she'd swung back the other way again. A discussion for another day.

Across the clearing, a team of four CSIs, suited and booted in white, shuffled around each other. One bagged soil samples. Another snapped pictures of everything, from the clearing itself, the rose bushes that lined a chunk of the perimeter, down to the hole by their feet. It was much larger now, carefully excavated. The remaining two waited until the snapping was finished, capturing everything in situ, before reaching in, one of them carefully lifting out the skull. He held it in both hands, like some kind of precious artefact, slipping it into a plastic evidence bag that his colleague held open.

Styles continued to watch as bone after bone followed, a grisly collection to be reassembled, a gruesome jigsaw waiting to be pieced back together.

'Anything you can tell me from that lot?' Styles asked the CSI closest to him. 'Best guess on how long, and male or female?'

'Literally best guess for now, so don't hold me to anything, but I'd say whoever this is has been here for a year, maybe more. Pretty sure it's female, though,' he said, and pointed to one of the evidence bags. 'This is the pelvic bone. See here, the pelvic inlet is a tiny bit more of a rounded shape than you'd see if it was male. It's only a slight difference at this age though, and can be hard to spot in many of them, but I'd say I'm about eighty per cent on it right now. The lab should be able to confirm it for you though. If I'm right, I'd say we're looking at a young female, probably no older than ten.'

It wasn't as if he hadn't already considered the possibility, but hearing it confirmed that the remains fitted Libby's profile cast a shadow over his mood. In the absence of anyone talking, above the rustling of suits, crinkling of plastic bags and scraping footsteps, he heard another noise. He couldn't quite place it at first, but it sounded electronic, like a series of tinny beeps. He pulled out his phone.

Nothing. He looked over at the CSIs, but none of them were holding or even reaching for any kind of device.

He skirted the edge of the clearing, angling his head, holding his breath as he waited to hear if it would be repeated. Nothing. He stepped into the treeline, branches whipping back into place behind him. No movement to suggest anyone else was out here. They had a man at the boat hire shack now, so it was doubtful that anyone else could have nabbed a boat and rowed over without being noticed.

Five seconds passed. Ten. Still nothing. Must have been hearing things. He shook his head and turned back towards the clearing. A flicker of light from a tree off to his right, blazing bright, like a camera flash, but gone the instant he took a step forward. Styles took a pace back, wincing as the same beam of light hit his eye. He took a quick scan around, but still nothing, save for the CSIs ten feet back through the trees.

He stepped carefully through the undergrowth, closing the distance, and that's when he saw it, wedged into a fork in a tree branch. A phone, some model of Samsung, perched six feet up, pointing in the general direction of the clearing. Styles reached up a gloved hand, taking it between thumb and forefinger, and turned it to face him.

The screen was on, a blur of green as he plucked it from its perch. His own face loomed large onscreen, peering out at him as he bent down, squinting to see against the reflection from what sunlight filtered through the canopy. In the top right corner, a smaller window, a woman's face, distracted, looking off to one side.

'What the bloody hell is this?' Styles said.

Amy Fitzwilliam's head whipped around, eyes wide in surprise, but only for a second. Shock gave way to an apologetic smile.

'Detective Styles, isn't it?' she said. 'Can't thank you enough for finding my phone. Whereabouts had I dropped it?'

'Six feet up a tree,' he said, no attempt to disguise his annoyance. 'Mind telling me what it's doing here?'

Rhetorical question. He already knew. Her own personal CCTV. She must have set it up before Porter found her creeping around earlier. He wished now he'd paid more attention to its position, to get a better idea of exactly what she'd seen. Porter would hit the roof when he heard. And that'd be mild compared to what Milburn would have to say, depending on what she might have heard. *No sense stressing over what you can't control,* he thought. *Might not even have captured anything.*

'So, I hear it's definitely a young girl you found out there then?' she asked, innocent, like butter wouldn't melt.

CHAPTER EIGHTEEN

Porter watched in horror as Amy Fitzwilliam gave her latest update. Behind her, the island showed no signs of life in the fading light. A reputable outlet like Sky wouldn't run with something like that as pure speculation. They had to have gotten the information from somewhere, even if it was utter rubbish. From where, though, or from who? And if it was true, if they had confirmed the remains to be those of a young female, why was the first he was hearing about it on national bloody television?

Simon Hallforth had edged inside the living room while Porter made sure Ally was alright. Her head bobbed up at the sound of him clearing his throat over by the door.

'You OK, Al?' Simon said in a timid voice.

'Do I bloody well look OK?' she snapped at him. 'Get out, just get out. You've done enough harm already.' For once he seemed lost for words, and she didn't give him time to recover. 'This is my flat now, and you' – she spat out the word – 'are not welcome. This is all your fault. Get out, get out, get out.'

Her voice rose higher each time, words blurred by tears, merging, coming out in a single breath.

Porter put an arm around her shoulder. 'I think it's best if you left now, Mr Hallforth.' Simon looked gobsmacked at the prospect of being ordered out of what used to be his home, but channelled any hurt he was feeling into anger, staring Porter out for a few seconds, then storming off down the corridor.

'Fucking incompetent coppers, and I'm the one getting grief.'

The door slammed behind him. Ally Hallforth shook as she sobbed, a mixture of grief and anger robbing her of the ability to speak. After a full minute, she peeled away from Porter.

'I'm sorry, Detective. He doesn't take well to being told what to do.' She wiped tear tracks from her cheeks with the heel of each palm. 'My God, I'm a mess.'

He grabbed a box of hankies from the coffee table, passed her one and waited while she ran it under each eye. It came away black with mascara from both.

'I can't believe my baby's gone,' she said, staring at the floor, speaking as much to herself as to him.

'Let me make a few calls, Mrs Hallforth. It's true, we did find human remains,' he said, pausing to let that sink in, 'but I only left the park an hour ago. There's no way we've gotten a positive ID in that time, let alone shared anything with the press.'

'Why would they say that on TV, then? They must have got it from somewhere.'

He shrugged. 'I honestly don't know, but I'm going to find out, I promise you that. Is there someone I can call to come and keep you company? I could arrange for a family liaison officer to come around?'

She shook her head. 'Thank you, but I'd rather just be on my own for a bit, I think. What happens now?'

'Now I'll speak to my colleagues and see where the reporters are getting their information from. If you change your mind about being on your own, let me know.'

He promised to call her as soon as he found out anything, and took the lift back down to his car. As soon as he was outside he called Styles.

'Have you seen the news?' he asked, no introductions.

'No, I'm still at the park, boss, but I can imagine.'

'What do you mean?'

Styles filled him in on the makeshift CCTV that the reporter had set up. Porter had seen journalists get creative before, but this took it to a new level. Any anger was tinged with a tiny bit of admiration. Thinking on your feet, on an island full of police officers, bang in the middle of a crime scene, suggested the kind of calmness under pressure you saw in journalists who spent their careers in warzones. Wouldn't stop him from lodging a complaint with her boss, though.

Parts of the investigation would be straightforward, with binary yes or no answers. It either was Libby they had found or it wasn't. If it was, what a shitty way for her parents to find out, especially if Fitzwilliam had managed to get actual footage. If it wasn't, then some other poor bugger had just had their daughter exhumed on camera. The press could be a useful tool in policing if the boundaries were set and stuck to. This had been irresponsible journalism, but it'd be the police, not the press, that people would be raising eyebrows at in tomorrow's tabloids.

'How did it go with Mrs Hallforth?' Styles asked.

'Oh, it was a barrel of laughs. She hadn't even seen the news when I got there, then the husband turned up and started shouting about it through the door.'

Styles groaned. 'You thinking we take another look at him if this is Libby?'

'I think we'd be daft not to,' said Porter. 'Once we know however long she's been there, whoever she is, we can see what we can get from the perimeter, any shops with CCTV, ANPR along the roads.'

86

It'd be a big job, he thought. They'd have a fairly wide time window to search through, hundreds of hours of footage, most of it probably not great quality, and that's if it still existed. Many places would delete it after a few months.

'What about the mum and brother?'

'Let's see who she is first, but yeah we'll need to go back to basics. Victoria Park is way outside the original search perimeter. It's gonna mean long days whoever we've found.'

'What's the plan then, boss?'

Porter looked at his watch. Just gone 8 p.m. 'Today, not much else we can do really. First thing tomorrow we look for every camera that covers any approach to the park, exits and entrances especially. Make sure the place is sealed off for the night once the CSIs are done. I want a couple of volunteers for overtime as well, for tonight at least. Wouldn't surprise me if that bloody journo tried a late-night boat ride back over.'

'Might not be willing volunteers, but I'll sort it,' said Styles.

'Get yourself away home once you have,' Porter said. 'I've got a feeling we've got a long few days coming up. I'll see you bright and early back at the station.'

'Ah, yeah, before I forget, it'll be around ten by the time I get in if that's still OK?'

'If what's still OK?' Porter asked, none the wiser.

'Emma's got a midwife appointment,' said Styles, bordering on apologetic. 'Mentioned it a few weeks back when we booked it.'

Porter had a vague recollection of an appointment, but there had been a few, and they blurred into one another.

'Oh yeah, of course. No worries, I'll just see you when you get in then. Oh, one more thing,' he added, 'get a patrol car to pop round and check up on Ally Hallforth, will you? She was pretty shook up when I left her, and I want to make sure her ex doesn't come back around and harass her as soon as I've gone.'

Styles promised to add that to his list. Porter ended the call and started his engine. No sign of Simon Hallforth, but with the light fading fast, shadows were pooling around the base of the tower. Plenty of dark corners for him to be lurking in, waiting for Porter to drive off. He squinted, peering into the gloom, seeing only a handful of optimistic kids chasing after a dirty grey football on Wanstead Flats behind the tower block. The enterprising junior car-park attendants who'd tried to fleece him on the way in were nowhere to be seen.

He pulled slowly away from the kerb, thinking through his options. It wasn't too late to call Evie back, tell her he was done for the day. Her place was closer than his from here. Worse ways to spend an evening, that's for sure. What if she was still at the station, though? He pressed a button on the steering wheel to kickstart the voice-activated dialling, but hit the cancel button part-way through the prompt. What about the bloody cat? He hadn't left enough food out back home if he stayed over at Evie's. Demetrious had enough attitude about him already without pissing him off by depriving him of dinner.

Porter wound his way home through thinning traffic. It had taken a while for it to feel like home after Holly died. For almost two years, he hadn't been able to bring himself to get rid of her things. Clothes, make-up, shoes, jewellery. A hundred odds and ends that she'd never use or wear again, but they'd been all he had left.

Evie hadn't chased after him. Not really. She'd made it obvious she was interested, but had let him make the decision in his own time. It wouldn't have worked any other way. The first date, a coffee, had felt surreal, like he was a kid again, not sure what to say or how to behave. Those that followed, drinks in pubs far enough away from the station that they wouldn't be spotted or bothered, had eased him into the idea of being with someone else. She hadn't pushed him, letting him take his time to come to the realisation that being with someone else didn't mean he had to forget about Holly.

Whether what they had was strong enough to stand any kind of stress-test, they'd have to play that by ear. For now, though, it felt good. Having someone who understood the job, the pressures that came with it. Highs and lows. Someone he could relax around, and not have to worry about placating them if he took a call at three in the morning that meant he had to jump out of a warm bed.

His brain cruised along in neutral most of the way home, carried along in that same current of thought. Home was a two-bed flat on Margaret Road in New Barnet that used to belong to Holly's grandmother.

Even before he closed the door behind him, a low rumbling like an idling engine filtered through from the kitchen.

'I know, I know. Sorry I'm late, D. You can call the RSPCA back and tell them to stand down,' he said, as a pair of unblinking green eyes stared at him from the shadowy three-inch crack between door and frame.

Porter slipped off his jacket and followed his disgruntled flatmate into the kitchen. By the time he flicked the lights on, Demetrious had slunk over to the corner, staring expectantly from Porter to his bowl and back again. Porter had always been more of a dog person. It hadn't been his decision to get a cat. Holly had turned up with him one day, rescued him from a local shelter, and Porter had moved one place down the pecking order. He couldn't imagine not having him around now, though. Up until recently, with Evie now on the scene, he'd had more conversations outside of work with Demetrious than any other living being. Everything from venting about Milburn to Porter working through his case strategies out loud.

He peeled back the foil on a pouch of food that didn't need the pictures of salmon on the front to give away the contents. Porter wrinkled his nose as he slid it into Demetrious's bowl. He pulled a sweet and sour chicken ready meal from the fridge for himself. Bachelor cuisine at its finest. He'd not eaten since lunchtime, and it barely touched the sides. It was tempting to double up and throw a second one in the microwave, but he fought the urge, and trudged through to bed instead.

The search had taken its toll on his feet; the visit to Ally Hallforth had done the same on his mind. He and Holly had talked about starting a family. No idea if that was on Simmons's agenda. Way too soon to know if he was ready to consider it with anyone else himself. All the same, he knew the last five months must have been some of the hardest a parent could face. The lack of resolution, the not knowing what had happened to your baby girl. Whether or not she was still out there. And after all that heartache, they might well have their closure now, in the most brutally public way.

He climbed into bed, hitting the pillow like a puppet with its strings cut, breathing slowing. His eyes snapped back open. Twisting around, he slid his bedside drawer open and saw her looking up at him. A photo from their wedding. Holly scooped up in his arms, one hand around his neck, the other stretching out to wave at the photographer. He'd stashed it here the first night Simmons stayed over. Feeling guilty on both fronts: that he'd felt the need to move it, but didn't want her to feel conscious of Holly staring at them.

He stared at it, floating back to that moment. Feeling her weight in his arms. The squeaky sound she made when he pretended to drop her. Porter lifted the frame out, traced a finger across her face, then carefully set it back on the bedside table, watching her watching him. Feeling the heaviness in his eyes. Seeing her face. The last thing on his mind before it all faded to black.

CHAPTER NINETEEN

He's been staring at the screen so long that when he blinks, fireflies star his vision. Sometimes he can bring himself to turn the volume up, but today isn't one of those. Today is one of his black days. Storm clouds gather in his head, a vortex of emotion so confusing that it hurts to try and make sense of it all.

The children rolling around on the TV screen are rosy-cheeked, padded coats and hair dusted with snow. The girl throws a snowball that hits the boy square in the face. He blinks in surprise, stunned for the briefest of seconds, before he roars a silent challenge back at her, scooping a double handful of powdery snow and charging towards her. The girl shrieks and turns to run. Even without sound, it echoes in his mind from the dozens of times he has watched before. It soothes him. A visual comfort blanket to ward off bad thoughts.

The boy is younger than her, but big for his age, and he catches her within ten feet, barging into her and knocking her to the ground, scrubbing snow into her hair and face. He can't help but smile, despite the darkness of his mood, at the sheer childish fun of it all, remembering it as if it were yesterday. Feeling the cold breeze sting his cheeks, numbing his fingers as he'd tried to keep the camera steady.

Then *she* comes into shot, and his hands grip the armrests reflexively, fingers digging into material hard enough to make the tips tingle. He swings from love to hate, and back again. He repeats the mantra.

It's my fault. All of it.

He's not sure any more whether that's true. Can't remember what it was he did, though the feeling of guilt weighs heavy as any anchor. There's a veil across it all, blocking his view whenever he tries to look back. She's the mother of his children. She's also the reason he lost them. The one who took them away. The one who can give them back. He still loves her. Doesn't mean to say he hasn't thought about making her feel an ounce of his pain. He'll do what he has to, though, to get them all back. Swallow his pride. Do whatever it takes.

He thinks back to the fairground, picturing the look on the girl's face as he walked towards her. Confusion in her voice as he took her hand. Fear in her eyes as he reached out a hand to stop her calling out.

CHAPTER TWENTY

Porter did a double take at the empty seat beside him, before he remembering Styles wasn't in until ten. Plenty to keep him occupied in the meantime. First on his list was a call to the pathologist, see what favours could be called in to fast-track the autopsy.

'I'm good, but even I'm not that good,' said Dr Isabella Jakobsdottir.

'Don't sell yourself short, Bella,' Porter said, dropping formality in favour of the shortened version. 'You don't even know what I'm going to say yet.'

'You're not going to say anything,' she shot back. 'You're going to ask, and no, I haven't started yet.'

'Hmm?'

'Your rush-job from yesterday. DS Styles caught me working late last night, and said he'd buy my lunch for a week if it jumped to the front of the queue.'

Not what he'd expected, and he made a mental note to add a drink to Styles's tab.

'Well, strictly speaking he said you'd be doing the buying,' she continued, 'but let's not split hairs. Anyway, it'll be done before lunch. Perfect timing when you think about it, seeing as you'll be buying.'

Porter agreed to turn up at noon, sandwich in hand. He scanned the office. A few of the faces from yesterday's park search were milling about. Quick check of the watch. Another forty-five minutes until Styles arrived. Made sense to go ahead with the morning briefing, and he could bring him up to speed when he got here. He stood up to round up Tessier, Williams and the others, but dropped back into his seat as his desk phone rang. He recognised the voice as Annette from the front desk.

'Got a fella here to see you, DI Porter. Have you got two minutes?'

'Not really,' he said, huffing at the timing. 'He give a name?'

'Uh-uh.' Sounded like she was sipping from a cup between every sentence.

'Did he at least say what it's about?'

'Mmm.' Another swallow. 'Didn't actually ask for you by name,' she said cryptically. 'Asked for whoever was in charge of the Libby Hallforth case.'

Porter rolled his eyes, knowing what was most likely coming. High-profile cases tended to tease all sorts out of the woodwork. People who'd confess to killing Kennedy if you caught them on the right day. They usually called up, but there were always walk-ins too. He thought fast, preferring to get the briefing done, tasks allocated and the team sent scurrying off to turn over rocks.

'Tell him I'm heading into a meeting. I'll send someone down to take his statement.'

'I think you might want to speak to him yourself,' she said, lowering her voice, as if he was standing right next to her, eavesdropping. 'He's insisting it's got to be the person in charge. He's got a little girl with him.'

* * *

94

Porter took the stairs two at a time, four floors down, thoughts skittering around his head, breathing fast. The majority of kids who went missing turned up within days, not months. Those that stretched out that long didn't tend to end well. And what? Now she'd just strolled into the station? Who the hell was the man she was with?

He reached the bottom of the stairwell and marched through the door into the reception area. A row of four hard plastic chairs lined the wall, all unoccupied. Annette looked startled when he appeared, putting a palm to her chest in surprise.

'Made me jump. You must have slid down the bannister, did you?'

'Where are they?' Porter asked, offering a quick smile to acknowledge her joke.

'Just stepped outside. He said he'd be right back, though.'

'And you just let him walk out?' he snapped, heading for the door.

She frowned. 'I couldn't exactly force him to stay, could I? Whoever he is, he's here voluntarily.'

She was right, of course, and he'd apologise for being snappy in a minute, but for now he had to find them. Had to see for Libby for himself. Outside the main entrance, a short flight of stairs led down to street level. Empty. Traffic grumbled past, bumper to bumper. Morning commuters strode past, earphones in, heads down, both for some, but no sign of a man and young girl. He looked frantically left and right, and did a double take back towards Edgware Road Tube station. A ramp led away from the entrance, and halfway down it a man stood, back propped against the wall. Not a face he recognised. He was eyes down on his phone, and hadn't noticed Porter yet. Nothing remarkable about him. Forties maybe, jeans and jumper, well-groomed sharp-edged beard.

Porter moved towards him, catching a flash of red, someone hidden behind him. The man must have heard him come out, sensed him at least, and looked around, straightening up as he clocked Porter's hard stare.

'You're the detective from the telly,' he said: a statement, not a question.

It took Porter a second to process, but then he remembered he'd been in the background as Amy Fitzwilliam had broadcast from the park. The man half-turned, reaching an arm behind him, guiding out a young girl. Around seven or eight years old. Postbox-red coat. Blonde hair scraped back into a ponytail. Porter blinked, doing another double take. Could literally have been the girl from their reconstruction.

Not Libby, though. His brain, bumped off kilter by the resemblance, clicked back into gear. Like her, but not her. Not quite. He breathed out, heavy, disappointed.

'DI Jake Porter. And you are?'

'Bruce,' the man said, extending his hand. 'Bruce Green. This is my daughter, Abigail.'

The girl looked uncomfortable, like she'd rather be anywhere but here. Thoughts zipped around Porter's head, bashing off each other, like flies against a window. This made no sense. It wasn't as if they were auditioning for lookalikes. All the same, he gave the girl a reassuring smile.

'And what can I do for you, Mr Green?'

'This is, uhm, well it's quite embarrassing really,' he said. 'All that fuss on the news yesterday. The missing girl. Thing is, we were in the park,' he said, letting a hand fall on his daughter's shoulder. 'I didn't even know anything about it until this morning, but I'm wondering if it was maybe Abigail that this lady saw. I'd hate to have been the cause of this, and, you know, got people's hopes up.'

Porter studied Abigail Green's face as her father spoke. She was probably closer to the girl they'd used in the reconstruction than Libby herself, in the shape of her nose and cheekbones. Still, there was no denying the resemblance. Could yesterday's search have all been a wild goose chase?

'What time were you there?' he asked.

'I'd say about noon,' Bruce Green replied, looking genuinely embarrassed. 'We only had a wander through for an ice cream. Abbs here wandered off while I was paying. It was at that cafe near the lake.'

'Why didn't you get in touch yesterday?' Porter asked, thinking of how many officers had combed the park all day, late into the afternoon. The wasted hours. Having said that, if they hadn't searched the park, they might not have found the body.

'My wife had seen it on the news yesterday, and she mentioned over breakfast how that little girl looked like our Abbs. I hadn't mentioned that we'd popped by the park, you see. She didn't know we'd been there to make the connection.'

Porter's frustration veered away from Bruce Green, circling aimlessly now, looking for a new target. It wasn't as if he'd knowingly wasted police time. One of those thoughts snagged on something. If that hadn't been Libby yesterday, and the body in the park was too old to be her, that meant a slim shard of hope. At least, that's the way Ally Hallforth would see it.

'Have we done something wrong, Daddy?' the little girl asked.

Bruce Green gave her an awkward smile, then looked at Porter, with a face practically pleading their case, eyebrows arched in a *help me out* kind of way.

'You and your dad have really helped by coming down here,' he said, crouching so as to be on eye level. 'You haven't done anything wrong.'

'Is that girl still missing?' she asked, in that blunt yet innocent way that only kids can.

Porter nodded. 'She is, but we're doing everything we can to find her.'

She looked about as convinced as he felt, and right now, he felt as optimistic as a turkey in the run-up to Christmas. Porter thanked Green for stopping by. Bruce Green couldn't have looked more relieved, and shepherded his daughter away, leaving Porter standing there wondering now if it truly was Libby waiting for him on the autopsy table. One way to find out.

Doctor Isabella Jakobsdottir was a bundle of energy, squashed into a compact frame. She only came up to Porter's shoulder if they stood side by side. Her hair was short, a pixie cut like Porter's sister Kat used to have, and light enough that it bordered on white rather than blonde. He'd never asked her age, but guessed it was early fifties. She was a constant hive of activity, always in motion. Even now sitting on the edge of a desk finishing off her sandwich, legs swinging like a kid on a wall, a swishing sound every time they grazed against each other.

'Thanks for this, Bella,' he said, knowing full well how busy she always was.

'It's you that'll get the dirty looks at the station for queue jumping,' she said, wiping a speck of mayo from the corner of her mouth. 'The living give me so much more grief than the dead. If I hadn't done it for you, Milburn would have probably called a favour in anyway with it making the news. You know how he needs to look good for the press. He's like a used nappy: self-absorbed and full of shit.'

Porter laughed for what felt like the first time in days. Bella was renowned for being as blunt as a hammer to the face, but it still tickled him when she came out with little gems like that. One to share with Evie later, Styles too. Even as he thought that, he noted the order he'd thought of them in. Fringe benefit of being part of a couple again. Having someone to share the daily highs and lows.

'Couldn't possibly comment,' he said, his broad smile showing exactly what he thought of her assessment. 'What's the headlines then?' he said, tilting his head towards the door to the next room where the remains from the park lay.

'Come on, let's walk and talk,' she said, pushing off the table, nailing the dismount like a gymnast. Her accent was a mash-up, having spent the last twenty years in London, with hints of her Icelandic inflection creeping in around the edges.

He followed her next door, seeing the remains for the first time. A length of blue paper towel was laid out on the stainless-steel table, bones arranged so as to reassemble the skeleton. You didn't need to be a pathologist to know they had been young when they died. Couldn't have been more than four feet in length. He'd stood through enough autopsies, seen people sliced open the day after they died, but this was different. Sadder somehow, seeing the fragile, delicate-looking bones.

'So, I've got a forensic anthropologist coming in to take a look later today, but the initial assessment they gave you from the scene looks right,' she began. 'We're most likely looking at a young female, aged around seven or eight from the development of her teeth, see the lateral incisors,' she said, pointing at a couple just off centre on the top and bottom rows.

'Is it too soon to have a DNA match to Libby Hallforth?' he asked.

'The DNA profile should be back by the end of the day, but I don't need that to tell you this isn't her.'

'What makes you so sure?'

'I could have told you that as soon as they brought her in,' she said, folding her arms. 'If this was Libby, there'd be much more connective tissue left, skin as well. Even accounting for where she was buried, the high moisture content in the soil, she wouldn't have decomposed this fast in five months.'

Porter nodded, already thinking about his next visit to Ally Hallforth, the questions she'd have. Now they knew this wasn't her daughter, what were they doing to find her again? His worry now was that Milburn would divert resources, him included, onto the body from the park. A missing girl was all well and good, but the body of a different seven-year-old was all over the news, and his boss was all about the optics, the perception of the force. There was every chance that Libby could slide to the bottom of the pile, for now at least, and that didn't sit well with him. It wasn't Milburn that the Hallforths would look to for progress, that they'd blame for lack of it.

'There's no sign of trauma, blunt force or otherwise. No nicks or scrapes on any of the bones. We've got a healed transverse fracture here.' She pointed at one of the legs. Porter could see a slight thickening around the tibia. 'It's an old one, though, too old to be relevant, although it might be useful down the line in helping to confirm an identity. But I do think we have a pretty good call for cause of death.'

Porter stared hard at the remains, scanning up and down as if it should be immediately apparent. Nothing jumped out, though. She leant forwards, pointing at a small arc of bone near the base of the skull.

'We've got an inward lateral compression fracture of the hyoid. And here,' she said, tracing a finger along the curve, drawing his attention to a broken fragment near the top of one side, 'you see this part, the greater horn of the hyoid has snapped, broken inwards. Points to strangulation.'

Porter clenched his jaw to the point of grinding his teeth. Any case involving kids always brought out a similar response. It was bad enough when one adult killed another, but to be able to do that to a kid . . . someone who could barely mount a defence against someone twice their size, more even. For people like that, a prison cell was way too good.

'OK, at least we have that, then,' he said.

'There's not a lot to go on for an ID,' she said, 'although there were a few bits she was buried with: clothes and a purse.' She gestured to a tray across the room, where the girl's last few possessions were laid out. 'Might be enough when we put the pictures out there, see if anyone recognises them and calls in. I've not looked inside the purse yet, but it'll all be sent off for testing today.'

His phone buzzed. 'Thanks, Bella,' he said, holding it up, showing her Styles's name flashing. 'I'll get him to take your lunch order when I'm done with him.'

She waved him away, smiling. 'Just put it on the tab for now.'

He headed out into the corridor, tapping to take the call.

'You enjoy your lie-in?' he asked.

'I wish,' Styles said. 'Don't get them as it is, and damn sure I won't be getting any for a few years soon enough. Where you at?'

'Just been to see Bella. I'm heading back now, though. Can you get everyone ready for a briefing in half an hour? I meant to do it before I left, but I got distracted. Lots to catch you up on.'

'Yeah, can do, but—'

'I'm just heading to my car now. I'll call you back when I'm on the road,' said Porter, scanning a row of signs on the wall, looking for a way out from the rabbit warren of hospital corridors.

'You're gonna want to hear this now, boss,' Styles said, all business, none of his usual jokes or banter on display.

'Come on, then,' said Porter, slowing to more of an amble.

'The midwife was ill, so Emma's appointment was cancelled by the time we got there. Thought I'd swing by the park on the way back to the station. Seems it wasn't just the one body out there.'

CHAPTER TWENTY-ONE

Déjà vu for Porter as he stood, suited-up in the clearing, for the second time in twenty-four hours. Today had a different feel to it, though. Clouds replacing sunshine, squeezed in on top of one another like dirty grey marshmallows. They hung low and heavy, waiting for the first drops to fall that would drag the rest down with them.

'How many are we up to now?' he asked, feeling perspiration prickle, pulling his shirt against his back.

'Eight more. Nine in total,' said Kam Qureshi, with a loud sigh from behind his mask. Porter had worked with the CSI on dozens of cases, knew Kam had been forced to work some pretty horrendous scenes, but this one seemed to have knocked the stuffing out of him.

There was something about the absence of violence in the clearing that gave it an eerie feel. It was an oasis of calm in the middle of one of the world's busiest cities. When he'd first stood here yesterday, it had had a tranquil feel to it before he'd seen the first body, splashes of colour hidden away behind the cloak of green trees. Now, it was as if vandals had ripped up a garden. Around half of the rose bushes were dug up, lying off to the side. Mini trenches excavated where they had been. Eight black plastic sheets lay on the ground. Some were just bones, picked clean by time and insects. Others looked more recent. Still been there a while by the looks of things, but clumps and strands of muscle still clung to the frame, like dirty papier mâché.

'What the hell happened here?' he said, as much to himself as anyone.

'We nearly missed it,' Styles said. 'Wasn't until after they'd shipped the first lot off to the doc that Kam spotted it.'

'Spotted what?'

'They thought we had the lot, but there was another fragment sticking out. Looked more like a tree root, apparently. When Kam went back for it, turned out it was a finger, attached to a full left hand. Trouble was, there was a left hand in the batch that had already gone.'

'Milburn's going to have a fit,' Porter said, knowing that his boss had a knack for looking past the human element, seeing the unsolved stats spiking upwards, one eye always on the headlines.

'After that they worked their way around the place,' Styles continued. 'Looks like there's two per bush judging by what they've found.'

'Jesus,' Porter breathed out.

'Gets worse,' said Styles. 'They're all kids. Every single one of 'em.'

They stood side by side in silence for a time after that revelation, Porter finally breaking the silence.

'Do have a best guess how long they've been there? Same as the first one?'

'Some of 'em, yes. Others look a bit more recent, not fully decomposed. Nothing fresh, though,' said Styles. 'We've got fragments of clothing for most of them. Scraps really, all filthy, and no real identifiers so far.'

'Hope Emma hasn't got any more appointments for a while,' Porter said, unable to tear his eyes away from the scene, like a macabre archaeological dig. 'Think we're going to be busy for a while.'

'If you two have finished whispering sweet nothings, I've got something else you might be interested in,' Kam called over his shoulder to them from where he knelt by the sheets of remains.

Porter and Styles headed over, careful to stick to the path of clear forensic stepping plates laid out across the clearing.

'What you got, Kam?' asked Porter.

'No idea if it's significant or just a coincidence, but look here.' He pointed at the remains furthest to the left. 'Here, this first one looks like a girl from the pelvic bone. She was under bush number one with this one here.' He pointed to the neighbouring plastic sheet. 'Pretty sure number two is a young lad.'

'OK,' said Porter, drawing that last syllable out, making Kam look up, realising his point wasn't landing.

'It's not just these two,' he said. 'All but the first ones are in pairs. One boy, one girl, a pair under each bush.'

CHAPTER TWENTY-TWO

'First person I hear use the phrase "serial killer" has to stick ten quid in the jar,' Porter said, looking from face to face around the briefing room, daring anyone to disagree.

'What else do we call someone who stashes that many bodies, boss?' one of the newer constables piped up.

'We call them sick, twisted and wrong, Glenn, cos that's what they are,' Styles cut in. 'But we don't get the tabloids all excited by thinking they're covering the next Hannibal Lecter.'

'What if they ask us outright?' Glenn Waters asked.

'Ask us what, Glenn?' Styles asked.

'Whether there's a serial killer wandering around London.'

'Then we use the most wonderful two words in the English language, Glenn: no comment,' Styles said. 'Oh, and that's a tenner in the jar as well, please.'

'Eh? I never . . . argh. Really?'

'Really,' Porter said, straight-faced, but as Waters rolled his eyes and looked away, Porter looked to Styles, seeing his DS give a wink and nod.

'You can pop it in on the way out when we're done,' said Styles.

PC Dee Williams, next to Waters, gave him a playful punch as pockets of laughter drowned out his grumbling.

'Enough of the small talk,' said Porter. 'Nick, take them through what we know so far.'

Styles took a step forward. 'We've got nine victims in total, eight of them buried in pairs. The first one we found was paired up. Odd one out is a boy. We're waiting on results for any DNA matches in the database, and should have tests back on clothes by tomorrow. The doc will be able to give us ages for the rest, but what we do know is that our first female was around seven or eight when she died.'

He paused, letting that settle in, seeing the rows of serious faces, all traces of laughter long gone.

'DI Porter and I will be speaking to Ally and Simon Hallforth again, as well as Libby's brother Marcus. Williams, Waters, the priority for you lovely lot is to start reviewing missing persons files. Whoever these kids are, someone has to have noticed they're not around any more. We know most about our first girl so far, so let's start with her and see where that takes us. We can focus on the others when we know more.'

Glenn Waters didn't exactly look thrilled at getting grunt work, but he kept his mouth shut.

'Gus and Kaja, you'll be heading back to the scene to speak to the park manager. We need a list of employees. Can't have been easy to get that many bodies over there. There's every chance that one of them either knows something or saw something.'

Kaja Sucheka was literally half Gus Tessier's size. Half-Polish, less than twelve months on the force as part of a fast-track intake. Normally that brought with it a sizeable helping of scepticism from some of the longer-serving officers, but she had a way of getting people onside better than most Porter had seen. Good with people.

Very good. She and Tessier would pair up well together.

'You should all have heard by now that the sighting we had can be ruled out, but we still want any CCTV we can get our hands on from the park and surrounding area. That island has a garden of remembrance type feel to it. Whoever's responsible might have been there in the not too distant past. Might feel like needle-in-a-haystack but it's too high profile to cut corners. Waters, you and Williams can take that too. Work out between you who does what.'

Styles nodded at Porter and took a step back, leaning against a desk.

'Thanks, Nick. OK, we all know what needs doing. Twice-daily briefings until further notice, 9 a.m. and 5 p.m. No comments to the press. Any enquiries come through me. Questions?'

Kaja Sucheka put a hand up. 'What about the Hallforth case, boss?'

Porter chewed on his lower lip. 'Still very much active, but this takes priority until I say otherwise. DS Styles and I will continue to chase up any leads for now.'

He hadn't spoken with Milburn yet, and wasn't sure how that would fly with his boss. The chances of not being collared for an update before he left the building again were slim to none. He'd work Libby's case himself if he had to. No way he could give up on it just yet. Too much of a coincidence for them to be looking for a missing seven-year-old and find a DIY graveyard full of kids around that age.

No more questions followed, and they dispersed in their pairs, leaving just Porter and Styles.

'Did you check in with Evie yet, boss?' Styles asked.

'Hmm?'

'About dinner?'

'Oh, right, shit, no I didn't but I'm seeing her after work.'

'No worries, there's no hurry,' Styles replied.

Porter hated letting things slip, no matter how small. He'd let a few little slips like that from Styles rub him up the wrong way, but he was getting just as distracted. Hard not to be when an already complicated case explodes in your face like an over-shaken can. One question kept circling, looking for a place to land. He was pretty sure he knew the answer, but tried not to let it become an absolute in his mind.

None of the bodies looked more recent than twelve months. Could someone capable of killing nine children really just stop like that?

CHAPTER TWENTY-THREE

'That poor woman,' Evie Simmons said, scraping froth from the top of her latte with a teaspoon. The station canteen was no Starbucks, but it'd do. 'Bad enough her daughter goes missing. I can't imagine what it must feel like to still not know, everything getting splashed across the telly now.'

'Mmm.'

This about summed up his conversational skills today. She'd noticed in the months they'd been together that he could be like this. Not in the heat of the moment. He was as good under pressure as anyone she'd worked with. But these little troughs where you had time to sit and reflect, it was as if he couldn't multitask, think and speak. Too caught up in untangling knots in his mind.

'How did you leave it when you called her, then?'

'Not a lot more I could tell her, really. They're all too old to be Libby, so doesn't matter to her what else we find out there.'

'Maybe, maybe not,' she said.

He frowned. 'What you do you mean?'

'I'm just thinking that there aren't many out there capable of doing whatever has been done to those poor kids. In one case you're looking for someone who's kidnapped a seven-year-old. In the other one you're after someone who kills kids around that age. There's no reason they can't both be the same person.'

'So, you're saying he keeps them all alive for months before he kills them?' Porter asked, scepticism clear to hear in his words.

Simmons shrugged. 'Can't rule it out, least not until you know who they are, how long since anyone last saw them alive.'

She watched the lines in his forehead soften as the logic in what she was saying sank in. He nodded, sipped at his coffee, splicing that possibility in with the dozen others jostling for position.

'You're right. Sorry, I shouldn't try and shoot you down like that. I know you're only trying to help.'

She reached over, placing her hand over his. 'It's fine, honestly.'

So slight she almost didn't feel it, but there was a definite twitch as she touched him. They hadn't come right out and broadcast being a couple at work yet. It wasn't an issue for her. Truth be told, she didn't even think it bothered him that much, the thought of others knowing. More likely that it was a reflex he might not even spot himself. More to do with being with anyone, not just her.

One of her best friends had likened him, and all men for that matter, to a pack of spaghetti. They could be brittle, not wanting to be forced into anything that wasn't their idea in the first place. Let things simmer, though, low heat for a while, and they'd soften, bend and let you in.

'The dad is a piece of work,' he said.

'Yeah, I saw him on his soapbox on Sky News earlier.'

'Don't get me started,' he said with a loud sigh. 'The son, Marcus, told Styles that his dad used to knock him around. Wouldn't surprise me if he did the same with his wife, or maybe even Libby.'

'He getting looked at again, then?' she asked.

Porter nodded. 'If I have my way, yeah. The two of them alibi each other for almost the full day, and we've got nothing to prove otherwise. Won't stop me from looking, though, assuming Milburn doesn't kick it to the back of the queue.'

They lapsed into silence for a moment, before Porter remembered his promise to Styles.

'Oh, before I forget, Nick has asked if we want to have dinner with him and Emma this weekend.'

'You asking me if I want to hang out with you and your mates in the park?' Simmons said, straight-faced.

A smile snuck around the edges, curling the edges of his lips upwards. 'There'll even be booze there. I can use my warrant card to get served in the shops.'

'Well,' she said, with an exaggerated roll of the eyes, 'I suppose I could cancel all those other grand plans I've got.'

'What about grand plans for tonight?' he asked.

She squeezed his hand, then sat back again. 'I'd love to say "none", but a girl's gotta work. I could come over later, though, if you're not going to be tucked up with a cup of hot milk by ten?'

'You know my routine so well,' he said. 'What you got on tonight, anything interesting?'

'We've got someone inside Nuhić's gang, low-level, but we're wiring him up for a meeting tonight. We arrested a few of Nuhić's dealers last week, and our man is in line for a promotion.'

Branislav Nuhić was a Slovenian who ran one of the gangs that had risen to fill the void left by Alexander Locke, formerly head of one of the largest criminal organisations in London, if not the UK. He was dead now, killed by a stray bullet as Porter tried to arrest him. Simmons hadn't been there to see the case through. One of Locke's men had put her in hospital, comatose and surrounded by more beeping machines than a supermarket checkout line. Almost killed her. She'd practically had to learn to walk again after suffering a near-fatal bleed on her brain. It had taken months of recovery and rehab, and at times she wasn't even sure she could come back, but here she was, trying to break up the multi-gang cockfight that Locke's demise had set in motion.

'You think Nuhić will be there?'

She shook her head. 'He keeps himself well insulated. Spends most of his time pretending to run the family bakery down by Creekmouth. We've still got a few rungs to climb before we're close enough to bag him, but he'll keep.'

Porter drained what was left of his coffee. 'Give me a shout when you're done playing cops and robbers, then. Might see you later.'

She promised to call him if she got done by midnight, and he headed off to see if Styles was still around. Simmons took the stairs down to the car park, texting her DI as she walked to her motor. Seconds later, an address popped up, the location of their surveillance van. She checked her watch. Traffic shouldn't be too bad this time of night.

With you in forty.

She didn't envy their inside man. Nuhić had a reputation for being creative with those who crossed him. No shortage of stories. One in particular stuck with her. There was little left by the time they found the body of a man who'd skimmed his own cut from Nuhić's profits. On all fours, feet and hands cased in concrete, stripped naked, gravy poured over him like a basted joint to attract the rats. Getting someone to turn on Nuhić was about as easy as striking a match on a bar of soap, but they'd done it.

The man in question, practically a kid really, Alfie Dean, had been making a few quid on the side selling his own product. Unfortunately for him, he'd been picked up doing it by one of the surveillance teams building a case on Nuhić. Simmons's boss, DI Aaron Maartens, hadn't expressly said as much, but Dean had been left believing if he didn't flip and inform for them that Nuhić might be made aware of his extra-curricular activities. Rock and hard place.

She pulled up on George Street, near Barking station, and a short walk around the corner from the apartment block at Anne Mews where tonight's fun and games would take place. Five minutes later, she walked through the door of a third-floor flat, joining DI Maartens, two plain-clothes PCs and a nervous-looking Alfie Dean. Dean was early twenties but probably still got ID'd in bars. Sharp haircut, shaved around the edges and styled longer on top. He could have passed for your average man-scaped teenager if he hadn't been sitting around a kitchen table with three coppers.

'Perfect timing,' said Maartens. 'Say cheese!'

One of the PCs spun a laptop screen around on the table to face her; there was a slight fish-eye effect, a little shaky but clear enough to recognise her own face staring back at her. From the angle, it had to be coming from somewhere around chest height on Dean, but try as she might, she couldn't spot the camera. Good news for Dean was that if she couldn't, chances were Nuhić's men wouldn't either.

'Third button down,' said Maartens, following her gaze. Dean smiled, but it was about as confident as a politician onstage, waiting for a count he knows he's lost by a country mile.

'Jesus, man,' Dean said, nerves upping his voice an octave, 'just me or is it hot in here? Can we just crack on?'

'You're all set, Alfie,' said Maartens. 'Now talk me back through it one more time.'

Dean rattled off his instructions at a pace. Always try and face whoever he was talking to for the camera's sake. Make sure there was at least one full sweep of the room. The meeting would be downstairs, in his flat on the second floor. After everyone left, he was to take the stairs back up here, where they would be waiting to retrieve the camera. Dean was moving up a rung, ready to run his own crew who would sell product in a defined area.

'Come on, man, I gotta go,' he said when he was finished. 'If I'm not in my own digs when they rock up it's gonna look weird.'

Maartens gestured towards the door, and Dean scuttled off without another word, the picture on the screen bouncing all over the place as he trotted downstairs.

'Knew I should have brought some teabags,' Maartens said, looking longingly at the kettle.

They didn't have long to wait. Less than ten minutes later, the tinny echo of a doorbell rang out from the laptop, and Dean muttered under his breath, swearing his way along the corridor. His visitors were all chips off the same block. Clothes so similar it could be a uniform. Low-slung jeans, hoodies so baggy they looked like the 'after' part of a weight loss ad.

Even though the whole thing was being recorded, Maartens scribbled notes in his mini Moleskine. He was old-school, a late joiner but with twenty years' service now, and tolerated technology when he had to. The tricky thing with Nuhić was pinning anything on him. He insulated himself with more layers than a pensioner in winter, and tonight was just one more step closer.

For God's sake, take a breath.

Might just be because she knew he was working for them, but he sounded nervous. Talked too fast. Laughed too loudly. Simmons noticed that while Dean dropped Nuhić's name in a few times, the others just referred to him as 'The Boss'. One of them raised an eyebrow as Dean name-dropped Nuhić for the third time in as many minutes.

'Dial it down, Dean,' Maartens muttered, picking up on the same nerves as Simmons.

The door chimed again, and Dean jumped up to answer.

'You expecting company?' one of the others asked, a hard-faced lad with a boxer's nose.

'That'll be the strippers,' Dean chuckled as he walked down the corridor, laughing a little too hard at his own joke.

Simmons looked from the screen to Maartens. Nobody else was due to join the meeting. This didn't feel good. She held her breath as the picture all but disappeared, Dean flush up against the door, spying through the glass peephole, presumably. A loud sigh.

'Not tonight, man, come back later.'

'I'm here now, though. Come on, I need to restock. It'll just take two minutes and I'm gone.'

The voice was muffled from behind the door. Not one Simmons recognised. Maartens didn't either from the frowns furrowing his forehead.

Another loud sigh from Dean. They saw his feet as he looked downwards.

'Two minutes, and I'm out of your hair,' the voice said, knocking again.

'Fine,' Dean huffed, 'but you wait outside. The usual?'

'Please. Thanks, man! Appreciate it.'

'Yeah, yeah, yeah,' Dean muttered, and they watched as he walked into his bathroom and lifted a mirror from the wall, exposing a hole behind, rows of small plastic pouches piled inside. Some had pills, others powder and, beside them, tightly bound rolls of banknotes.

'This is just to keep my cover.' Dean's explanation for their benefit, whispered through the speakers. 'One of my guys after more gear to sell. I don't do this, they ask questions.'

Maartens chuckled. 'Selling a few pills is the least of your worries right now, mate.'

Dean grabbed an assortment of bags, powder and pills, and headed back to the door. Simmons leant back, tipping her chair onto two legs, using the break in action to stretch, yawning so wide her jaw clicked. She watched as Dean opened the door. The face waiting in the corridor made her jerk forward, chair thumping on the floor. She'd seen it before. Earlier today on Sky News. He looked less riled up now, bluster all used up in front of the cameras. No mistaking the face, though. Grinning, shifting from foot to foot as if the floor was burning up. Simon Hallforth.

CHAPTER TWENTY-FOUR

Porter blinked in disbelief as he listened to Simmons. Simon Hallforth, whose daughter was missing. Working for Dean, who worked for Branislav Nuhić. The names crashed together in his head. What the hell was Hallforth doing mixed up with these men? What might it have cost him? Libby's name flashed through his mind. Knowing the kind of man Nuhić was, Porter would put nothing past him. Had Hallforth betrayed him, sending Nuhić after his family, a greater punishment than any beating?

'What does this Alfie Dean have to say about Hallforth?'

'Just that he's as much a customer as an employee. That's why he started dealing, apparently. Needed the extra cash to buy his own gear.'

'Well, this is going to make for an interesting chat with Mr Hallforth now, isn't it?'

'What do you mean?'

'Styles and I are following up with him and his ex-wife tomorrow.'

'You can't grill him on this, Jake, not yet.'

'You said it yourself. If he's in deep with Nuhić there's a good chance Libby's disappearance is linked. If it's not then that's one hell of a coincidence.'

'And that's why he can't know about this. How else do you explain finding out about his little habit without exposing Alfie Dean?'

Porter stopped in his tracks. He hated to admit it but she was right. As much as he wanted to grill Simon Hallforth, shut him in a claustrophobic room and look him in the eye when he asked if he'd put his own daughter in danger for the sake of a cheap high, he knew it'd hurt more than help at this stage.

'Alright, fair point,' he said. 'But we can't ignore the connection, so what do you suggest?'

'How about letting me take a shot at the mum?' she asked. 'She's clearly come to her senses if she's left him. If we can get anything from her that sends us down the same path, then it's fair game.'

Porter mulled it over. Blurring of boundaries never sat well with Milburn. He'd left a voicemail for Porter to brief him first thing tomorrow, but he knew his boss was likely to insist all hands on deck for the Victoria Park case. Unlikely that he'd sanction Simmons's time being spent on a five-month-old case instead, assuming he found out, that is.

'It'd have to be an unofficial one for now. You know what the super will say.'

'I can keep a secret if you can,' she said.

'Deal. If you can do that first thing, I'll hang fire on speaking to the dad again in the meantime.'

'So now that we've practically solved the case,' she said, 'I think a celebratory drink is in order.'

'Think we've missed last orders,' he said, knowing full well what she was getting at.

'I'll take my chances your place doesn't get raided, then.'

'I'll make sure your name's on the VIP list,' he said.

He ended the call and peeled himself off the couch, picking a cushion off the floor, scanning the room, remembering the mess he'd left in the kitchen, crumbs and empty packets. Demetrious watched him through slitted eyes from his spot on the armchair.

'What?' Porter asked the cat. 'Just picking up a few things so it doesn't look like a squat. You might think about pulling your weight round here one of these days.'

A long, slow blink was all he got in response. As he hastily worked his way around the flat, making the place presentable, he peeked around his bedroom door, spotting the wedding photo he'd left out. Back it went into the drawer, and he was surprised to note that it didn't feel wrong to stash it. Maybe this time it could stay there. Should stay there. They'd been together almost eight months, depending on when you class the whole 'couple' thing becoming unofficially official, and Evie was spending more and more time here after work. The photo had become more of a habit and less of the crutch it used to be.

He heard Holly's voice in his head. She could still make him smile.

About bloody time.

CHAPTER TWENTY-FIVE

It was a misunderstanding, he tells himself. The girl from the fairground. Nothing wrong with his eyesight, just that sometimes everything goes into soft focus, like an old home movie. Not the first mistake he's made. Hopefully the last, though. There had been such a strong resemblance. Uncanny, the way she'd looked, moved even. If he could only get five minutes with *her*. Explain what this was doing to him. Being kept apart from his children. It's a physical pain, an ache in his gut, as if he's been sucker-punched if he thinks too hard about it.

That's the problem, though. He can't find her. Each time he's seen the children, she's never around. They're always on their own. That, or with other people, strangers, like she's farmed them out. Too busy to take care of them herself, too precious to leave with him. She's careful, alright. Moves around as much as he does, keeping one step ahead.

He's pretty sure he saw his son yesterday. Right here in Oxford. What were the chances, that he just happened to be here working for a few days? All happened too quick to be sure, the boy sitting on a double decker bus, framed in the window, generic-looking school uniform on. It pulled away from the stop, driver oblivious to his waving. He'll wait there tomorrow. Same time, same place. The following day too if he has to. When it comes to his children, there's nothing he won't do. Nothing.

CHAPTER TWENTY-SIX

'Your concerns are duly noted, DI Porter,' said Superintendent Roger Milburn, chair creaking like a floorboard as he leant back. 'I'm not saying the Hallforth case is dead in the water, but even you have to admit, an island full of bodies trumps it for now.'

Even you. The inference being that he was an outlier, a dissenter. Like his opinion was at odds with the entire Met Police force.

'I'm not saying it doesn't, sir, but—'

'Then why is there a "but" at all?' Milburn shot back.

'I just think it'd be wrong to shelve it when it's back in the public eye after the reconstruction.'

'And you think it'll stay that way once the *Evening Standard* is running headlines about serial killers?'

Porter toyed with mentioning the ten quid fine rule, but knew it'd cost him more than it'd cost Milburn.

'We didn't have anything tangible on the parents at the time, sir, but now we know the father has links to Branislav Nuhić, that opens up a whole new line of enquiry . . .'

'. . . that you cannot use as leverage with Simon Hallforth,' Milburn finished for him. 'I will not have you torpedo one case to chase another, all the while leaving potentially the biggest murder inquiry you've ever worked on to gather dust. That's assuming you still want to work it, of course?' Milburn raised his eyebrows in challenge.

Porter knew what his boss said made sense. He genuinely believed he could work the two, but recognised the look he was getting for the *you just try me* that it was. Styles would follow Porter's lead, do whatever he could to keep all plates spinning. That plus Evie's help might just be enough. Regardless, it wasn't worth losing the Victoria Park case. *Pick your battles*, he told himself, *and this isn't one.*

'Course I do, sir. You're right.'

The last few words felt awkward, but Milburn swallowed them down, happy that, once again, he'd got his way. Porter left him be, after promising to update him personally after each briefing, including the one he was heading to now.

Styles had been tasked with herding everyone in for the morning briefing, and Porter was pleasantly surprised to see not only were they all there, but that Styles had a spare coffee waiting for him.

'How was our glorious leader?' he asked.

'As glorious as ever,' said Porter, squashing down a dozen more accurate replies. 'Right, let's get cracking. Gus, Kaja, you're first up. What did our park manager have to say for themselves?'

'Oh, he was a barrel of laughs, boss,' said Kaja Sucheka. 'Poor sod couldn't have been more nervous if we'd slapped the cuffs on him. Didn't help that he kept looking at Gus like there was a chance he'd end up under a rose bush if he didn't cooperate.'

Tessier shrugged. 'Dunno what his problem was. He'd be safe. I hate gardening.'

'We did get a list of names, though. They use a mix of permanent staff employed by Tower Hamlets Council, plus some third-party contractors. There's a dozen in the first pot, and we're waiting on word back around how many contractors. They use a company called Nexon.'

'I've heard of them,' said Styles. 'Think they're a French company. Got a load of contracts in the public sector.'

'OK, good work. Let's get those dozen interviewed ASAP, and we can work on the contractors when we get the info through.' He turned to Waters and Williams now. 'How about you two? How big a list do we have reported missing in the right age range?'

Dee Williams beat Waters to the punch. 'So, going off the age plus how long she's been down there, we've got a total across the thirty-two local authorities of seventy-four. Should be able to narrow that down later today or tomorrow when we get results back around ethnicity and any more distinguishing features like that leg break.'

'I'll check in with Dr Jakobsdottir. Might even spring for dessert if we get our tests back today,' he said, looking towards Styles.

Williams, however, didn't get the reference, but smiled anyway. 'Will do, boss.'

Porter debated sharing the intel they now had on Simon Hallforth, but decided against it, for now at least. The more who knew, the higher the chance that word might get around. These things had a way of bubbling to the surface, and as much as he wanted to force it down Hallforth's throat to find out if it had a bearing on Libby, he couldn't let Evie down like that.

'OK, lots to crack on with,' he said, rubbing his hands together. 'I'll see you all back here for five, and remember, if any press asks, what have we not got on the loose?'

Silence all round. They were fast learners, even Glenn Waters. No extra cash heading into the charity jar. Styles hung back.

'You want to head and speak to the parents first thing, or you want Milburn to see us working the park case first?'

He signalled with a flick of eyes, and Porter saw Roger Milburn from the corner of his eye, walking the length of the office, glancing his way but not bothering to stop and talk.

'Oh, you know me,' he said, picking up the phone. 'Perception is reality.'

Styles recognised one of Milburn's own overused quotes, and bit back a smile until the superintendent was out of sight.

'You remember to speak to Evie yet?' he asked.

'Hmm? Oh, yeah. We'd love to. Let me know when works.'

'Emma said to suggest this Saturday. Any good?'

'Yeah, sounds good.'

'You know,' said Styles, leaning in, about to share a secret, 'I had Unsworth in my old team ask me about you two today. Seems there's a scandalous rumour going around that you two might even be . . .' He paused for effect, looking both ways, before whispering, 'An item.'

Porter rolled his eyes. 'And it'll be all over *Hello!* and *OK!* magazine before you know it. It's like being back in the bloody playground.'

'I might be able to make a few quid,' said Styles. 'I can be that insider they always quote from. You know, "a source close to the couple said . . ."'

'Oh, speaking of Evie, she's doing us a little favour this morning.'

Porter ran him through what he and Evie had agreed last night, how it needed to stay between them for now. Not for onward distribution, and definitely not for Milburn's ears. Styles mimed pulling a zip across his lips. Porter checked his watch.

'She should be there now in fact. I say we give her an hour, then once she's checked in we go and speak to Simon Hallforth. Actually, scratch that. Divide and conquer. You take Hallforth. I'll take the brother, Marcus. Lemme just check in with the doc and then we'll head.'

Isabella Jakobsdottir picked up on the first ring. 'Spooky,' she said. 'I was just about to call you.'

'That's what they all say, but then they never call.'

'Really? That's not what I hear these days, Detective,' she said, but carried on speaking before he could ask what she meant. 'Some interesting little titbits for you to start the day. First things first. Cause of death looks the same on all nine. Same inward lateral compression fracture of the hyoid. Should have toxicology back this afternoon, but in the absence of anything contributory showing up, I'd say it looks like straightforward strangulation on all.'

Death broken down into a series of clinical observations, as if it was the most everyday of occurrences, mundane. Although good to have confirmation, Porter had second-guessed this, so it didn't come as a huge revelation. The time passed since death was a significant complication. Had they been recent, the bodies could have held a wealth of clues. Marks on a neck to indicate hand size. Skin under fingernails from a struggle. Most, if not all of that would have long since deteriorated, beyond use.

'Got a bonus prize for you as well, though,' she said. 'I know they were recovered in a particular order, boy, girl, boy, girl. Doesn't stop there though. All the boys were aged around six, and the girls around eight, so you've got four matching pairs. Make of that what you will.'

CHAPTER TWENTY-SEVEN

Simmons knocked for a third time, deciding she'd give it a ten count then give up. Shuffling from behind the door, a sign that patience had paid off. A few seconds' delay, time taken to check through the peephole who was disturbing her. Finally, the door opened. Ally Hallforth looked older than on the footage Simmons had seen, but she supposed losing a child would do that to you. The woman before her looked hunched as they took their seats in the living room, posture eroded by months of constant pressure and speculation.

'Detective Porter sends his apologies,' she said. 'With what we found at the park, things are a little crazy right now, but he wanted me to reassure you that just because Libby wasn't amongst those we found, we're not losing sight of her due to the new investigation.'

Ally gave a thin-lipped smile. One that spoke of a dozen other reassurances over the months, none of which had brought her daughter back, but thankful for what little belief it let her hang on to.

'He asked me to follow up on a few things with you, see if we can't shake something new loose. I was going over interviews from back when she disappeared, and one of my colleagues had spoken to your son, Marcus. I understand he and your husband didn't get on too well?'

'Ex-husband,' she said, wrinkling up her nose as if she'd caught a whiff of something bad. 'Least he will be soon.'

'Ex-husband, sorry.'

'They were as bad as each other sometimes. Almost like they got their kicks out of winding each other up.'

'Marcus mentioned a number of occasions where things had gotten physical,' Simons said, leaving it hanging open rather than ask an outright question.

'Simon doesn't do well with anyone standing up to him,' she said, eyes fixed firmly on the floor. 'It was just easier to let him have his way, you know? Made for an easier life. That and I hated it when he kicked off in front of the kids. Marcus, though, he's just as stubborn as his dad.'

She paused there, sniffing loudly. Not a pleasant trip down memory lane by any means. Simmons fought the urge to prompt her. Old wounds needed to be probed carefully.

'It's not easy to talk about. Never have really, but if he's already told you, there's no point saying otherwise. He's many things, my boy, but he's not a liar. It's true, Simon wasn't shy about dishing out a slap or two.'

'Just to Marcus?'

Ally looked up, a fierce look in her eyes, cornered. Only for a beat, though, shoulders slumping again. 'I know what you're thinking. Why did I stay with him? Where the bloody hell was I supposed to go? And he wasn't all bad. Not at first anyway, not until . . .'

'Until what?'

'He never hurt me, not really. Was more of a slap across the cheek, usually after a night out with his mates from work. One time he gave Marcus a bloody nose, when he was twelve, maybe thirteen.'

'What about Chloe, Libby?'

She shook her head. 'Grabbed a hold of them a few times when they were having a tantrum, a bit too rough, you know, but no worse than that.'

'Most kids who run away, Ally, they do it to escape stuff at home or school. I get that you might not have wanted to say at the time. You were scared of what he'd do, how he might react, but we need you to think back. Was there anything around then, an argument, Simon getting drunk, anything that might have made her think running away was the best option?'

'He was a shit to me the day we lost her, but that was after we couldn't find her. Nothing she would have seen. Is that what you're saying now, then, that you think she ran away instead of someone taking her?'

'We're not putting all of our eggs in one basket, Ally, but yeah, we need to go back over all the possibilities.' Time to gently steer the conversation. 'You mentioned about him going out a lot with work mates. Remind me what he does for a living.'

There it was, so fast, easy to miss if she wasn't looking for it. Ally's eyes darting around the room, looking for a way out. One hand rubbing the other, thumb grinding into her palm. Not a question she was comfortable answering. Time for some subtle pressure.

'Ally, if there was anything Simon was into, anyone suspicious he was hanging around with, we need to know. Maybe Libby disappeared, but if she didn't, if she was taken, we need to know who else might have had access to her.'

Ally Hallforth's face spoke of an internal struggle. No denying she had something she wanted to share. She was at a crossroads alright, mouth twitching, tongue wetting her lower lip.

'I know what it's like to be scared,' Simmons said finally. 'I was hurt not too long ago, at work. Could have died, apparently. I nearly didn't come back to work.' She felt a prickle in her eyes as she shared. 'Wasn't anyone I knew who did it, but you're not the same afterwards. There's that little voice that tells you to keep your head down, out of harm's way.'

She paused, making eye contact with Ally, willing her to open up.

'I'm not saying I know what it's like to have that feeling at home as well as work, but you're stronger than you give yourself credit for. You might have put up with it for years, but look at you now. He's not here, and you're standing on your own two feet. All I'm interested in is finding your daughter, Ally.'

Ally sniffed, ran a hand under her nose. Took a deep breath and held it for a few seconds, then deflated like she had a slow puncture.

'He was a mechanic. I mean he still is, but that's not all.'

Bingo.

CHAPTER TWENTY-EIGHT

Simon Hallforth hadn't moved far. His first floor flat on Reynolds Court was less than half a mile from the place he once shared with Ally. A boxy block, four storeys, and five across. A row of seven padlocked doors lined the back lane. Wheelie-bin storage, maybe? Styles trudged up the concrete staircase and almost toppled backwards when he got to the top, hands up to avoid bumping into the figure that appeared.

Simon Hallforth scowled, but his face dropped when he recognised Styles, whatever curse he'd been about to spit out dying on his lips.

'Mr Hallforth, DS Styles. Have you got a minute?'

'I remember you, and no, I'm on my way out.'

'It'll only take a few minutes, sir.'

'Like I said, I'm busy.' A smug smile reinforcing that he had better places to be, people to see.

'Surely not too busy to talk about your missing daughter, though,' said Styles, enjoying the twist to Hallforth's mouth as it hit home. 'Maybe we could pop back inside for a chat?'

'Here's fine,' said Hallforth, clinging onto what little control he had over the situation.

Style shrugged. No skin off his nose. 'I know my boss spoke to you yesterday about the sighting.'

'Yeah, fat lot of good that bloody reconstruction has done you.'

'You', not 'us'. Wordplay, sure, but interesting to note.

'We're going back over everything, and some new information has come to light. Are you sure you wouldn't rather pop back inside?'

'I said I'm fine here, didn't I?' he said, but Styles saw Hallforth's eyes narrow, trying to work out what was heading his way.

'Have it your way. We're looking at anyone who might have come into contact with Libby, or had access to her. Anyone who might have a reason to take her.'

'And? You did that already. Didn't get you anywhere, though.'

'That was before we received information that you had ties to a local gang.'

It was as if Styles had slapped him across the face. His mouth worked soundlessly, eyes wide in surprise. A few seconds of paralysis, before he snapped back into action.

'The fuck I am. What you talking about? Whoever said that is full of shit.'

'You're denying it, then?' said Styles, opting to prod him a little more. Men like Hallforth struggled to wind it in once they'd lost the plot. Often ended up running their mouths off when they didn't mean to.

'Dunno what you're on about, Officer,' he said, puffing his chest out. 'I'm a mechanic, not a bloody gangster.'

'We know the gang deal drugs in this area. I'm not here to arrest you over that, but if there's a chance that anything you're mixed up in might have spilt over into Libby's world, we need to know. If it helped us get her back, you'd likely get a free pass anyway.'

Not likely, of course, but Hallforth had to believe there was an upside to him talking.

'Where the hell have you got this rubbish from anyway?'

'Not at liberty to say just yet, sir, but you're missing the point. If there's anyone from that part of your life who you might have pissed off, anyone who would want to teach you a lesson, we—'

'It's her, isn't it?' Hallforth said, narrowing his eyes. 'That bitch up the road. It's not enough she thinks she's too good for me now, she's got to try and get me banged up as well.'

'This isn't about you, sir,' Styles reiterated, patience wearing thin.

'You don't deny it, then?'

'What? Oh, you mean who told us that—'

'Don't bother,' Hallforth said. 'You'd done it right off the bat I might have believed you, but I know it's her.'

'Is that because nobody else knows about your extra-curricular?' said Styles.

They stared at each other for a few seconds, before Hallforth stepped to one side, moving past Styles, who reached out a hand, grabbing his arm.

'Get your hands off me,' he said, pulling the arm back.

Styles held up his hands, backing away a step. 'I'd think about cooperating if I were you, Mr Hallforth. You might need us onside if Mr Nuhić starts asking why a police car was parked outside your flat.'

'What's that supposed to mean? I've not told you anything!' Hallforth was practically shouting now, face flushed with colour.

Styles smiled. 'You've told me more than you think.'

'You're off your rocker, mate.'

'Really? Funny, you didn't bat an eyelid when I mentioned your boss's name, let alone ask me who I was talking about.'

Another strike. Hallforth was lost for words again, but the delay, even just for a second, was all the confirmation Styles needed. Hallforth stared him out for another few seconds, then disappeared down the staircase. Part two of Styles's plan was to follow Hallforth now, see if he ran straight to anyone else in Nuhić's crew, maybe even Dean. If he spilt to Alfie Dean that the police were looking for links to his daughter, Simmons would find out. In theory that would mean it was less likely there was any internal squabbling, if he was willing to confide in his own. The flip side of that, of course, was that Libby could be a casualty of the struggle for power between the rival gangs jostling for top spot now Alexander Locke was long gone.

That would put Hallforth between the proverbial rock and a bat-shit Slovenian sociopath. Don't help the authorities, and risk never seeing your child again. Go to the police for help, and risk disappearing yourself. Maybe the rest of your family too.

Styles waited a five count, then trotted downstairs after him. Hallforth's silver Ford Mondeo spun its wheels as it barrelled out onto Cobbold Road. Styles quickened his pace, gunning the engine and just rounding the corner in time to see Hallforth disappear left onto Harrow Road. Definitely a man in a hurry. Suggested he was panicking, acting on instinct.

It wasn't until he skewed right onto Montague Road, rear wheels drifting a few feet, that Styles realised what was about to happen. Up ahead, the Mondeo screeched to a halt outside John Walsh Tower. He wasn't running off to one of Nuhić's men. He was going after his ex-wife.

CHAPTER TWENTY-NINE

Eve Simmons checked her watch. Almost ten-thirty. The family liaison officer should be here any minute. Ally Hallforth had barely moved in the past half-hour. Legs folded up under her, scrolling mindlessly through Facebook.

She could have sworn she remembered Porter mentioning that he'd already arranged for an FLO. God knows Ally still needed one. Not around the clock, but she'd been getting calls from the press after the false sighting. A few had even chanced their arm and doorstepped her. She tried again to put herself in Ally's shoes. It was one thing to watch others go through this kind of trauma, another entirely to live it. It had been hard enough when she'd been hospitalised, not knowing if she had the strength to make it back to any kind of normality. She'd felt helpless, but this was a whole different level. At least she'd been able to influence her own recovery. All that Ally could do was sit there and hope they did their jobs well enough. Wait for a phone call or a knock at the door, with no guarantee as to what kind of news it'd bring.

She'd fobbed Maartens off with a fictitious doctor's appointment. But that wouldn't buy her much longer. Another ten minutes tops, and she'd have to leave Ally Hallforth to wait in alone. The banging on the door made her jump, looking across to Ally, seeing the fear in her eyes.

'Open up, you bitch. I know what you did.'

Not the FLO, then. 'Your ex-husband?' she asked Ally in a low voice. Ally nodded, her whole body a bundle of nervous energy.

'Don't worry,' Simmons said. 'I'll take care of it.'

She strode down the short corridor and called through without opening the door.

'Mr Hallforth, this is DS Simmons, Met Police. Ally's not up to visitors right now, so can I suggest you head off until you've calmed down a bit.'

'I don't care who you are. Open this bloody door. She doesn't get to slag me off then hide behind you.'

'I've got another officer on the way, sir. Threats aren't going to help you here.'

'Then I'll wait till they get here. You'll have to open the door then.'

Simmons's mind flashed to her baton, safely tucked away in the glovebox downstairs. It wouldn't exactly be reasonable force at this stage, more's the pity. Her pulse hammered; the first time she'd been in any real confrontation since she came back to work, and here she was cowering behind a door. Sod him. A scrawny little shit like that wasn't going to intimidate her. He was nothing like the gorilla of a man who'd smashed her head off a wall. Before she thought too hard about it, she wrenched the door open.

He'd been inches away, peering pointlessly through the glass peephole, and jerked back as she stepped into the frame.

'Sir, you need to leave now, please.'

'Or what?' he said, taking a half-step back, spreading his arms in a *what you gonna do* gesture.

'Just go, Simon.' A timid voice came from behind her. She turned, saw Ally's face peering around the corner. 'Please, just go.'

The sight of her was like a starter's pistol. He lurched forwards, catching Simmons off guard, dipping his shoulder as he collided. The impact ripped her hand from its grip on the frame, spinning her around against the wall. She hit it with an *oofff* as the wind was knocked out of her, but recovered quickly and followed Hallforth along the corridor.

Ally stood behind a large armchair, feinting one way as he went the other. He made a feint of his own, lunging the other way as she scooted off to one side, grabbing a handful of hair, dragging her towards him. All his attention was focused on his ex-wife, so he didn't realise Simmons was there until her foot connected with his knee.

His grip loosened, and he flopped into the chair like a puppet with strings cut, with a surprisingly high-pitched whine.

'You bitch, you've broke my kneecap,' he snarled, flecks of saliva bubbling down his chin.

'Simon Hallforth, I'm arresting you for assaulting a police officer,' she said, breathing hard, more from the adrenaline rush than exertion, as she rattled through his rights. 'Stay down, or the other one will be next.'

The look he gave her could have curdled milk, but he clutched at the damaged knee, no attempt to stand. Footsteps hammered along the corridor and set her heart hammering again. Had he brought one of Nuhić's men with him? She readied herself, sliding a step over to the corner of the wall, one eye on Hallforth to make sure he didn't try anything, both fists held high, ready to block or strike.

She acted on instinct as the figure barrelled around the corner, catching Styles a glancing blow on the shoulder.

'Woah, easy there, killer,' he said, backing away.

She breathed out hard, laughing in spite of the tension, maybe because of it. 'Too late, mate,' she said, nodding towards Simon Hallforth. 'You want a job doing properly, you send in a woman.'

Styles gave Hallforth a once up and down, nodding his approval. 'Looks like you've all worked your differences out nicely.'

'Don't suppose you saw the FLO on your way up, did you? I called one in an hour ago.'

Styles's face dropped. 'Shit.'

'What's wrong?' asked Simmons, puzzled.

'I was meant to sort one yesterday. If they'd been here you'd have had backup from the off. Porter's going to kill me.'

CHAPTER THIRTY

Simon Hallforth had a face like a smacked backside as Porter walked into the interview room. He looked down at the heavy strapping around the damaged knee, gave a half-smile, appreciating Evie's work.

'You'll not be laughing when I sue your stupid mate that did this,' he spat out.

'Knock yourself out,' Porter shot back as he sat down. Styles slid into the seat next to him, and Porter reminded himself there was a time and place for any recriminations, and now was neither.

'Ally's already given a statement that you assaulted both her and my colleague, so good luck with that. If I were you I'd be more concerned right now about what Branislav Nuhić will think when he finds out one of his men, and I use the term loosely, has been arrested.'

'Don't know no Nuhić,' he said.

'I'll let you off with the double negative,' said Porter, holding up a hand to Hallforth's solicitor, a portly man by the name of Steven Linton, to acknowledge the grammatical swipe.

'My client denies all knowledge of Mr Nuhić, and has no links to Mr Nuhić's business, whatever that may be.'

'Is that right?' Porter mused. 'Be that as it may, you're already charged with two counts of assault, and I think we both know not even Mr Linton here will help you wriggle out of those. All I'm bothered about today, Simon' – Porter leant forward, low voice but no mistaking the hard edges – 'is where your daughter might be right now. Let me tell you where I'm at with that, because the simplest explanations are usually the right ones. Now we know you have form for knocking around women and children, we'll be looking at you again through a microscope. You can't account for that entire day, and if there's anything there to find, make no mistake, I'll find it.'

'Detective, please,' Linton cut in. 'As rousing as your soapbox moment is, my client isn't under arrest in connection with his daughter's disappearance. I'd suggest we keep on track here?'

Porter gave Linton a polite, thin-lipped smile. 'Let's do just that, then, shall we? The other school of thought is that Libby's disappearance has something to do with Branislav Nuhić, either at his command or because of the ongoing struggles he's currently having with rival gangs in the area.'

'At the risk of sounding like a broken record, Detective, my client denies—'

'All knowledge of Mr Nuhić, and his business interests. I know, I remember that part. What I'm curious about, then, if your client has no links to the biggest drug lord in the area, is where he got the stash we found in the wheelie-bin lock-up behind his flat?'

Linton turned to Hallforth, who said nothing, his face dropping a few shades on the Dulux colour chart.

'Did I forget to mention, Simon, we got a warrant to search your premises, including your little lock-up? Nice little nest egg there. So, now you're either competing against Nuhić, and I'm not sure he'd take kindly to that, or you're on his team. But like I said' – Porter leant back, as relaxed as if he were having a natter across the dinner table – 'I'm all about Libby here. There's something about that day you're not telling us. We know you and your wife weren't together the whole time up until Libby's disappearance.'

Linton leant in, speaking into Hallforth's ear, too low for Porter to hear. Hallforth wouldn't look Porter in the eye as he listened, turning to whisper a reply to Linton. They repeated this three more times, until Hallforth finally looked back at Porter, leant into the table and spoke.

'I don't know no Nuhić,' he said, speaking slowly, as if to a child. A pause, his mouth twisting as if what came next carried a bad taste. 'Stuff in the lock-up, s'mine. The day at the fair, I was, ah, I was off selling to customers. My customers, no one else's.' He sat back, arms folded, but the body language was all wrong. Far from confident, one tic after another, nose twitching, licking lips, eyebrow raised.

'You're your own boss, then?' Styles chipped in, clear from his tone he didn't believe a word of it.

'That's right,' said Hallforth.

'And who were these customers you sold to?' Porter asked.

Hallforth rolled his eyes, looking over Porter's head. 'I dunno all their names, do I? Don't have to. They know me, they know where to get their gear.'

'So, what, you took out an ad in the *Evening Standard* saying you'd be there, big sale, one day only?'

Hallforth smirked. 'No, but I like that. Maybe I'll do that next time.'

'Your wife went to get coffee,' said Porter. 'You were apart for ten minutes, give or take. What did you do during that ten minutes? Where were you, who were you with?'

The corners of Hallforth's mouth curled into a cruel smile. 'It's not me you wanna be asking, mate.'

'Who else should we be asking, then?' said Styles.

'You really think she went for coffee?'

'You think she didn't?'

'I know she didn't.'

'And where do you think she was?'

'Oh, I know exactly where she was.'

Porter leant forward, tired of the verbal sparring. 'Tell us, don't tell us, I don't really care at this point. You're the one up shit creek.'

'I know where she was because she was one of my best customers,' he said, leaning back, hands behind his head, relaxed, just chewing the fat with his mates. 'She was off shooting up. High as a kite she was. Could have done anything and she'd not even remember it.'

CHAPTER THIRTY-ONE

Two days by the same stop, same time. Buses came and went. A procession of blurred faces, but the boy doesn't reappear. There's a conflict in his mind he can't quite reconcile. A disconnect. No tracking back to a last happy memory, unable to pinpoint when he last held them, heard their laugh, played with them. The version of himself he's seen in the home movies looks younger than the face staring back at him from the mirror. How long has it been exactly since those were shot? Years. Then why does it feel like only yesterday when he watches them? Why are those versions of the children from years ago the same as how he sees them now?

His memory is like an old TV set, tuning ever so slightly off, fuzz around the edges. Maybe that's why he's made so many mistakes. Last week wasn't the first time he was certain one or both of the children were standing right there in front of him. It's as if he gets caught up in the moment, overwhelmed by the thought of getting his life back, having them back as part of it, that it knocks the dials in his head a notch, skewing his vision. In those moments, his whole being sings with joy, reunited with his boy and girl, pieces of his life reassembled.

The crash that follows is every bit as intense, only in reverse. The realisation that it's somebody else's child he holds in his arms. Disappointment and devastation, twin birds swooping in to peck away at his happiness, leaving him adrift, looking into frightened eyes. His own personal *Groundhog Day*, destined to replay until he gets it right. It'll happen one day. After that there'll be no more mistakes. No regrets.

He looks around the hotel room, feeling as alone as he ever has. *Click.* The television pops into life, the newsreader's voice better company than his own thoughts, even though he usually avoids it where he can. He wanders over to the kettle, stands as it grumbles into life, and stares at the small red light glowing near the base, until a series of words from the TV pops his daydream bubble.

Nine bodies . . . Victoria Park . . .

He whips around, trailing hand knocking the cup flying, spinning onto the floor. Sees a familiar vista on screen. An island in soft focus, behind a female reporter. A familiar face flashes on screen, the girl from the funfair. No mistaking her for Marie this time. Thinner around the nose, higher cheekbones.

Children . . . Roses . . .

His skin prickles, goosebumps popping like Braille. His garden. His children. Ruined. Spoilt. Shock turns to anger. Anger into resolve. Someone will answer for this. They don't understand what he does, and why he does it. Who's going to watch over them now they've been taken? He moves on autopilot, ramming clothes into a rucksack. One way or the other, he'll have his children back.

CHAPTER THIRTY-TWO

Ally Hallforth pushed both palms against her temples, stretching the edges of red-rimmed eyes.

'You don't understand what it was like living with him,' she said between sniffs. 'He was the one who got me on the stuff in the first place. Next thing you know he's giving me grief for using too much. I'm clean now. Have been for nearly five months, ever since . . .' Her voice trailed off, fresh tears trickling down her cheeks.

'What about your husband's statement, then?' Styles asked. 'Had you in fact gone to inject heroin when Libby went missing?'

Her head dropped forwards, shaking with silent sobs as she nodded.

'He's mixing with some bad people, Ally. Really bad. Bad enough to hurt him, or those close to him if they thought he'd done them wrong. I need you to tell us what you actually remember from that day.'

'I hate him,' she said softly. 'Everything that's happened, it's all his fault. I hate him.'

'What do you mean it's his fault, Ally?' Porter asked.

She closed her eyes, exhaled loudly, and when she spoke, there was a dreamy lilt to it, like she'd just woken up.

'We'd had a bust-up a few days before. I accused him of having an affair with Ellie from two doors down, and he wouldn't give me any gear. By the time we went to the fair, I was all strung out, you know. Nearly didn't even go, but Libby was harping on about it, doing my head in, about how we'd promised to take her.'

Porter clenched and unclenched his fists under the table, anger bubbling beneath the surface, imagining Libby's world, walking on eggshells with two junkie parents, left to wander off with God only knows who, while one dealt drugs and the other shot up.

'I wanted to call you lot sooner. That part was true,' she said, with a sad shake of her head. 'But he convinced me that she'd turn up. That if I called and you lot saw me high like that, that you'd take her away. He'd get banged up, and then she'd have no one.'

'So what made you come clean about his drug dealing now?'

'I knew after Libby, I had to clean up for Chloe's sake,' she said. 'He wouldn't leave me alone. Kept calling round, pestering me when I went out. I just want him out of my life for good.' She looked up, nervous glances at both Porter and Styles. 'What happens now? Am I going to be arrested?'

'You're not under arrest, Mrs Hallforth,' said Porter, leaning forward, elbows on the table. 'I will have to pass on this information to social services, though. They'll want to speak to you and your ex-husband.'

'But I'm clean now,' she said in a shrill voice. 'I don't do that shit any more. They can't take Chloe! She's all I've got left. They won't take her, will they?'

'Not up to me, Mrs Hallforth,' said Porter.

The lack of any visible sympathy set off her sobbing again. Porter couldn't decide whether she deserved his pity or not. She'd been dealt a crappy hand alright, but if your kids weren't motivation enough to straighten yourself out, he didn't know what was. She may well have found that strength for Chloe, but it had come way too late for Libby.

'What happens now?' she asked once she had reined her emotions back in, for now at least.

'Now we look at the possibility that your husband's drug dealing played a part in your daughter's disappearance,' he said. 'Simon has been charged with two counts of assault, and possession of Class A substances, but for now, you're free to go.'

He and Styles watched as Ally Hallforth was escorted out of the room by a uniformed constable. As soon as the door was closed, Porter dived in where he'd wanted to go all day.

'Simple job, Nick, get an FLO there. Why was there nobody with her when Evie called round?'

'Boss, I—'

'You've seen what an odious little prick Hallforth is,' he spat out. 'They could both have been hurt, or worse.'

'I know' – Styles held up his hands in apology – 'and I'm sorry. Had so much going on. I just forgot. Won't happen again.'

Porter had been spoiling for a bigger argument, but the fight went out of him as he looked at Styles, saw the genuine regret etched on his face. He stood up, clapped Styles on the shoulder.

'Come on, let's get this briefing done and get home. It's been a long day.'

They headed back to their desks, Styles popping around the others, tapping shoulders and pointing towards the room they had set up for the investigation. Porter had asked Dee Williams to check whether they'd had any more results back from the lab, and he assumed that was a yes, seeing her already in there, scribbling on the whiteboard.

It took five minutes, Glenn Waters hurrying in last, clutching a takeout coffee cup from the cafe downstairs. Porter had seen him scurrying out as Styles was rounding them up. Priorities. He'd have a word later.

'Looks promising, Dee,' he said, as she clicked the cap on her pen. 'Want to kick us off with what came back?'

She looked tired, but her face brightened. 'Bit of progress, actually, boss. The DNA profiles from all nine have been checked against the database, and we've got four matches,' she said, tapping her pen against the board.

She'd drawn nine columns, a picture pinned in place above each with a round magnet like a mini hockey puck. On the right-hand side, a blown-up aerial photo; numbered locations for each body fanned out in a semicircle on the east side of the island.

'The aerial shot is Google Maps, last updated five years ago. Notice you can't see the clearing, so that narrows down our window. No way those roses would have grown like that without the direct sunlight.'

Porter nodded, impressed at her attention to detail.

'Numbers one, three, four and six now have an ID,' she said, with a single tap against each.

Annelise, Shelley, Christopher, Francesca.

'Of those, only two were reported missing in London, though. Numbers three and four lived in Peterborough.'

'Shelley and Christopher Downes,' Styles said. 'Let's use the names now we have them.'

Williams lost her train of thought for a second, thrown off-stride, but recovered, nodding. Porter knew what Styles was getting at. They needed people to care about these kids. Not just the team around him looking for a killer, but the media, the public, anyone they'd be appealing to for information. Little things like this made a difference, humanised the victims, a constant reminder of who they did this for.

'They're the only actual brother sister pairing, though,' she continued. 'None of the others are related.'

'Have the parents been contacted yet?' Porter asked.

She nodded. 'We've been out and spoken to all three sets of parents. Peterborough sent someone to call round to save us the trip, but we'll get up there and speak to them in person tomorrow.'

'None of them went missing in or around the park, though, sir.' Glenn Waters spoke up, clearly not wanting to be left out. 'According to the parents, none of them had ever been to Victoria Park before.'

'So what's so special about the location, then?' Porter asked, more of a rhetorical question, but Gus Tessier spoke up.

'Definitely special to someone, boss. That rose garden would have taken a bit of work. Some thick branches cut through to make the space. It's lot of trouble to go to, to bury a body.'

Porter nodded. 'Mmm, didn't exactly look overgrown either. Whoever did this has been back to do a bit of weeding since he buried them.'

'It's like they've made a memorial,' Styles said.

'We're looking for a keen gardener, then?' said Kaja Sucheka. 'Let's get some surveillance on B&Q.'

That got a chuckle from the room. You had to find humour where you could. A job like this would weigh you down without it.

'Here's hoping that's exactly what it is,' Porter said.

'You honestly think he'd come back?' Williams asked.

Porter didn't bother to pick her up on the assumption their killer was male. Statistically speaking she was on safe ground, but they couldn't afford to rule out a woman, however unlikely.

'Maybe not literally standing on the shore of the lake, not with all the press coverage, but around the park somewhere, it's a possibility. That place means something to them, enough to create their messed-up garden, so they might not be able to resist.'

'Wonder what the press will start calling him,' said Waters. 'They love a good corny name for a serial killer.'

Porter looked at Waters like he'd just farted. 'That's a tenner, Glenn, and a new rule while we're at it. No nicknames. The press are bad enough without us dreaming up that shit. Anyone else wants to christen our killer, that'll cost you another tenner.'

Waters scowled at his own schoolboy error, digging through his pockets, a handful of change jangling as he counted.

'No coins, Glenn. That goes for the rest of you too. I'm not having a jar full of pennies.' Porter gave Styles an accusing look.

'As if,' Styles said.

'Anyway, getting back on track,' Porter said with a half-smile. 'Anything else, Dee?'

She shook her head. 'Still waiting for results on the clothes and few possessions that they were buried with. Nothing conclusive from CCTV either. We've got footage on some entrances but not all.'

'OK, let's get some plain clothes in there to keep an eye. I want two in there on rolling shifts while it's open, and any cars in the area keeping an eye when it's not. Kaja, Gus, you're next up.'

They looked at each other, both standing up, turning to face the others, Sucheka dwarfed by Tessier.

'We've run background checks on all of the permanent staff,' Sucheka began. 'Couple of them have form for minor stuff, one assault, one for possession, but nothing that stands out. Still digging, though, so watch this space. Interviewed 'em all as well. Apparently, the islands aren't part of the regular park maintenance schedule.'

'Something that anyone who worked there would know,' Tessier chipped in. 'Give us another day and we'll have the contractors named and interviewed as well.'

Porter nodded his approval. 'Our timeline is somewhere between twelve months and five years. I want records for former employees

150

going back that far as well. Anyone who's ever planted a flower or cut a blade of grass. Kaja, Gus, I'll leave that with you.'

'No worries, boss.'

Porter paused for a beat, rethinking his decision to keep Nuhić a secret. When had he become so mistrusting? That was for the likes of Milburn, to limit information, to manage in silos. Not his style. He decided to bring them up to speed, and ratted through what had come to light.

'I'll be following up the Nuhić angle with DS Simmons. In the meantime, Simon Hallforth isn't going anywhere. Nick, now we know his true colours, I want his life turned inside out, all his known associates checked out. Anyone that could bear him a grudge, and for those of you that have spoken to the man, that could be quite a lengthy list.'

Styles nodded. 'I'll have another chat with Marcus Hallforth as well,' he said. 'Might be that he saw people coming and going from the flat. He could help narrow it down.'

'That's a good shout,' Porter said, checking his watch. 'Right, that's it for today. Get yourselves away, and let's have a good run at this tomorrow. Any questions?'

A full complement of shaking heads. It was almost 6 p.m. on a Friday; nobody needed telling twice. They disappeared faster than bargains in the Boxing Day sales, leaving just him and Styles.

'Sorry about snapping earlier,' Porter said. 'You know, about Evie and the FLO. Just that with what happened last year . . .'

'Honestly it's fine, boss, I'd have been the same,' he said.

Porter doubted that. Styles was one of the most laid-back people he knew, but he left it there, happy that waters had been smoothed. A quick time check showed him he had an hour before he was expected at St Cuthbert's School hall. He and Evie had been invited by his nephews, Tom and James, to their school play. They seemed more excited by Evie coming than anyone else due to attend, including their uncle Jake, and even their own mum. Was it really that much of a novelty that he actually had a girlfriend now? What with that tonight, then dinner with Styles and Emma tomorrow, he was almost starting to feel comfortable being someone's other half again. Almost.

CHAPTER THIRTY-THREE

Tom and James barrelled towards her, although she couldn't tell which was which yet. Literally carbon copies of one another, they'd already cottoned on to the fact, aged only six, that being able to pose as each other was one of the best games that twins could play.

One clinging to each leg, she turned and shrugged at Porter, as if to say he had some stiff competition. Words tumbled out from both, overlapping into a stream that she had to really concentrate on to follow.

'Did you see . . .'

'What did you think of . . .'

'Did you like . . .'

Porter's sister, Kat, stood off to one side, smiling, shaking her head, revelling in Porter's apparent awkwardness at actually being out in public without wondering if they'd be spotted by anyone they knew. He definitely had a tough outer shell, but she couldn't blame him after what happened to his wife. Losing a spouse young was bad enough. Worse still that it was a hit-and-run, an unsolved one at that.

She'd taken an instant liking to Kat Porter. Felt like that had been mutual. They'd even met for coffee a few times without Jake there. Kat and her mother were iterations of the same person, in looks and personality. Jake's mum and dad, Harriet and Richard Porter, had welcomed her with open arms too, but Evie sensed a wariness with Harriet. Nothing bad, or disapproving. More along the lines of a mother watching out for her child, worried in case he got hurt.

The twins buzzed around her legs for another minute, before peeling away, running along the corridor to repeat the process with Porter's parents. With them out of earshot, Kat asked Jake about the coverage she'd seen in the news.

'I know you can't tell all the gory details, but where do you even begin working out what kind of sick bastard could do that kind of thing to a child?' she said, watching her own two pogo up and down against their grandfather's legs. 'The mother of that other girl as well, Libby, wasn't it? I don't know how I'd cope if anything happened to my two.'

She and Porter said nothing, both giving her matching raised eyebrows that said, *We hear you.*

'Sorry, not exactly family-friendly chat, is it?' Kat said. 'I'll shut up now. Well, maybe not shut up, but pick something nicer to waffle on about.' She rested a hand on Evie's shoulder, gesturing down the corridor with the other. 'You do realise they've got you up there with Uncle Jake and Batman, right?'

Simmons looked at her, then to Porter, feeling the faintest hint of a blush. 'They're adorable. If I ever have kids, I'd want them just like that.' She saw a twinkle in Kat's eyes, realising she'd just given her a perfect in to ask about something she and Jake hadn't even talked about in any way shape or form.

'How many do you want?' Kat asked, diving in headfirst. Simmons saw Jake trying to pretend he hadn't heard, and failing miserably. She tried to fob Kat off, make a joke of it, save the conversation for another day, a more private setting.

'Ah, we'll see. I struggle just looking after myself these days, without having anyone else depending on me. Besides, it's hard enough to climb the ladder at work without taking a year off, you know.'

'You'd be surprised how quickly you adapt,' Kat said, 'especially when you get a bonus one you hadn't planned for.'

Simmons looked to the twins again, still on the move, no off switches. She had nothing but respect for Kat. She did want kids, but the thought of two at the same time was a little terrifying. She turned to face Kat again, sending her what she hoped was a strong *can we please change the subject* look. It seemed to do the trick, and right on cue the twins charged back towards them, begging to be allowed to go back to Grandma and Grandad's for ice cream.

'Way too late, my little terrors,' Kat said.

It took them another full minute to be persuaded to let Simmons and Porter head off. She meant what she said, they were adorable, but as she climbed into the car, she noticed he'd not said much since that last exchange.

'Don't worry, I'm pretty sure it's still you and Batman fighting it out for the top spot.'

He smiled, but didn't say anything as they pulled out of the car park.

'Everything OK?' she asked.

'Yeah,' he said, glancing over, smiling again, but a tired one. 'Just been a long day, that's all.'

'We still on with Nick and Emma tomorrow?'

'Yep.'

Monosyllabic, even by male standards. 'Don't blame him for Simon Hallforth being a dick,' she said. 'Wasn't his fault.'

'Eh?'

'I know you were annoyed at Styles for forgetting to arrange an FLO for Mrs Hallforth, but there's no guarantee they'd have even been there

155

the whole day. Don't get me wrong,' she said, reaching over and squeezing his leg, 'it's nice to have someone who worries about me, but it's not like we work in Tesco. Things like this are bound to happen sometimes.'

'Maybe,' he said, 'but doesn't mean we can't try and keep the risks to a minimum.'

'And I do. It's not like I go out looking for fights,' she said, raising her fists like a boxer, dragging some humour into it. 'But you can't wrap me up in cotton wool, not when we do what we do.'

'I know, I know,' he said, suddenly sounding exasperated. 'It's just that I almost lost you once already. Shit like that just seems to happen to people around me, and . . .'

She knew exactly where he was coming from. Not just her. Holly. Her words came out sounding harsher than she intended.

'I'm not her, though, Jake. I'm not Holly,' she snapped, snatching her hand back from his leg.

She couldn't have stunned him silent better if she'd slapped him across the face. Glancing across, she saw his grip on the wheel tighten. The leg she'd been squeezing jiggled ever so slightly, as he bit down on whatever he wanted to say next. The silence lasted a full thirty seconds, until she caved.

'I'm sorry. I didn't mean to snap like that.'

'No, it's me being stupid,' he said, and she could tell he meant it. The car slowed as they pulled up at a red light, and he looked over at her. 'I can still picture you all wired up in hospital. Wasn't that long ago. It was hard enough losing one person I care about. Can't help but get a little worked up about that kind of thing happening again, you know.'

He reached over, put his hand over hers. 'Can't help being an irritating, overprotective, grumpy old git, but if you can put up with that, the rest isn't so bad.'

The lights cycled through amber and green, and they set off again, falling into easier conversation, and by the time they got back to her place, the dial was as good as reset. She was a firm believer in clearing the air, and far better this had been done tonight than hang over into dinner with Styles tomorrow evening. She was really looking forward to that. Styles was impossible not to like, one of those people who could put anyone at ease, and Emma sounded lovely too.

Guaranteed there'd be some shop talk, even with one non-copper at the table, but she was looking forward to a slice of normality, to just be one half of a couple instead of part of a task force. To talk about normal things instead of who was selling what drugs on which turf. Everyday things like . . . She closed her eyes, groaning inside as she had a flash-forward of what tomorrow's dinner conversation might go like. Emma Styles was expecting any time now. She could see the look on Porter's face already, reddening cheeks, shifting in his seat. The thought made her smile. What the hell, bring it on.

CHAPTER THIRTY-FOUR

The dreams are always a variation on a theme. Marie and Ben in the back seat, not a care in the world except who gets to go next with I spy. They're strapped in behind, he's driving, and she's there in the passenger seat beside him. The destination varies. This time they're off to the beach. Gabbling from the back seat, extracting promises of ice cream, chips and some of that bright blue bubblegum-flavour fizzy pop, enough sugar to give an elephant diabetes.

Up ahead, a bend in the road. One he's sure they passed a few miles back. He looks in the rear-view mirror, seeing the children impossibly far away, as if he's looking the wrong way through binoculars. His wife in the seat beside him, however, is the polar opposite, close up and HDTV clear. The trio of freckles on her cheek. Every pore in her face, as if he's examining her through a microscope.

No traffic on the road. Can't remember the last time they passed another car. Trees and hedges either side whip past, smudges of greens and browns. His foot floats above the accelerator, barely touching but it's enough to propel the car forward like a missile. He takes the corner, impossibly smooth for the speed they're travelling, but he's the only one who notices.

Nearly there. Not long. Straight road ahead now, stretching to a point on the horizon. He feels himself relax; tension seeps from his shoulders as he sinks into his seat. The steady hum of the engine as he doesn't so much drive, but flow over the tarmac. It's the change in sound he notices first. Makes him glance back at the kids again, voices filtering through from the back, crackling, like a bad phone line. Their features start to shift, rippling, never constant. He knows it's them. Recognises their voices, so why can't he see their faces?

He turns to ask his wife, words booming in his head, but he isn't sure he actually speaks them out loud. Her mouth opens, forming around words, but no sound comes out. He stares, studies her, tries to second-guess what she's telling him. Behind him, the children's faces are now nothing more than smooth ovals of skin. No eyes, nose or mouth, but somehow, impossibly, still talking, laughing.

I spy with my little eye.

His wife grabs his arm, eyebrows arched in alarm, imploring him, but to what end he has no idea. Ruby red lips framing a black oval. He looks down, sees her nails digging crescents into his flesh, but there's no pain. She tugs at his arm, pulling towards her, making the wheel jerk. The car swerves, flirting with the grass verge. A stale odour fills his nostrils, familiar but foreign, having no place in the car.

He wrestles with the wheel, righting them, but she grabs at him again. Before he can react, arms swarm from behind, two, no, four of them, thin and childlike but with surprising strength, pinning him to his seat. The faceless figures in the mirror are still strapped in, so if not them, then who?

His wife reaches over, silently screaming inches from his face, eyes and mouth wide in an oval trio of alarm, a real-life Munch's

The Scream. He strains to break free, but instead can only watch as the wheel is yanked a full one-eighty. From the blur of trees, one emerges, snapping into focus, filling the windscreen as if he's static and it's the tree that rushes towards them.

His eyes snap open, and he's back in his bedroom, chest heaving as if he's been running. It takes a few seconds until he can move, synapses firing, kicking back in, telling him he's alive. Reality comes crashing back in. Victoria Park. The children, taken from him. They're not there any more, no idea where they'll be now, but he needs to be close to them, and that's as good a place to start as any.

CHAPTER THIRTY-FIVE

Marcus Hallforth had traded up, no doubt about that. Not exactly a palace, but no shopping trolleys in sight, or carpet of broken glass to greet him, as Nick Styles walked up the short path to the house. A step up from Fred Wigg Tower, and a healthy distance from his dad. That had to have been a big selling point.

Styles had tried to catch him last thing yesterday on the way home, but had to make do with leaving a voicemail. This morning was the only time he was free over the next few days, so Styles dragged himself out of bed, Saturday morning lie-in sacrificed for the greater good. Couldn't hurt to clock up a few extra brownie points with Porter as well, after his recent cock-up.

It had been a blessing in disguise that Marcus couldn't meet last night, as it happened. It gave Styles time to get his brain in gear, spot some dots that hadn't been joined yet. Ones that led to some interesting questions for Marcus. Might be that Marcus would regret not being available last night.

Marcus opened the door before Styles could even knock, jacket on and phone in hand, on his way out by the looks of it.

'Morning, Marcus. You wouldn't have been trying to head out and leave me hanging, would you?'

Marcus Hallforth looked offended by the very suggestion, but Styles wasn't convinced. 'Thought we'd said half past,' he said with a casual shrug. 'Got to get something for breakfast. Can we walk and talk, cos I gotta work after this?'

Styles debated insisting they went inside, but had a feeling that he'd probably get more time on the walk than he would inside.

'Just heading to Maccy D's along the road,' said Marcus, gesturing along the street. 'What was it you wanted to see me about, anyway?'

'Have you spoken to your mum?'

Marcus kept his eyes on the pavement as he walked, hands deep into the pockets of an oversized jacket that looked way too warm for the weather.

'Yeah, she called me yesterday.'

'Why didn't you tell us about your dad, Marcus? When I spoke to you months ago, you told me then about his temper. Why keep the rest a secret?' he asked, the assumption being that Marcus had known, of course. He might not have, but Simon Hallforth didn't strike Styles as the world's greatest criminal. More like the kind who'd strut around, pretending to be the big man.

'Didn't want to get Mum in trouble,' he said. 'It's his fault she got into that shit in the first place, no reason she should get dragged through the mud as well.'

'There's a chance that your sister's disappearance could have something to do with your dad's activities, Marcus. We could have done with that info months ago, so I need to know.' Styles put out a hand, stopping Marcus with a light touch to the arm, fixing him with a hard stare. 'Is there anything else you're not telling us? Anything you might be holding back, no matter what the reason?'

Marcus took a step back, looking Styles up and down. 'What you trying to say?'

'Nothing,' said Styles, hands sliding into pockets. 'Just thought if you'd kept that to yourself, even with good intentions, that it was worth checking again.'

'Nah, that was it. Like I said, bad enough she had to put up with him, but she's all Chloe's got now, and she's doing much better. Cleaned herself up, for now anyway. If he gets sent down, she might even stay that way.' It didn't sound like he believed his own words.

'Here's hoping,' Styles said, and genuinely meant it. 'She's done the hard part.' He pulled a notebook from his pocket, flicking through until he found what he was looking for. 'When we first spoke, you said you'd been at home with your girlfriend, Susie, wasn't it? Susie Lim?'

'Yeah,' said Marcus, sounding wary, clearly wondering where Styles was going with this, as they rounded the corner, Marcus picking up pace like he had somewhere to be.

'I spoke to Susie back then. That's pretty much what she said too.'

They were level with McDonald's now, and crossed the road in silence.

'You coming in, or waiting here?' Marcus asked.

'I'm good here,' said Styles, leaning against the wall, seeing the glance Marcus gave back over his shoulder. Wondering if it was nerves, or just instinct.

Marcus came out five minutes later, carrying a bulging brown paper bag in one hand, drink clutched in the other.

'Look, I don't mean to be rude or nothing, but once I have this' – he held up the bag – 'I've got to work. Was there anything else you needed?'

'You and Susie still together?' Styles asked.

Marcus scowled. 'Why all the questions about Susie?'

'I don't get out much these days,' said Styles. 'When I couldn't reach you last night, I ended up online. Bit of Facebook, little bit of Instagram, you know how it is. Don't do much personally, but you'd be amazed how handy it can be for work. Take Susie, for example – she's got her profiles wide open. Don't even have to be her friend to see her posts or pictures. All just there for anyone to scroll through.'

'You been stalking my girlfriend?' Marcus shot back, any trace of the helpful teenager long gone.

'Stalking's such a strong word, Marcus. I didn't even start off looking at her. Shall I tell you how I ended up on her Instagram page?'

'Do what you like,' said Marcus, setting off back in the direction of his flat. 'I ain't got time to stand around and listen, though.'

Styles caught him up in a few long strides, keeping pace as he talked.

'Seems the funfair was part of an Epping Forest Council series of events. They even had their own hashtags. Wasn't quite big enough to get the fair trending, but when I had a search for the "Epic Epping" hashtag, corny I know, you'll never guess whose face I saw.'

Marcus clutched the bag to his chest, picking up his pace. 'No idea.'

'If you were at home with Susie all day, Marcus, then why are you on one of the Instagram posts from the fairground?'

CHAPTER THIRTY-SIX

'It's not what you think,' said Marcus, all traces of attitude gone, bag and cup hanging by his side. He practically vibrated on the spot, and Styles tensed in case he bolted.

'Then why don't you tell me what I should be thinking, Marcus.'

Marcus Hallforth leant back against the nearby wall, letting his paper sack of food flop from his hand onto the pavement, cup still in the other hand. He breathed out, loud and heavy, looking both ways along the street. Styles moved in a half-step, into his personal space, letting him know he was within reach if making a run was his plan.

'I went there to keep an eye on her,' he said at last. 'Dad was being a dick about Libby going. Mum was all kinds of strung out, like she hadn't had a hit in days. I was amazed they still went. Least I was until I saw him dealing behind one of the stalls.'

'Do you remember who he was selling to?' Styles asked.

Marcus shook his head. 'Wasn't close enough, and besides, I was trying to keep an eye on Libby.'

'Did she know you were there? Libby, I mean.'

A rapid shake of the head. 'Nah, she wouldn't have left me alone if she'd seen me. Wasn't worth the kick-off there would've been with Dad if that happened.'

'So if you were there keeping an eye on her, how come you didn't see where she went?'

'I just lost her in the crowds,' he said, taking a long pull on his drink. He was still looking anywhere but at Styles, barely making eye contact, bordering on impatient, as if this was an inconvenience.

'You just lost her?' Styles repeated back to him.

'Yeah.'

'And did you look for her?'

Marcus gave him a look like he'd just suggested the earth was flat. 'What? Course I did. Why would you even ask that?'

'Oh, I dunno, Marcus, maybe because I still think you're not being completely honest with me. Maybe because you could have told me this months ago and had your sister safely back home.'

'And said what? Dad might be a dick, but we both know who he works for. What they do to people who talk to the police. All I could have told you was that I saw a few deals. That doesn't bring Libby back. All that does is land me in the shit with bad people. People worse than Dad, who hurt other people for fun. You think I wouldn't have told you this back then if it made even a tiny bit of difference?' he said, holding up finger and thumb a centimetre apart. 'I'm out of there now, away from Dad and his mates. Trying to make something of myself, and I ain't getting dragged back in for some bullshit like this.'

'You finished?' Styles said, leaning in, one hand on the wall, towering over the younger man. Marcus went to speak but thought better of it, clamping his mouth shut again.

'Here's what happens now,' Styles said. 'I'm going to need you to come and give a revised statement down at the station. Maybe it helps us, maybe it doesn't, but it sure as hell isn't going to hurt Libby, is it? That's who this is about. You with me?'

Marcus nodded, sullen like a scolded schoolboy.

'You say you only saw a few deals. What's to say Libby didn't see the same? What if one of Simon's customers didn't like being spied on by a young girl? You see where I'm going with this? So we're going to talk it all through, get descriptions of anyone you remember, and see where that takes us.'

Marcus agreed, but it was with all the enthusiasm of a man consenting to a root canal without anaesthetic. Styles stepped back and watched him hustle down the street like he was on fast-forward. Did he think Marcus could have hurt his sister? Styles still thought not, but there had been something else. Styles wouldn't have expected him to be exactly in his comfort zone, blindsided outside McDonald's and backed up against a wall, but if he had to plant his flag anywhere, he'd say that the kid had been scared. Plenty angry too, sure, a fair helping of indignation. But the way he acted, the way he spoke, Marcus Hallforth was scared, but Styles couldn't escape the feeling it wasn't just of Nuhić. If not him though, then of what, or of who?

CHAPTER THIRTY-SEVEN

Porter tipped a ladle-sized spoonful of Thai green curry sauce over his rice. Beside him, Evie Simmons shifted in her seat. Emma Styles had spent the last few minutes shuttling between dining room and kitchen despite her husband's protests that he should do the running around, and Porter sensed Evie wasn't comfortable talking shop in front of someone not on the force. Not specifics, anyway.

Emma finally eased herself into a chair, one hand rubbing her bump like a crystal ball, the other reaching for a mini prawn cracker, dipping it into the sweet chilli sauce. Styles moaned as an orange trail dotted across the tablecloth towards her, but she cut him off mid-grumble.

'It's not as if you'll be washing the tablecloth anyway, so shush your face.'

'You know I would if you'd let me.'

'And I also know you'd put it in with your red boxers and stain it pink,' she said, reaching for a second cracker.

'Red boxers? We talking Spider-Man ones?' Porter said, never one to miss a chance to poke fun at his DS.

'Yeah, d'you want them back?'

'Shush you two, and eat your food,' Emma said, nudging her husband, knocking his forkful of rice back onto the plate.

'Jesus, we can't even keep the peace at the dinner table, never mind the streets,' said Porter. 'Speaking of work, any follow up from Marcus's statement?'

Styles had filled Porter in on his walk-and-talk with Marcus Hallforth, but not the follow-up this afternoon at the station.

'Said he saw Simon Hallforth selling drugs to two separate men. He gave us a couple of pretty generic descriptions that could fit half of London. Average height, average build, you know the type. Not much to go on, but I'll get Sucheka or Williams to check against the list of people we interviewed at the fair back then.'

'What's your take on Marcus, then?'

Styles rested his fork on his plate. 'If you mean could he have done something to his sister, nah, I don't think so. Having said that, we know he's held back on us already, and you should have seen him. Jumpy as hell when he knew we can put him at the scene. Suppose if I was his age and my dad worked for a bloke like Branislav Nuhić, I might be a bit skittish as well, though.'

'How far off making a move on Nuhić are you?' Porter asked Evie.

She pointed at her mouth, the universal *I'm chewing* sign. 'A way to go yet,' she said eventually. 'He hardly ever pops his head up in person. If we moved now, we'd take out a half dozen of his men, but they'd be replaced before we got them back to the station.'

'And there's no way Milburn would let us anyway. No way he risks what you've built so far when I can't even convince him there's a link between your case and mine.'

'You've been helping the guys out, though, I hear,' Emma said.

Simmons shrugged. 'Just a few bits, some intel and an interview.'

'Mmm, Nick told me what happened at that block of flats. Are you OK?'

Porter saw Styles's expression shift, uncomfortable, hoping his omission didn't get another mention.

'I'm fine,' Simmons said. Porter didn't doubt it. She was one of the most resilient people he knew. Didn't stop him from worrying, though. 'He was just an angry little man anyway. Besides, Nick was there a few seconds after I tackled him anyway.'

'Oh, he's all about the cavalry charge is my Nick,' Emma laughed.

'This is really good by the way,' Simmons said, tapping her fork on the mound of rice piled on her plate.

Emma smiled her thanks. 'Aw, glad you like it. This one would eat nothing but his grandma's bloody recipes if he had his way, so it's nice to mix things up a little when we have guests.'

Styles's family were originally from Barbados, and his grandma Clara had given them a thick sheaf of photocopied recipes last time they visited. Her scrawl looked like a spider had walked in ink then breakdanced on the page, but Emma had managed to decipher it faithfully enough to do them justice. Porter had been a willing guinea pig on more than one occasion.

'How long have you got left to go?' Simmons asked.

'Less than a fortnight now,' Emma said, raising eyebrows in mock alarm. 'I'm going to give him a few months off before we start trying again.'

Styles half-choked on his food, grunting to clear his throat, as Emma patted his back.

'How about you, Evie? Do you want a family?'

'Em,' said Styles, recovered now. 'Bit heavy to land that on them.'

'Just blame it on the hormones. I can get away with most things these days,' she said, winking at Simmons.

Porter felt his cheeks redden. Hard to tell if Emma was asking just to be nosy, or because she enjoyed making him squirm. If he didn't know better, he'd say she was in cahoots with Kat, after her attempts to broach the subject last night. He was still trying to come up with a suitable fob-off to change the subject when Simmons answered.

'Not sure I feel grown up enough yet myself,' she said, sidestepping for now. Definitely a conversation that couldn't be put off for ever, Porter thought. He'd always seen one, maybe two in his future back when Holly was alive. That hadn't changed. It just felt like more of an abstract concept that it would have to be with someone else. Onc for when it was just he and Evie, no prying ears.

'On to more light-hearted matters – any news on the Victoria Park murders?' Emma asked, taking the hint to change subject, throwing it out to the table.

Porter caught another of those looks from Simmons, one that said, *Should we really be talking about this here?* There were limits to what he'd share, but Emma was as safe a set of ears as anyone not on the payroll, and thanks to Sky News, most of the country had heard about the case. Seen footage of the secret garden.

'We've identified a few of the bodies, but no real leads on who might have put them there yet. We're hoping they might have been back to visit, maybe been caught on camera.'

'All a bit creepy if you ask me,' she said, shivering like someone had walked over her grave. 'Building a little shrine like that. Takes all sorts. Those roses did look beautiful, though, like something fresh from the garden centre. All those different colours. So sad, though, to think of those kids buried there for so long. Bet their parents must have had such a horrible time.'

Something pinged in Porter's mind halfway through Emma's mini monologue. It wasn't just that notion again that it was a place to visit, rather than just a dumping ground. No, it was the flowers themselves

171

his mind flashed to. Emma's comment about the range of colours. All the bushes had looked different. Porter had no idea how many different types of rose there were, but many killers had a signature. A method of killing, posing of bodies. What if the roses were somehow involved like that, linked in with the pairings, which he was sure also had to mean something?

The others kept talking around him, but his thoughts leapfrogged ahead as he kept tugging that thread, past the notion that they had to identify the victims first to be able to work back from there. The location wasn't exactly an opportune spot to dump and run. It had been carefully chosen, crafted even. What if the roses had been picked just as carefully? An integral part of whatever their killer had created. It might be nothing, but Porter had a feeling nothing was on that island by chance. He filed it away to follow up on Monday morning.

Despite all the chatter about Branislav Nuhić, he couldn't shrug off the feeling that the island was linked to Libby. That whoever had put those children there, it was too much of a coincidence to think they weren't also the prime suspect for Libby's disappearance. Problem with that, though, was he knew what happened to kids taken by that person. To go down that route meant admitting the chances of finding Libby alive were pretty much nil, and he couldn't quite bring himself to do that. Not yet.

CHAPTER THIRTY-EIGHT

Monday morning, and London slumbers as the sun flirts with the horizon a little after 6 a.m. Traffic on Old Ford Road is light, cabs mainly, paying no attention to the man with his baseball cap pulled low, hands in pockets. Although it would be barely any different if it were rush hour. He doesn't attract a second glance, everyone else lost in versions of their world. Sitting on buses with heads in newspapers, or walking along, bowed over their smartphones.

A street sweeper rumbles past close by as he passes St Stephen's Road, and along towards the Lord Morpeth pub, complete with its mural of the suffragette campaigner, Sylvia Pankhurst, that dominates one side of the building. Even with the tables outside cleared, the smell of stale beer soaked into the cracks makes him wince and want at the same time. When was it he last had a drink? Like many things these days, it's hazy. He doesn't remember it being a conscious decision, only that he's a better man without it. Close to the man, the father, the husband they deserve.

The road bears right over the Hertford Union Canal, and the road begins to hug the edge of Victoria Park. He needs to be careful. The news footage showed plenty of policemen scuttling about like ants in the background, spoiling *his* island. Some of them might have stayed behind. He can't risk being seen.

A steady pace takes him past the row of closed curtains, houses as asleep as their owners. Over in the park, a couple of early morning joggers wind their way around the path, headphones in, matching stride for stride, not looking at each other, let alone him. Up ahead, his destination rises above the row of townhouses, appearing like a magic trick. Lakeview Estate, a pair of matching tower blocks joined by a series of walkways between each floor. Eleven storeys of perfectly placed concrete perch, with a line of sight over the trees and across to the lake.

Less than five minutes later and he's up on the roof, lying in a prone position like a sniper, focusing a compact set of binoculars past Grove Road and into the park. He sweeps around the shoreline, but barring a few ducks out for a morning paddle, it's deserted. No sign of movement over on the island. Why would there be? They've taken his children. All the same, he had to come, has to see for himself. The island is calling him, a siren song too strong to ignore.

He runs his gaze along the perimeter, as far along Old Ford Road as he can see, and back towards the roundabout below him at Crown Gate East and Crown Gate West, each a trio of red brick pillars, topped and tailed in white, and his heart pounds out an angry rhythm as he sees the figures. Two of them, a man and a woman. The woman looks like the reporter he saw on the news a few nights ago. The man carries what looks like a camera on his shoulder. They go to cross Grove Road, over towards the west gate, when another pair step out from behind a clump of what looks like pampas grass, just inside the park, arms stretched out, barring entry, moving them on.

Safe to assume the two inside the park railings are police. Who else would be hiding in there at this time of day? The park doesn't have any security of its own. Neither looks like the man he saw on the news yesterday, Detective Porter. He is the one with answers. The one who will know where the children are. Will he come back today? No rush. He settles in to wait.

CHAPTER THIRTY-NINE

'You've got to be bloody kidding me?' said Porter.

'Wish I was, boss,' Dee Williams replied. 'Me and Glenn had the stupid o'clock shift keeping an eye out at the park. They pulled up right over there in their Sky News van, so hardly incognito if our guy had rocked up.' She pointed over the road to indicate where she meant.

'Thank God you did, or we'd being seeing footage of roses all over the breakfast news. What the hell good did they think filming an active crime scene would do?'

'She reckons they were only going to do shots from the edge. To be fair, all the boats were locked up, so they'd have had a job getting over. I asked them to stay till you got here, but she blathered on about another story she had to chase up.'

'You'd be surprised at how resourceful some of those bastards can be,' Porter said. 'Where's Glenn now?'

'I told him to get away to bed,' she said. 'Only needed one of us to brief you.'

Not for the first time, Dee Williams impressed Porter with how willing she was to stick her hand up for absolutely anything. She was one of those people who practically hummed with energy, like a live power cable. Did she ever run out of battery?

'OK, thanks, Dee. You do the same. You must be knackered. I've got Glenn and Kaja on their way here now, so I'll hang on till they get here.'

She offered to stay, but he waved her away, checking his watch. Kam Qureshi had said to give him a call this morning. He apparently knew someone who could help prove or disprove Porter's theory, after Jake had spent chunks of Sunday turning over different possibilities, pulling them apart, and seeing how easily they went back together.

The more he thought about it, the more it made sense that the rose garden itself had some sort of significance. He'd logged on, looked through the photos they'd taken before digging the roses up and, sure enough, not all the bushes looked quite the same. Seemed to be a couple of different types. They'd all still be across there. Kam had arranged for the bushes to be re-potted, preserving them. It stood to reason that as they'd been growing in the same soil the bodies had lain in, they might contain trace evidence. What if the perp had snagged on a thorn, Kam had argued? Left a pinprick of DNA behind?

Porter walked slowly into the park, taking his time, looking around and wondering which entrance their killer had used when he brought the bodies. Another possibility bounced up and down in his head, like an attention-seeking child. Bodies uncovered in pairs. What if the pairs had been buried at the same time? Could one person have transported both without being seen? Had he been going about this all wrong, sending his team searching for an individual? It wouldn't be out of the question for there to be an accomplice.

Despite the temperature creeping up into double figures, he felt the breeze chill him, tickling the strands of hair around his ears, making his scalp prickle with tiny pins and needles. He looked around:

dozens of people going about their days, not one of them appearing to pay him a blind bit of notice. If that were true, why could he not shake the feeling, a slow crawl down his neck and across his back, that someone was out there, watching the park, watching him?

CHAPTER FORTY

'Ah, there you are, Porter. Just in time.'

'For what, sir?'

'I'm running a press conference at ten on the Victoria Park case.'

'Do you really think that's wise, sir?'

The words slipped out before he could stop himself. Milburn's face darkened as he tilted his head downwards a half inch, so he could give Porter the full schoolteacher effect of looking over the rims of his glasses. Porter reworded hastily before Milburn could speak. 'What I mean to say is one of our working theories is that the island is like a shrine for them. Somewhere they might visit again. More press coverage might scare them off.'

'More press coverage?' Milburn repeated. 'More than that part where you let a news team trample over the scene and hide cameras? I think that ship has sailed, don't you?'

'Not necessarily, sir,' Porter protested. 'I don't mean your average perp just popping back to admire their handiwork type of affair. This

179

place was special to them. Maybe special enough to take a chance when they think we're all done with it.'

Porter held back mentioning his theory about the roses for now. Without any hard facts, Milburn would swat it away.

'And in the meantime, I just pay overtime to have officers taking nice long walks in the park?'

'No, sir, I don't—'

'There's a press conference arranged for lunchtime. When I said you were just in time, I meant to start prepping for it, not for me to ask your permission to do it. One dead child is bad enough, but nine? Might have been different if we could have controlled the narrative, kept the numbers out of the public domain for the time being, but seeing as you couldn't manage that, we need to get out in front of this and dictate the flow of information. The bloody *Standard* have already thrown in their first serial killer strapline.'

No sense arguing, Porter thought. When Milburn made his mind up he was like a truck with its brakes cut. He'd keep going until he hit something else big enough to stop him.

'You'll be leading, I assume, sir?'

Milburn gave a curt nod. 'I'll read out a statement, and you can field any questions, or any you can actually answer at least. We'll be appealing to anyone who has visited the park in the last few years, asking if they've noticed any unusual activity, anyone clambering round on that island, that type of thing. I take it we still don't have IDs on all victims?'

Porter shook his head. 'Working on it.'

'OK, so we also include an appeal for anyone with a missing child that fits the age profile, for any links to the park, anyone who might have taken their child there before they disappeared.'

Times like this, Porter wished Milburn would stay behind his desk, stick to the politics and leave him be. A press conference at this stage could do more harm than good. Asking parents if their kids had been to the park could bring dozens, hundreds even, of calls flooding in. They'd already confirmed that several of those they'd identified had never set foot in the place, so if there was a link, it was unlikely to be that. Some battles weren't worth fighting, though, especially not with stubborn bastards like Roger Milburn.

Rock and a hard place though. If they didn't feed the press something, unchecked speculation could be just as bad. Worse in some cases. Best case, a flood of calls. The flip side, maybe someone sees someone acting suspicious, takes matters into their own hands.

'I've asked Anthea in comms to pull a statement together. Let's meet in my office half an hour before to go over it.'

Porter barely had time to nod agreement before Milburn was marching off down the corridor. Quick check of the watch. Half an hour before he had to be in the superintendent's office. No time to go and see Kam until afterwards. He headed back to his desk, doing a mental run through of what he'd say to the usual press conference questions, wondering whether somebody out there would be watching who knew the children. Cared about them. Had killed them.

CHAPTER FORTY-ONE

Milburn oozed confidence as he read out his pre-prepared statement, a politician addressing his constituents. The questions that followed were almost exclusively batted to Porter by his Teflon-shouldered boss. Did they have any suspects? How were the children killed? Should the public be worried that a serial killer was stalking the streets? With the likes of that last one, he sometimes wondered whether they expected or even wanted anything other than a vague answer that would give them leeway to speculate, spicing up their headline with some kind of cheesy pun.

He was getting ready to finish up and close it down when a familiar voice piped up, one final spanner slipped into the spokes of his day.

'Detective Porter? Amy Fitzwilliam, Sky News. What can you tell us about links between this case and the disappearance of Libby Hallforth?'

Subtly different from many of the others. Open-ended, assuming. Porter took a sip of water, working through the best way to answer, the one that left the least gaps to poke back through.

'At this stage we're not treating the two as linked, but as you know, I'm leading on both, so if any links do present themselves, I'll be sure to investigate those thoroughly.'

'So Simon Hallforth being arrested is purely a coincidence, then?' she asked, sweet as a daughter wrapping dad around their finger.

They hadn't gone public with that. How the hell did she know? No time to question where her information came from. Better to act like it was a throwaway soundbite, something he cared as much about as what he'd had for breakfast.

'Mr Hallforth has been arrested,' he confirmed, seeing it land, rippling around the room in a dozen surprised faces, impressed and annoyed that she'd been the only one to know. 'But it's not in connection with either his daughter's disappearance or the Victoria Park case.'

'What's he been arrested for, then, and how likely is it he'll be charged?' she fired back, not giving anyone else in the room time to react and piggyback on her success.

'As I said, Miss Fitzwilliam, it's an unrelated matter, and we're just here to talk about Victoria Park today. Now, if there's no more questions,' he said, pushing up and away from the table, ignoring the clamour of whats, whys and whens that flew his way from the assembled journalists. Milburn fired up a winning politician's smile and followed Porter through a door, and back into the corridor beyond.

'You want to tell me where she's getting her information from?' he snapped, after checking the door was closed.

'We've got a tight team, sir. No way this came from one of them,' Porter said.

'You'd stake your reputation on it?'

'I would,' Porter answered, no hesitation.

'In that case, you just did. I find out this came from your team, it's on you.'

'With all due respect, sir, does it really matter that they know he's banged up? Doesn't affect our other cases.'

'It's the principle. We need to control the flow of information. We lose that, we lose credibility.'

There was more to it than that, though. Milburn had become Porter's boss, when his previous one, George Campbell, was found to have been in the pocket of Alexander Locke, the very crime baron that Porter had been tasked to take down. Campbell was guilty by association in a number of deaths, and it had been swept under the carpet, all in the name of avoiding giving the Met a bloody nose. Granted, the evidence against him had been circumstantial without Locke alive to corroborate, but Milburn would dance around the facts like Fred Astaire if he deemed it in the interests of the force. He'd done it then, and he'd do it again in a heartbeat.

'Speaking of controlling information,' he said, checking his watch, 'I'm due in the deputy commissioner's office now to bring him up to speed. Call me if anything breaks.'

And like that, he was off again, dropping his orders like a mic on stage, walking off with no right of reply.

Porter shook his head, pulled out his phone and called Kam Qureshi. It seemed to ring forever, and Porter was wondering if something was up with the voicemail that should have kicked in by now. He was about to end the call and take his chances dropping by when Kam answered, breathy, as if he'd sprinted to grab his phone.

'Now a good time?' Porter asked.

'There's never a good time,' Kam said. 'Just degrees of inconvenience.'

'Well, here's hoping I'm the least inconvenient problem you have today,' Porter said, getting back to his desk and dropping into his chair. 'You said to give you a call anyway?'

'Mmm.' Something between a swallow and a slurp. 'Sorry, protein shake. Yes, so your text said you need to speak to someone about roses. I assume it's not just you getting romantic in your old age?'

Another side reference to him and Evie, or just Kam's attempt at humour?

'Yeah, something like that.'

'There's a guy I know at Kew Gardens. Helped me out with a case a few years back, you remember the Leo Olivera case?'

Porter hadn't worked the case himself, but knew the detail. Leo Olivera was a Brazilian, living in London, who had killed his mistress when she called things off. He'd denied having been at the scene, or even seeing her at all that week, but the nail in his coffin was pollen. He'd sent her flowers earlier on the day she died, and when the police had arrested him, they'd found traces of pollen on his sweater, from the same flowers that had only been in her apartment for less than an hour. Turned out he'd watched them getting delivered, then called her, trying to woo her back. Apologies and begging turned to anger and broken windows. She had thrown the bouquet at him when he got inside, and enough had stuck to make the case tight enough to see him get life.

'Wasn't one of mine, but yeah.'

'His name's Marc Booth. I'll text you his number. He's expecting your call.'

'You're a legend, Kam.'

'Flattery gets you everywhere. Got another little extra for you to perk you up. We gave the roses a once over and found a few bits and pieces. Don't get too excited, I'm not talking enough to give you someone's name, age and inside leg measurement, but there are some trace fibres snagged on a few thorns. Goatskin, if you can believe it.'

'Goat.' Porter sounded as confused as he felt. 'What did they do, swim across? I didn't see anything like that on the island.'

Muffled laughter from Qureshi. 'Not from a live goat. The guy isn't making pagan sacrifices. No, goatskin is used in some of the higher-end gardening gloves apparently.'

'So good enough to match if we find who owns the gloves?'

'Should be, yep.'

'Seriously, mate, I owe you.'

'I'll stick it on the tab, shall I?' he said. 'Still got a few results to come back from the bits and pieces we found with the bodies, clothing fragments and the like. I'll let you know as and when.'

Porter thanked him and signed off. Quick glance at the time. Five whole minutes since he'd walked out of the press conference. Might as well pop back up to where his team sat and see if the tip-off calls had started rolling in while he waited for Kam to text through details of the Kew Gardens guy.

Styles looked deep in conversation with Gus Tessier as he walked in. They both clocked in around the six four mark, but with Gus's bulked-out physique, it looked like Styles could fit in his jacket twice over. Styles looked up as Porter joined them.

'True what they say, the camera adds ten pounds. You look much better in the flesh.'

'I bet you say that to all the guys,' he batted back. 'You saw the press conference, then?'

Styles nodded. 'Our friend from Sky News, she's a bit of a terrier, isn't she?'

'Don't get me started,' Porter said. 'Need to have eyes wide open around that one.' He turned to look at Tessier. 'Did we get anything back on the contractors, Gus?'

'Thirty-four in the last five years, boss. Working through them now. Some are still with Nexon, others have left, but we'll work through that,' he said in his low rumble, like an idling motorcycle. 'Give me till tomorrow. Speaking of which, I'd best get back to it.'

'What next, then, boss?' Styles asked, leaning back in his chair. 'We working both cases today, or sticking with the park?'

There'd be headlines and photos from today's conference in the evening editions. Porter knew what Milburn would say, but he couldn't bring himself to abandon Libby just yet. A half-formed plan pressed its nose up against the glass in his mind. Not without risk, but what didn't have a slice of that these days?

'Bit of both. I've got something I need you to chase up,' he said, running Styles through his theory about the roses, and the fibres Kam had found.

'You think they're like a calling card, then?'

'Careful,' Porter wagged a finger. 'You know who leaves calling cards, don't you? And yes, I will make you pay the tenner if you say it. I'm thinking more of a tribute. Whoever planted them, he had to know his stuff. What they'd need to grow. How much light, water, general maintenance, that sort of thing.'

As if on cue, Porter's phone buzzed. A text from Kam with the number he'd promised, which Porter then forwarded to Styles.

'How about you? What you up to while I call Kew Gardens?'

'Easier if I tell you later,' Porter said. 'That way, you can't get in trouble for not trying to stop me.'

'Cos of course I've got a good track record of stopping you from doing what you want,' said Styles, smiling, but Porter could see the concern in his eyes.

'I need to speak to Evie about something. I'll be a couple of hours tops. Cover for me if Milburn comes sniffing.'

He left Styles to chase up the rose line of enquiry, grabbed his car keys and headed downstairs. Traffic was light for the time of day, and his drive took around forty-five minutes. Long enough for him to question the sanity of what he was about to do. Short enough for him to avoid changing his mind. He called Simmons as he pulled up at his destination.

'To what do I owe the pleasure?' she asked.

'Can't it just be because I wanted to hear your voice?' he said, making the most of the light mood before he soured it.

'Could be, but it isn't, is it?'

'Nothing gets past you. You should be a detective.'

'Mm-hmm,' she said, waiting him out past the jokes.

'We might actually be making some progress in the park case,' he said, giving her a whistle-stop tour of where they were at. 'Just as well, cos that's all Milburn wants to talk about. As far as he's concerned, Libby Hallforth is yesterday's news until this gets wrapped up.'

'I'd love to contradict you, but I know what he's like,' she said. 'You know if there's anything else I can do to help, I will.'

'I know,' he said, a sigh giving away his mood. 'That's why I called actually. I'm following up a lead on her case today, but I didn't want to get you in any trouble.'

A pause. 'What kind of trouble? Jake, where are you?'

'I'm down at Creekmouth Industrial Estate,' he said, waiting for the penny to drop. That took all of one second.

'Jake, you can't!' She spoke low and urgent, clearly somewhere she couldn't raise her voice, no matter how much she wanted to.

'I can't sit around and do nothing, Evie. The longer she's missing, the less people care. I figure your team will have eyes on the building, so they'll see me go in. I want you to go and see DI Maartens. Tell him you have reason to believe I'm heading to Creekmouth, and that you tried to talk me out if it. Should save you from any fallout. If I don't call you back in half an hour, you might want to send someone in looking for me.'

He batted back her attempts to change his mind, and told her again to call Maartens, then hung up and went to meet Branislav Nuhić.

CHAPTER FORTY-TWO

On the face of it, the building was a bakery factory. The loading bay to the right was full, six trucks decked out in the blue and white company colour scheme. A steady stream of men decked out in white overalls carried trays from inside the building, sliding them into racks inside the vans.

Porter hadn't clocked any surveillance when he'd parked up, or as he crossed the road. No bad thing. Hadn't expected anything else. They were hardly going to be sitting across the road in a squad car with blues and twos flashing. Of course, he could be wrong. Might be that there were no eyes on the place. When Simmons had told him about the other night, she'd said that it seemed clean.

He walked straight up to the main doors and into a cramped reception area, complete with a woman behind the desk who looked like she'd been baked in one of the ovens herself. She was the sort of brown you can only get from being basted in a vat of fake tan, sixty-ish at a guess, and she stared at him over thick black-framed glasses.

'Can I help you?' she asked, a hint of an accent blurring the words around the edges. Not strong enough to place, but he guessed it'd be Slovakian. Family business, family employees.

'I'm here to see Mr Nuhić,' he said, the smile on his face feeling about as genuine as a politician justifying his expenses.

'Who are you, please?' she asked, impatient, as if he'd interrupted another conversation she'd rather get back to.

'Detective Inspector Porter, Met Police,' he said, holding out his ID.

'He is not here,' she said, sounding proud to turn him away. Was she a relative? Porter wondered. Quite literally keeping it in the family.

'Would the answer have been different if I'd been here to buy some bread?'

She shrugged. 'He is not here. What do you want me to say?'

'When will he be back?'

'Maybe today, maybe tomorrow. Who knows,' she said, still seeming to take pleasure in her role as gatekeeper.

'Could you call him, ask him for me?'

She shook her head. 'Mr Nuhić doesn't have phone.'

'No phone?' Porter asked, as if he'd not heard properly the first time. 'No mobile?'

'No.' Another head shake, arms crossed, everything about her body language telling him to get lost.

'Got to be kidding me,' Porter muttered, turning away.

As he looked back towards her, a phone rang somewhere behind the counter. She answered, eyes fixed on him as she spoke in her native dialect, lips barely seeming to move. He listened intently, hoping that one or two words might be anglicised enough to get an idea of what was being discussed, but he was out of luck.

She didn't so much replace the handset as drop it into place.

'You wait. Someone will come.'

'Someone?'

She didn't answer. Just inclined her head and sat back down, only her head visible above the counter now. Clearly customer service didn't extend to small talk. He looked around, but there was nothing else to see really. No window behind her into the bakery beyond. The far corner of the room caught his eye, though. A tiny black orb fixed to the ceiling tile. He couldn't see the lens thanks to the dark glass, but he'd bet any money it was fixed on him right now. Made him wonder how much call a bakery had for security, and how easy it'd be to get into the building beyond for a look around.

Less than a minute passed before a door set in the wall behind reception opened, and a man stepped out. Porter recognised him immediately from pictures he'd seen. The man himself. Not a henchman in sight to play up a Bond villain image. Hard to say exactly how old he was, late fifties maybe, with a face that looked like he'd sucked too many lemons as a kid. Short greying hair, bordering on a military cut. Smart trousers, white shirt, sleeves rolled halfway up his forearms. Not an imposing figure, at least not physically, but when you had men working for you who did the kind of things Porter had heard about, you didn't need muscles to inspire fear.

'Mr Nuhić,' Porter said, a trace of surprise in his voice. 'My name is—'

'Detective Inspector Porter, yes, yes, I heard. You were looking for me? What could a policeman possibly want with a baker?' Same accent as the receptionist, only stronger. All a bit Bond-villain-esque.

Porter took a step forward, hands on the counter. 'I hear you're a man who doesn't waste his words, Mr Nuhić, so I'll do you the same courtesy.'

Nuhić nodded, looking vaguely amused. Held out his hands in a *be my guest* gesture.

'I'm investigating the disappearance of a young girl. She went missing five months ago. You might have seen on the news – Libby Hallforth.'

Nuhić folded his arms, and Porter could see the ghosts of old faded tattoos, the outlines but not the actual design.

'And what has this girl got to do with me?'

'One of your, ah, employees, Simon Hallforth. Libby is his daughter.'

'My employee, you say?' He shook his head. 'I don't think so. I know every person who works here, and we have nobody by that name.'

'I never said he works here,' said Porter, his emphasis on the last word.

Nuhić just stared, with flat dark eyes that reminded Porter of a reptile. Cold, unblinking. After a beat he gave what Porter supposed was meant to be a smile, but looked more like he just had wind.

'Why don't we go back to my office?' He gestured towards the door. 'If it sets your mind at rest, I can show you my personnel records.'

He flipped the hatch over on the reception desk, took a step to one side and motioned with open palms for Porter to join him.

Why had he come here if not to speak to the man? Granted, heading into the belly of the bakery, with no idea what actually lay beyond the door and with a man of Nuhić's reputation, it was a risk. Policemen were generally sacred, off limits, even to the most extreme of the underworld. Hurt a member of the force, and a wave of blue would crash down on you. Nuhić didn't strike Porter as the most rational of men from the stories he'd heard, though.

If there were any of DI Maartens's men outside, they wouldn't be able to see him once he stepped through that doorway. Porter's scalp tingled with nervous energy. He hesitated, only for a second, before stepping through the opening, hearing Nuhić follow, fighting the urge to look back as the door closed behind him and wondering if he'd just made a huge mistake.

CHAPTER FORTY-THREE

The biggest surprise was how normal it all looked. A dozen men and women in overalls, nets or paper caps pinning hair in place, stood at workstations. Some preparing dough, others shaping it, shovelling it onto wide wire trays and sliding them into huge ovens. The smell tickling his taste buds was enough to remind him that he hadn't eaten since an early breakfast. He was doubtful that Nuhić's hospitality would extend to a few slices slathered with butter, though.

They cut along the side of the building and finished up in an office, small and sparsely furnished. A desk with a chair either side, a laptop with the screen facing away from him and a row of three filing cabinets in the corner.

'Please, sit,' Nuhić said, walking round the desk and taking his own advice. 'What makes you think this man, what's his name again, that he might work for me?' He started tapping at keys as he spoke, poking with both index fingers. He spun the screen around so it faced Porter. 'You see, he isn't there.'

A long list of names ran down one side, a mixture of surnames starting with G and H.

'There's only the two of us here, Mr Nuhić. I think we can dispense with the notion that the only way you make a living is from baking bread.'

'You're right, we make pastries as well,' Nuhić said, looking almost amused at his own joke.

'You just asked me what his name was again as you were searching, but you managed to get just the right part of the list to show me he wasn't on it. Safe to say, he doesn't bake your buns for you.'

Nuhić rasped a palm over the blanket of stubble covering his chin. 'What exactly is it you think I do, Detective Porter?'

'I'm not here for you,' he said. 'Or your men. I'm not wired up, trying to get you to incriminate yourself. I just want to find the girl.'

Nuhić gave him another poor attempt at a smile. More of a twitch around the mouth that never touched the eyes.

'If you were wired, you would have set off sensors in my door,' he said, nodding as if to confirm that wouldn't have ended well. How many of the staff here weren't just bakers? Porter wondered.

'Let us say that I did know this man, Simon? Let us even say that he might have done some work for me. I'm a big family man, Detective Porter. The lovely lady on reception, even she is family, my cousin. But family and certain parts of business have to stay separate. So I ask you, why would his daughter have anything to do with my business?' Emphasis on the *his* and *my*.

'I've met Simon Hallforth quite a few times now. Let's just say he's no stranger to running his mouth off. Rubbing people up the wrong way, you know what I mean? We received a tip-off that he dabbles in selling drugs. One of our theories is that he might have pissed off the wrong person. That they might have taken her to teach him a lesson.'

'And you think that I did this?' he asked, an angry rumble to his words.

'No, that's not what I'm saying,' Porter said, even though he wouldn't rule it out privately. 'From what I hear, you'd be more likely to take it out on the man himself. But what if it was one of your competitors?' He leant forward, trying to convey the urgency. 'She's only seven years old.'

'And to come to me, you must be desperate, yes?'

Porter nodded, surprised by his own honesty. 'Yes, I'd say we are. If there have been any . . . shall we say, disagreements between you and any competitors around the time she went missing, it would help our case considerably if you shared that information.'

Nuhić leant back, rubbing both palms together. 'If I am the man you say I am, Detective, then you must know I'm hardly likely to speak out of turn about these things, these disagreements. No, that sort of man, he would sort things like this out his own way.'

'You have two daughters,' Porter shot back, Nuhić's obtuseness starting to rub against him like sandpaper. 'What would you do if this happened to one of them?'

'No man would be foolish enough to touch my daughters,' he said, evidently finding the notion almost laughable. 'But if they did, I would do what had to be done, just like any father. Like I'm sure Simon will continue to do when he gets released from his cell.'

The reference made Porter's thoughts grind to a halt for a split second, the inference clear. Nuhić knew they'd arrested Hallforth. What he'd do when Simon got out was anybody's business.

'He assaulted one of my officers,' Porter said. 'Nothing to do with your business. Things just got heated about his daughter's case.'

He stared at Nuhić across the desk. As much of a dick as Simon Hallforth was, Porter didn't want him in the firing line for this. He'd likely do time anyway for the assault on Simmons. There was a good chance that Maartens would offer him a deal to flip on Nuhić. That's what Porter would do in his place. Chances are, though, Simon would rather do the time than have to look over his shoulder every time he popped to the shops for a pint of milk.

'If you say so,' said Nuhić, but Porter suspected he would be making enquiries of his own as to what Simon Hallforth had and hadn't talked about. Maybe, though, just maybe, that would extend to looking at who Simon might have pissed off enough to lash out at his family. Nuhić wouldn't tolerate anyone harming his people. They were an extension of himself, and if he let that slide, what message did it send?

'All I'm asking, Mr Nuhić, is that if you did hear anything that could be linked to Libby's disappearance, you could let me know.'

He pulled out a card with his details on, and slid it across the desk. Nuhić looked down, but didn't make any move to pick it up.

'You think she is still alive then, or . . . ?'

'Honestly, I don't know. I want to say alive, but she's been gone a long time now,' Porter said, hearing the regret in his own voice.

'And if I did this, if I found anything that helped, you would what, owe me a favour?'

Porter's turn to smile. 'We don't do favours, Mr Nuhić, but you'd certainly have my gratitude.'

Branislav Nuhić flicked his hand in a dismissive gesture. 'Gratitude, I have no use for gratitude, unless it brings favours; a mutual understanding, if you will. If I find this is the doing of a competitor, you would of course act upon this, yes? Lock them up and throw away the key?' He mimed the action as he spoke.

'As long as we have proof, yes, you have my word,' said Porter.

'And maybe even your colleagues that take such an interest in me would be grateful enough to find another hobby.' Not even a question, Porter realised, just a statement of fact that he knew he was under surveillance. He made a mental note to mention it to Maartens.

'You have my card,' Porter said, rising to his feet. 'Thank you for seeing me.'

'One question before you go, Detective Porter. You say you wonder if Mr Hallforth has offended anyone enough to go after his family. Has he said himself who he thinks may be to blame?'

Porter shook his head. 'Wouldn't even admit to knowing you, let alone your competition. Told us he works alone, and hasn't got a clue.'

Nuhić shrugged. 'Maybe he doesn't work for me after all, then?'

Porter followed Nuhić as they retraced their steps back through the bakery, and it wasn't until he was back in reception that he realised how warm he'd been back there. Whether it was heat from the ovens, or sitting across from a man they believed responsible for some shockingly violent acts, he didn't know, but either way, sweat prickled his forehead and along his spine as the cooler air hit.

Nuhić held out a hand, and Porter felt the strength in his grip as they shook, resisting the urge to squeeze back. No time for pissing contests. He glanced back as he walked through the door and out towards the road, but Nuhić had already vanished back inside, leaving only the harsh stare of his cousin on reception.

No guarantees that Nuhić would give him the whole truth, even if he did find something. At this point, though, he'd grab that with both hands if it meant finding Libby, alive or not. More pressing would be the flak he'd almost certainly get from Maartens and Milburn. It was worth it to shake the tree, though. If it worked, most wouldn't care how the results had been achieved. If it didn't, he could live with that too. At least he'd have tried. What it'd cost him remained to be seen.

Branislav Nuhić watched the policeman leave, a grainy grey figure on a screen set into a bank of CCTV monitors. In his line of work – his real profession, not the bakery – attention from the police was a hazard of the job. This, however, wasn't something he'd expected to land at his door. He'd only met Hallforth a handful of times. Remembered him as a talker. Running his mouth off about how he could sell ice to Eskimos and sand to Arabs. He'd made money so far, sure, but was it worth the hassle of detectives barging into his place of work like this? One of his other men had vouched for Hallforth. Maybe it was time to question the strength of that now.

A few of the screens were set up sequentially, covering the stretch along the front of the building and down along the side. The effect was such that Detective Porter seemed to walk through the side of one monitor and into the next.

Of course, Nuhić knew they were watching him. You didn't get to where he was, do the things he'd done, without attracting the attention of the authorities. They had set up shop a few months back, in an old furniture wholesaler up the road. They'd been discreet about it, but they'd need to be far better to squat right on his doorstep and go unnoticed. They watched him, he watched them. He had a one-man outpost a few hundred yards further up the road.

If they were watching him, they would be looking for one of two things. A stupid mistake on his part, or a way in, to get close enough to where the mistakes didn't have to be big ones to sink him. Even if Hallforth kept his mouth shut, he'd need to take extra precautions. Insulate. His man down the road answered on the first ring.

'The man who has just left. Follow him. I want to know where he goes, who he speaks to.'

'Just follow?'

Nuhić watched as Porter pulled away and drove out of shot. 'For now.'

CHAPTER FORTY-FOUR

Despite years of living in London, this was Styles's first visit to Kew Gardens. As he wandered through the triple-fronted Victoria Gate on Lichfield Road, he imagined himself coming back here with Emma and a faceless mini Styles. No idea yet whether they were having a boy or a girl. As tempting as it was to find out, it was one of life's true surprises and neither wanted it spoilt before time.

He glanced at his phone, following the pulsing blue dot on the map, guiding him along a long straight path before cutting in to the right towards his destination, the recently renovated Temperate House. It made for an impressive sight as he came out past the flanking trees and into a clearing. The largest Victorian glasshouse in the world, it reminded him of a giant glass marquee tent. It stood almost twenty metres high, an elegant canopy of steel and glass, home to a vast collection of plants from around the world. Pity the poor bugger who had to clean the windows.

He'd agreed to call Marc Booth when he arrived, and when his host came out to meet him he wasn't what Styles had expected after speaking to him over the phone. He'd sounded young, vibrant, full of life. He was definitely the latter two, but was pushing seventy. The outdoor life suited him, though, and he had as much exuberance about him as a man half his age.

'Kam said this is to do with those bodies you found in Victoria Park?' Booth asked, his accent the very definition of English country gentleman.

'That's right.' Styles nodded. 'They were planted above the bodies, and someone had been tending to the area, so we're wondering if there's anything special about them, any way to trace back to a supplier if they're rare. That type of thing.'

'Let's see what you've got, then.'

Styles placed the storage box he'd brought with him onto a nearby bench, flipped the lid off and lifted out the first of five evidence bags, each containing a cutting from one of the rose bushes. Booth picked up the one closest to him.

'May I?' He gestured as if to open the bag.

Styles nodded. 'These are just cuttings, it's fine to handle them.'

Booth reached in, lifting out the single stem, letting the bag fall back inside the box. He rolled it between finger and thumb, causing the buttery yellow petals to twirl. He gently probed the bloom with a finger, separating the petals, peering between them, then raised it to his face, closing his eyes as he inhaled the perfumed scent. He repeated the process with the other four.

'Been a few years since I worked with roses in particular, so you'll excuse me if I'm a little rusty,' he said, 'but these are exquisite. This one' – he held up the first flower again – 'is a shrub rose. They all are actually, variations on a theme. Perfect for the kind of conditions Kam described. They'll make do with four, maybe five hours of sun, plenty of moisture.'

'Call me a heathen, but when I buy some for my wife, they all look the same,' Styles said. 'We're working on the basis that whoever did this, these meant something to them. Maybe they're a rare type, particular to certain areas, that sort of thing. Is there anything unusual about these that you can tell me about?'

'They do look familiar.' Booth nodded.

'You recognise them?' said Styles, hopeful.

'Yes, and no,' said Booth. 'This one, for example.' He held it out towards Styles, as if closer inspection would reveal its secrets to him. 'Have you heard of Daniel Grantham?'

Styles shook his head. 'Someone you work with?'

Booth smiled. 'I wish. No, Daniel Grantham is one of the best-known rose breeders in the country.'

'Rose breeder? How do you breed a rose? I thought you'd just plant it?'

'There are over one hundred and fifty species of rose, Detective, and that's before you start factoring in hybrids. Men like Daniel Grantham create new varieties all the time.'

'How exactly do you create a new rose?' asked Styles, his forehead creasing at what he'd thought would be a simple enquiry growing legs and running off in a completely new direction.

'It's not that complicated, to be honest.' Booth shrugged. 'Anyone with a bit of time on their hands can do it. It involves collecting pollen from one rose, then you apply that to the stigmas of another plant that you've already prepared. What you get are rose-hips, seed pods, that form. You harvest the hybrid seeds from those, plant them and, hey presto, you've bred a new rose.'

It sounded like way too much hard work for Styles when he could get a bunch delivered from his local florist, but he kept those thoughts to himself, not wanting to rain on Booth's parade. Something Booth had said a moment ago bounced back into his mind.

'When I asked if you recognised them, you said "yes and no". What did you mean by that?'

'Ah yes, sorry, I tend to go off on tangents if you get me started. I asked about Daniel Grantham because this looks a lot like one of his hybrids that we had here as part of an exhibition last year.' He held it up again, a conductor raising his baton. 'Very similar to one he bred; he calls it the Poet's Wife.' Booth chuckled. 'They do have some overly grand names, but it's all part of the fun of creating them: you get to name them like children.'

'Similar, but not the same?' Styles asked.

'That's right,' he said. 'The scent is a little different. I remember that one being a little citrusy. This one, not so much. The petals' – he stroked a finger over them again – 'these are a little less densely packed.'

'How about the others?'

'Mmm, this one could be the same.' Booth picked up a second stem. 'This one looks a lot like one of my favourites, a breed called Tranquillity. Couldn't say for sure with the other two. Whoever picked them has good taste, though. If I were you I'd get in touch with Daniel. He'll tell you for sure if these are his.'

'Where can I find Mr Grantham?'

'His centre is out west, towards Reading. A place called Kiln Green.'

'Don't suppose you have a number for him? Best if I give him a quick call, then, make sure he's in before I drive out there.'

'He'll be there, Detective. He eats and sleeps there,' Booth said, holding out his phone so Styles could copy the contact info.

'Bit of a workaholic, then?'

'The worst kind. Still is, even though he's a few years older than me as well. Literally lives there in an old farmhouse.'

Styles thanked him and headed back along the path to Victoria

Gate. His maps app said he'd be there in a little over forty minutes. No way could he make that now and be back in time to meet Emma for lunch at noon. Strictly speaking, Porter had asked him to run down the Kew Gardens contact. He could always head back to the station now, get one of the others to follow up with Grantham while he had lunch.

There was a nagging feeling, though, that he'd not been pulling his weight as much lately, even without the cock-up that had put Simmons in a jam. Porter hadn't said as much, but Styles felt it. There wasn't an atmosphere as such, but he'd sensed Porter's frustration a few times recently. He took out his phone to call Emma, but thought better of it. She'd pluck at the heart strings, try and persuade him to go with plan A. She'd probably succeed, too. All the more reason to drop her a text instead.

Hey Em. About to start an interview. Probs going to overrun so won't make lunch. Make it up to you tonight – takeaway – your choice. x

Not a lie, just a gentle stretching of the facts. The tiny bubble popped up showing her impending reply.

You had me at takeaway. Go get 'em. x

His thoughts turned back to the flowers as he reached his car. Two of the four possibly coming from the same place – if Grantham confirmed it, that is – could be a coincidence, but that wasn't the feeling he was getting. Everything about the island, the clearing, the way it had been carefully carved out, just didn't feel like anything had been left to chance.

Styles suddenly had a thought. Who would the flowers be more precious to than the man who'd created them? What if he was walking in there to meet the person responsible for all of this? He shook it off, remembering Marc Booth mentioning that Grantham was a few years older than him. That put him floating around his mid to late seventies. It was hardly as if Styles was going to call in for backup on the vaguest notion of a hunch. He could just imagine the stick he'd get back at the station. They'd be leaving roses on his desk for years.

He tapped David Grantham's address into his satnav and pulled out into traffic. What's the worst that could happen?

CHAPTER FORTY-FIVE

'Do you have any idea how much shit you've caused me?' Eve Simmons was in his face from the second he climbed out of his car. Angry, but the controlled sort that carried more weight than an all-out shouting, bawling verbal kicking.

'What was I meant to do? Sit around and wait another five months, and hope that Nuhić decided to help out of the goodness of his heart?'

'Alright, let me put it another way,' she said, hands on hips, practically barring his way back into the station. 'How would you feel if I ran into the middle of one of your cases, kicked it all over like a bully to a sandcastle?'

'So, I'm a bully now, am I?'

'That's not what I meant,' she said with an exasperated sigh. 'We might not be there yet, but we're as close as anyone's come in months to getting to him. Now that's all compromised, thanks to you.'

'Don't be daft,' he said, 'I did no such thing. We've got Simon bang to rights from Ally and Marcus's statements plus his little pharmacy in the lock-up. This doesn't compromise your inside man in any way. Besides, Nuhić already knows you're watching him.'

'Eh? What? How would he know that? And how do you know he knows that?'

'He as much as told me so. And I have no idea how he knows,' Porter said, throwing up his hands. 'He's a drug dealer. They're all bloody paranoid, aren't they?'

'He will be thanks to you barging in there,' she shot back.

'Look, Evie, I'm sorry if I've pissed you off, OK?' he said taking the heat from his voice. 'You know I wouldn't have done something like that just for the hell of it. I just thought after the sighting in the park, we were finally getting somewhere, you know? Then all this shit kicks off on that island, and it's like Libby Hallforth is a second-class citizen, even though she's been in line longer. I had to try something.'

'Maybe you did, but you should have talked to me first.'

'I did,' he protested. 'I called you before . . .'

'I mean talked it through before you went over there. You didn't call to have a chat about the rights and wrongs. You called to tell me what you were going to do, and that's not how this works, Jake. You can't just do what you want and expect to talk your way out of it after the shit hits the fan.'

'Usually works out alright for me, to be fair,' he said, attempt to lighten the tone as her point hit home.

'Yeah? Well if you'd heard what Maartens was calling you half an hour ago, you might not be feeling quite as bloody flippant about it all.'

'I'll speak to him and make it right,' Porter said. 'But I think this is our best lead for a while. Hallforth is a wrong 'un. I still wouldn't rule him out completely. Once he finds out we've spoken to Nuhić, though, that might make him more cooperative, to think that his boss suspects him of already talking to us. You've met him. You really think it's a stretch to imagine him pissing off some pretty nasty people? The kind bad enough to teach you the kind of lesson that only needs giving once. I know I said it might be Nuhić's competitors, but it's more likely to be Nuhić himself, after what we've heard about him. Maybe it was to teach Hallforth a lesson. Maybe Libby just saw something she shouldn't have.'

'You really think he'd hurt a seven-year-old girl?'

Porter nodded slowly. 'I hate to say it, but yeah. I think he's the kind of man who doesn't like to have to give a message twice, so he makes damn sure it lands the first time. The sort of man you'd be too scared of retaliating against, even if he hurt your family, for fear of what he might do to the ones that were still around.'

Simmons took a step back now, spent, the fight in her melting away.

'I don't want to argue with you about shit like this, Jake. If this is going to work outside of work, we've got to keep some ground rules here too. If we're a team off the clock, we need to be on the same team at work as well. I get where you're coming from, I really do, but Nuhić is no joke. If he had anything to do with this, he's not exactly going to hold his hands out to be cuffed, is he? If he'd hurt a kid, who's to say he wouldn't have a pop at a copper as well?'

'That wouldn't end well for him,' Porter said.

'Yeah, probably wouldn't, but for all you know you might not have walked out of that bakery, and that's a pretty shitty ending too.'

She looked up at him, eyes wide blue pools that he could fall into. Anywhere other than the station, and he'd pull her in close, wrap his arms around her. He hated the fact that being here made him feel like he couldn't. They stayed like that for a few seconds, before the moment passed. She took a half-step back, turning to let him past.

'I'd give Maartens another half hour if I were you.'

'Sounds like good advice,' he said, smiling.

'You might want to give Kam Qureshi a call, though. He came looking for you earlier. Said he had something for you.'

'Did he say what?'

'Yeah, the bodies from the park. The tests came back on the clothes they were buried in, and it's an odd one.'

CHAPTER FORTY-SIX

The entrance to Daniel Grantham's premises reminded Styles of a farm. He clocked the blinking LED in the treeline above, CCTV watching any comings and goings. Not quite the full relaxed rustic look once you spotted that. Was there much call for security in the flower business? he wondered. Industrial rose espionage, perhaps?

A mini tractor, more like a golf cart, zipped through the gates and past him while he stood rooted to the spot. The piss-take down at the station would have lasted a lifetime if he'd been done over by something that size in a hit and run.

A concrete circle acted like a roundabout just inside the gates, a spur off either side and, straight ahead, a smaller set of gates, thin metal bars with the initials D and G housed in between the wrought-iron rods. Wooden trellises stood either side, and through the gates, Styles saw enough roses to have Valentine's covered for a small town. Unsure which way to head, he was mid *eenie meenie minie mo* when a figure approached from behind the gates.

The man who opened them could have been Marc Booth's brother. Similar tanned, weathered look, but the sort earned through years of working outdoors, not wasted on a sun lounger.

'You wouldn't be Detective Styles by any chance, would you?'

Just the slightest hint of a Highland burr, enough to suggest he'd lived south of the border for most of his years.

Styles nodded. 'That would make you Mr Grantham? I tried calling a few times earlier, but your line was engaged. Business must be good.'

'The very same. Don't worry, laddie, Marc called ahead, told me you needed my help, so here I am,' he said, spreading arms wide. 'Is this them?' he added, nodding to the box under Styles's arm.

'Yep. Is there somewhere we can go and talk, maybe a little more private?'

'We can use my office,' Grantham said, gesturing for Styles to follow him through the gates. Either side of the path was an explosion of colour, a gauntlet for hay fever sufferers to run. Roses with such vivid hues and tones that it was like looking at nature on an HDTV.

'Makes the raggy ones I get from Tesco for my missus look like weeds,' he said.

'Not even a fair comparison, Detective,' Grantham said as they headed inside.

Where they finished up was more greenhouse than office. Glass walls, benches lining two sides, littered with pots, gardening tools and several pairs of gloves, longer than the usual gardening variety Styles had seen.

Grantham caught his gaze. 'Rose gauntlets. I'd be scarred for life without them. Now let me see what we have.'

He nodded towards the box Styles carried. Styles put it down, took the roses out of their bags and laid them side by side on a clear part of a bench. Grantham didn't pick them up straight away. Instead he leant in, touching them lightly with his forefinger, squinting through glasses that could put a telescope lens to shame.

'Marc Booth seemed to think these might be some of your creations.' He pointed towards the two Booth had highlighted earlier. 'How easy is it to tell?'

'I might have jam-jar bottoms for glasses, Detective, but I can still tell a Roald Dahl from a Rambling Rector.' Styles blinked in confusion. Grantham might as well be speaking Spanish, and the older man must have seen the baffled look.

'Varieties of rose, two of my creations.'

It felt like the equivalent to Styles of distinguishing between wines. Red, white and rosé in his book. Anything deeper than that was lost on him. Roses might be red, white, or any number of other shades. They were still just roses. He had a feeling saying that out loud now would be the equivalent of calling Grantham's kids ugly, so he kept those thoughts to himself.

'Mr Booth said this one was close but not quite,' he said, tapping a finger on the bench near the one Booth had called Tranquillity.

'He's no fool, that one,' said Grantham. 'It's not far off my Tranquility. One step removed, maybe two, but the petals are slightly differently shaped, and the scent has lost a note.'

'So somebody has tampered with your creation?'

'What they do once they buy them, however misguided, is up to them I suppose, but yes, at first glance that's what it looks like.'

'And the other?'

Grantham inspected the other rose. Peeling petals back with his finger, peering inside the folds, rolling stems between finger and thumb. After a minute, he looked up, taking off his glasses and rubbing the bridge of his nose.

'I'd say the same about this one too, a version of The Poet's Wife. Decent efforts, actually. Whoever did it knows their stuff. This one' – he pointed to a third rose, an apricot-coloured bloom – 'is a spin-off from my Roald Dahl. I can see from your face you're not sure of the names. It's just a little indulgence. Gives them a slice of personality, don't you think?'

Styles shrugged, nodding, not sure what to say on that. Instead, he decided to steer back towards the case.

'Would you happen to have a list of customers who've bought those varieties from you? Maybe a list of your staff here as well?'

Grantham laughed, bordering on a snort. 'I probably do, but there'll be hundreds of customers, thousands even. As for staff, I've got a dozen. Sometimes a few more in the busier periods.'

'Could I get that going back the last five years?'

'My son insisted everything went digital a while back now, so I can get him to email you the list, customers and staff, for all the good it'll do you.'

'You've got a family business, then?'

Grantham nodded. 'I'm more of a part-timer these days. Stick to what I love, creating new flowers. My son runs most of the business side of things now, you know, the marketing, website, does the books and all that stuff. Has done since . . . well, for a while now.'

'Since what?'

'Oh, it's nothing,' Grantham said, waving a hand, laugh a little too forced. 'Family stuff that's all in the past. Tell me, Detective, this secret garden you found in the park, what was it like?'

An image flashed in Styles's mind. The clearing. Contrast of colour against green. Blooms arcing around in a semicircle, reaching up to the sunlight.

'It was well hidden,' he said finally. 'Well looked after, too, like someone had been tending it.'

'And it was on an island, you say?'

He hadn't – said it, that is. He hadn't mentioned it. It'd been all over the news, though. Grantham could easily have seen it there.

'It was, yes.'

'Those poor, poor children,' said Grantham. 'All that time just a stone's throw away from people walking past, or sat drinking their coffee.'

'Have you been to the park before, sir?'

'Hmm?'

The older man looked like he'd been somewhere else, eyes snapping back into focus.

'You said "drinking their coffee". There's a cafe that looks out over that part of the lake. I'm just wondering if you've been there yourself?'

'Not for a long time,' he said. 'I used to take my grandchildren there, when they were younger. They used to love to feed the ducks, even though they'd end up eating as much of the bread themselves.'

Styles saw he'd lost him again, eyes drifting off a few inches as he strolled through the memory.

'Do you still get to London often, then?' Styles asked, not quite sure of where he was heading with this himself. Those bodies hadn't been there more than five years. The idea that this old man could, even back then, have broken into the park, hauled them over there, dug graves, just seemed ludicrous. Yet here he was, standing with the person who had created the original versions of the flowers that had grown around bone and skin, who knew the location. Freely admitted having been there. Would he really do that if he was responsible? It took all sorts. Whoever had put those kids there wasn't of sound mind, so who knows what they would or wouldn't do. Some liked to go back to their own crime scenes, even ones the police were still cataloguing.

Could Daniel Grantham be both that man and the one stood here today? It wasn't even like there was an easy way to start probing without just asking him outright. It's not as if they had a specific time of death for any of them to ask him outright where he'd been. Styles filed it away for now as something to mention to Porter. There were subtle enquiries they could start off with. Find out what he drove, check any ANPR and

CCTV that went back far enough for the first body. The former was kept for up to two years, so worth a punt.

'No, I haven't been into the city since the start of last year. Like I said, my son deals with most of the business side now. I'm getting lazy in my old age. Tend to wait for folk to visit me instead,' he said with a chuckle.

'These flowers, then; if they're a step removed from your originals, is there any way to determine who it was that bred these versions?'

'That's like showing an artist a forged painting and asking them to tell you who drew the copy,' he said with an apologetic smile. 'Course, I'm not saying just anyone can do this, at least not professionally anyway, but no, I couldn't tell you just from looking.'

Styles shrugged. 'I did think it was probably a long shot.' He began bagging up the flowers, slipping them back into the evidence box.

'Sorry I couldn't help more,' Grantham said. 'On the plus side, it's the most excitement I've had in months. If you leave your details, I'll get my son to email over the list of customers.'

'I'll leave you to it then, sorry to bother you,' said Styles, picking up the box and turning to leave. His foot caught on something, making a scuffing noise as he almost stumbled and put a hand out against the bench to steady himself. He'd managed to stand on the fingers of one of those extra-long gloves he'd seen when he first came in, his other foot snagging in the opening.

'These look a bit posher than the black rubbery ones my mum wears,' he said, picking it up and laying it on top of its twin. 'Leather?'

Grantham nodded. 'Goatskin.'

CHAPTER FORTY-SEVEN

'You're sure?' Porter asked, regretting the stupid question as soon as it popped out.

'Because of course I'm usually the poster boy for wild speculation.' Kam Qureshi's response was pure sarcasm with raised eyebrows thrown in for good measure.

'How about I just shut up and listen?'

Kam inclined his head, placated. 'So, as I was saying, not only were they all wearing pyjamas, but they were matching. Boys match with boys and girls with girls. Same type of cotton fibres. Don't get me wrong, most of them are a bit worse for wear, but a couple of the labels are intact, and I've been able to do some magic with imaging on the writing. All of 'em are from Next.'

'Great work, Kam,' said Porter, but even as he did, common sense kicked in. All well and good knowing the source, but that in itself didn't get them much closer to their killer. Those pyjamas had likely sold in their hundreds, thousands even, at a national retailer like

Next. No, it was more of an insight into the mind of who was doing this, rather than their identity.

The chances of all nine of them being taken while wearing the same outfits was astronomical, so Porter felt on fairly safe ground assuming that they'd been dressed like that by whoever killed them. Before or after death? Impossible to tell after this long. The layers of ritual were building up, though. Buried in pairs, one boy and one girl. Each pair around the same age. Each wearing mirror image outfits. Laid to rest, as opposed to buried to cover up; at least that's how it was beginning to feel. Their killer saw them as children, not just victims. The way they'd been buried preserved that notion in Porter's mind.

'Don't think it's going to help us much at this stage,' Kam said, as if he read Porter's mind. 'Not unless you bust into a house and find a stash of last season's PJs.'

'Nah, maybe not. Could come in handy later, though. I'll take anything I can get at this point.'

'You manage to speak to Marc Booth yet?'

'I sent Nick to see him,' Porter said. 'Had something else I needed to handle this morning.'

'Oh yeah? Anything interesting?'

It was as if they had rehearsed the timings as he saw Styles walking into the office. Saved by the bell, no need to offer up an explanation.

'Speak of the devil, Kam, he's just walked back in. Gotta go, but thanks again.'

Styles walked towards him, narrowing his eyes, giving a disapproving parent to naughty child look.

'I'm guessing you've spoken to Evie, then?'

'She called me when I was driving back from Kiln Green.'

'Where the bloody hell is Kiln Green?' Porter asked. 'You were meant to be at Kew.'

'I went there first, then . . . Never mind changing the subject. I could have come with you, boss. Why didn't you just take me along?'

Porter felt a genuine twinge of guilt, knowing if the roles were reversed that he wouldn't have been happy being kept out of the picture.

'No point us both getting in trouble.'

As true as that was, it wasn't the only reason. Styles had gotten hurt pretty badly when they took down Alexander Locke and his gang. His wife had gone as far as trying to persuade him to transfer back to Specialist, Organised & Economic Crime Command, where he'd started off his career. Porter already felt responsible for him, for his safety, even before he learnt Styles was going to be a dad. Doubly so now. Chances of Nuhić doing anything stupid for the sake of a fishing expedition had been pretty slim in his opinion, but with Emma weeks away from giving birth, he'd sooner stick himself in harm's way than face her if he let anything else happen to her husband.

'And are you? In trouble, that is? What's Milburn had to say?'

'Nothing yet, but I'm sure he'll take great pleasure when he does. Have you eaten yet?'

'No, literally just got back.'

'Come on then, my shout. Let's catch up over a bite.'

They headed along to Bake & Cake on the corner of Edgware Road and Broadly Street, Porter going first, describing the encounter with Nuhić as they waited to get served.

'You think he knows more than he's saying?' Styles asked.

'Well he's saying nothing, so wouldn't take much, but yeah, wouldn't surprise me if he does.'

'What about Hallforth? You think Nuhić believes he's keeping his mouth shut? Wouldn't want to be in his shoes either way.'

Porter shrugged. 'He as much said that if it was anyone in his crew, he'd want to take care of it himself. Swear I saw his eyes light up at the thought that it might be one of his competition, thinking that we'll do him a favour and take one of them down for it.'

'What's our play now, then?'

'Depends if Hallforth gets bail. If he does, and Nuhić thinks he's guilty, he'll try and clean house to stop us looking too closely. We keep an eye out and see what happens. If it's one of his rivals, there's a chance he'll reach out, let us do his dirty work.'

'And if it's neither?' Styles said, letting the elephant well and truly into the room.

'If it's neither, then . . .' Porter didn't want to admit it, but if the Nuhić angle didn't play out one way or the other, it'd put them right back where they were before the false sighting. 'Let's cross that bridge when we come to it. Anyway, what about you? How was Kew Gardens, and what the hell is at Kiln Green?'

Styles gave him a summary of his mini road trip as they headed back into the station, not looking convinced by his own theory about Daniel Grantham, but Porter nodded along, letting him finish before chipping in with questions.

'It's as good as any lead so far. We might not be able to pinpoint our guy from his DIY roses, but it'd be a pretty big leap to think Grantham has no significance at all, even if it's just that we're looking for one of his customers. Not as if they can just go to B&Q and grab a few of his, is it?'

'He's sent over a list of people who've bought any of those varieties from him, but it's going to take some going through. Tell you what, though, lovely place he's got there. Might take Emma for a trip up after the baby's here. Her mum's into her gardening, and Em's been stuck for ideas for a birthday present.'

'Chat with a scary gangster, wander around a rose garden?' Porter made a weighing-the-scales gesture with both hands. 'Sounds like you've had the rough end of the deal.'

They exited the lift, heading back towards their desks. Milburn walked towards them from the far end, beckoning towards his office with an imperious flick of the hand.

'You can mock all you like, but I nearly went down in the line of duty out there. Tripped on one of these massive leather gloves he had. Reminded me of the ones vets wear, you know when they're shoving their arm up a cow's backside.'

Porter started to laugh, but it caught in his throat.

'Leather gloves? Wasn't goatskin by any chance, was it?'

'Yeah,' said Styles, looking as impressed as a kid who's just seen the rabbit pulled out of the hat. 'How did you know that?'

CHAPTER FORTY-EIGHT

Sweat cools on his back, a hundred tiny pinpricks of relief. The detective walked right past him and didn't so much as glance in his direction. From his table outside the Maitrise Hotel, he watches him walk back towards the station. He isn't alone. A tall black man ambles alongside him, both clutching matching sandwiches and takeout coffee cups. Doubtful that they'll have his children inside the police station. No, more likely they'll be in a hospital somewhere. Lying on a cold table, nobody close by to take care of them. Ripped from the comfort of their garden. Sadness and anger swirl around him in equal measure.

He has nowhere else to be today. Only has eyes for this building, and the man who might lead him to his children. There is another thought that circles like a shark hemming in a shoal. The notion that they might be beyond his reach for good. That he has failed them, the same way he has failed Marie and Ben. Even the hint of it, allowing the possibility to squat nearby, makes a lump form in his throat. After everything he's been through, the catalogue of mistakes he has made, he isn't sure how he could cope with that. If he could cope at all.

Unable to visit them, unable to take care of them, to whisper to them, reassure them. Pressure starts to build, beginning in the pit of his stomach, swelling up through his chest, beating its fists at his temples. They've been part of him for so long now, a plaster over the wound of his own fractured family, that the absence of them is a physical ache, only surpassed by his longing to see Marie and Ben. That ache grows as he watches the two policemen disappear into their building, swelling, taking on dark form.

He has experienced troughs to rival the deepest ocean trench over the years, but nothing quite like this. The pressure becomes a buzzing in his head, and the white noise of the city around him fades until nothing else remains. The policeman can't stay in there for ever. He'll be waiting right here until he does, and he'll find a way back to his children, all of them, no matter what the cost.

CHAPTER FORTY-NINE

Milburn glared at him as he entered the office, and Porter clocked Maartens over to the left, standing, arms folded like a bouncer about to take great delight in telling a spotty teenager to get lost.

'You can stay standing,' Milburn said in a clipped tone that Porter recognised from previous bollockings. 'I'm guessing you might have an idea why DI Maartens is here? Why he's pissed off?'

Porter pretended to think for a second. 'Did he not manage to get Take That tickets for the gig at the O2?'

Roger Milburn sneered, glancing over to Maartens as if to say, *Can you believe this one?*

'You think pissing your colleagues off and pissing all over their hard work is funny?'

'With all due respect, sir, I—'

'That's one thing you've not shown any of today, DI Porter. Respect.' Milburn shot him down before he could finish his sentence.

'Six months we've been on Nuhić. Six bloody months, to get a man in there without him raising an eyebrow, and now he's going to think that every *Big Issue* seller on the street is a copper with eyes on him.'

'Look, I'm sorry if you think I jumped up and down on your case, Aaron, and I hate to be the bearer of bad news, but he knows you're there already. He said as much this morning.'

'He what? What the bloody hell did you tell him?' Maartens took a step closer, working his jaw from side to side.

'What did I tell him? Come on, Aaron, I'm not an idiot. I ignored the comment. If I'd denied it, I'd have looked defensive; if I'd confirmed it, I'd cock up your surveillance. I'm not bloody stupid.'

'Yet you went to see the head of one of the biggest organised crime gangs in London, when you knew the case against him was at a delicate stage. If you've jeopardised that in any way, or put our informant in danger, I'll see that you're held to account, you can be sure of that.'

'There's no risk to your inside man,' Porter said, looking over at Maartens. 'I have Simon Hallforth's ex-wife, a witness independent from your case who gave us the drugs angle, so there doesn't have to be any overlap, and it's currently the best line of enquiry we have into Libby Hallforth's disappearance. You both remember her, don't you? I know she's not making the news this week, but doesn't mean I'm going to sit on any possible line of enquiry while there's a chance we might find her.'

'Oh, come on, man, she's most likely dead and you know it.' Milburn was usually one to hide any anger behind a more officious tone, but there was a real snap in his voice now. 'The immediate threat to our informant and the people who shoot up that crap Nuhić peddles, not to mention the person who killed nine kids is still walking the streets – all of that outweighs that girl now. I know you find that unpalatable, but that's just the way it is. We all have to make hard choices, and this is one of those.'

'You're suggesting I stop looking for the girl, sir?'

Milburn glared at him. 'Don't you get clever with me, Porter. I'm telling you to prioritise how you spend your time, and not run around like a law unto yourself. We're a team here,' he said glancing over to Maartens. 'Even if you're not acting like part of it at the moment, that's what we are, and I'm telling you now, you'd better bloody well get yourself back on board with the rest of us.'

Porter stared at a spot just over Milburn's head, his face impassive, but inwardly slating his boss. Of course he would rather Porter spent all his time on the Victoria Park case and forget about Libby. That's what was getting the tabloid inches, so that's what he'd bang his drum about. All about the optics, that one. It wasn't that Porter didn't want the park case solved as well. What Styles had uncovered this morning definitely had legs, as good as anything so far, but there was something about Libby's case that niggled him like sand in a shoe after a beach trip.

Everyone close to her had lied in one way or another. You'd think when a loved one disappeared, a little girl, that self-preservation would be sent to the back of the class like a naughty kid at school. But they had all held back, partly lies, some just selectively withholding. Either way, it had cost them valuable time. Might even have cost a seven-year-old girl her life.

'Are we clear?' Milburn sat back, arms folded in a *here endeth the sermon* pose.

Porter nodded, biting down, swallowing the answers he'd much rather give.

Milburn glared at him, eyebrows arched, waiting to hear the words. 'Yes, clear, sir.'

'Good, now where are we with the park case?'

Porter brought him up to speed on the morning's findings, outlining plans to dig into Grantham, continuing to pursue identification on the other bodies. Milburn nodded, asked a few questions, finishing up with a veiled threat, his usual style.

'Of course, if you're struggling with both cases, I can always reassign one of them?' The inference being that Porter couldn't cope, or that he wasn't up to the job. No way was he about to give Milburn an easy stick to beat him with.

'It's alright, sir, I can manage both.'

'Good, in that case you'd better go and crack on,' he said, and with a flash of a cold smile, Porter was dismissed. Maartens followed him out into the corridor, and he drew level with Porter within a half-dozen steps.

'That the last we'll see of you down Creekmouth, then?' he said, inching closer just outside of Porter's personal space.

'It's all yours, Aaron.'

Maartens sighed, took a half-step back and shook his head. 'Simmons says you're a good guy. I get that it's hard when there's kids involved, but I can't have you busting in on the middle of my case again. I see you down there again, and my men have orders to keep you away. Understand?'

Truth be told, Porter had no intention of heading back there. The trip to see Nuhić had been a one-bullet-in-the-gun type of effort. Either Nuhić would bite, or he wouldn't. Porter had no leverage, nothing to press home.

Maartens backed off another few steps, still facing Porter. 'If you'd asked, we could have worked something out, you know. Let you go see him when the timing was better.'

Better timing? A seven-year-old girl was missing, probably dead, and this dick was worried about timing.

'That everything?' Porter asked.

Maartens gave a big toothy smile, like a shark, and backed away, turning to walk down the corridor without another word.

Deep breath. Rise above it.

Porter headed back to join Styles just in time to see him polish off his sandwich. Porter's waited next to his coffee, both untouched after having been dragged straight in to see Milburn from their trip along the road.

'What did he say?'

'In a minute,' Porter said. 'I want to talk about Grantham first. Kam found traces of goatskin leather on some of the thorns from the island. What can you remember about them? Were they branded? Any damage, or marks?'

Styles huffed out a loud breath. 'Brown, more like normal leather on the hand part and suede style on the parts that cover your arms. Don't remember any branding. You really think . . .'

'That plus the flowers, it's a coincidence, don't you think?'

'Yeah, but I don't even know for sure they were his. He could say they belong to one of the staff, and he was borrowing them. Maybe they even share a pair? For all we know, every member of staff has a pair.'

'I know, I know,' said Porter, looking around his desk as he thought, as if the answer was on a stray Post-it waiting to be found. 'We ask him to see them without a warrant, and we tip him off. No way we have enough for one, and if it is him he can get rid of them before we come back.'

'We need more,' Styles agreed.

'Let's get his car run through ANPR for starters, see if he's been anywhere near the park or the victims we have IDs for.'

'I'll crack on with that while you grab your lunch. What about the customer and staff lists he sent through? Still worth checking?'

Porter thought about it, but only for a second. 'Yep, still needs following up.'

It'd be a schoolboy error to do anything else. Wouldn't do to let confirmation bias slip in, the tendency to favour information that fitted the prevailing theory you were chasing.

'Pass it on to Dee or Gus. ANPR takes priority. If we find anything we can be back out there with a warrant. Kam reckons he'd be able to match the fibres to the glove if we get the right one, or at least match to the brand.'

'I'm on it,' said Styles, rising from his chair. 'You didn't tell me what Milburn said?'

Porter gave Styles the headlines. Stick with the park case, keep the Hallforth case at arm's length until further notice. Essentially give up on Libby. Not something Porter could bring himself to do, no matter what Milburn threatened. He'd find a way to keep both plates spinning.

'What are you going to do, then?' Styles asked.

'Whatever I have to.'

CHAPTER FIFTY

Any chance of juggling both cases relied on momentum, generating it, capitalising on it. Porter couldn't afford any downtime. Watching Styles vanish, presumably to find Dee or Gus, Porter tore off a chunk of his sandwich and called Marcus Hallforth. The younger man didn't exactly sound overjoyed to hear who was calling, but Porter didn't care. No sense in taking it personally. He was trying to find a young girl, not win a popularity contest.

'We're going to need you to come in again, Marcus. Got some more mugshots for you to look at.'

'I did that already,' Marcus grumbled.

'Well, now I need you to do it again. Those were fairground employees. These are different.'

'Different how?'

'These are people who worked with your dad.'

Worked with. Made it sound like mates on a factory production line.

'You mean the Slovakian guy? Nah, I ain't having them thinking

I'm a grass. I've heard the stories. Wouldn't last five minutes.'

'They'll never even know you've pointed them out. All I need you to do is look at a few pictures, tell me if you saw any of them at the fairground that day.'

Silence bar some background noise, traffic on the other end maybe.

'Come on, Marcus. You're her big brother. If someone doesn't step up soon, I don't know whether we'll get any closer.'

'Don't see how it matters. Even if I see someone who was there, what does that prove?'

'Nothing on its own, but we've got to start somewhere. Come on, Marcus, this has pretty much ground to a halt. If you don't help me out, I don't know if I'll be able to kickstart it again.'

Porter wasn't above using a little emotional blackmail now and again, but Marcus was more hesitant than he'd expected.

A few seconds' pause. 'Alright,' he said finally. 'I can come in after work. About seven o'clock?'

Porter did some quick mental maths. He'd promised Kat, not to mention Tom and James, that he'd make their after-school football match. Five o'clock kick-off. Three quarters of an hour there, the same back. He could make the match, but he'd need to sack off the post-match pizza.

'I'll see you here for seven,' he confirmed. The boys would be disappointed, but he'd make it up to them. He'd been threatening for ages to take them to a Spurs game, and they were away at Chelsea this weekend. As good a chance as any to make good on that promise, as long as nothing kicked off at work.

Time for one extra roll of the dice while Styles was off doing his thing. He wasn't done with Simon Hallforth just yet.

Hallforth looked far from pleased to see Porter again. A quick glance, then he turned, stared up into the corner with a loud sniff but said nothing. The same solicitor sat by him, Steven Linton. Give the man a beard and red suit, and he had the build for Santa Claus. Hallforth looked positively dwarfed by him.

'So, we've spoken to your ex-wife again, and your son, Marcus. Funny, but they both seem pretty sure you know Branislav Nuhić.'

'Yeah? What a surprise. They would say that, wouldn't they?'

'So, they're mistaken then?'

'Course they're bloody mistaken. I already told you I haven't got a clue who you're on about. That all you dragged me out of my cell for?'

'Not quite, no.' Porter was amused by Hallforth's swagger. The little man puffing up his chest routine. He stopped deliberately short there, letting the silence rattle Hallforth's temper up another notch.

'Well, come on then?' Simon snapped.

'I do hope you haven't called me in just to run over the same accusations my client has already denied, Detective?'

'Course not, Mr Linton.' Porter gave him a tight smile. 'No, I actually had a chat with somebody else this morning, and your client's name came up.'

'And who would that be?' Linton asked.

'Whoever it is, they're a lying bastard,' Hallforth chipped in.

'Really?' Porter leant back, amused by the build-up. 'You'd say that to Mr Nuhić's face?'

Hallforth's face was a picture, frozen like a snapshot as the name seeped into his brain. Eyes widening as it hit home, fear washing over him, but quickly replaced by disbelief, and a mask that screamed bravado, no matter how fake.

'Bullshit. As if he'd sit and chew the fat with you.'

'Ah, so you do know him, then?'

The mask fell for good this time, he and his solicitor turning to look at each other, Linton giving a disapproving shake of the head.

'Alright, I've heard of him,' Hallforth said, words rushing out now, 'but that's all.'

'Let's cut the shit, Simon,' Porter said, leaning forward, elbows on the table. 'I had a chat with him this morning, quite a long one actually, at his bakery over in Creekmouth.'

Didn't hurt to embellish a little. Wasn't as if Hallforth or his solicitor could corroborate what was said at the bakery. Neither could Porter for that matter, but this wasn't testimony in a court. He just needed to see what he could shake loose. If anyone within Nuhić's crew had had a hand in Libby's disappearance, scaring Simon into talking was his best bet. His only hope. No way would the Slovak give up any of his own men. They'd end up wearing concrete shoes in the Thames, or crammed into a barrel and dropped off a bridge.

No smart-arsed comeback from Hallforth this time. Porter took a small amount of enjoyment from seeing him squirm. It wasn't hard to second-guess the kind of thoughts running through his head now. Self-preservation. The best route to stay alive, never mind out of jail.

'Now, he didn't implicate you in any illegal activity. Couldn't do that without throwing himself under the bus, and he isn't going to do that, especially for the likes of you. He knows you've been arrested, though. Interesting that he'd keep tabs on you, if didn't know each other quite well, and I'm guessing you're not best mates, so I'm sticking with you two working together. Now,' he said, leaning forwards, lowering his voice as if about to share a secret, 'what do you think Mr Nuhić made of you being in here?'

Linton leant in, whispered something in Hallforth's ear. The little man grimaced, as if whatever had been suggested was as unpalatable, if not more, than where Porter was leading him. Porter waited him out. Watched as Hallforth wrestled with his choices.

'Assaulting an officer, and possession with intent? You'll be looking at a nice chunk of change inside. Five years at least, I reckon. If only you had something to trade up, you know, help reduce the sentence.'

'He'll kill me,' said Hallforth quietly.

'Sorry, didn't catch that.'

'I said he'll kill me,' he said again, more forceful this time. 'Knowing him he'll probably do it either way just to be safe. Jesus!' Hallforth flopped back in his chair, hands running through his hair, down to cover his face, only for a second.

'Help me and I'll help you, Simon. Maybe your boss knows something about Libby, or at least knows who you might have pissed off enough to do something to her. It's the best lead we have for her at the moment. Whatever you are, you're still her dad. Worst case, if there's nothing you can give us there, you can talk to my colleagues about his business. Help us take him off the streets, Simon.'

Hallforth gave a bitter laugh, not an ounce of humour. 'Feel like I've just landed in an episode of *Line of Duty*. Isn't this the part where you say how you'll protect me?'

'We will,' Porter urged. 'He's far more important at this stage than getting you banged up. Not just for Libby either.'

Linton whispered into Hallforth's ear again, and the smaller man listened, thought for a second, then nodded.

'My client would want written agreement that all charges against him are dropped in exchange for his help, but making that request is in no way, shape or form an admission of prior knowledge of Mr Nuhić's business.'

'If it helps find Libby or take down Nuhić, we can look at that.'

'Not "look at", Detective. It has to be in place before he'll talk any further about this.'

'I'll have to speak to the super first, but in principle, yes, we can do that.'

However this played out, Porter wouldn't want to swap places with Simon Hallforth. If Nuhić was every bit as bad as the stories, Hallforth was right; he'd probably try and kill him anyway, just on the off chance, regardless of whether he kept schtum and went to jail, or flipped and worked with them. Men like Nuhić had a long enough reach that you couldn't be sure of safety even if you spent most of your day in a cell.

Porter left the two men in the room to carry on their part of the conversation, promising to call Linton as soon as he'd spoken to Milburn. Gus Tessier was looking around the office, and when he clocked Porter, he gestured for him to head over.

'What's up, Gus?'

'Just thought I'd let you know the latest on the contractors from the park. We've spoken to most of them now, and done all the background checks. Most of them are clean. One stands out, though.' Tessier held up a sheet of paper that Porter hadn't spotted him holding by his side. 'Christopher Hargreaves. Did a short spell inside for exposing himself to a twelve-year-old boy at the school he worked at for kids with learning difficulties. He's still on the sex offender register.'

Porter scanned the info on Hargreaves as he listened. Fifty-three years old. Sentenced six years ago, to five months. Unlikely that he'd disclosed this to his employers at Nexon, or he'd surely not have been allowed to work in an environment where he'd come into contact with so many young children.

'Have we spoken to him yet?'

Tessier shook his head. 'Literally just got the info five minutes ago. Just thought you'd want to know.'

'Good work, Gus. He goes to the top of the list for ones we still need to speak to, then. How many others left?'

Tessier slid a second sheet out from behind the first, a printed email from someone in Nexon HR. Numbered with names, phone numbers and email addresses. Twenty-five of the thirty-four had been highlighted.

'Those ones we've spoken to,' said Tessier. 'Ones not highlighted are still to do.'

233

Porter scanned the list of names, staring hard at each one, as if some hidden info would be revealed. Halfway down the list, he heard footsteps behind, fast and purposeful, Styles's voice coming from over his left shoulder.

'Boss, you got a minute?'

'Course, what's up?'

'It's Daniel Grantham. When I asked him, he said he hadn't been into London. He lied.'

CHAPTER FIFTY-ONE

'Lied about what?'

'We were talking about the park, and I asked him if he got into London much. He said he hadn't been in since the start of last year, but his car pinged on ANPR near Stratford on three separate occasions. First was 18th August last year, second was 10th November, and the last one was 26th January.'

Styles looked like a kid expecting praise from a parent. It took a few seconds, but Porter caught on.

'Isn't that . . .'

'. . . the day Libby Hallforth disappeared? Yep.'

The three of them shared the same look now, the one that said something previously stalled had been jump-started. No sense sitting on it. Might as well get out there and put him on the spot today. Porter checked his watch.

'We heading, then?' Styles asked, tilting his head towards the door.

Porter had a sudden thought, checked his watch and scrambled to make plan B. No way he could get out to Kiln Green and back in time to see the boys play football. He pictured the disappointment on their faces, the disapproval on Kat's, and made his decision.

'You go. Take Gus with you.'

'What about you?'

'Got somewhere I need to be this afternoon, plus meeting Marcus Hallforth later to look at some mugshots from Nuhić's crew.'

'As long as that somewhere isn't another trip to a bakery in Creekmouth,' Styles said, only half-joking.

'Not this time, I promise. You two go. Should be able to handle a pensioner between you no matter what he has to say. I'll be back here by seven at the latest if you come back in, or you can give me a call after you've seen him if you need to head off.'

He saw the relief on Styles's face. It wouldn't normally bother him to work evenings, but Porter had noticed they'd been fewer in number the further Emma went into her pregnancy.

Styles and Tessier disappeared, leaving Porter to shut down his PC and head out to the car park. Even though rush hour was a little way off, traffic was already starting to thicken as roads became clogged arteries. He trundled up Edgware Road, over Regent's Canal, part wishing he'd decided differently, part proud he'd picked family over work for once.

The Grantham connection had already been too interesting to ignore, and would have pinged an alarm even just with the lie about travel, but the date of that third trip took a coincidence and ramped it up to the next level. The possibility that the two cases were linked, previously based on nothing more than a gut feel to do with victim age, had just become very real.

Of course, there was always the possibility that it was nothing more than a lapse in memory, a blurring of time as Daniel Grantham got older. But the way Styles told it, he'd been very specific, saying that his son picked up any business trips into the city. That left option B, that he was indeed lying, but why?

Porter beat the amber light coming past Kilburn High Road station, looking guiltily around as if he expected blue lights to flash and pull him over. A quick involuntary glance in the rear-view made him feel slightly less guilty when he saw a white van, two back, floor it to get through. He shook his head, taking back the moral high ground. He didn't think much else of it for the next five minutes, noticing the van sitting three cars back now, chancing another set of lights that he'd made comfortably. Just a driver with a chip in their shoulder thinking they owned the roads, or something else entirely?

He put it to the test, indicating, pulling over, stopping outside a Tesco Extra on Cricklewood Broadway, watching to see if the van followed suit. It kept coming, no sign of indicating or slowing down. Past him in a flash, but Porter tensed. It couldn't have been level with him for more than a fraction of a second, but he was sure of one thing. The driver had been looking across at him.

He went to pull out, give chase, follow them until a chance presented itself to confront them. A horn blared, and he slammed on the brakes, narrowly missing a BMW. He watched the van continue up the road, trying to time a gap in the traffic, but when he finally managed to rejoin the road, the van was nowhere in sight.

CHAPTER FIFTY-TWO

Styles looked across at Tessier, hunched over the wheel, wondering if the car looked tilted to the right from behind. The initial rush following his discovery of Grantham's lie had receded on the forty-five-minute journey, and he was starting to think bringing Gus along might have been overkill. The guy could probably bench-press Styles and Grantham combined. Styles had a foot in height and forty years on Grantham and, despite the connections building up, Styles couldn't shake the notion that for a man like this to have been able to commit as well as cover up these acts, at his age, felt like a stretch. Nonetheless, all roads seemed to lead to Kiln Green at the moment.

They pulled up in the same spot Styles had previously. He checked his watch. A little after four. No guarantee Grantham would be here still, but better to take a chance than call ahead and warn him. Besides, there was always a chance they could talk their way in and get another look at those gloves even if he wasn't.

The main gates were still wide open, and as they approached, a mop-haired young man appeared from the left-hand spur that ran off the circular concrete area, pushing a barrow full of soil. He was headed straight across their path, lost in whatever tunes pumped through his headphones, noticing them late and almost steering into them.

'We're looking for Daniel Grantham,' Styles said, as the lad popped one headphone out.

'I think he's in the side garden,' he replied, looking Tessier warily up and down.

They followed his directions, coming out into a walled garden about the size of a five-a-side football pitch. Winding paths disappeared between bushes sporting an outrageous display of colourful blooms. Styles had never been the green-fingered sort. Mowing the lawn was his definition of gardening, but even he took a moment to appreciate the canvas Grantham had stamped his mark on. He told Tessier to stay put while he wandered around the path, unsure if this was the only exit. Didn't hurt to block it off, and also made for a less intimidating sight with only him doing the searching.

It didn't take long. He found Grantham sitting on a low plastic stool, secateurs snipping at a bush like a sculptor. Styles couldn't help but glance at the hands wielding them, wondering if they had the strength to overpower, to choke, to bury. He was wearing a pair of those long gauntlet-style gloves, different to the pair Styles had seen, though. Grantham glanced up as he approached, eyes squinting against the sun, and took a few seconds until Styles saw recognition dawn.

'Detective Styles, did you forget something?'

'Afternoon, Mr Grantham. No, I just have a few more questions I'd like to ask you if that's OK?'

Grantham took off a glove and dragged the back of his hand across a sweaty forehead, before standing up. Styles saw the secateurs dangling in the other, still gloved hand, choosing to ignore them and fix a friendly smile instead.

'Of course, ask away.'

'I thought we might use your office again,' Styles said, tilting his head up at the sky. 'Take a break from the heat.'

'Erm, yes, of course. Follow me.'

He set off deeper into the garden, away from where Tessier stood waiting. Clearly more than one way in and out of the walled garden.

Styles debated leaving Tessier where he was, but thought better of it.

'I've got a colleague along for the ride with me, just back by the entrance,' he said. 'Mind if he joins us?'

He didn't wait for an answer, and popped his head back around the corner, waving for Gus to follow.

'This is Detective Constable Gus Tessier,' he said, noting that unlike most people, Grantham showed no reaction to Tessier's size, instead offering a short hello and welcoming nod, before leading them out of a side gate, and around into his glass-walled office.

'Can I get you gentlemen a drink?' he asked once they were inside.

'We're good, thanks,' said Styles, answering for both. 'Sorry to trouble you again so soon, Mr Grantham, but there's a few things I needed to follow up on, to do with the case we spoke about.'

'Of course, please, ask away,' the older man said, bending slowly, reaching underneath the bench and opening a small fridge that Styles hadn't noticed on their first visit.

'When we spoke about Victoria Park earlier, you mentioned you used to take your grandchildren there.'

'Yes, that's right,' he said, twisting the cap off a bottle of water and taking a sip.

'And you also said you hadn't been into the city since the start of last year.'

'Mm-hmm,' said Grantham.

'When we have a case like this, we come into contact with a lot of

240

people,' Styles said, treading carefully, aiming for as soft a set-up as possible in case he was wildly off the mark with this. 'And where there's any kind of connection, we look to rule people out of our enquiries, even where there's no direct evidence of them doing anything wrong. With the flowers at the scene being from your collection, I'm sure you can understand why we'd be interested in talking to you.'

Grantham's eyes narrowed a touch. 'I can, Detective, but I'm not sure what more I can tell you?'

'Let's just say you're somebody we'd love to rule out,' Styles said bending the truth diplomatically. 'Here's the thing,' he said, watching closely for a reaction. 'Your car was picked up on three separate occasions heading into London over the last twelve months.'

'Must have been my son,' Grantham said. 'He uses it now and again.'

Styles shook his head. 'I'm wondering if you remember why you went into London on . . .' He took out a notebook, flicked to the right page, and read out the dates. '18th August, 10th November and 26th January?'

Grantham replaced the cap on his bottle, put it down and folded his arms. 'There must be some mistake, Detective. I'll ask Harry. I'm sure it'll have been him.'

'The images show you as the driver, Mr Grantham. There's no mistake. It's a while back, though, so I can understand you making a mistake with dates, but it'd really help us to know why you travelled in on those dates.'

'Wait a minute, didn't they say on the news that those bodies you found had all been there quite a while? Why would it matter to you even if it had been me driving?'

'The January date in particular would be really useful to us,' Styles continued as if Grantham hadn't even asked a question.

'What's so bloody important about January?' Grantham asked, trending more towards irate and impatient than kindly grandfather.

'A young girl went missing that day, Mr Grantham. She still is.'

Grantham's face was somewhere between disbelief and denial.

'And what? You think I had something to do with that?' he said, his voice rising now, shifting from one foot to the other, clearly agitated.

'As I said, Mr Grantham, with you previously saying you'd not been there in over a year, we'd just like to rule you out and move on.'

'And I'd like you to leave.'

'Excuse me?' It was more of a reflex response from Styles. He'd heard Grantham fine. Just hadn't expected him to put up the defences quite so vociferously.

'I was happy to speak when you were asking for help. I gave it, and now you've got the nerve to turn this back around and say, what? That I hurt these children? That I killed them?'

'I never said that, Mr Grantham, I just—'

'Oh no, you were far too polite to come out and say it. You just want to "rule me out",' he said, making air quotes for the last three words. 'Well, I'm not prepared to stand here in my own place of business and be accused like this, so if you want to continue to rule me out you can do it through my solicitor.'

Styles held Grantham's angry gaze for a second, gave a slow nod and looked across at Tessier, who returned the gesture.

'You're sure you'd rather not talk this through with us now, sir? It'd be much easier for everyone if we just kept this less formal, no need to come down to the station, that type of thing?'

'I'm happy to do whatever my solicitor advises. Stephen Holmes, of Holmes, Friedman and Warner,' he said, uncrossing his arms, burying hands deep in pockets. 'Now if you'll excuse me, I've still got a lot to do. You know your way out.'

He turned away, hauling a bag of compost from underneath one of the benches, dropping fistfuls into a row of small plastic pots. Styles looked at Tessier, who shrugged and headed for the door. Styles joined him, stopping level with Grantham.

'Give me a call, either with a time you and your solicitor can come in, or just to talk. Either way we'll speak soon. One child is missing. Nine are dead. This isn't going away, and the sooner you get out from under it, the sooner you can get on with doing what you do best.' He pointed through the glass at the bursts of colour, beautiful even through dirty panes. 'Enjoy the rest of your day, Mr Grantham.'

They walked back to the car in silence, and it wasn't until they'd pulled back out into the road that Tessier spoke.

'Went quite well, I thought.'

Styles turned to him, about to ask if he'd even been in the same room, when he saw the smile split Tessier's face, and the big man laughed. Styles shook his head, looked back at the road, but couldn't help bust out a smile of his own.

'Doesn't exactly make him look less suspicious, does it?'

'Definitely hiding something,' Tessier agreed.

'Oh shit,' Styles said, slapping a palm off the wheel. 'I forgot to ask him about the gloves. Probably wouldn't have let us near them anyway, the way that went.'

'Don't know about that. I got plenty close,' Tessier said, reaching into his pocket, pulling out a clear plastic bag and holding it out so Styles could see the brown leather glove inside.

'Gus, what the hell did you do?'

'He's hiding something. Either he's our guy, and we need to move fast to stop him hurting anyone else, or he's hiding something bad enough to lie to the police. Either way, we need to know.'

'And what? We just pop back tomorrow and say the glove we stole matches evidence at a mass grave? Come on, Gus, it won't stand up at the station with his solicitor, never mind in court.'

'You want us to go give him it back?'

'We do that now, he'll have us both up in front of the IOPC.'

'What then?' Tessier asked, slapping the bag against a palm.

Styles gripped the wheel, stared at the road ahead, thought of Libby Hallforth. Asked himself how far he was willing to go to get justice.

Damned if you do, damned if you don't.

CHAPTER FIFTY-THREE

Porter didn't see the van again. Twice he thought it had been lurking half a dozen cars back, but when he slowed down, pulling over a few times, it turned out to be a completely different vehicle. The feeling stayed with him all the way to the match, a slow-spreading itch across his shoulders and down the back of his neck. Eyes on him from somewhere, someone, but who?

He pulled up five minutes before kick-off, just in time for the twins to sprint across, ignoring the shouts from their coach.

'Uncle Jake, Uncle Jake, Uncle Jake.'

Two voices blurring into one, both bouncing like Tigger, balls of energy. He bent down, promised a pound per goal and saw their eyes widen, spending the money before it was earned.

One last glance over his shoulder, back at the car park and beyond onto the road, but no van in sight. He turned, seeing Kat waving at him from the touchline, and sent the boys scampering back to join their teammates.

'Thought you were a no-show,' she said when he reached her.

'Promised, didn't I?'

'Like that's stopped you before,' she said, immediately regretting it. 'Sorry, sorry.' She held up one hand, bending down and grabbing a thermos with the other. 'You're getting better, I'll give you that. More down to Evie if you ask me, though.'

'Hey, I've sacked off interviewing an important suspect for this match, I'll have you know.'

'Oh no,' she said, hand to her mouth. 'You mean a shoplifter might walk free all for the sake of the big game?'

'Yep, all your fault,' he said, making no attempt to dodge the half-hearted punch to the arm.

She poured a coffee for each of them, and they settled into the usual flow of pseudo-barbed banter that siblings excel at. Prodding, poking, but never causing any actual harm. The ref blew his whistle to start proceedings, and it felt good to switch off, even for a short while, lose himself in the flow of the game. Sixty minutes later, and three quid lighter thanks to two goals from Tom and a belter from James, he walked with them back to the changing rooms, digging in his pockets for change.

'Mine was better, though,' said James.

'I get more money,' Tom said, half-smirking.

'Not fair.' His brother pouted. 'I would have had two if that stupid idiot hadn't fouled me.'

'You set one of Tom's up, though, mate, so that gets you a bonus fifty pence,' Porter said, flipping him an extra coin. James's face lit up. Tom frowned, but only for a moment, then Jake saw him nod after a second, seeing it for the peacekeeping gesture that it was. Switched-on kids, these two.

'So you and Evie seem to be getting on famously still,' Kat said, not quite a question, not quite a statement, and looked over at him, clearly expecting a response of some sort.

'Yeah, she's nice, I like her.'

'*She's nice, I like her,*' Kat mocked in a bad impression of him. 'You need to rein in those feelings there. If you're not careful someone might think you actually care about the girl.'

'Yeah, well . . .' He started to respond but stopped mid-sentence, looking over Kat's shoulder, off beyond the car park. A white van, sitting parked up on the main road. No logos or markings, just the dark outline of a person in the driver's seat.

'Wait here,' he told her, and set off in a jog towards the van, a few hundred yards away. He hadn't even covered half of the distance when it started to move. No indicators, just whipping its front end around in a tight one-eighty and zipping off, out of sight before he could reach the spot it had occupied.

Porter was breathing heavily, part exertion, part adrenaline. Who the hell was following him, and why? He wasn't imagining this. He kicked himself for reacting in the first place. Why had he not just made a beeline for his own car, walking so as to not alarm them, then driven up and boxed them in?

Glancing back towards the changing rooms, he saw Kat watching him, too far away to see her expression, but if she thought for a second that he'd brought danger anywhere near her kids, she'd tear a strip off him. Was it danger? Impossible to say for sure, but surely nothing good could come from having your own personal stalker. His phone rang before he had time to catch his breath.

'You OK, boss?' Styles asked.

'Yeah, I'm fine. What's up?' said Porter.

Styles gave him a run-through of the trip to Kiln Green, and Porter used it as a chance to slow his breathing down, scanning the road. Kat had gone inside now. He'd smooth things with her in a minute.

'I want him in first thing tomorrow,' Porter said when Styles had finished. 'Who's his solicitor?'

'Already on it. Called them on the way back. He'll speak with Grantham and let us know.'

'What about the gloves?' Porter asked. 'You get another look at them?'

Was it his imagination, or did Styles hesitate a beat too long? 'Nothing on that front yet.'

'Alright, it'll have to be enough for now to just get him in, find out what he's hiding. So, he literally gave away nothing when you saw him?'

'Not when we saw him, no, but there's something else about those trips he made in.'

'Come on then, don't make me beg.'

'It's not just that he came into London. Gus has been looking back through the ANPR data on his phone. He didn't just come into the city. He tracked through the full journey, and Grantham's car was clocked on all three occasions passing within a few miles of the Hallforths' flat.'

CHAPTER FIFTY-FOUR

It was fair to say Styles had looked better. He had mentioned Emma's pregnancy-related insomnia a few times now, how he'd likened her constant shuffling in bed to sleeping next to a sack full of hyperactive hamsters. Porter clocked the dark circles under his eyes. He knew better than most how it felt. To not find any peace at night, bordering on light-headed from tiredness. Not so much now, but in the months that followed Holly's death, a crap night's sleep had become the norm.

'We still on for the interview with Grantham at two?' he asked.

'Hmm? Oh yeah, his solicitor called back to confirm the time.'

'OK, leaves us plenty of time to go over the approach, then.'

'Yeah, about that . . .' Styles began.

Porter recognised that tone in his sergeant's voice, knew he wasn't going to like whatever came next.

'I need to head off around half one. Emma's got an appointment.'

'Another one?'

Styles nodded. 'Yeah, sorry, boss. I should have mentioned it earlier, just with everything going on, it kinda got lost in the mix.'

'It's fine,' Porter said without missing a beat. 'Lemme see the map. You can still help me prep.'

Styles looked relieved, a naughty schoolkid told that he'd been spared detention, and slid a printout from Google Maps across the desk, red dots scattered across it.

'OK, so these are the cameras that picked him up. You can see he comes into London, along the A406, literally a couple of kilometres from where Libby lived. Epping has far fewer cameras. There's ways and means of driving as far as the visitors' centre without getting spotted if you know what you're doing.'

'What about links to any of the Victoria Park victims?'

'None that we've found so far, but I've been looking at his website. When it comes to roses, he's like royalty. He's had exhibitions at Kew, the Chelsea Flower Show. He even had some of his flowers used as part of the last royal wedding.'

Porter shook his head. The more connected Grantham was, the worse it'd be if Milburn got a whiff. Not that the super would stand in the way of a righteous arrest. Far from it. The positive press inches it would bring would be music to his ears. Anyone with a public profile made him massively overcautious, though, to the point of being obstructive in the name of thoroughness.

'Question is, if he's not our guy, then what the hell is he hiding that he'd risk being tarred as a suspect?'

'I've got a feeling it'll be like pulling teeth,' said Styles. 'Speaking of awkward folk, did Marcus Hallforth pick out any familiar faces last night?'

Porter had sat with Marcus the night before while he pored over faces, members of Nuhić's gang and known associates. He'd drawn a blank, and sent Porter home in a grumpy mood that he'd had to make a real effort not to take out on Simmons.

'Nothing,' he said to Styles, shaking his head. 'He's another one. All these people and their bloody secrets. Most of 'em come out eventually anyway. Bunch of bloody timewasters.'

'What about the son?' Styles asked. 'Runs most of the business now, apparently. Grantham said something about his family, how he used to do more with them but stopped, and went all cagey. If the two don't see eye to eye, might be worth speaking to him? Find out what he has to say about dear old dad?'

'Good shout,' said Porter. 'Will you have time to pick that up before you head off?'

'Yeah, course I can. You sure everything's OK, by the way? You really sounded weird on the phone yesterday.'

'It's nothing,' said Porter, then changed his mind. Sod being insular; if someone was following him, who better to have on his side than one of his most trusted friends? 'Just that yesterday, I could have sworn someone was following me around.'

He talked Styles through the sightings of the van, right up to the incident after football.

'Jesus! Who do you think it is?'

Porter shook his head. 'Honestly, I have no idea. Probably that bloody news anchor, sniffing round, trying to catch me out and make me look stupid again.'

'Yeah, maybe,' Styles said, but the looks they gave each other suggested neither was convinced. They bounced a few other ideas off each other around how to approach a man like Grantham. Someone clutching secrets to their chest like a kid hogging their favourite toy. It still felt like a long shot in many respects, but if this man knew where Libby was, alive or otherwise, Porter needed leverage, a way inside to make him crack.

Styles checked his watch, trying to look nonchalant, but by the third time, Porter sent him on his way. No point them both incurring Emma's wrath for him rocking up late.

Half past one. Porter killed time by reading through the notes of some of the interviews Tessier and Sucheka had done with Victoria Park staff. His phone buzzed at five to the hour. Grantham and his solicitor were here.

He was on his way downstairs to reception when Styles called.

'Managed to speak to Grantham's son on my way out, boss. Had a few interesting things to share.'

Porter paused mid-step, listening intently as Styles recounted the call, frowning as he tried to slot these new pieces into place.

'Good work, mate, now go find Emma before you blame me for running late,' he said, signing off.

He stood halfway down the last flight, letting what Styles had just shared soak in, mind racing as he decided how best to use it in the upcoming interview. Could go one of two ways, but Porter wasn't the sort to tiptoe, not when so many had already suffered. Time to apply a little pressure to see if his man would buckle.

CHAPTER FIFTY-FIVE

Stephen Holmes, of Holmes, Friedman and Warner, looked every inch the first name on the letterhead. Filling out his tailored suit, testing seams that were likely stitched at least ten pounds ago. He barely glanced up as Porter walked into the interview room, turning instead to whisper something to Daniel Grantham. His client looked just as Styles had described. Smartly dressed, countrified gent chic, tweed jacket and ticking all the right boxes for a harmless grandfather figure, but Porter fancied he caught a hard edge to the older man's look as their eyes met.

'Mr Grantham, I'm Detective Inspector Jake Porter. Thank you so much for coming in,' Porter said, and ran through the formalities before starting the recording.

'My client is here voluntarily as a courtesy, Detective,' Holmes jumped in. 'And doesn't take kindly to the way he was treated by your colleague yesterday.'

'I can only apologise if anything came over the wrong way, and

'I'm sure this is something we can clear up relatively quickly, but as you've no doubt seen on the news, this is a pretty serious matter we're looking into.'

'Which as far as I can see only links to my client insofar as whoever is responsible may possibly have been a customer. My client has provided a full customer list of anyone purchasing the varieties you specified, but your colleague,' he said, referring to lines of illegible scribble, 'Detective Sergeant Styles, went as far as to insinuate that my client might have been involved in the disappearance of a young girl.'

'That's not quite how I heard the conversation went,' Porter began, putting a hand up to ward off a comeback from Holmes, 'but be that as it may, if your client was caused any distress by my colleagues yesterday, I can assure you both it wasn't intentional. You understand, though, that we have to follow the evidence where it leads us, and in this case, it led us to you, Mr Grantham, or to your roses at least.'

'And I told your man yesterday, I have thousands of customers. All I do is grow and sell flowers. Other than tell you who I sell to, I really don't see what this has to do with me.'

'No one wants to agree with you more than I do, sir,' said Porter. 'And I'm sure you're as keen as we are that we rule people like yourself out, and find the person responsible. Makes it all the more puzzling why you wouldn't account for those trips to London. It'd help us tick you off and move on a lot faster.'

There was a brief pause as Holmes leant in, whispering to Grantham. 'Nothing to account for, really,' said Grantham finally. 'Just popped in to catch up with a few friends.'

'And which friends would they be?'

'Just a few former colleagues. A couple of them work in parks across London. I supply quite a few, so it pays to keep my hand in to make sure they keep buying from me.'

'Yet when you spoke to Detective Styles, you said your son does that part of the business, and that you hadn't been to London for over a year.'

'Memory isn't what it used to be at my age,' Grantham said, tapping a finger against his head. 'The days just seem to whizz past. Just got my dates wrong.'

'Which parks did you visit?'

'Not Victoria if that's where you're going with this.'

'Which ones, then?'

'Does it matter?'

'Indulge me,' Porter said with a friendly smile. 'Talk to me about the January one.'

Grantham looked at him like a schoolteacher humouring an inquisitive child. 'If you must know, I visited Marc Booth at Kew, then on to Valentines Park. Old friend of mine, Jim Oswald, runs the place. Had a coffee with him and stayed maybe an hour. He'll tell you the same if you call him.'

'Unless I'm mistaken, Detective,' Holmes cut in before Porter could ask another question, 'that's essentially the information your man asked for yesterday. My client has shared details of his trip, given you a corroborating witness, so unless there's anything else, I think we can call it a day and let you get on with keeping our streets safe.'

Holmes had a pomposity about him, the sort of person that Porter took great delight in cutting down to size, pulling the rug from under their feet. Now seemed as good a time as any to start.

'Tell me about your grandchildren, Mr Grantham,' he said, ignoring Holmes, watching Grantham instead for a reaction.

It was like watching a ripple spread in a pond. A host of twitches and tics, starting from the eyes, spreading outwards.

'What?' The question came out croaky, hoarse, caught off guard.

'We spoke with your son earlier, on the basis that he runs a lot of the business side now. You'd told my colleague that you'd been to Victoria Park before with your grandchildren, but not for a while.'

'Detective—' Holmes began, but Porter spoke over the top of him, still fixed on Grantham.

'I know the memory isn't what it used to be,' he said, mimicking the tap against the side of his head from earlier, 'but your son told us what happened to them, how they died. Boy and a girl, I believe, and how they were the same ages as the bodies we found in Victoria Park.'

CHAPTER FIFTY-SIX

Stephen Holmes clamped a beefy hand on Daniel Grantham's forearm.

'I don't know what exactly you think you're doing, Detective, but I think we've reached the limits of my client's patience and cooperation.'

He started gathering his things: notepad, pen. Grantham still looked a little dazed, and Porter pressed a little harder.

'I know what happened to them, Mr Grantham. To your grandchildren and your daughter. I know about the car crash.'

Miles Grantham had shared the sad tale with Styles. How his sister, Samantha, and her two children, Marie and Ben, had died in a car crash. Their father had been driving, three times over the limit. As happens all too often, fate was overly cruel, killing Samantha and her kids, sparing her husband, or at least his life anyway. He stood trial for death by dangerous driving once he had recovered from his injuries. No surprises when he was convicted.

The flowers. The leather rose gauntlets. The concealed trip on the day Libby disappeared. Porter knew coincidences existed, but when a host of circumstantial pieces started to float into view, you ignored their collective weight at your peril.

'That must have left such a hole in your world,' Porter said, feeling the echo from his own, still there regardless of his own life partially rebuilding. 'Can't even imagine what that would do to a person. Losing them like that, to have them ripped away. Could quite literally break someone, make them see things through a broken lens. Do things to get back to that perfect family life. Things that might be so wrong but they just can't see it for grief.'

The only sign Grantham had heard him was a slow shake of the head, lips pressed together in a thin line.

'The parents of those nine children are grieving just as much. Libby Hallforth's parents, too. All I want to do is help them with that. To stop any more parents from having to go through the same. I'd hope someone who's experienced that first-hand would want the same.'

'We're done here,' said Holmes, pushing up from the table. 'If anyone speaks to my client again without coming through me first, we'll be looking at a harassment case. This is nothing more than a fishing expedition, and now you're looking to question a man's grief for his grandchildren. I've half a mind to speak to—'

'Sit down, Stephen.'

Grantham's voice was weary, as if he'd not slept in days. Anticipation fizzed through Porter. The old man's posture softened, the precursor to something, but Porter didn't want to jump the gun and hope for too much.

'Daniel, I'm not going to sit here and let them accuse you of—'

'Please' he said, sounding hoarse, but with the strength creeping back in. 'It's alright. Sit back down.'

Holmes looked from Grantham to Porter and back again, wearing a *can you believe this guy* expression, but did as his client instructed.

'I'd strongly advise you and I have a conversation before you answer any more questions, Daniel.'

'Understood, but really, it's alright.' He leant back, taking slow measured breaths, building up to something. Porter wanted to jump in, press home the advantage, unpick whatever thoughts were tangled around Grantham's tongue. It took a long few seconds, but when the old man finally spoke, he was calm and measured.

'Have you lost someone close, Detective?'

'My wife,' Porter said, nodding. No benefit from keeping it to himself. Might help establish a connection. 'Died in a hit and run.'

Grantham looked him straight in the eye, held his gaze. 'I'm so sorry for your loss. Did they catch them?'

Porter just shook his head in response.

'That's what people don't get. Those who haven't been through what we have. They don't get the sense of injustice. Your wife's killer is walking around out there, no need to answer for what they did. My son-in-law nearly died from his injuries, but in the end, he pulled through. He was spared and they weren't. He went to prison, but is that really a good enough punishment for what he did? A few years in exchange for a life? People like him, they get to walk around, breathing the air that my grandchildren should be breathing.'

His eyes glistened, not quite full, but damp with emotion.

'You're right,' Porter said. 'It's not fair, but we can't make up our own rules and punishments.'

'Can't we?' Definite steel in Grantham's words now.

Porter shook his head. 'That makes us as bad as they are. The kids on the island in Victoria Park, they're the real victims here. The way they were buried, it meant something to whoever put them there. Dressed up cosy in their pyjamas, laid out in pairs. You can't bring Ben and Marie back, Daniel, but you can help give the parents of those kids some peace. Help me to help them. We still need names for half of them. What were their names, Daniel?'

Grantham had been staring at the wall, but his eyes snapped

back to Porter now. 'You still think this was me? Have you not been listening to a word I'm saying? I have no idea who put them there. This is about my trips to London. To Valentines Park.'

Porter frowned. 'What does Valentines Park have to do with Victoria Park?'

'Nothing. It has to do with my son-in-law, Graeme.'

'You've lost me. What's somebody who's locked up got to do with any of this?'

'He's not a prisoner any more.'

Porter did a double take. 'He's been released? Since when?'

Grantham leant forwards, moving fast for his age, shaking his head. 'He's been out five years now. Twelve months is all he served. Appealed based on some sort of cock-up regarding the tests on his blood alcohol level.'

Porter hated being blindsided like that, but shook it off and continued, committed to the line of questioning now.

'All the same, Mr Grantham, whether he's in or out, it's you I'm interested in right now.'

'Don't you see?' Grantham said, half-shouting now. 'I didn't hurt anyone. I could never hurt a *child*.'

There was something about the way the emphasis kicked in at the end of the sentence.

'But . . .' Porter prompted.

'But I could damn well hurt someone who would.'

'What are you saying, Mr Grantham?'

'I'm saying that my son-in-law deserves to die for what he did to Ben and Marie, and Samantha.' He added his daughter almost as an afterthought. 'I went to Valentines Park to find him, and make him pay. I went there to kill him.'

Two trains of thought raced neck and neck through Porter's mind. First, and most obvious, was that Daniel Grantham had just admitted to plotting his son-in-law's murder. Out of the blue, and not where Porter had thought this was heading at all, but something that couldn't be ignored.

On top of that, however, his theory about Daniel Grantham being on some kind of grief-triggered spree, blinded to his own actions, had taken a sideways shunt onto another track entirely. Graeme Gibson had suffered loss too, maybe even more traumatic, with him being the cause. Could he be the man they were looking for, or was this a clever play from Grantham? A misdirection. Porter's pulse quickened. Either way, it felt like things had crested, about to pick up pace on the way down to the finish.

'Where is he now? Your son-in-law?'

'Last I heard he was working in Valentines Park.'

'And you went there to confront him on 26th January.'

Grantham nodded. 'I did. A friend of mine told me he'd been doing some short-term contract landscaping work there. Those first two trips,' he said, looking down at his hands, thumb absentmindedly stroking the knuckles on his other hand, 'I saw him, both times, but it was like I was paralysed, you know. There was this man who'd killed my daughter, my grandkids, and I wanted to hurt him. Make him suffer, and I just . . . I couldn't do it. I couldn't even bring myself to confront him. Then that last time, that was the anniversary. I'm never in a good place around then, and I came in for a third trip. Went for a quick drink to find the courage to go and confront him, at least. One led to far too many, and it was like a dam had burst, all that hate and anger pouring out, fuelled by the whisky. This time, I thought, this time I can do it. Make him pay.'

His voice tailed off, and Porter noticed a tremor in his hands.

'Daniel, why don't we take a break?' asked Holmes, one last attempt to counsel restraint.

'What's the point, Stephen? Hmm? They know now, about him, about Samantha. And it's not as if I've actually done anything.'

'Why now?' Porter asked. 'If this happened six years ago, why go after him now?'

'Couldn't find him,' Grantham said simply. 'He worked alongside me for years. He was almost as good as me when it comes to roses. Almost. There was no way he wouldn't drift back to it in some way, so I put out a few feelers, and just waited.'

Watching him unload was a peculiar experience. Shrugging this weight off didn't make him lighter. On the contrary, it was as if talking about it doubled the load, pulling him downwards, shoulders slumping, folding in upon himself. Something Grantham had said floated back to the front of Porter's mind. He fired off a quick text to Dee Williams – one question – then turned his attention back to the two men opposite.

'The crash, can you tell me what happened?'

'Samantha was a fighter,' he said, sounding every inch the proud father. 'He was a troubled man. Liked the drink too much, but she stuck by him. Even when he accused her of cheating on him, raised his hand to her, she stuck by him. I begged her to leave him. Even squared up to him one time. Told him to leave my girl be. They'd had an argument the day she died, a big one.'

'How do you know that?'

'She texted me. Asked if the children could come and stay the night. Said that she and Graeme had some things to work out. That was how she put it. Couldn't even bring herself to slag the man off to me, not properly. I didn't see the text till it was too late. I tried calling her, but by then . . . If I'd seen the message earlier, the children would have been with me. They'd be alive.'

His words came laced with emotion now, voice thick around the edges, and Porter wondered if he'd opened up to anyone about this. Possibly not. Maybe not even to his own son, out of some misguided guilt.

'Your son-in-law, is he a violent man?'

'You want to know if I think he could be the one who buried those children in the park?'

'Do you?'

Grantham didn't hesitate. 'I want to say no, but I just don't know.'

Porter felt his phone buzz, glanced down and saw a reply from Dee Williams that stopped him in his tracks. A list of names, contractors from Nexon who had worked at Victoria Park. Nestled halfway down, there he was. Graeme Gibson.

CHAPTER FIFTY-SEVEN

He listens to the newsreader's voice drifting through the car speakers, regurgitating the same lies, carbon copies of previous hourly headlines.

Police would like to speak to a man in connection with the investigation into the bodies found at Victoria Park. Graeme Gibson was found guilty of death by dangerous driving, in a crash that killed his wife and two children six years ago. Police have asked members of the public to contact them if they see Mr Gibson, but not to approach him themselves.

He squeezes his eyes shut, so tight that when he opens them, pinpricks of light cartwheel across his vision. Why are they lying about his family? He would never hurt Ben and Marie. He has raised a hand to Samantha in a fit of temper, but he was another man back then. It must be the police, he decides. That detective. They don't understand about his other children, the ones in the park. How he has cared for them better than their own parents ever did.

Each time has brought conflicting tides of elation and hope, but ultimately regret. Their resemblance to Ben or Marie has been without question at the time. Spotted alone in shopping centres, out on streets, loitering in fairgrounds. Sometimes they come with him willingly, others need to be told, forcibly brought with him in some cases. Only later, in the quiet of his allotment, no longer caught up in the moment, do the masks slip away, replaced by frightened unfamiliar faces. Similar age, build, hair, but not them. Not his children. He tries to reassure them, comfort them. That's when the edges blur, slipping into soft focus. When things snap back . . . well, he doesn't like to dwell too much. All he can do then is look after them. Dress them up warm, like he used to his own children. Take them to the park, looking out over the lake that Ben and Marie love so much.

Love, or loved? If the headlines are to be believed, everything about them is past tense now. It's lies. Has to be. The detective, the one he has followed, is trying to lure him out. They don't understand. The children in the park, they are better off with him than they ever were with their parents. People who left them to wander unchecked, unsupervised, unloved. He'll never do that with Marie and Ben when he finds them again. Never let them out of his sight.

He presses the heels of both palms into his temples. Tries in vain, as he has so many times before, to dredge up more recent memories than the home movies. Nothing. It's as if he's flicking through a book, but someone has torn out the last fifty pages.

His children in the park have consoled him, been a comfort in his darker moods as he searches for his son and daughter. Listened to him ramble on, reliving moments spent with Ben and Marie. They're as much family to him now as his own flesh and blood. He needs them every bit as much. They should be with him, in his garden, not hidden away in a dark room somewhere.

The policeman, Porter. That's the route to take. Everyone has something they hold precious, that they'd do anything for. For him it's his children. He doesn't know Porter as such, but he can hazard a guess as to what would compel the policeman to give his children back to him.

Across the road, and a half-dozen doors down, two boys hustle down a short driveway, jostling for position. Even from here the similarities are unmistakable, each a clone of the other. A woman joins them, one hand jangling keys, the other elbow deep in a handbag. Doors open, slam and the engine purrs to life. Seconds later, the woman jumps out again, striding back to her front door, disappearing inside.

He doesn't hesitate, no pause for thought. He's out of his own car and walking towards theirs a matter of seconds after she goes inside. 'Whatever it takes,' he mutters.

An eye for an eye.

CHAPTER FIFTY-EIGHT

Styles clicked the icon showing a boxy camera, seeing a miniature of his own face in the bottom corner as he waited for Skype to connect. The melodic chimes seemed to tinkle for ever. Was that something on the corner of his mouth in his video feed? Remnants of breakfast? The call connected as he started to lean forward for a closer look, and he jumped back, shoulders squared, one hand brushing against the corner of his mouth, hoping he'd send whatever it was flying.

A voice drifted through his laptop speakers as he waited for the video feed to kick in.

'Hi . . . Hello . . . Can you hear me?'

'Hi there, yep, I can hear you. This is Detective Sergeant Nick Styles. Thanks for—'

'I can't see you yet,' the voice interrupted.

'That makes two of us,' Styles said, and they both waited out the next few awkward seconds, like an uncomfortable silence on a first date.

The face that popped on screen, looking a mixture of surprised and flustered, reminded Styles of Richard Branson. Well, maybe Branson if he'd let himself go a little. Thicker around the cheeks and neck, beard an inch longer, and wearing glasses with lenses thick enough to be spares for the Hubble Space Telescope.

'Ah, much better. Hello, Detective.'

'Hi, Doctor Larsson. Really appreciate you taking the time to speak to me.'

'Not at all,' Larsson said, a hint of an accent around the edges that Styles couldn't place. On the dove-grey wall behind him, one either side, were what looked like framed diplomas, like twin epaulettes on Larsson's shoulders, although Styles couldn't make out the writing.

'The warden said you needed to speak to me about Graeme Gibson. He said it was urgent. Is he alright?'

'What can you tell me about him, Doctor?'

'That depends on why you need to know.'

Styles paused a beat, deciding how much to share with Larsson.

'We need to speak to him about a sensitive case we're investigating. His father-in-law believes Graeme might still be . . .' He paused, searching for the right words. 'Suffering from his accident, from losing his family.'

Larsson nodded slowly, leaning forward, elbows on the table, resting his chin on clasped hands.

'Tragic, tragic thing. To lose your family like that . . .'

'Mmm,' Styles murmured in agreement, waiting for the doctor to speak again, but Larsson just stared back at him.

'How long did you treat him for?' Styles prompted.

'All in all, around nine months,' said Larsson. 'His physical injuries had healed by the time he was sentenced – well, those on the outside at least – but his problems ran a lot deeper than that.'

'How so?'

Larsson gave a wry smile. 'Come now, Detective, you know there are limits to what I can discuss about a patient.'

'I'm aware of that, Doctor Larsson, but there's more at stake here than you realise.'

'Has Graeme been arrested? Charged with a crime?'

'No, but—'

'There were many things discussed at his trial,' Larsson interrupted. 'That's all public record. How his defence tried to argue diminished responsibility, using his bipolar as a mitigating factor. That I can talk about. What we spoke about in the sessions we had, I'm afraid that falls under doctor–patient confidentiality.'

'In most cases that'd be true, sir, but I don't believe it is here.'

'And why would that be?' Larsson leant back in his chair. Styles could practically see the condescension coming of him in waves, so sure of himself.

'General Medical Council disclosure guidance, paragraphs sixty-three through to seventy. Disclosure is allowed in the public interest if it's likely to prevent death or serious harm.'

Styles kept glancing down at the notes in front of him, thankful this wasn't a face-to-face so he could peek at his messy scrawl. He made a mental note to buy Dee Williams a coffee for raising the disclosure point before he made the call, giving him a chance to check and prepare.

'Death or injury?' Larsson huffed. 'I must have done over fifty sessions with Graeme while he was here, and don't get me wrong, he had his demons to battle with, but what happened to his family was an accident. He isn't capable of actively choosing to hurt someone, let alone kill them.'

'We have information that suggests otherwise, Doctor,' said Styles.

'Well, I'm afraid if you expect me to share my information without knowing yours, that's just not how this works,' he said with a shrug.

Enough of the tiptoeing around. Who knew where Gibson was now, what the consequences might be of him being out there an extra day, maybe more.

'Have you seen anything in the news about Victoria Park recently, Doctor?'

Larsson's eyes darted side to side for a second, widening as it hit home.

'You don't mean . . . not those bodies they found?'

Styles said nothing, letting it sink in.

'Surely you don't think that Graeme could have anything to do with that? Losing his own kids almost broke him. I honestly don't think . . .'

'We've already released his name to the press as a person of interest, and yes, there's enough linking him to the case to make us worried about what he might be capable of, so anything you can share that helps us understand him, maybe even find him, would be a big help.'

Larsson looked off balance for the first time. 'But by the time he was released, we'd made such progress.'

'People have already died, Doctor. Children. I'd hate for any refusal to help us to come back and bite you, especially when, as you say, you'd done good work with him,' Styles said, playing to the ego.

'I . . . uhm . . . well, hmm.' Larsson looked flushed now, leaning forwards, steepling his fingers, blinking furiously. Styles waited him out. Only took another few seconds.

'If I share my thoughts with you,' Larsson began, 'I'm assuming my name could be kept out of any press releases.'

Styles nodded. 'You have my word.' Chances were if Gibson was their man, Larsson would change his mind and look for a pat on the back for playing ball.

'OK, well, let me see then . . .' Larsson seemed to relax a little at the prospect of anonymity. 'Graeme is a complex character. On one hand, he was all about his family. To hear him, they were his world, the kids especially.'

Styles sensed a 'but' coming.

'Things are rarely straightforward for people by the time they become a patient, though. With Graeme, he didn't have the best childhood. Mother who left when he was eight. His father was an alcoholic, no other real family support network to speak of. That fractured family feeling echoed into his own marriage.'

'How do you mean?'

'It's unusual for a mother to leave her family. Far more likely to be the father. It was as if her leaving him behind with a father that spent as much time in the pub as with his own son, probably more, left him with a sense of fragility. That if she could leave him, anyone could. Sadly for him, and his family, it meant that he was looking for it around every corner.'

'He thought his wife wanted to leave him?'

Larsson nodded. 'It was a vicious circle of the worst kind. He'd read into something and accuse her. She'd changed her make-up, bought a new dress, didn't return his calls fast enough. Sent him into a spiral, accusing her, drinking more, even becoming physical on occasion. All things more likely to make her want to leave.'

'And what can you tell me about the accident itself? What did he say about that?'

Larsson shrugged. 'Exactly what he said in court. That he didn't remember getting in the car, let alone crashing it. He'd been drinking for hours before that at a local pub. She was late picking him up. One of the regulars was outside smoking when he came out, and saw him climb in the driver's seat, kids in the back, threatening to drive off without her if she didn't get in. The crash was a few miles from there. There was some footage from a dashcam coming the other way. Only a brief glimpse, but they managed to enhance the image. It showed his arm reaching over, looked like he had a handful of her hair. Arguing about something.'

'So how do you treat someone who doesn't even remember their crime?'

'By looking at the root cause of his unhappiness. What caused him to behave like that. He might not have remembered the event itself, but he remembers his behaviour leading up to it.'

'And from what you said earlier, you don't think he poses a danger. Is that because the only trigger was his wife?'

Larsson nodded. 'Exactly right.'

'So if he can't remember the accident, did he at least show any remorse that his family were dead?'

'That's the thing, you see, Detective,' said Larsson, shaking his head ever so slightly. 'He wouldn't accept that they were dead. Denied it right up to the day he walked out. He said it was all a cover-up, some sort of plot to help her leave him, that he'd been set up somehow.'

'Set up?' Styles said incredulously. 'There would have been photos of the scene at the trial. How did he explain those?'

'Said it was all manufactured. What I suppose you'd call fake news these days.'

'So, he thinks what, that his wife and kids are in hiding somewhere?'

Larsson leant back again, spreading his hands wide. 'Nonsense, I know, but the accident caused severe swelling to his brain, bleeding as well. The brain, memories we have stored, it really doesn't take much to shake something loose when it comes to car crashes. It might have come back to him by now, who knows?'

'When he left your care, would it be a leap to say he might go looking for his family?'

'I'd say that's exactly what he'd do. In fact, he talked about it frequently. I think it's more of a leap to say that he might start hurting people, children.'

'All the kids match the ages of his children, and he had access to the park after hours. Let's just say we'd love to rule him out, but we need to find him first. Did he say anything about what he planned to do after he was released? Where he might go?'

'Nothing specific, no.' There was little of the confidence left in Larsson's voice, as if mention of the children had brought home how serious this was. 'But he was adamant that he'd find a way to make things right. To get his family back together, no matter what it took.'

The silence that followed those final five words hung heavy. Styles focused on them, and the man who had first said them. Reunite a family at all costs. One that didn't exist any more except in Graeme Gibson's mind. A man who had done terrible things, suffered unimaginable loss. Styles's thoughts flicked to the island garden. Its inhabitants buried close, each one touching distance from their neighbour. A family plot.

'Not my preference to have shared Gibson's name with the press,' Porter said to the room. 'But who am I to question our illustrious superintendent?'

'Do we drop Grantham now?' Sucheka asked.

'Not drop, but shelve for now. It's still all circumstantial with him, but we can put Gibson in the park. He will have had access to the place after hours as well, easier to move bodies around.'

'What about motive?' asked Tessier.

'Nick's had some interesting calls today,' Porter said, indicating for Styles to share. His phone rang as Styles started to speak, Kat's name and picture lighting up his screen. He hit reject, knocked it onto silent, and carried on.

'Spoke with his probation officer, and a psychiatrist based at the prison he did his time in. Seems that the car accident that killed his family left him with selective amnesia. When he came round after the accident, he refused to accept his family were dead. Said it was all lies to keep his kids away from him.'

'So, he has no memory of the accident at all?'

'Nope. Last things he remembered with any clarity were a few days before it happened. He's done contract work for Nexon for the last five years. Had jobs all over the country. The ages of his kids match the ages of those we found at the park, so the working theory at the moment is that it's some kind of attempt to replace the family he lost, although why he kills them instead of just keeping them alive, we don't know.'

'Any luck on his whereabouts?' Dee Williams asked.

Styles shook his head. 'He's got a one bed flat in Forest Gate. We sent a car round an hour ago, but no answer. Neighbours haven't seen him in a few days either.'

'That's just down from Wanstead Flats, isn't it?' asked Glenn Waters.

'Gold star for Glenn,' said Porter. 'When we find him, and we will find him, we'll be speaking to him about Libby Hallforth as well.'

Porter glanced at the picture they had stuck on the whiteboard, committing it to memory. A shot of Gibson taken pre-trial, but after his release from hospital. Bruises spreading under his eyes like stage make-up, stubble roughing up his jawline, eyes looking through the camera and beyond.

'We've got eyes on his place if he turns up back there,' Styles said. 'Also, I spoke to someone at Nexon earlier. They told me Gibson is still down against the Valentines Park contract, but he hasn't showed for work these last few days.'

'What do you need then, boss?' Sucheka asked.

'We've got a list of his previous jobs from Nexon. Dee and Glenn, you two pair up, and Kaja and Gus, if you can work together. Between you, I want each place checked out, park managers spoken to, and get around as many as you can in person. If we're lucky, someone he worked with might remember something to point us in the right direction. Any mention of a girlfriend, friends from work, that kind of thing. I want to know which parts of the parks he worked in. Have a word with Kam, tell him we need some of his people sent out with you.'

The unspoken part of that, what every one of them in the room was thinking right now, fearing, was that Victoria Park might not be the only secret rose garden in London.

'Only other thing registered in his name at the moment is a plot at Leyes Road allotments, down near the ExCeL. Nick and I are going to head down there now and take a look.'

He saw Styles reach into his pocket, checking his own phone, frowning.

'She's not gone into labour already, Sarge, has she?' Waters said, laughing louder at his own joke than anyone else.

'Don't recognise the number,' he said, holding the screen to Porter. 'Am I OK to take it just in case?'

'Course you are.'

Styles answered, turning away and wandering over to the window. Porter opened his mouth to continue the briefing, but whipped his head to look at Styles, wondering why his partner was saying his sister's name.

'Kat, Kat, it's OK. Calm down. He's here. Let me put him on.'

Porter took the phone, looking to Styles for an explanation, finding none.

'Kat? What's the matter?'

'It's the boys, Jake, they're gone. Someone took them.'

CHAPTER FIFTY-NINE

Two faces stare back at him in the rear-view mirror, features rigid, frozen in place, too scared to move a muscle. There were shouts at first, as he backed out of the driveway. Fingers tugging at door handles that had already locked. Palms slapped against the headrest, grasping at his shoulders. That has since migrated into tense silence after he braked hard, twisting around and snatching mobile phones from their hands, throwing them out of the window to shatter on tarmac.

He doesn't want to hurt them. Tells them this and genuinely means it. They're a means to an end, but he knows that if it comes down to it, he'll do whatever he has to. This isn't like the other times. There's no mistaking either of these boys for Ben. They mean nothing to him, but they mean something to Detective Porter. To the woman he saw last night. His wife, girlfriend maybe? No, when he followed them home from the football game, Porter hadn't stayed long. He had come back out after an hour, heading back to a house near Pinner. Family, then; sister, maybe?

A pen rolls back and forward on the passenger seat, next to a white napkin, as he takes a corner, waiting for the next round of headlines and the confidential police hotline number. This happens on his terms or not at all. The fate of the two boys will rest with the detective. He isn't asking for anything that isn't already his. He saved them, all those children. Saved them from a life where no one cared enough about them to keep them safe. But they saved him in return, in those darker moments, when he felt at the bottom of the well, looking up at a pinprick of light. Caring for them. Tending to them. Giving him a reason to keep going, even when at times the search for his own children seemed an impossible task.

He glances in the rear-view every thirty seconds or so, watching the boys, checking the traffic behind them. Until he makes contact, they have no way of knowing who he is, how to find him. This is about more than just getting the children back now, though. Once he does, he can't stay here. Can't return them to the park. The search for Ben and Marie will be harder now.

The landscape changes as he drives. Less residential, more industrial, fewer prying eyes. Another glance in the mirror. The stares looking back at him are somewhat glassier now, the shock of the situation well and truly set in. What will Ben and Marie think of him when they're finally reunited? Of the lengths he's gone to in order to make that happen? He hopes they'll understand, that he never gave up trying. That's what a parent does: they go the extra mile for their kids. Make the hard choices. Even do the wrong thing for the right reasons.

He offers up a silent prayer. Hopes that the detective loves these boys as much as he loves Ben and Marie. That he'll make the right choice for them. The alternative doesn't bear thinking about.

CHAPTER SIXTY

'Two minutes.' Kat sniffed. 'Wasn't even that long. I came out and they were gone.'

'Did you notice anyone hanging around the street?' Porter asked. 'Anyone acting suspiciously?'

She shook her head, fresh tears flowing freely down her face. 'Who would want to hurt my boys, Jake? You have to get them back. Promise me you'll get them back.'

'I promise,' he said, breaking one of his own rules. Never make a promise on the job that you can't guarantee. 'We've got half the force looking for your car. We'll find them, Kat.'

'Who would do this, Jake?'

He wanted to tell her he had no idea, but an image of the van from yesterday swam to mind. A coincidence? His own paranoia? Either way, he couldn't bring himself to lie, not even a little white one, so instead he just reached out, pulling her in close. She didn't resist, and it was as if the action scraped away the last ounce of control she had. His hard-faced, tough-as-nails, handle-anything-life-can-throw-at-me sister melted into him, and stayed there.

Whoever it was, he'd make damn sure not only were they found, but that everything was done to the letter of the law. Overriding his anger that someone had messed with his family was an overwhelming urge to make sure they couldn't wriggle out of what they had coming to them.

'I've spoken to Dad. He and Mum are on their way over to sit with you. Will you be OK until then?'

She lifted her head away from his chest, wiping tear-trails from her cheeks and sniffing.

'I'll be fine. Go, please, find my boys.'

He kissed her forehead and headed out, leaving a uniformed constable parked outside the door. He jumped into his car, connected to Bluetooth and scrolled to find Styles in his contacts.

'You at the allotment yet?' he asked, when Styles picked up.

'Ten minutes out. Anything?'

'Not yet. Should have ANPR any minute, but there's no guarantee whoever took them actually triggered any cameras, and that's if they even stay in their own car.'

Could be that this was a simple crime of opportunity. Someone passing by, hearing the idling engine, seeing the empty driver's seat and taking a chance to make an easy buck. There'd been similar cases before, and kids had been left on street corners once the thief realised the empty car they'd nicked had passengers. This felt different, though. Kat didn't live in that kind of neighbourhood, and the inescapable feeling that he'd been followed not once, but twice, just felt like too much of a coincidence. What if whoever drove the white van had seen him with the boys? Maybe targeted them because of him? The thought that they might come to any harm because of their connection with him made his stomach swoop.

'Call me as soon as you get there.' A double beep on the line.

Another call coming in, this one from the station. 'Got to go.' He toggled to the second call.

'DI Porter.' A snap to his voice, no time for pleasantries.

'Boss, it's Dee. We've had a call come in, someone looking for you.'

'I'm a little busy at the minute, Dee,' he said, pulling away from the kerb.

'You're going to want to take this one,' she said. 'This guy, says he has the boys in the back of a car.'

CHAPTER SIXTY-ONE

The seconds of silence as he waited for the call to connect stretched to the point where Porter thumbed the button on the wheel to up the volume, wondering if he'd lost connection. There was a brief series of sounds, like someone fumbling for the handset, and Dee Williams came back in the line.

'Connecting you now, boss.'

'You better be recording this, Dee,' he said, but she'd already gone, replaced by static and soft breathing.

'This is DI Porter,' he said. 'Who am I speaking to?'

Something between a grumble and a cough, someone clearing their throat. No background noise that he could make out. Nothing to give away a location. He hoped to God that Dee and the others were tracing it if the call was genuine.

'My name doesn't matter. All that matters is that you do what I ask.'

The voice was soft, giving nothing away, no anger, no fear, nothing.

'And what is it you want?'

'You have something of mine, now I have something of yours.'

'Let me speak to Tom and James,' Porter said.

'Not how this works. You get them back when I get my children back.'

'Your children?'

'From the park.'

'Graeme? Is that you?'

A pause before the man responded. 'I get my children back, you get yours back.'

'Your children? Do you mean Ben and Marie?'

Another pause. 'I heard those lies about them on the radio. Saying they're dead. That I killed them.' Porter caught a hint of something now, anger. Milburn's press release had gotten under his skin. Sounded like the prison psychiatrist had been spot on. Gibson believed they were alive, out there waiting to be found.

'We don't have Ben or Marie, Graeme,' he said, 'but I'm happy to help you look for them. How about you drop Tom and James off somewhere? Tell me where to pick them up, and then you and I can talk.'

'So, they're not dead, then?' he shot back. 'I knew it. I knew that was just . . . how could you think I'd believe that?'

'You're right,' Porter said, thinking on the fly, how to play this with a man not entirely rooted in reality. 'You sussed us, Graeme. It won't happen again. You just tell me where and when, and we'll meet up and talk this through.'

'You're not bloody listening.' Gibson came back louder this time, tense and snappy. 'There's no talking to do. You took them from me. The others. I need them back. They need . . .' He trailed off, and Porter could hear the breathing on the other end a little more ragged.

'Graeme, whatever happens, I'm going to need proof that Tom and James are alright before we do anything.'

Silence apart from breathing, becoming slower, more measured, back under control. Porter slowed at a set of lights, watching pedestrians amble past him, oblivious to what was playing out right in front of them.

'Tomorrow,' he said finally. 'I'll call you tomorrow and tell you where to come. Only you. Bring my children to me, alone, and nothing happens to your boys. You want them back, do what I say and it'll all be fine.'

Click. The line went dead. Porter stared at the console for a beat, then hammered his palm against the wheel. Once, twice, a third time.

'Aggghhhhhh.'

His frustrated groan filled the silence, loud enough for the last of the pedestrians to hear, frowning as they squinted to see through his windscreen. Not the time to let his anger get the better of him. *Stay cool*, he told himself. Had to do this as a copper, not their uncle. He called Dee as he started up again, crossing the junction.

'Please tell me you got something from that?'

'Too short to trace, boss,' she said, sounding like she'd let him down personally.

'ANPR?'

'We got a hit a couple of miles from your sister's house, heading east towards Edgware, but nothing since then.'

'I had a white van following me yesterday. Get hold of someone from Nexon. I want to know what he drives for work, whether he has access to any of their vehicles. Get those checked out too.'

'Will do, boss.'

Porter ended the call, gripping the wheel tight, wondering where the hell the boys were, how scared they'd be. If anything happened to them, he'd never forgive himself. How would he face Kat? His parents? Knowing that they were taken because of his job, because of him. He could have stopped this in its tracks. Twice yesterday he'd seen the van. Known something was wrong. Gibson must have trailed around after him, watching him. Watching the boys. Jesus, he must have literally followed Porter back to Kat's house. How had he not seen that?

Kat's words echoing in his head.

Find my boys.

He'd promised her he would. Gibson hadn't given him any proof of life, though. No chance to speak to the boys. What if it was too late, if that promise was already broken?

CHAPTER SIXTY-TWO

Styles crawled his way through a bottleneck of traffic courtesy of whatever convention the ExCeL was holding this week. Leyes Road allotments were set back from the main road, just past the ExCeL and penned in behind six-foot-high gunmetal grey fencing. No houses overlooking them, backing onto the Royal Docks Academy playing fields. Isolated enough to guarantee privacy, but close enough by to be accessible. A short drive from Libby's home at Wanstead Flats. Another short hop to the west took you to Victoria Park. Three points on a triangle.

He climbed out of the car and looked around. The gates stood open, two cars parked on a tight rectangular area that might fit half a dozen at a push. Neither of them was Kat's, but that didn't mean that Gibson and the boys weren't here. He could have switched vehicles by now. If he was, it wouldn't hurt to make things a little more difficult for him. Styles jumped back in the car, reversing up to the gates, blocking off the car park.

He wandered towards the two vehicles, glancing up at the power lines above humming like angry bees. A quick glance through the windows of both gave nothing away. An envelope on one passenger seat, face down. Yesterday's *Evening Standard* in the other. Nothing to indicate Porter's nephews had been in either car, though.

Walking deeper in, looking both ways, the plots sprawled out from a central crossroads, spreading out either side of the paths. Gibson's plot, according to the guy from Newham Council, was in the far north-east corner. A crunch of tyres on gravel behind him, and Styles turned to see a grubby once-white Ford Fiesta pull up, Newham Council logo splashed across the side.

The driver didn't so much climb out as heave himself through the open door. He had the kind of beer belly that took years of hard work to cultivate, and a swollen red drinker's nose to complete the look. He reached back into the car, re-emerging with a pair of bolt cutters, and lumbered towards Styles.

'You the chap from the police?'

'Detective Styles,' he said, nodding, holding out a hand that the big man took an age to get close enough to grasp. 'Thanks for coming out so quickly.'

'Phil Woods,' he said, grabbing Styles's hand with a clammy one of his own. 'What's he gone and done, then? Better not be growing anything dodgy in there. You hear about people having their own weed farms.'

The last part came out with peculiar emphasis, like he was trying it on for size, showing that he knew the lingo to impress the cool kids.

'Can't really say just now,' said Styles. The guy clearly hadn't heard the press release, naming Gibson as a person of interest. Best keep it that way, crack on, fewer questions and less time wasted. 'Really do appreciate you letting me take a look around, though. Are there any limitations on access for people who have an allotment here?'

Woods shook his head. 'They get a key for the front gate, then they come and go as they please. Even get some of them up here with torches in the winter months.'

They bore right at the mini crossroads, limited to the ambling pace of Woods, finally stopping at the far end of the path.

'This is his, here,' said Woods, pointing to the last plot on the left. Nestled in the shadows of the electricity pylon, looming over them like a mini Eiffel Tower. Where most of the plots had been bordered by fencing no more than a foot high, more of a token border, this one was better protected. Dark green polythene mesh fencing wrapped around the plot, coming to just above the top of Woods's head, sealing it off from prying eyes. It helped that Styles had six inches on the council man, and he saw the top of a greenhouse poking up, set back from the entrance. Two posts either side of the entrance, and a wooden gate, padlocked. Compared to neighbouring plots it was practically Fort Knox, but Woods stepped forward, snipping off the padlock like slicing through butter.

'We don't mind them putting up stuff like this, but they all sign to say we can have access if we need it. Whatever he's done, if it's worth a visit from you chaps, I don't think he'll be chasing us for the cost of a new lock.'

He stepped to one side, gesturing Styles to have the honours, staying close enough to peer in himself.

'Thanks, Phil, I'll take it from here,' Styles said, seeing disappointment ripple over the big man's face, his excitement done for the day.

The gate swung open with a soft groan and he stepped inside, pushing it closed behind him. He stood still, listening, sweeping eyes across the allotment. A greenhouse in the north-west corner, a shed of similar size opposite. The whole thing was maybe ten metres square, big in comparison with the other plots, and filled with enough roses that Styles could be standing in an offshoot of Daniel Grantham's garden.

No sounds other than the fizzing of power cables overhead, and the dull hum of traffic back out on the road. Styles walked slowly up the centre, row upon row of roses flanking him. Brilliant whites, creamy yellows, slashes of crimson. He studied them, wondering if any were the exact varieties from the park. He walked over to the greenhouse, peering through dusty glass panes. A wooden trestle table ran the length of one side: stacks of plant pots, a trowel, a bundle of bamboo canes. Nothing out of the ordinary, no sign of life.

He walked across to the shed next, noting the relatively new-looking padlock, tugging it against the clasp to be sure, then retreating back to where Phil Woods waited. He returned with the bolt cutters, and the padlock hit the ground with a solid *thunk*.

Only now that the door was open did he notice there were no windows. No lights hanging anywhere by the looks of it, so he flicked the torch on his phone into life and shone it inside, sending shadows slithering away. Empty, apart from an old, well-used armchair in the near right corner, a slight bow in the centre of the cushion, shaped by years of pressure. He went to step inside, but stopped, foot hovering a few inches above the ground. Not only no windows, but no floor either. The whole shed sat on bare earth.

Styles squatted down, holding the torch inches away from the ground, sweeping it back and forward, his other hand holding onto the doorframe to steady himself. The soil was packed down closest to the door, a strip around three feet wide, but beyond, the rest of it looked loose. Not dark and freshly turned, but drier, more greyish brown and crumbly, as if the remaining area had been dug up and refilled.

Styles reacted before the thought even registered, shooting back to his feet, stepping back away from the door. It looked like a pre-dug flower bed, ready to plant.

CHAPTER SIXTY-THREE

Styles was slouched against the side of his car, tapping away on his phone, when Porter pulled up. Beyond him, he saw a line of police tape across the entrance to the allotments, a uniformed officer standing guard, clipboard in hand to sign people in and out of the scene.

'How you doing? And Kat for that matter?' Styles asked him as he climbed out.

'Shit, and shittier. What have we found then?'

'Enough,' Styles said. 'They're still working their way around the rest of the allotment, but the shed . . .' He trailed off, clearly bothered by what he was about to say. 'They found another body buried there. A young girl, except this one is, ahm, it's more recent. Few months tops.'

'Libby?'

'Don't know yet. It's a girl, so maybe. There's more. A box behind the chair. Looks like he's kept some of their things. A scarf with a name tag in: Shelley Downes, one of the girls we ID'd. A New York Yankees baseball cap with another name in we don't have. Alex Southern. Dee's checking the name out as we speak.'

'Ah, shit,' said Porter, turning away. As much as it seemed nailed on that they had their man, the new discovery dampened any enthusiasm, serving only to reinforce the danger Tom and James were in.

'Kam's in there now,' Styles went on. 'Reckons at first glance we've got the same varieties of rose as well. He's got an interesting theory you need to hear.'

Porter followed Styles into the allotments, signing into the scene, suiting up, and stopped short of Gibson's plot when Kam Qureshi came out, pulling his mask down as he exited through the gates.

'Ah, just on my way to see if you were here yet. Saves me the walk. Has he told you?' he asked, nodding towards Styles.

'Didn't want to steal your thunder,' Styles said.

'This is partly speculation for now, but doesn't hurt to share these things when you're pretty sure you're right,' he said, ever the modest one. 'I've done a few basic tests across a selected number of spots in the allotment. Sampled the soil and tested for a few things, nitrogen and phosphate in particular. Every sample tested high for both.'

He looked from Porter to Styles and back again, shaking his head at the lack of reaction.

'When a body decomposes, it releases large amounts of both into the soil. Normally that'd help kill off any plant life that dared to share the same space, but here's the thing. After a year, sometimes a little longer, those same chemicals can make things grow like crazy. With the samples we took from the island, the soil the roses were planted in tested differently than samples a few feet out. I'm betting that if we compare that to the soil we've found here, it'll match.'

'You're saying he used soil from here to bury the children?' Porter asked, still not clicking to what was getting Kam so animated.

'Yep. I think he buried them here first, waited for the bodies to release their nitrogen and phosphate, and used it as bloody fertiliser for his little garden.'

Porter grimaced at the thought. Pictured Gibson shovelling soil into sacks, transporting it, soaked with the essence of his victims, across to the park. A thought hit him square on and full force. What if there had been no sighting of Libby in Victoria Park? What if Madeline Archer had decided to walk her dog somewhere else, and they'd never descended on that place, finishing up on the island? The boys would be home now with Kat. *Can't afford to think like that.* It would paralyse him, and now more than ever he needed to be on point.

'How soon before we know whether that's Libby in the shed?' he asked Kam.

'Couple of days, unless you want to dig deep and expedite it,' Kam said, rubbing two fingers against his thumb in the universal gesture.

'Do it.'

Kam nodded and excused himself to head back into the allotment. Porter stared after him, lost in thought, until he felt a hand on his shoulder.

'I got this, boss,' said Styles. 'Go and see how Kat's doing. I'll call you the second we find anything.'

'She's fine. My folks are heading around there now, and . . .'

'And that's all the more reason you should be there, together,' Styles said. 'If it makes you feel better, come back after a few hours. You get to see your family, and I can pretend we really struggled without you, and how it's not the same without you around. It's win-win. Besides, you can get Kat to talk you through the last few days in more detail, see if there's anything she remembers that might help.'

Porter smiled, even in the middle of this whirlwind of a day, more in appreciation than humour. He clapped a hand against Styles's upper arm.

'You know what, I might actually do that. Just for an hour, mind. Doesn't hurt to let you think you're actually a decent copper now and again.' Then, after a second, more straight-faced this time: 'But seriously, mate, thanks.'

Styles gave him an *it's nothing* shrug, and Porter walked back to his car, wondering all the way if Tom and James had trodden this same path at any point today. He signed out on the clipboard, stripped off his Tyvek suit and headed back to his car. Time to stop being a copper for the next hour, and just be part of a family.

CHAPTER SIXTY-FOUR

Walking away from his sister's house, Porter felt drained. No other way to put it. His own worry for Tom and James was bad enough, but the last hour with Kat had been a full-frontal emotional assault. Watching it play out on her face, permanently pink eyes from crying, hankie scrunched in one hand like a comforter. Staring at a new spot on the wall any time there was a lull in conversation, which made for large chunks as they all processed what was happening.

His mum was putting on a brave face, Dad too, but it wasn't too hard to see the fear if you looked, carved into every line and wrinkle. The question they didn't want to ask out loud. Would they get to see their grandchildren again? Then there was him, just as afraid as they were, but they didn't need to see that, not now. Alongside that, a rising sense of unsettling energy, the need to be out there doing something, even just driving around looking for Kat's car. Stupid notion, he knew. The chances of finding that needle in the haystack of London on pure chance was astronomical. All the same, he couldn't sit here into the evening. Just wasn't wired that way. He called Styles for an update.

'Kam said he'll have the results by late morning or early afternoon. We've managed to keep the allotment away from the press for now, but wouldn't surprise me if any of them follow the trail and start poking around.'

'What about the stuff in the box, what was the name in the hat again?'

'Alex Southern,' Styles reminded him. 'And Dee's got a hit on that. Six-year-old boy. Went missing down in Brighton on a day out with his family three years ago.'

'I'm heading back over there now. Should be with you in half an hour.'

'No need. They're done. Kam's disappeared, and we've left two cars with a couple of plain-clothes in each, watching the road from both directions in case he heads back. Replaced the padlock as well. Obviously the second he tries his key he'll know, but it'll buy us a bit more time if he tries it.'

'What about you?'

'Need to pop home for a bit. Em's been having a few twinges, so she's getting nervous, but if Gibson pops up, I'll be right back in. How are we going to play it when he calls tomorrow?'

Porter huffed out a loud breath. 'Honestly, haven't worked that part out yet. There's no way we can hand over the children, but can't see him settling for anything less.'

Even as he said it, a little voice whispered inside, saying if that trade got the boys home, it was worth every ounce of grief he'd get from Milburn, the press, anyone with a conscience. He shook it off, knowing that it could never happen. Maybe they could string him along, though. Sell him a dummy, trade bones, but not *the* bones. Would he honestly know the difference if Kam, Bella Jakobsdottir, anyone on that side of the fence, doctored a man-made skeleton, knocked about and dirtied to look the part? Some of the bodies they'd found still had connective tissue attached. Parchment-thin skin, strands of muscle. Surely they could mock that up?

'Think all we can do for now is be set up for when he calls, and do what we can between now and then to get a step ahead, try and find him first.'

'I'll give you a call after I've checked in at home,' Styles said. 'If you're still at the station, I can pop back and chip in.'

'Appreciate that, mate. I need to pop home first and feed the cat in case it turns into an all-nighter. Don't worry about calling if she needs you.'

'I'll call,' said Styles. 'This is about your family and, well, that's as good as being my own, so go home, and I'll see you later.'

As much as Porter had meant what he said about Styles staying at home, he knew his partner had his back, and that he'd call, and probably come in even if Emma wasn't keen.

'We'll see. Anyway, gotta go. Catch you later.'

He hung up, checked his watch. Seven o'clock. Demetrious would almost certainly be waiting by the door, judging him with those big green pools for eyes. He wound his way back home, through the echoes of rush-hour traffic.

Cars zipped past as he trudged up the short path to his front door, their headlights sending shadows grasping for his feet, then retreating in time with the vehicles. Then it was as if someone had hit a mute button. No more traffic, just the sound of key rasping in lock, and he headed inside. He'd told Styles an hour for his ETA back at the station, but as soon as he fed Demetrious, maybe grabbed a bottle of water, he might as well head straight back in. No sense hanging around here. Besides, he wasn't about to relax any time soon.

No sign of Demetrious as he wandered into the kitchen to grab a drink. Tom and James's picture stared back at him from the fridge door, sucker-punching him with fresh waves of guilt. Porter grabbed a foil pouch from one of the cupboards, catching a fishy whiff when the top ripped off. He squeezed it into Demetrious's bowl, tapping the plastic on the floor to lure him in.

A bottle of water from the fridge next, maybe even a sandwich for the road. The kitchen blinds were still closed from this morning, and the fridge light cast a cold glow on the floor. Not much choice on the sandwich front. Looked like a toss-up between cheese or cheese.

A flicker of shadow down by his feet. Demetrious on the hunt for dinner. Porter grabbed a chunk of cheddar and the tub of butter, turning towards the bench. He realised something was wrong around the same time the blade touched against his throat. The movement behind him not his cat. It hadn't registered on a conscious level until now, but there'd been no sound. None of the usual impatient purring, a mini engine on permanent idle, that signalled the start of every meal. When the voice came from behind him, it was barely above a whisper.

'Do what I say and it'll all be fine.'

The same words he'd heard on the phone hours earlier. Same voice. Graeme Gibson.

CHAPTER SIXTY-FIVE

'Can I turn around?' Porter asked, heart pounding so hard it felt it might leave an imprint on his chest.

'Not yet.'

Gibson sounded tired, as if every word was a physical effort. Porter scanned the bench, looking for something, anything, he could use as a weapon. Why couldn't he have been messy for once, have a few knives scattered on the worktop?

'Are the boys alright?'

'They're fine. They'll keep being fine as long as you do what needs to be done.'

Porter focused on staying as relaxed as possible. Easier said than done. Someone in Gibson's state of mind wouldn't need much of an excuse to pull the blade across. He rested his palms on the bench, a show of hands to prove he was no threat, that Gibson held all the cards.

'Where are they?' Gibson asked. 'Where are my children?'

Porter almost asked which ones he meant, the actual ones, or his adopted ones from the park, but held off. He knew what Gibson was getting at. No point in winding him up. Probably a waste of time focusing on Ben and Marie Gibson too. He could show him news articles about the accident, but Gibson would call it fake news. Christ, he could probably take him to their graves and Gibson would probably accuse him of staging that as well.

'They're safe, Graeme. They're at St Leonard's Hospital.'

'You're going to take me to them, now, tonight. No one else, no backup, just you and me.'

Porter felt a swoop in his gut, wondering if this had been the plan all along. Promises of a call tomorrow just for show. Either that, or could be that Gibson was losing what little grip he had, slipped his tether and drifting.

'You know we can't just walk in there and carry them out, right? I'm going to need to make a few calls first, get things ready, that way we—'

Gibson's knife hand twitched, an ounce of extra pressure. Not much, but enough to make him catch his breath, wondering if it had broken the skin yet.

'No calls. Just you.'

'Whoa, whoa, whoa, Graeme,' he said, his whole body stiffening. 'We're just talking here. There has to be a way through this, for the boys, for both of us.'

'There is: just give me back my children,' Gibson said, practically pleading.

'OK, OK,' said Porter. 'But if we're going to get them, you're going to have to let me turn around and get my car keys.'

What the hell did Gibson think was going to happen? That he could march Porter in there at knifepoint, and they would just walk out with nine bodies? No sense thinking through logistics. All that mattered right here and now was that they weren't leaving this kitchen on anything less than Gibson's terms, and standing here, cut off from any backup, wasn't going to get the boys back any faster.

Porter's eyes were fixed at a point on the tiled wall when something skittered across the kitchen counter.

'Put this on.'

He looked down, saw a cable tie, one end pushed through the locking mechanism to form the loop, but left loose like one oversized DIY handcuff. Porter hesitated, but only for a second. As he reached out, slipping his left hand through the loop, it registered that Gibson had made his first mistake. Porter would be incapacitated much more effectively with hands behind his back, but leaving him to put them on meant more freedom of movement. That, plus cable ties weren't as inescapable as most people thought, too many believing what they saw on TV. Just needed the right opportunity, one without a knife at his neck. Porter put his other hand in, positioning the locking mechanism in the centre, reaching down and cinching it tight with his teeth.

'Tighter,' Gibson instructed.

Porter did as he was told, to the point of plastic biting into his wrists, letting his hands fall in front of him when he was done. The pressure on his throat disappeared, and a hand on his shoulder spun him around.

Gibson looked older than the picture Porter had seen, longer hair growing down over his ears, a little greyer around the temples. He had a sharp face, all angles and edges, and his eyes never seemed to rest on one thing for long, constantly searching. Porter glanced down at his hand, looking for the weapon. It hung in Gibson's right hand, but the grip was tight enough to see his knuckles blanch from where Porter stood. It looked like a pruning saw, similar to one his mum had. Plastic handle, fine-toothed blade. Capable of cutting through branches as thick as his arm without too much effort, so no doubt as to the damage it could do to his throat. Dark spots speckled the blade. Rust, or worse? When he spoke, it was quiet, the kind of tone you'd use in a library.

'We'll take your car. You drive. I see anything that suggests you're not doing exactly what I need . . . well, I don't think either of us wants to see what happens then.'

'I want to help you, Graeme, but if you hurt me, I can't help you get them back.'

'There's plenty more of you who can,' he said, flat, no emotion. 'The tall one you had coffee with, the woman who you met at the park gates the other morning. If that's what you want, I can leave here now and go find one of them to take your place?'

Not an option, least of all because Gibson wasn't about to leave Porter alive and well, and able to call for help.

'Alright, Graeme. We do it your way. Can I get my keys?'

'You won't need them.'

Gibson's vehicle, then. Mistake number two would be letting him see what he was driving around in. Halfway along the corridor, Gibson a few steps behind, Porter paused, mind flashing back to when he first came home. Why he came home.

'Where's my cat?' he asked. 'What have you done with him?'

He turned to see Gibson looking genuinely hurt. 'You have a cat? I've not seen any cat. Wait, you think I would . . . ?' He shook his head in disgust. 'Even if I had, I wouldn't hurt it. I'm not a monster.'

Porter almost laughed out loud. This man who had done unspeakable things, however noble the reasons in his own twisted mind, was taking the moral high ground. Gibson reached out, putting a hand on his shoulder, pausing him by the front door. He grabbed one of Porter's jackets, draping it over his hands, covering the cable tie.

Porter looked both ways along the street as they made their way down the path, mind working overtime to figure out how to play this. Gibson held out a key fob, clicked a button and a white van parked nearby chirped in response. He started to usher Porter towards the rear doors when Jake's phone rang. It sounded unfeasibly loud, amplified by the tension. He looked back, seeing Gibson shaking his head.

'Leave it. Just drive.'

'That'll be my partner,' he said. 'We'd arranged to speak. If I don't talk to him now, he'll just keep ringing. He'll think something's happened.'

Gibson looked spooked, on edge. It just re-enforced Porter's feeling that he was balancing on a razor-thin line of self-control. Wouldn't take more than an ounce of pressure to push him off.

'I won't say anything. You have my word, I'm not going to risk the boys' lives.'

That seemed to strike a chord with Gibson, and he took the phone out from Porter's pocket with one hand, opening the passenger door and gesturing for Jake to get in with the other, pruning saw held just between thumb and forefinger for a few seconds. For the briefest of seconds, Porter considered making a grab for it with his tethered hands. Not worth the risk. Not yet.

'Make it quick,' he said, tapping to answer and putting it on speakerphone, glancing around to scan the street.

Porter nodded his thanks, slid onto the seat, and tried his best to sound nonchalant as he spoke.

'Nick, what's up?'

'Hey, boss, just checking in to see if you're still heading back to the station. Emma's fine, not a contraction in sight, so I've got the all clear to come back out to play.'

'You know what, I'm just gonna call it a day,' said Porter. 'See if I can get some sleep, and just be ready for tomorrow.'

'You sure?' said Styles, sounding surprised. 'There's got to be more we can work our way through. Kaja and Gus should be back in soon as well. It'll be interesting to see where they got to with that list of his previous jobs.'

'Yeah, I'm sure, mate. Why don't you have the night off as well? I'm just going to kick back here, wait for Holly to get back from work, and have a quiet night in,' Porter said.

He held his breath, waiting, hoping that Styles was astute enough to pick up on the nearest to an emergency flare he could think to send up. If he answered without thinking, contradicted in any way, there was every chance Gibson would see it as a betrayal, and Porter didn't want to think about what that might mean.

The next words out of Styles's mouth could literally mean life or death for him, for the boys.

CHAPTER SIXTY-SIX

'I'm just going to kick back here, wait for Holly to get back from work, and have a quiet night in,' said Porter.

Styles frowned. His gaffer had clearly been working too hard. Initially his mind went to a dark response, to tell him he'd be waiting a while, but there'd be no real humour in that. Even he had standards. Why would he say something like that, then? After watching how difficult it had been for him to come to terms with losing Holly, this just didn't seem the kind of slip of the tongue he would ever make. Why, then? What possible reason could . . . unless . . .

The call went dead, no standing on ceremony, no goodbyes. Maybe he was seeing things that weren't there, but the reference to Holly really bothered him. The only explanation that made sense was that Porter had meant to say something else. Had wanted to, but couldn't for whatever reason. Styles looked out of his car window, at the closed curtains, a soft glow around the edges. Emma was already expecting him to head back into work for a few hours. Wouldn't be so different if he used the time to check up on Porter. Best case, he'd casually drop by and have his boss give him a funny look on the doorstep. Worst case, well, no sense in letting his mind run away with itself just yet, although the knotting feeling in the pit of his stomach kept getting heavier, tighter. Not good.

He put the car into first and pulled away, calling Porter back. If the boss sounded weird again, he'd not question it, just see it as confirmation that something was definitely wrong. Voicemail. He didn't bother with a message. Emma was next.

'Hey, Em, just popping over to Jake's for an hour, maybe less.'

'Everything OK?' she asked.

'Yeah, it's all good. Just need to prep for tomorrow. Work out what he wants to do.'

'Why not ask him round here instead?' she said. 'There's plenty left over from tea.'

'Nah, just as quick for me to pop round.'

'What do you mean just as quick? I've just seen you drive off.'

'Exactly, I'm on my way now.'

'What are you not telling me?' she asked.

'Nothing,' he said. 'Well, probably nothing.' God, he hated the fact sometimes that he couldn't lie to her. Was he so bad at it, or was she so good at sniffing him out? He told her about the reference to Holly.

'I don't understand,' she said.

'Me neither, but he's been under a lot of pressure, even before the boys were taken, and he's not picking up now. I just want to make sure he's alright, then I'll be straight back home.'

'Alright then,' she said, but sounded far from convinced, worry creeping in around the edges. 'Call me when you're heading back.'

He promised to do just that and ended the call, trying Porter one last time, but same result. He debated trying again, but opted to concentrate on driving instead. This wasn't like Porter in so many ways. To come out with a bizarre statement like that, then not take his calls.

Probably nothing, he kept telling himself.

CHAPTER SIXTY-SEVEN

Styles's name flashed up a third time.

'No,' said Gibson from behind him. 'Just get in and sit down.'

He opened the double doors of the van, and Porter was halfway to ducking his head as he climbed in when he saw them. Tom and James were up at the far end, backs against the wooden panelling. They had carbon copies of his cable tie restraints, and each had a rag stuffed in their mouths, brown packing tape holding them in place.

Porter had seen some pretty horrific things in his time on the job, things that had squeezed a tear out of some of the hardest officers he'd known. He'd walked through the lot. Only losing Holly had cut him deep enough to draw tears, but this felt pretty damn close.

They looked terrified, eyes wide, at once taking in who was joining them and pleading for help. Tom saw him first, muffled grunts the best he could manage. James looked up at the noise, seeing his uncle, blinking back fresh tears. Porter bit down hard on his bottom lip, shaking his head.

'It's OK, boys, it's going to be alright.'

He did his best reassuring gesture, holding his hands up, regretting it when the sight of his own bound hands seemed to spark them off, chests heaving, sucking in air through their snotty noses, breath crackling. Porter turned to Gibson, gave him a glare that could cut glass. Gibson said nothing, just raised the pruning saw, using it as a pointer, directing Porter inside. Porter heard him climb in behind him, and tensed as Gibson grabbed him by the loop of his restraints. Gibson produced another tie from his pocket, threading it through a steel loop set into the wood panel, fastening Porter in position to the left of the boys. He tested it once, twice, then retreated out of the van, slamming the door behind him.

Porter looked down first at Tom, then at James, as the van started up. He was facing front, not enough leeway in his restraints to even think about reaching them to peel the tape from their faces. Instead, he just spoke to them, a soothing voice trying to transport them away from all of this. Talked about their mum, how happy she'd be to see them again. How they'd go to the Chelsea game this weekend, burn their mouths on hot chocolate and slop match-day pies down their tops. Slowly, almost imperceptibly at first, they started to calm down, uncoil from their shells, breathing slowing. He lost count of how many times he told them everything would be alright, hoping that his words conveyed how serious he was. That he'd do whatever it took to keep them safe, even if it meant putting himself in harm's way.

A small window set in the same internal wall gave him a view of the street. Not far off eight o'clock, and the sun had dipped low behind the cityscape. Every time they came to a junction Porter scanned ahead, watching, looking for anyone close enough who might look into the car. Would they even be able to see this far into the vehicle?

If this had been tomorrow, Porter's phone and his every move could have been tracked, guiding Gibson into a net he didn't even know was closing. As it was, they moved quietly through the city, unnoticed, unobserved. Whatever went down tonight, he was on his own.

By the time they approached St Leonard's, Porter felt surprisingly calm, as if his body had adjusted to this new norm. He noticed that Gibson had parked along the side of the building, rather than the front. No real surprise there. He'd hardly want to announce his arrival or intentions. Porter had spent the journey trying to figure out how Gibson would play this. Would he leave them tied up, march in and take what he wanted by force?

Up ahead, a door slammed shut. Footsteps along the side, and Porter saw Tom and James tense up as the rear doors were pulled open. He turned to see Gibson climb in, face blank, on autopilot as if it was just another day at the office. One hand held the pruning saw, the other a pair of secateurs, and Porter instinctively moved his body across to try and shield the boys.

Gibson didn't seem to notice, instead moving to Porter's right, sliding the secateur blades either side of the cable tie anchoring Porter to the van, snipping it and leading Porter outside to fresh waves of groans from the twins.

'Listen carefully,' he said. 'When we go in, this stays on.' He tugged at the original tie binding Porter's hands. 'If you speak out of turn, they die. If you try and warn anyone, they die. I've got nothing left to lose. Look at me,' he said, stepping to within a foot of Porter. 'Look at me, and tell me if I'm lying.'

Gibson's eyes stopped their usual wandering, fixing on Porter, boring into him with a force that left little room for error. No mistaking his tone, either. He would follow through, and not lose a second's sleep because of it. Porter nodded.

'We do it your way, Graeme. Nobody else has to get hurt,' he said, all the while working the angles. If they went inside, if other people became involved, Porter couldn't guarantee how they would react. All that mattered right now was getting the boys to safety. Any have-a-go heroes inside could put them, and him, in jeopardy. He had to do something before they got inside.

Gibson turned side-on, tossing the secateurs back inside, transferring the pruning saw to his left hand and reached out to close the doors. Porter moved on instinct, lifting his hands to head height before slamming them towards his stomach, popping his shoulder blades towards each other. He grunted with the impact, the tie pinging apart. Gibson spun back to face him, blade in the hand furthest away. Only one door had been shut, and Porter could see the twins over Gibson's shoulder, faces now a mask of panic, about to watch their would-be saviour fight for his life and theirs.

The force he'd used to break his restraints had left him bent forward, and he used this to his advantage, charging forward, below Gibson's swinging arm, catching him in the chest and driving him back against the door. Porter heard both the loud *ooofff* as air was driven out of Gibson's lungs and a muted crunching sound, ribs maybe. He pulled back six inches, digging a shovel hook into Gibson's side, but Gibson twisted a fraction. Porter's fist landed square against the door, and white-hot lances of pain shot through his fingers and up his arm.

Gibson pushed Porter away, swinging a punch of his own that Porter was able to slip easily. The counter was there for the taking, but throwing it would mean using his injured hand. It throbbed as if he'd dipped it in a deep-fat fryer. He used it to feint instead, flicking a jab towards Gibson's jaw, following it up with a cross that connected with Gibson's cheek, but it wasn't a clean shot, and he seemed unfazed.

309

Porter's eyes flicked down to the weapon in Gibson's right hand as his opponent finally seemed to remember he was armed. Gibson opened his stance, whipping the blade in an upwards arc. Porter jerked away, but a fraction too late, feeling a sting across his cheek. He staggered backwards and to the side, tripping over the kerb and onto the pavement, one hand out to break his fall, the other going to his face, coming away red.

He felt the impact before the pain. The hand he'd put out was the same he'd punched the side of the van with, and as soon as his weight bore down it buckled like wet cardboard. He gasped, rolling over onto his side, away from the van, from any follow-up strike. When he looked up, Gibson had moved in, standing over him, breathing hard, in through the mouth and out through the nose, like he was psyching himself up.

'I told you,' he said in a voice ragged around the edges. 'I told you, all I wanted was my children, and you had to . . . you couldn't just . . .'

His head weaved from side to side, forehead creasing like crumpled paper, as if trying to work out how he'd got here, where it all went wrong.

'I didn't want to hurt them,' he said. 'None of them. I thought they were . . . they looked like them, like my Ben and Marie. I just wanted to bring them home, and you,' he said, pointing the blade at Porter, 'all you had to do was give them back. I'm all they've got. They need me.'

He sounded pleading now, losing what tenuous grip he had on reality, spare hand rubbing at his temple. Porter looked beyond him. Guessed the van to be about ten feet away now, Gibson halfway between him and the twins.

'We can still get them, Graeme. We can go in there now and bring them out,' Porter said, pushing up on his good hand, pointing with the broken one towards the building.

'That's what you said before,' Gibson sneered. 'Then you did this, tried to ruin it all. No, this time I do it myself. You don't get to ruin this.'

'What now, then?' Porter asked.

Gibson looked down at him with sorrowful eyes. 'I'm sorry. Truly I am,' he said, changing to a reverse grip with the blade, moving towards Porter. Jake watched as it came closer, the teeth of the saw arcing in a wicked smile. Everything seemed to slow, and all he could think was that he hoped the boys wouldn't suffer. That Kat would forgive him.

CHAPTER SIXTY-EIGHT

Gibson had covered half the distance to where he lay when Porter heard it. Loud, blaring: a horn. Gibson slowed, looking up, and Porter saw lights swooping past him, washing over the road, across Gibson's body. An engine roared, the light doubling in intensity, searing Gibson's eyes closed. Porter whipped his head around, saw the vehicle hurtling towards them. He threw himself to his left, away from the road, reaching out with his injured hand without thinking. The pain was white-hot, liquid, flowing up his arm. Barely time to process it when he heard the impact. A sickening symphony of crunches and cracks. Something landing further along the pavement like a sack of wet laundry. Tyres screeching, metal scraping against metal.

Porter moved using his heels and good hand, pushing backwards crab-style, and looked back towards the van. A second vehicle, another van, had collided with Gibson's, front wheel up on the kerb, driver's side pressed up against the rear corner of the parked van.

Gibson lay motionless on his side, facing away and almost wedged up against the side of the building, looking of all things like he was in the recovery position. Even from his low vantage point, Porter saw a dark stain spreading over pavement. He sat up, holding his injured hand to his chest, wincing, teeth gritted. Only for a second, though. The boys. They'd still been inside when the van hit! The impact had sounded harsh, enough to throw Gibson ten feet. He went to scramble to his feet as he heard a door open.

The man who slid out the passenger side, his saviour – Porter had seen the face before. The last sixty seconds had shaken his head like a snow globe, and he frowned, trying to place it. Short hair, bordering on military. Boxer's nose, teeth stained like a forty-a-day smoker. It wouldn't quite register at first, but as he stared, brain on overdrive, it clicked into place with sickening clarity. The face, the white van. The man who had been following him. Not Gibson. Who, then? No time for small talk. The man reached into his inside jacket pocket, and Porter readied himself for one last charge.

CHAPTER SIXTY-NINE

Porter came up into a crouch, injured hand out to ward off, pushing forward. Whatever weapon the man had, whatever his motives, the boys were all that mattered. He lurched forwards, off-balance, desperate, but faltered when he saw what the man held. A phone. Porter couldn't have been more confused if he'd pulled a rabbit out, magician style. Phone in one hand, the man held up a finger, telling him to wait. When he held the phone towards Porter, he could see a call connected, a number he didn't recognise. He reached out, taking the phone, plucking it from the other man's hand suspiciously, like it was wired to shock him.

'Detective Porter, you are alright, yes?'

It took Porter a moment to recognise the accented English, but when he did, it sent his mind into a fresh spin cycle.

'Nuhić? What the hell?'

'You're welcome.'

'What did you do?'

'What did I do?' The Slovak mirrored his words back at him. 'I think I just saved your life.'

'Have you been following me?'

'Now, now, Detective. Just right place, right time is all. My man happened to see you, called me and asked if he should help.'

'And what, you told him to kill someone?'

'Someone holding a knife over you, yes?'

'I saw him, his van, yesterday. Twice.'

'You must be mistaken, Detective. Why would he be following you?'

'You tell me, you bastard.'

'Hey, without me, without Józef there, you wouldn't even be alive to call me names. You don't want to say thank you? Fine, but a little respect wouldn't kill you.'

The inference in the words seemed clear: respect wouldn't kill him, but there was plenty that would.

'You want me to say thank you? For killing a man? My nephews are in that van. You could have killed all of us.' Fresh waves of anger washed through him with every word.

'Or I could have left your friend there to do it,' Nuhić said simply.

'You know I can't just leave it at that,' Porter said. 'You killed him. He died, right in front of me.'

'And you are alive. That will have to be enough. Would you be kind enough to put me on speakerphone for a moment?'

Porter looked back at Nuhić's man as he took the phone away from his ear, tapping to switch to speaker. A volley of Serbian rattled out. Porter might not understand it, but the man in front of him clearly did, nodding as he listened. When Nuhić finished speaking, he started a slow walk backwards, using one hand to move his jacket to reveal a handgun tucked into the waistband.

'My man is leaving now, Detective. I wouldn't try and stop him if I were you.'

Porter clenched the phone tighter, wishing it were Nuhić's neck. He took an instinctive half-step towards the retreating Józef, only to be met with a smug smile, one finger wagging a warning, the other hand patting the pistol grip that jutted above his belt. Porter read and reread the licence plate, committing it to memory, knowing it'd probably be stolen or fake. Józef climbing back into his van acted as a trigger for Porter. He ran towards Gibson's van as the other pulled away, wrenching open the doors.

The twins flinched as light flooded back in, not knowing what had happened outside, or who was clambering into the van.

'It's me, boys. It's Uncle Jake. It's alright. Everything's going to be alright.'

He put the phone down by the side, twisting back towards the entrance, grabbing Gibson's secateurs and cutting the boys free. Tape came off their makeshift gags without too much fuss, but neither managed a word at first. They both flung themselves at him, nestled against his chest, trying to hide tear-stained faces.

'They are OK, I take it?'

Nuhić's voice seemed louder in the confines of the van. Porter had assumed Nuhić had ended the call when his man left. Hadn't thought to check, his only concern being to free the boys.

'They're OK,' he replied.

'Good, good,' Nuhić replied. 'So, you're alive, they're alive. In my book, that means you owe me, Detective, and one way or the other, I will collect.'

The line went dead, screen fading. A problem for another day. He'd keep. All that mattered right now was that they were safe. Porter kept his arms around them. Didn't want to let go, but the scene outside was still vividly fresh in his mind. He spoke softly, explaining to the boys that he had to go back outside. The prospect of staying back here alone, even for a minute or two longer, sparked panic in their eyes, and he agreed to let them out as long as they sat in the front of the van, well away from where Gibson lay in a broken heap.

He shepherded them around the side, watching them slide across the driver's seat, and headed around the front. The crimson halo pooling around Gibson's head was the size of a dinner plate, his eyes closed and skin already a pale imitation of a few minutes ago. Porter touched two fingers to his neck, and almost lost his balance, rocking back in his heels as he felt the faint *duh-dum duh-dum* of a pulse. He was alive! Porter searched his pockets, found his own phone and dialled 999 first, then Kat.

She arrived minutes before the ambulance, and the reunion, watching the boys piling out from the van when they saw her, was something Porter knew would stay with him for a long time to come.

A blur of green and yellow burst into the edges of his vision as a pair of paramedics skidded to a halt next to Gibson, a second pair making a beeline for the twins. Kat looked aggrieved at having to let go of them, but she stepped back, letting the paramedics give the twins a once over. He hadn't seen any physical damage, but the mental scars would take time and help to heal.

One of the paramedics ignored Porter's protests of being fine, and strapped his wrist and hand up, slipping a makeshift sling around his neck. He, Kat and the boys were ushered into one of the ambulances, leaving their colleagues working on stabilising Gibson before they moved him. Porter had little voices whispering into each ear, one hoping Gibson would pull through so he could stand trial for what he'd done, the other hoping he never woke up, fuelled by white-hot hatred for what the boys had been through.

He called his parents en route, putting them on speaker so they could hear the twins, who remarkably seemed to be getting more animated already, almost like they were on an adventure. They promised to meet them at the hospital, and he took advantage of the downtime as they drove. Calling Styles was next, and his DS was silent as he rattled through what had transpired, albeit a less dramatic version, trying to keep the adrenaline levels down for the boys' sake. Better they didn't focus too much on what might have happened.

'Jesus,' Styles exhaled when he'd finished. 'Poor buggers, tied up in the van all that time. Must have been terrified.'

'They weren't the only ones,' Porter admitted.

'I'll come pick you up when they're done,' Styles offered.

'It's fine, I'll just get a cab. Don't want to get in Emma's bad books for dragging you out this time of night.'

'I've just pulled up outside your place,' Styles said. 'Thought you'd been drinking when you mentioned Holly, so I came to put you to bed. You left your front door open, you know.'

Porter laughed. 'Don't suppose you want to do me a favour, then?'

'Whatever you need?'

'Make sure Demetrious hasn't gotten out.'

'I'm on it. Be with you in an hour, give or take.'

Porter ended the call, leant back in his seat and closed his eyes, happy just to listen to the boys and Kat chattering away. Once at the hospital, they were whisked off into A&E, to be checked over again, more thoroughly this time. Porter was led away for an X-ray, leaving Kat and the boys in the capable hands of the hospital staff. He had to wait his turn, and took his place in amongst a handful of others. An elderly lady clutching her hand to her chest, accompanied by a younger lady, her daughter maybe. A young boy, still in full football kit, minus one sock to reveal a foot twice its normal size, already an impressive shade of purple-ish blue. His mum beside him, looking the more worried of the two.

He looked around, realised he was the only one here by himself. Styles would be here soon, but that didn't mean he had to be alone while he waited. He slipped out his phone and tapped to dial Evie Simmons. Times like this it was nice to have someone, even if they couldn't do anything, but now, more than any time since they'd started dating, he just wanted to hear her voice.

CHAPTER SEVENTY

Nick Styles took the corner into the hospital car park a little faster than he should, whipping into a space he saw someone vacate, not realising until he climbed out that another car had been patiently waiting for the same spot. No time for niceties, but he didn't dare look back at the older lady who cursed after him as he trotted across the car park.

He asked at reception and was directed into a private room where he saw Kat Porter and her twin boys. No sooner had he asked how they were doing than Porter came through the door, arm pinned across his chest in a sling.

'How you doing, boss?'

'Don't think I'll be learning piano any time soon,' he said, and a chuckle spread around the room.

'You got a minute?' Styles asked, gesturing out to the corridor.

They stepped outside, leaving Kat on the bed, Tom one side and James the other.

'Didn't want to bring him up in there,' Styles said, 'but I asked about Gibson on my way in.'

'And?'

'And they're not sure whether he'll make it or not yet. He's on his way to surgery. Internal bleeding, possible fractured skull.'

'Couldn't happen to a nicer bloke,' Porter said.

'You were a little vague on how he ended up on the pavement,' said Styles.

'Didn't want to say too much in front of the kids,' Porter said, 'but we've got Branislav Nuhić to thank for that.'

He talked Styles through the sequence of events, how he'd thought Gibson was set to finish him off. How Nuhić's man had been the one he'd seen in the van, presumably keeping tabs to make sure their investigation didn't come any closer to his business.

'Hate to ask, boss, but if he hadn't been there, did he have you? Gibson, I mean?'

Porter considered this. Wanted to believe that he could have prevailed. Dodged whatever attack Gibson had launched, and overpowered him, but deep down he knew he was lucky to be sitting here, talking, breathing. That didn't mean he felt indebted to Nuhić, not in the true sense of the word. Whatever debriefing Milburn subjected him to, he'd already decided to edit that part out, where Nuhić claimed to have a favour owed.

'Honestly? I don't know. Probably did, yeah.'

They lapsed into silence for a moment, letting that alternate universe dissolve, the one where Gibson wasn't mowed down, where he had kept moving forward.

'Did they say when you can all go home?' Styles said, changing the subject.

Porter shook his head, pointing to his injured hand. 'Not yet. Pretty sure I've broken something, and they haven't said about the boys yet. You can get yourself away if you like, though. Evie's heading in. Wouldn't take no for an answer, so she can run me home.'

'I get it, three's a crowd,' Styles said, grinning. 'Might leave via Gibson's operating theatre, trip over a wire or two, see if any plugs pop out.' He reached out, patting Porter on the arm. 'Glad you're in one piece, though, boss.'

Porter winced, and Styles realised that he'd jolted the injured side without realising. No time to apologise, though, as a nurse busted around the corner, almost bumping into him, stopping short, and had to look up thanks to almost a foot's height difference.

'Detective Styles?'

'Yep,' he said, frowning, glancing from her to Porter and back again.

'You need to come with me.'

'Come where?'

'To the maternity ward. Your wife's just been admitted.'

CHAPTER SEVENTY-ONE

A shaft of sunlight lanced through the gap between curtain and wall, making Porter blink fireflies away when he opened his eyes. Eve Simmons nestled into him, tucked neatly under his good arm. He looked down, feeling a smile creep across his face. Today would be a good day, he decided. A glance across at his bedside clock: five past six. No need to disturb her just yet. He had a ten o'clock with Superintendent Milburn, but could easily justify another hour's worth of lie-in.

When she'd turned up at the hospital last night, it had hit home that he really wasn't alone any more. Someone cared about him, wanted to be there for him, look after him. He closed his eyes, drifting in and out for another hour, before slipping out of bed and getting dressed, and heading through to stick the kettle on. He fired off a text to Kat, checking what kind of night the boys had had. They'd been allowed home, with a referral to a counsellor to help come to terms with their ordeal. Three dots appeared almost instantly as she typed her reply. Probably hadn't slept a wink herself.

Took them a while to drift off but all good. Still out now.

*Hate to ask but need them to give a statement today or tomorrow latest.
I can be there with you though.*

They agreed that he'd come and pick them at three, take them in and
be there all the way through. Evie padded in before he'd managed to
make his cuppa, wearing one of his hoodies that came down to miniskirt
length. She circled her arms around him, nuzzling into his chest.

'Morning,' she said, looking up at him, pushing up on tiptoes, giving
him the kind of slow kiss that seemed to go on for ever. 'How you feeling?'

'I'm all good,' he said, holding up his broken wrist. 'You think the
other kids at school will sign my cast?'

She rolled her eyes. 'I'm sure they'll draw much worse than their
names on it if you ask them nicely.' She took a half-step back, her smile
replaced by a more serious look. 'Glad you're OK, though. It's meant to
be you that worries about me, not the other way around.'

'I had him covered,' Porter said, tapping his cast against the side of
his head. 'This is just a flesh wound.'

She gave his chest a half-hearted shove, spinning away, back towards
the bedroom. 'Get dressed,' she called over her shoulder. 'I'm buying
you breakfast. Any news from Nick, by the way?'

'Shit, forgot to check.' Porter rattled his cup back onto the counter,
clicking into his messages. Sure enough, one unopened from Styles,
timed at a few minutes after five this morning. He opened it and the
screen filled with a tiny scrunched-up face.

*Em wants to have Holly as a middle name, but said I'd need to check
in with you first!*

Porter stared at the tiny person that had just tilted Nick and Emma's
world on its axis. He nodded slowly, a faint smile as he headed into the
bedroom to show Evie. He approved the name one hundred per cent.
Knew Holly would have too.

CHAPTER SEVENTY-TWO

'And this mystery man, this saviour of yours, you couldn't persuade him to stick around?' Milburn asked, sounding slightly dubious. 'Regardless of which way things go with Gibson, we need to track them down. Can't have people mowing each other down, even in situations like this.'

There he goes again, thought Porter. All about the optics, not endorsing someone taking the law into their own hands, even when that action probably saved the life of an officer, not to mention his nephews.

'I'm sure the CPS won't throw the book at them, but we need to tie up the loose ends. Damn shame Gibson hasn't woken up yet.'

'I spoke to the hospital on the way in, sir. They say he's stable now, just a case of waiting for swelling to go down in his brain, see how he goes after that.'

'And he really expected you to waltz in there and bring him out a trolley-full of bodies? I knew the man was certifiable, but that's a special kind of crazy.'

Porter just shrugged, said nothing.

'What about CCTV from the surrounding streets?'

'Nothing, sir. Already been checked.'

'And forensics on his allotment and vehicle?'

'Spoke with Kam Qureshi this morning. He's confirmed the body in the allotment isn't Libby Hallforth, so that case stays open. Initial findings show correlation between soil found at the allotment with soil the roses were planted in at the park. We're pretty sure he buried them there for a while, let them decompose, then moved them to the park.'

'I've seen some messed-up stuff in my time, but this is right up there with the worst of 'em,' Milburn said. 'And he thought he was what, protecting these children?'

'That's the gist of what he said, sir. That they looked like his kids, that they needed him to look after them.'

Milburn shook his head. 'Well, if he wakes up, we can hear it from the horse's mouth, but for now, it's a win for us. There'll not be many like this,' he said, giving Porter a knowing smile. 'A double-figure win, no less.'

A reference to the body count, of course. Milburn was happy on both counts. A murderer caught, and a boost to the solve rate. To Porter, the numbers involved were a source of infinite sadness, little to celebrate.

He left Milburn to work on a statement for the press, heading out into a relatively quiet office. No Styles; he'd be away for a spell with Emma and the baby. The rest of his team was nowhere to be seen. Instead of sitting at his desk, he hovered by the window, looking down at people scurrying along Edgware Road. He hovered there, pressing his forehead against the cool glass, and knew where he had to be before news of Gibson's capture splashed across every front page.

CHAPTER SEVENTY-THREE

John Walsh and Fred Wigg Towers, twin castles guarding the edge of Wanstead Flats. They barely cast a shadow in the midday sun. No kids playing outside today, as he headed up to the top floor to see Ally Hallforth. Milburn was due to speak to the press at two this afternoon, and as part of that would be talking about the discovery at the allotments, and the ongoing search for Libby, who they now believed to have been another of Gibson's victims. The last thing he wanted was for Ally to get yet another update via Sky News. She deserved to hear it face-to-face. That, plus he wanted to look her in the eye, tell her he wasn't giving up, that her daughter wasn't getting pushed to the back of a queue.

He rapped on the door, waited, knocked again after thirty seconds, and was ready to try third time lucky when an old lady came out of the lift, looking like she was dressed for an Arctic winter and laden with shopping bags.

'If you're looking for Alison, she's not in.'

'I was starting to wonder,' said Porter. 'Don't suppose you happen to know when she's due back?'

'Don't know about that,' she said. 'She's not been gone long. Said she was off to see her boy, no idea when she'll be back, though.'

Porter thanked her, offered to help her in with her bags, but she puffed out her chest.

'I can manage just fine, but thank you for offering, young man.'

Been a while since anyone called him young. He checked his watch. Still enough time to catch Ally at Marcus's place. Two birds with one stone. He jumped back in his car, using the journey to map out what he could do while they waited for Gibson to wake up. Every place he'd worked at would need to be checked. Tessier and Sucheka had ticked a few off the list yesterday, but Nexon had confirmed it wasn't just confined to London. They'd need to reach out to other forces, coordinate multiple locations. Porter hoped it would be a fruitless exercise. That the Victoria Park location was the only one special enough to warrant Gibson creating his garden. If what he said was true, he wasn't a predatory killer, preying on victims at random for the sheer thrill of it. He'd believed, at least for a time, that he was reunited with his own children, thanks to the still-scrambled signals in his brain. After the illusion wore off, what else could he have done? This misguided notion he had that they were better off with him than their families, even if that meant being part of his garden, had fuelled what happened.

Marcus answered quickly, already wearing a jacket as if he'd been hovering by the door, expecting someone.

'Marcus, can I come in?'

'I'm heading out actually. Going round to see Mum.'

'I can save you the bother,' said Porter. 'I've just been round to hers and a neighbour said she's on her way here. I wanted to see you both anyway. We OK to wait inside?'

Marcus didn't look happy at the prospect, but opened the door anyway. 'Living room's in there. Back in a sec, I'll stick the kettle on.'

Porter wandered through into a living room that was surprisingly tidy and well decorated for someone of Marcus's age. Looked cleaner than Porter's own place if he was being brutally honest. He heard the whisper of the kettle kicking into life, and footsteps disappearing down the hallway, to the bedroom or bathroom presumably. He made himself comfy on the sofa, taking the time to reply to a few texts and emails. Marcus reappeared a few minutes later, passing him a mug of tea, enough steam rising off it to fill a sauna.

'There you go. Be with you in two mins. Just need the loo.'

He disappeared again, leaving Porter to search for a coaster. None in sight, so he made do with a folded copy of yesterday's *Evening Standard*. His eye was drawn to a frame on the far wall, collage style, pictures of Marcus and Libby. A single one dead centre with Ally in too, but in the main it was all brother and sister shots. He was still staring at it when he placed his cup on the paper, not realising his hand had strayed too far. The edge of the cup hit the bump of the fold, and the top inch of tea spilt out in a tan-coloured mini tsunami, pooling on the coffee table, splashing the nearby TV remote.

'Shit,' said Porter, jumping up, picking up the remote, shaking it as if that'd fix everything. He used the edge of his hand to drag the edge of the spreading pool back, stopping a waterfall hitting the carpet. He shook his hands out, droplets flying everywhere, and headed into the kitchen to find something to mop it up with. A quick scan of the counter and he grabbed an oversized kitchen roll, and used a few sheets to blot up the bulk, a few more to wipe the streaks away. As long as the remote still worked, Marcus would be none the wiser.

He headed back into the kitchen to hide the evidence, and pushed the pedal to open the bin, dropping the stained pale-brown soggy sheets in. He'd removed his foot and half-turned away, when he paused, frowning. Turning back to the bin, he pressed to open it again, reaching in, moving the balled kitchen roll to one side.

No. Fucking. Way.

CHAPTER SEVENTY-FOUR

Porter heard Marcus call out, presumably from the living room, wondering where Porter had gotten to.

'In here, Marcus. I'm in the kitchen.'

Marcus's face appeared around the door, looking deeply suspicious, as if he'd found someone rooting through his stuff.

'What you doing?' he asked.

'I spilt my tea. Needed something to mop it up,' said Porter.

Marcus's frown disappeared at the innocent enough explanation, and Porter let him have it with both barrels.

'Where is she, Marcus?'

Marcus stared at him, face a blank mask, but only for a second. 'Where's who? My mum, you mean? She ain't here yet, you know that.'

'Where is she?' Porter repeated.

'Who? Who are you on about?' Marcus spoke slowly, like talking to a difficult child.

'Your sister,' he said simply.

'Man, you must have hit your head on something, cos you've lost the plot.'

'Really?' Porter asked, with raised eyebrows, taking a step towards Marcus, bringing one hand from behind his back. 'Then I guess it's you who wears the bright red hair bobbles, then? Funny, didn't think you'd have the length to manage a ponytail.'

The frayed, snapped ends of the red bobble hung down over his fingers like a worm. Marcus's eyes bulged when he saw it. His breathing picked up pace, and his tongue darted in and out, licking dry lips. Porter tensed, ready for him to either lunge towards him or bolt. Fight or flight. But instead, Marcus did something Porter hadn't expected. He started to cry.

CHAPTER SEVENTY-FIVE

Five months ago

Libby sees something move, a reflection in her camera screen. She turns, looks up at the man standing behind her, phone dropping to her side, all thoughts of *Pokémon Go* forgotten. He makes a surprised noise, as if she's magically appeared out of thin air. He has sad eyes, staring at her. Looks like he's going to speak, but nothing comes out when his mouth opens.

'Are you OK?' she asks.

It's like someone pressed play, starting him up again. 'I am now.'

'Are you lost?'

'No, no. I was just looking for you and your brother.'

That's a weird thing to say. She doesn't even know him, so why would he be looking for her? Maybe Marcus knows him?

'Why?' she asks, in that blunt way only kids can.

'What do you mean why? I've come to take you home.'

Alarm bells sound, heart fluttering in her chest like a butterfly beating its wings. She knows she isn't meant to talk to strangers. She's already broken that rule. But going home with him? No way. She leans to one side, looking beyond him, back to the safety of the fairground. Sees flashes of colour as people breeze past the gap between stalls. Wishes she hadn't wandered off.

'I can't go home with you,' she says, hearing the wobble in her own voice. 'Mum always says I shouldn't talk to strangers.'

'I'm not a stranger, though, Marie, am I? I'm your dad.'

Her heart changes from a butterfly to a hammer. Feels like it's about to bash straight through her chest. She notices now how nervous he looks, the way he shifts from one foot to the other, as if the ground is too hot. Her churning stomach feels like that time she ate too many sweets and was sick all over the couch. There isn't much room to squeeze past him. What if he reaches out and grabs hold of her? She could turn, run, find her mum and dad, but it's as if her legs are carved from stone.

'My name's not Marie, and you're not my dad.'

He gives a weird kind of laugh, and she feels goosebumps pop along her arms. Something about the way he's staring at her. Like he's looking through her, not at her.

'Come on now, sweetheart. Let's not be silly, eh.'

'My mum and dad will be looking for me,' she says. 'I need to go and find them.'

She takes a half-step back, but he reaches out before she can take another, grabs her by the arm. She opens her mouth to scream but before she does, there's a blur of movement, someone bustling along the gap between stalls, bumping into him. No, not bumping. Shoving. It's her brother, Marcus.

'Whoa, what you doing, man? Get your hands off her.'

The man lets go of her wrist, staggering into the side of the stall. Marcus doesn't hang around. He takes her hand, tugs her around the corner and out of sight.

'Come on,' he says, and she glances back over her shoulder as she follows. No sign, and they whip around the next corner, heading back to the main stream of people. They burst out, almost knocking a little boy over. Would have if he hadn't been holding his mum's hand.

'Sorry,' they call in unison, him trotting and her skipping their way back towards the car park.

They don't stop until they get to the rows of cars, and he hunkers down, bringing himself to her eye level. She likes that he does this. Makes her feel as big as him.

'Where are Mum and Dad?' he asks. 'They should have been looking after you, not leaving you to wander off with blokes like that.'

He sounds angry, and she feels her eyes begin to fill now that the excitement of their escape is wearing off. Her bottom lip starts to tremble, and she bites down, holding her breath to try and stem the tears, but they come anyway.

'I wasn't going anywhere with him, I promise I wasn't.'

'I don't think he was going to give you much choice, Lib. Proper creep, that one.'

She sniffs, long and loud. 'Can we go and find Mum and Dad now?'

He looks around as if he's scanning for their faces, but when he looks back at her, he's smiling a sad smile that confuses her.

'Marcus?'

'I've got a better idea, Lib. Why don't we go back to mine, get some popcorn and watch a movie?'

CHAPTER SEVENTY-SIX

Porter waited him out, gave him time to regain his composure. Marcus sniffed loudly, dragging the back of a hand across his nose.

'I had to. Had no choice. If I'd left her there, he would have beaten her the same way he beat me, or worse. Mum might be clean now, but she wasn't strong enough. Not back then. This was the only way out, the only way she'd be safe. You think – what? That I should have left her there with him? Nah, man, no way.'

'Marcus . . .' Porter began.

'No, you don't understand, man. I lived that, the life she would have had. Took me years to get out. Couldn't even tell you how many times he got heavy handed. Do what you want with me now, but I did what needed to be done.'

'Marcus, please tell me you haven't . . .'

Marcus's face contracted into a cobweb of creases. 'Whoa, wait, you think I would hurt her? You lost your mind? She's fine. She's here.'

'Here?' Porter said, pointing a finger towards the floor. 'In this flat?'

Marcus nodded. 'She's in her room.'

Porter followed Marcus down the short corridor and into a small bedroom. No sign of a little girl. No pictures on walls. A plain cream duvet. No toys, nothing. Marcus walked over to some double doors, a walk-in wardrobe, maybe, and Porter waited in the doorway as he knocked gently.

'Libs?' he called softly, resting his head against the door. 'I've got a, um, a friend here. It's OK to come out.'

Porter swallowed, breath catching in his throat, as the door opened, just a crack at first, then a foot. A small face peered out, like an animal emerging from hibernation. She looked even younger than the pictures he'd seen, if that was possible. Her hair was darker, not blonde any more. More of a mousey brown, and longer, down past her shoulders. She was cross-legged, sitting amongst a castle of cushions. Stuck on the wall was a round LED push button light. In her hand a copy of *Harry Potter and the Philosopher's Stone*.

'This guy is a policeman, Libs. It's OK. He's going to keep you safe.'

Marcus hunkered down, held his arms out to her. She looked at Porter, sizing him up, then back at Marcus. Trust in her brother won out, and she rolled forward onto her knees, closing her book, and crawled out towards him. Marcus scooped her up, bouncing her in his arms, trying to keep things light, no easy feat in the circumstances.

'This is Detective Porter. Detective Porter, this is Libby.'

'Hey, Libby. How you doing?'

'I'm OK,' she said, resting her head against her brother's.

'I've been looking for you for a very long time,' he said, feeling a little tongue-tied. He had always assumed if he'd found her, it would have been in a locked room somewhere, kept captive, frightened for her life. But this was a new one.

'Looking for me?' she said. 'I haven't been anywhere. Just here.'

Such a beautifully simple view of the world. Got to love kids and their no-nonsense way of seeing things.

'Well, it looks like your brother has been taking good care of you.'

'He has,' she said. 'Marcus has been teaching me how to make my own games, and Susie's going to teach me how to ride a horse.'

Porter's eyebrows raised at the mention of Marcus's girlfriend, something to shelve till later. 'That sounds fun. Not in the flat, though, I hope?'

Libby laughed. 'No, silly, in a field.'

'Ohhh, of course. Makes sense. Probably couldn't get up the stairs to get in here anyway.'

He looked at Marcus, saw the nervous smile. There would be no quick, clean way to put the pieces back together, or to sugar-coat for Marcus how bad this looked for him.

'What now?' he asked, as Porter came into the room, peering into the wardrobe.

'That's my den,' Libby said proudly.

'Looks like a good one,' said Porter, turning back to Marcus. '"What now" is I have to call this in. We have to let your mum know that Libby's alright, then we all need to head down to the station, take statements and see where we go from there.'

Porter left out the fact that someone from child protection would be called in. That this might be the last time Marcus saw his sister, for a little while at least.

'Why do you need to let Mum know I'm alright?' Libby asked.

'She's been worried about you, Libby. She thought something bad had happened to you.'

'Something bad?' Libby said, screwing her face up. 'Why would she think that?'

'Because you've been with Marcus for quite a while, and she didn't know where you were.'

Libby gave him an *oh, is that all?* look. 'It's OK, she knows I'm here. She said it was OK for me to stay. She's coming over soon. You can ask her then.'

Porter clocked the moment Marcus's face fell, eyes closed, a soft exhale. 'That right, Marcus? Your mum knew all about this?'

'Not at first,' he said, sounding like a naughty schoolboy. 'Not till after all that stuff with the park. She was clean by then. Really trying, you know. When she thought that . . .' He left it hanging, not wanting to spell it out with Libby there. 'That nearly broke her all over again. I was worried she'd slip back, so I brought her over, told her what I'd done. We agreed Libby would stay here till things died down again.'

Jesus, Porter thought. Could this get any more convoluted? Libby needed to be the focus, though; everyone else could wait.

'Tell you what, Lib, how about you read some more while me and the detective have a chat in the living room?'

Libby settled back into her den of cushions, instantly lost in the pages, and Porter followed Marcus back out along the corridor.

'If anyone gets in bother for this, it should be me,' said Marcus, back in the living room. 'Mum didn't know, not back then. How bad will it be for me?'

Time to rip off the plaster. 'Honestly, not great. Don't get me wrong, she looks well cared for, well looked after . . .'

'We've been home-schooling her and everything,' said Marcus. 'Me and Susie. She's never been left on her own, or anything like that.'

'We'll need to speak to Susie as well. I know you did what you thought was right, Marcus, but there were other ways to handle this. You could have called child protection, you could have—'

'I did that already. Twice. Nobody did anything.'

That tweaked a memory. The two anonymous calls social services had taken. Missed opportunities to have stopped this in its tracks, way back.

'I'll be honest, and it won't be me that decides this, but there's a good chance you could be looking at charges for wasting police time at the very least.'

'Ah, shit, man.' Marcus stomped over to the window. 'If I get banged up, if you go after my mum as well, Libby'll have no one. She'll get farmed out to some foster family. You know what, though?' He turned back, and Porter saw the fierce look in his eyes, fanatical almost. 'If it gets Dad out of her life for good, it was worth it.'

Marcus headed back into Libby's room as Porter started making calls. Setting wheels in motion that might ultimately keep a family apart, instead of reuniting. He couldn't just brush it under the carpet, though, not with something that had been so high profile. He stared out of the window as he spoke, seeing Ally Hallforth appear around the corner. She walked with a spring in her step. Why wouldn't she? She was on her way to see her baby girl, blissfully unaware that yet another hand grenade was about to be thrown her way.

She disappeared from sight, angling towards the entrance, and Porter wandered down the corridor to let Marcus know she was there. He paused by the door, looking in to see Marcus lying on the bed, Libby curled up against him. He was reading to her from her Harry Potter book, and Porter could see from her face that she'd dived head first back into the world of wizardry and witchcraft. Ally would be here any minute. He'd decided to drive them all to the station himself. That'd give them a window to breathe, soak in the new world view, contemplate the scrutiny of their lives that lay ahead.

As he watched Libby and her brother, he reminded himself that this outcome was beyond his wildest expectations. She was alive, and unharmed, physically. This was a win, so why was it starting to feel like something less?

CHAPTER SEVENTY-SEVEN

The last seven days had been like being swept up in a whirlwind, buffeted on all sides by a horde of people wanting a piece of him. Since Libby's re-emergence the day after a suspected serial killer was taken into custody, the press had been hailing Porter as a hero. Doorstepping him at home, chasing him for a quote on his way into the station. He'd even made an appearance in the *Sunday Times*, a satirical cartoon depicting him being sworn in as the replacement for St Jude, patron saint of lost causes, holding a clipboard mandate to find the £350 million that the Brexit Leave campaign had promised would find its way to the NHS.

Needless to say, that had prompted a wave of piss-take at the station. Someone left a framed mock-up of a *Hello!* magazine cover, cartoon at the bottom, his head photoshopped into a picture, shaking hands with the Pope.

Saint Jake negotiates world peace, impeaches President Trump and secures Christmas number one.

Never underestimate the creativity of bored coppers.

Interviews with Marcus, Libby and Ally hadn't revealed a great deal more than he'd been able to pick up last week in Marcus's flat. It wasn't complicated. Marcus admitted he'd planned things to an extent. The what, more than the when. Stumbling across Libby, cornered by the man who Marcus had identified as Gibson from photographs, had been the proverbial straw that broke things. Seeing how far removed from parents Ally and Simon were being, he'd acted on instinct, jumped in his girlfriend's car and taken Libby home with him. The mystery of her phone, cracked screen, the blood, was solved too. Dropped on a long detour to the car park, the screen had smashed and she had cut her finger trying to swipe it back to life.

Between he and Susie Lim, they'd basically stepped in as parents for the last five months. Bought a load of clothes from charity shops, set her up in the spare room, explained to her that Simon worked for some dangerous people. Marcus had planned to somehow get Chloe out as well, but that, he said, would have looked too suspicious coming so soon after Libby. Besides, after Ally kicked Simon out and started to sort herself out, Marcus had seen a future where he could eventually come clean, tell her what he had done. That Libby was safe.

Throughout Libby's interviews, she'd stuck up for her brother all the way through. Said it had been like a long holiday, that she'd enjoyed learning stuff with Susie more than she ever had at school. It was harder to get her to open up to questions about Simon. Porter had seen the wariness drop over her face like a mask. Even when she was told that Simon had been arrested, that he couldn't hurt her, it took a while to coax answers out.

What Porter hadn't seen coming was the approach from the solicitor that Marcus had instructed. A young lady called Amina Baqri, from Pringle & Bailey, had been kicking up a fuss on his behalf, asking some pretty searching questions about how the Hallforth family had been let down so badly, victims of a broken system that should have protected all three children, long before one of them cracked under the pressure and took matters into his own hands.

She was also shining a spotlight, albeit not quite as bright, on missed opportunities by the Met. They'd searched Marcus's flat when Libby first went missing, but knew now that Susie Lim had taken her round to her place for the day. Could they have done more? Porter genuinely didn't think so, but even if they had, would that have worked out best for Libby? She would have been returned to Ally and Simon. They might never have found out about his links to Nuhić, the threat he posed to his own children.

Porter didn't want to jump the gun, but with Baqri snapping at the council's heels, public pressure mounting, social media sparking all sorts of debate around public interest and whether punishing a young man for protecting his sister was serving it, anything was possible. If he was honest with himself, once he got past the initial sting of having been lied to, he didn't see any good coming from splitting up the siblings that Marcus had risked everything to keep together. If everything aligned, if Marcus walked free, if the family were left to rebuild and restart, he would be at peace with that.

Styles would be off for another week's worth of paternity, but he'd insisted Emma was OK with visitors. Evie had tried to mask the smile, but her face had lit up at the prospect of going to meet the new addition. When Styles came to the door, he looked like he'd just made a breakthrough after an all-nighter at the office. Tired, but looking a little smug. He shook Porter's hand, gave Simmons a hug and ushered them both inside.

Emma looked up as they entered the living room, rocking ever so lightly back and forth, baby draped over her shoulder. She had that same look of exhausted happiness, and Porter couldn't help but smile as Styles crouched down beside them, pulling back a corner of muslin cloth. The little face he revealed wasn't as smushed-up as the one from the picture. She'd filled out a little, tiny chest puffing in and out at a fair pace. Reminded Porter of a little bird, so frail-looking, hands encased in scratch mitts, cheek pressed against Emma's shoulder making for a scrunched-up face.

'Allow me to do the introductions,' Styles said, clearing his throat like a master of ceremonies announcing the special guest. 'May I present Hannah Ruth Holly Styles.' He half-bowed to complete his act.

'She's adorable,' said Simmons. 'And you look amazing,' she added to Emma.

'Thanks,' said Styles, jumping in. 'I've been using this new moisturiser, takes five years off, they reckon.'

She and Emma shot him the same glance, shaking heads, attention going right back to the baby.

'Hannah Ruth Holly,' said Porter.

'My dad's mum was Hannah, and Em's mum is Ruth,' said Styles, the third one needing no explanation.

'And I'm sure the initials being HRH is just a happy accident?'

Styles couldn't hide a half-smirk. 'Yeah, I can't lie, that sold me on having the three. She's going to have one hell of a signature.'

He followed Styles into the kitchen, catching him up on the latest with both cases. Graeme Gibson still hadn't woken up. Porter had been in to see him twice on the off-chance, but both times he just stared at the tubes and wires, wondered if it would be kinder to pull them all out. A different brand of justice.

By the time they wandered back through, Simmons had taken up residence on the couch next to Emma, and had commandeered the baby, cradling her in her arms, talking softly. Porter stared for a moment, imagining what could be, somewhere down the line. She looked up, as if she'd felt his gaze. Smiled at him, and he felt the faintest of flutters.

Standing there, watching domestic bliss unfold before him, he was sure there'd be some wisecrack from Styles any second, but it never came. Instead, Styles patted him on the shoulder, and gestured towards the baby.

'You want a turn next?'

'No rush. Let Evie have a spell first.'

'Don't use me as your excuse,' Simmons said, rising to her feet and sliding Hannah into Porter's arms.

She was so light, he barely felt anything, like holding air. She stared up at him with wise eyes, the occasional slow blink, sizing him up.

'We were wondering as well,' said Styles, clearing his throat, 'if you'd do us the honour of being her godfather?'

Not often it happened, but Porter was lost for words. He just nodded at first instead, then found his tongue.

'Not sure I'll be the best influence ever, but yeah, I'd love to.'

That prompted grins all round. Even looked like they were getting one from Hannah.

'Don't flatter yourself, Jake,' Emma said. 'It'll just be wind.'

More smiles. After the maelstrom of the last few weeks, he could do with more days like this. A buzzing broke the spell, and he looked around for his phone.

'Think I left it in the kitchen,' he said, offering the baby back to Emma, but Styles had already disappeared to fetch it. Porter heard him speaking to someone, and when he came back in, he held out the phone, hand covering it and speaking in a stage whisper.

'It's the gaffer, your gaffer, I mean. Sounds a bit weird.'

Hannah screwed up her face as he passed her over to her mum, a cry starting low, working its way up, like an air raid siren. Some set of lungs on her for one so small.

'I'll take it outside,' he said, lifting the phone to one ear, poking a finger in the other to block out Hannah's wail.

'Boss, it's Porter, What's up?'

'Where are you, Jake?'

Porter picked up the vibe that Styles had. The super sounded a little off, distracted. The use of his first name wasn't the norm either. Clearly there was about to be an ask of sorts, some kind of favour. He opened the front door, wandering halfway down the garden path. When he turned, he could see the others through the window, Emma in the act of passing Hannah to Evie for a second bite of the cherry.

'It's my weekend off, boss. I've popped round to visit Nick and his wife, meet the new baby.'

'I know you're not due back in till Monday, but I need to see you, today if possible.'

'What about?'

'It might be better if we spoke in person.'

'And it can't wait until Monday?'

'I don't think that'd be a good idea.'

'What about DI Pittman?' Porter asked. 'He's covering. Can he not pick up whatever it is?'

'I'm not trying to assign a case, Porter; this is something different, personal.'

So, his gut had been right. Something personal, something he wanted doing off the books as a favour maybe. He genuinely toyed with the idea of a brush off, of calling his bluff and just saying he needed downtime after everything that had happened, but he knew he'd never hear the last of it.

'I haven't got my car here, sir. By the time I make it home and drive back in it'd be over an hour. Give me the headlines over the phone and you can fill me in on the rest when I get in.'

Seconds of silence as Milburn hesitated. Had it not been for a slight rasp in the super's breathing, Porter might have thought he'd hung up. Porter heard a deep breath being sucked in, let out in one long sigh. When he eventually spoke, it reminded Porter of his press-conference voice. Slow, deliberate, as serious as a judge dishing out a sentence.

'There's been an assault, near Clapham Common, early hours of this morning. Young man, no ID yet.'

'Any witnesses?' Porter asked. 'Do we have a timeline?'

'No to both.' It was as if Milburn was choosing his words carefully, keeping something back.

'Look, boss, it's OK, I'll pick it up. I can take my time back next weekend instead.'

'I, ah . . . I can't let you do that. Pittman's already on the scene.'

'Then why do you need me?' Porter was lost as to the point of this entire call. Was the victim someone Milburn knew? Someone he was close to?

'The young man, we got a hit on his prints.' Milburn hesitated again.

'Who is he?' Porter asked, wishing his boss would just cut to the chase.

'We don't have an ID. The hit was from an old case. I'm just going to come out and say it . . .'

Finally, Porter thought.

'They matched the prints we found in the car that killed your wife, Jake. Whoever he is, he was also in the car that killed Holly.'

Porter was looking through the window as Milburn dropped the bomb. Watching them inside, laughing. Hannah back with her mum now. Evie still cooing over her, one of her fingers held tightly in Hannah's fist. His future framed inside, behind a pane of glass, while out here, his past came pouring back, washing over him, a coating of all the old anger, grief and frustration. A wave smashing into a ship that hadn't long been steadied.

Milburn's voice chirped away in his ear, asking if he was OK. He felt scooped out. Hollow. Only one way to fill that void back up. Justice. Revenge. Somewhere on that sliding scale would do.

Whatever it takes.

ACKNOWLEDGEMENTS

It's still a little surreal to think I have anything published, let alone the fact that this is my third book. As ever though, it's far from a solo journey, and there's a long list of thank yous to dish out for folk that have helped me along the way.

My agent, Jo, and all the team at The Blair Partnership, thank you for helping Porter and Styles continue to find a home on bookshelves.

The team at A&B – Lesley, Kelly, Susie, Daniel, Kirsten and Christina, thank you for everything you do to help polish, shape and release the books into the wild.

To the Durham Crime Book Club at Waterstones, led by the force of nature that is Fiona Sharp, thank you for your continued support and shoutouts on social media.

To all the other booksellers and bloggers who help not just me, but countless other authors, to get our stories heard, you folks rock.

I'm lucky to have a very supportive family too. My mam and dad have always been there for me whenever I've needed support or advice on anything in life. Hope I've made you both even half as proud of me, as I am to be your son.

When I wrote the acknowledgements for *Nothing Else Remains*, my daughter Lily hadn't joined the family officially yet, but now she's here, along with Jake and Lucy, the three of them provide more than enough motivation for me to keep bashing these stories out in the hope that one day this writing lark might even become a full-time job.

My in-laws, Jude and Malc, and my bro-in-law Mike, thanks for all your support, for reading some terrible early drafts, and Jude in particular for her part in persuading me not to kill off Evie Simmons in the first draft of book 1. Both she, and I, are glad I took the advice.

To Mik, my festival partner-in-crime, and the man known universally in Harrogate as 'that bloke in the dress by the bar', it's definitely been more fun becoming part of the crime-writing community with you along for the ride. Keeping everything crossed that you'll be writing your own set of acknowledgements this time next year.

No thank yous would be complete without the biggest of all to my wife, Nic. Jointly responsible for Evie Simmons being resurrected, my chief proofreader, confidante, fish to my chips, bread to my butter, and all-round soulmate. Love you, even if you do put the cream on your scone before the jam, when everyone in the civilised world knows that it's jam first #teamjam.

ROBERT SCRAGG had a random mix of jobs before taking the dive into crime writing; he's been a bookseller, pizza deliverer, Karate instructor and football coach. He lives in Tyne & Wear and is a founding member of the North East Noir crime writers group.

robertscragg.com
@robert_scragg